PRAISE FOR THE RILEY O'BRIEN & CO. ROMANCES

"If you like tension filled and chemistry charged romance, this is the series for you. I want more of Riley O'Brien & Co. right now!" – Book Briefs

"This series and author are a true gem in the Contemporary Romance genre!" – The Book Reading Gals

"Ms. Sutton really knows how to capture a reader's heart with her characters!" – The Sassy Bookster

"Where do I begin my obsession with Jenna Sutton and her Riley O'Brien & Co. series!!! Obsession would totally be an understatement about the love I have for the story lines, characters, and writing style illustrated by Ms. Sutton in these beautiful series." – Owl Always Be Reading

"If you haven't picked up Jenna Sutton's Riley O'Brien & Company Series yet, you absolutely need to check out this series. Every installment whether long or short is packed full of great characters, heart-felt emotion, solid storytelling, some good steam and lots of pleasing romance!" – BFF Book Blog

"Ms. Sutton has become one of my favorite authors, and the Riley O'Brien & Co. books one of my go-to series." – Panda & Boodle Book Blog

PRAISE FOR *THE PERFECT FIT*

"There are some stories that just make you happy when you read them. *The Perfect Fit* is exactly that kind of tale. Jenna Sutton has delivered a story that's so bright, charming, and heartwarming that I couldn't put it down." – Wit & Sin

"I fell in love with the two characters and was thoroughly entranced by their romance." – Smitten with Reading

"Sexy and sweet, it'll pull at your heart strings and have you laughing out loud as two very special people find just a little magical when they least expect it." – Herding Cats & Burning Soup

"This novella is wonderful; not too long or short, paced liked a dream—this amazing slow build and burn of two people coming together, first in friendship and then, ultimately, in love. They're so right together. *The Perfect Fit* is the perfect title for the love story of Margo and Zeke." – Give Me Books

"Sutton delivered another standout story for this series. Both likeable characters with big hearts trying to deal with their vulnerabilities and flaws…" – Confessions From Romaholics

Forever

in

Blue Jeans

Jenna Sutton

FOREVER IN BLUE JEANS/published by Jenna Sutton
Copyright © 2017 by Jenna Sutton

Digital ISBN: 978-0-9974032-3-7
Print ISBN: 978-0-9974032-4-4

Publishing history: Jenna Sutton eBook edition/March 2017; Jenna Sutton print edition/March 2017

Published in the United States of America

Cover photos: Couple image © kiuikson/Shutterstock; Denim seam © vadimmmus/Shutterstock

Cover design by Asha Hossain Design.

Copyediting by Graham Toseland of Polgarus Studio.

Formatting by Polgarus Studio.

Contents

The Perfect Fit...1

A Kick in the Pants... 137

Will Never Fade 297

The Perfect Fit

CHAPTER ONE

Foolhardy. Silly. Unwise. Asinine. Imprudent. As Margo Lange gazed up at the tri-level Victorian, nerves knotted her stomach and made her palms sweat.

She was starting to think that moving to San Francisco had been a stupid decision. Even though living in the Bay Area had been a lifelong dream, maybe she should have stayed in Ithaca.

She was familiar with the college town in central New York, having attended Cornell University for veterinary school. The cost of living was much cheaper there, and cheap was good. She had hundreds of thousands of dollars in student loans piled on her shoulders and no safety net. The cross-country move had drained her checking account, and her family and friends were equally cash-strapped.

Although Margo had researched San Francisco before making the decision to relocate, she'd underestimated the cost of housing. She had spent the past six days touring apartments, and it hadn't taken her long to realize that the only places she could afford were dumps.

She wasn't spoiled. She wasn't used to luxury. She could handle dinky, dingy, and dirty.

But she couldn't handle dangerous.

The apartments in her budget had been in parts of the city that made her heart pound with fear. And after what had happened in Ithaca, she craved safety more than she craved Reese's Peanut Butter Cups when she was on her period.

With the moving truck scheduled to arrive any day now, she was desperate to find a place. And this tidy-looking Victorian could be the answer to her fervent prayers.

Roby tugged at his leash, just enough movement to grab Margo's attention. She glanced down at the four-year-old Doberman Pinscher she had rescued from a kill shelter in Ithaca.

"Do you like it?" Margo asked.

Roby looked around, as if he were giving careful consideration to her question. His cropped ears pointed toward the overcast sky, and she rubbed the top of one between her thumb and forefinger.

The house was situated on a quiet street in Pacific Heights, one of the most exclusive and safest neighborhoods in the city. On this Saturday afternoon in early March, a lot of people were out and about. She'd seen several women power walking with baby-filled strollers, a few runners in brightly colored athletic gear, and a couple of families riding bikes.

Her potential home wasn't one of San Francisco's famous "painted ladies"—houses that incorporated three or more colors to emphasize architectural details. This particular Victorian was painted a color somewhere between lavender and violet with bright white trim around the windows and eaves.

From the outside, it seemed like the perfect fit for her and Roby. It even had a backyard. But the trade-off for an affordable apartment in a safe neighborhood with space for a big dog was a roommate.

Roby nudged her thigh with his snout, a not-so-subtle encouragement for her to move. She loosened his leash, and he leapt to his feet. As they made their way up the shallow steps, she took note of the huge glazed planters flanking the front door. Pansies overflowed the pots in a spill of yellow, white, and purple.

Spotting the directory next to the door, she pushed the black button for apartment 1B. She waited for a voice to come through the speaker, but instead heard the unmistakable buzz and click that indicated the door had been unlocked.

She stepped inside. The wide-plank oak floors gleamed under the sunlight that filtered from the stained-glass transom. The smell of lemon lingered on the air, tart and fresh. She hoped the apartment was as nice as the entryway.

Following a well-lit corridor beside the wide staircase, she found the right apartment. She took a moment to wipe her perspiring hands on her jeans and tuck the escaped strands of strawberry-blond hair back into her ponytail.

After taking a deep, steadying breath, she knocked. The door was solid wood under her knuckles, and her knock barely made a sound. She knocked harder, and the door swung open abruptly, her fist still in the air.

A broad chest covered in a maroon thermal T-shirt filled her vision, and she looked up, way up. Words stuck in her throat.

This was the man her uncle Dave had served with in Iraq?

The man arched a dark eyebrow. "So, you're Reno's niece, Margo?"

Remembering that her uncle's Army buddies referred to him as Reno instead of Dave, she nodded mutely. She still hadn't found her voice. She, who was *never* shy, *never* speechless.

This was Major May?

"Ezekiel May," he said, extending his right hand.

5

She automatically did the same, forgetting for a moment that she held Roby's leash. She awkwardly transferred it to her other hand, and his hand engulfed hers, huge and strong and warm.

"Most people call me Zeke," he added, his voice deep and kind of growly.

She didn't reply. She just stared. She couldn't help it.

He wasn't what she had expected. Not even close.

When Margo had realized she would need someone to help share the housing burden, she'd asked her family and friends if they knew anyone in the Bay Area looking for a roommate. To her surprise, Uncle Dave had responded almost immediately, passing along the phone number of one of the former soldiers he knew.

According to Uncle Dave, Major May had recently moved to San Francisco. He had assured her that his buddy was a "decent, honorable man" who would be a trustworthy and trouble-free roommate.

Uncle Dave was in his late fifties, and she had expected Major May to be around the same age. But he wasn't. He was at least twenty years younger. And he was, quite possibly, the most handsome man she'd ever met.

Thick, short hair the color of milk chocolate. Eyes just a shade lighter, with tiny lines radiating from them, either from laughing or squinting into the sun. A straight, bold nose. A strong jaw and full lips surrounded by a sexy dark scruff sprinkled with gray.

He wasn't just handsome. He was gorgeous.

"You're not what I expected," she blurted out, unintentionally.

"No? What did you expect?"

She floundered for an answer before finally replying, "You're a lot younger than I thought you'd be."

The corner of his mouth kicked up in a cynical smile. "I don't feel all that young."

Curious, she asked, "How old are you?"

He didn't blink at her rudeness. "Thirty-six."

Eleven years older than she was. Not a huge age difference, but not a small one, either.

Zeke abruptly dropped her hand, as if he'd just realized he was still holding it, and she tucked it in the pocket of her jacket. Her fingers tingled, and she clenched them into a fist.

He looked down to where her dog sat, his silky head resting against her thigh. "This must be Roby."

"Yes, it is," she confirmed. "Can you say hello, Roby?"

Roby perked up and obediently held out his front paw. Zeke bent down with his palm open.

"Hi there, Roby," he said, gently grasping the dog's rust-colored paw. "It's nice to meet you." He looked up at her. "It's nice to meet you, too, Margo. Want to see the apartment?"

She hesitated for a moment. She hadn't lived with anyone since her days in the dorm at Michigan State, before she'd moved to Ithaca to attend vet school.

She didn't want a roommate. She really didn't want to live with a complete stranger, even one who had her uncle's stamp of approval. And she wasn't sure she wanted to live with a man, especially one like Zeke May.

But she was sure of one thing: she needed a place to live.

"Yes, I'd love to see it," she said.

With a nod, Major May … Zeke … used his big body to open the door wider and beckoned her inside with a wave of his hand. He had texted her a few pictures of the apartment prior to their appointment, so she had an idea of what to expect. But the space looked even better in person.

The hardwood floors from the entryway continued into the apartment, a rich shade the color of whiskey. She wondered if they were original. They were in good shape, with only a few blemishes here and there.

Long windows allowed plenty of natural light into the spacious living area, which was painted a neutral color. A burgundy leather sofa and recliner surrounded a square coffee table made of crates. Matching end tables flanked the sofa, and lamps sat on top, their bases reminding her of circular metal sculptures.

The furniture, while a little worn, was still nicer than anything she'd ever owned. And everything was neat and clean, which she attributed to his stint in the military.

"Are you sure you're okay with a dog living here?" She smiled ruefully. "Roby is housebroken, but I've always let him up on the sofa to snuggle."

Zeke leaned a shoulder against the wall and crossed his arms. She could see the muscles in his arms bunch and shift under his shirt, and she had a sudden urge to touch them. She, who *never* noticed the size or shape of a man's muscles.

"It's not a problem as long as Roby doesn't want to snuggle with *me*," Zeke assured her.

Wisely, Margo kept her mouth shut. Once the dog got used to Zeke, he'd definitely want to snuggle with him.

You might want to snuggle with him, too, a voice inside her whispered. The thought made her face hot, and she glanced toward the dining area, hoping Zeke wouldn't notice her red cheeks.

She focused her attention on the bar-height dining table and stools. Despite their modern design, gray concrete tops, and stainless steel bases, they didn't look out of place.

Moving into the kitchen, she evaluated the stainless-steel

appliances, granite countertops, and butcher-block island. Although she didn't cook very often, she enjoyed having the space when she needed it.

Zeke's voice floated from the dining area. "Reno told me that you got Roby after someone broke into your apartment in Ithaca."

Walking toward him, she replied with a simple "Yes." She wondered if Uncle Dave had mentioned that the home invasion had occurred while she'd been there, sound asleep. Afterward, she hadn't been able to sleep for weeks.

Zeke eyed the ninety-pound canine. "I doubt anyone would try to break in with Roby here."

She nodded. "Dobermans are bred to be protectors. If their bark doesn't scare away burglars, their bite will."

"You can take him off the leash, if you want, and let him nose around."

She unclipped Roby's leash from his collar, and he loped off, most likely heading for the kitchen in hopes of finding a few crumbs. She doubted he would discover any, given how clean the floors were.

She walked farther into the living room, her heeled boots sinking into a rug with an intricate design in hues of wine and dark blue. It looked expensive, even to her untrained eye.

"This is a beautiful rug," she said.

He was silent for a beat, an unreadable expression chasing across his face before it disappeared. "I brought it back with me from Afghanistan a few years ago."

"I thought you served in Iraq."

"I did."

"Afghanistan, too?"

"Yes."

Before she could ask any more questions about his time in the Army, he pushed away from the wall and walked across the living area. She had to force herself not to stare at his butt, perfectly outlined by the worn denim of his jeans. Then she noticed he was limping a little, favoring his left leg, and she wondered if he had sprained an ankle or something.

"Follow me," he ordered. "I'll show you the sleeping quarters."

She laughed under her breath. Sleeping quarters? *You can take the man out of the military, but you can't take the military out of the man.*

As she followed him into the hallway, she asked, "How long have you lived here?"

"Almost seven months."

He passed a closed door. "That's my room." He continued and stopped at the next doorway. Flipping on the light, he said, "This would be your bathroom. I have my own, attached to my room, so we don't have to share."

That was a relief, but she wished her bathroom was attached to her room, as well. She didn't want to run into him in the hallway while wearing only a towel. She was going to have to buy a robe.

Stepping to the side, Zeke allowed her to enter the bathroom. With its granite countertops, silver mosaic tile backsplash, and charcoal-colored slate floor, it reminded her of a spa. But it didn't have a bathtub, only a glassed-in shower.

"No bathtub?"

"No."

"That's disappointing. I love to take baths when I've had a long day."

She loved to soak in warm, scented water while reading an engrossing romance novel and drinking a glass of wine. It was a perfect way to wash away a difficult day.

After a brief hesitation, Zeke said, "There's one in my bathroom. You can use it whenever you want." He disappeared from the doorway. "Turn off the light behind you."

He obviously was used to issuing orders and having people obey them without question.

She did as he instructed and then followed him to another open door. He stopped beside it.

"This would be your room."

She entered the room, flipped on the lighted ceiling fan, and turned in a full circle to take in the space. It was large—larger than any bedroom she'd ever had. Since it was at the back of the house, the room had windows on two sides. Wooden blinds covered the panes, slanted just enough to let in a bit of light.

She crossed the shiny hardwood floors to the door in the corner. Opening it, she discovered a walk-in closet and gasped in delight.

"A walk-in closet," she murmured reverently.

Hearing a muffled chuckle from Zeke, she turned toward him. He had stepped into the bedroom, and they stared at each other, a few feet separating them. Although his eyes never wavered from hers, she got the feeling that he was assessing her, from her wispy ponytail to her thrift-store boots, and everything in between.

"How old are you, Margo?"

"Twenty-five."

"Twenty-five," he echoed softly.

She wondered what he was thinking. Was he worried that she was too young or too immature to be a responsible roommate? Was he worried that she would stay up all night partying or bring home strange men for wall-banging sex?

She almost laughed at the idea. Over the past four years, the only reason she'd stayed up all night was to study for a test, and she hadn't brought any men home, for any reason. And she'd never had wall-banging sex, either.

"Would you like to see the backyard?" he asked.

She nodded enthusiastically, and a minute later, they stood in the backyard. Roby immediately darted toward the back of the small lot to hike a leg on the Japanese maple.

A breeze shook the branches of the tree, and Margo shivered. It was a bit chilly, but if she had been in Ithaca, she'd still be wearing winter gear.

Standing beside Zeke, she was intensely aware of his height and breadth. Not for the first time, she pondered the idea of living with a former soldier. He would provide even more protection than Roby.

But what could she offer him?

"Why do you want a roommate?" she asked baldly. Why bother beating around the bush?

"I *don't* want one, but I can't afford this place on my own. It's too expensive." He sighed. "My first roommate didn't work out, and I need some help with the rent."

"What happened with your first roommate?"

"He was a pig."

She couldn't help but smile at his obvious disgust. "As a vet, I feel compelled to tell you that pigs are actually very clean animals. In general, they prefer not to soil the areas where they sleep or eat. And they only roll in mud to cool off because they don't have sweat glands."

"Okay, then, my previous roommate wasn't a pig." He paused for a moment before asking, "What's the dirtiest animal you can think of?"

She considered his question. Cows were yucky; they constantly leaked methane gas, producing up to a half a gallon of farts per minute. But hippos were the worst.

"Hippos. They urinate on other hippos, and when they're really mad, they kick their feces on them."

Zeke stared at her for a moment before bursting into laughter. It rumbled up from deep in his chest. It sounded as if he hadn't laughed like that in a long, long time.

"My former roommate was a hippo."

"Well, I'm not, but sometimes I leave dirty dishes in the sink or kick off my shoes by the front door. Is that going to bother you?"

He shook his head slowly.

"And Roby sheds. I groom him regularly, but he still sheds. Not a lot, though."

"I have a vacuum." Zeke cocked his head. "So, what do you think?"

The apartment was perfect. So was the backyard. But she didn't know what to think about Zeke.

Instinctively, she knew he would be a distraction—one she didn't need. She had more important things to worry about. Things like establishing herself as a valued member of the veterinary practice she'd joined, building a loyal clientele of four-legged patients, and feeding her bank account so it had more than a hundred bucks in it.

She had no backup plan. She had to succeed. And a handsome roommate would undoubtedly be a temptation.

Beggars can't be choosers, she reminded herself. And at this point, she definitely was a beggar.

"When can I move in?"

CHAPTER TWO

Zeke crept from his bedroom at six o'clock the next morning. He was trying to be as quiet as possible, but he lacked the stealth that he'd possessed before losing half his leg in Iraq a little more than two years ago.

He didn't want to wake up Margo, who was sleeping on the sofa in the living room because her furniture hadn't arrived yet. Although he had suggested that she sleep in his bed and let him take the sofa, she'd declined his gentlemanly offer with a vehement "No!"

The idea had clearly horrified her, but he had no idea why. Maybe she was scared of him. Her behavior when they'd first met certainly indicated that might be a possibility. When he'd introduced himself, she'd just stood there silently, her blue eyes the size of saucers.

He sighed. That was the last thing he wanted—a roommate who acted like a fraidy-cat when he was around.

Maybe she had mistaken his offer as a come-on. Should he reassure her that he wasn't interested in her? He wanted a roommate, nothing more. And even if he wanted a lover, which he didn't, he wouldn't pick someone like Margo.

As he crossed the threshold to the living room, he was surprised to see that Roby was the only warm body occupying the sofa. The Doberman was lying on his side, his sleekly muscular form stretching the entire length of the cushions. Apparently, Roby already considered Zeke a friend; his appearance warranted nothing more than a brief lift of the dog's head before it flopped down again.

Glancing toward the dining area, Zeke spotted Margo. She was perched on one of the barstools at the table, her small frame swathed in a gray Cornell University sweatshirt and plaid pajama pants. He was wearing almost the same thing, but his sweatshirt was U.S. Army issue.

Her hands were wrapped around a coffee mug—his favorite mug—but he didn't smell the enticing aroma of coffee. She must drink tea.

"Good morning," she chirped.

He barely bit back a groan. Was she a morning person? God help him.

"Morning," he replied.

He knew he sounded like a bear that had just emerged from hibernation. Hell, that was exactly how he felt: irritable, hungry, and itching to tear a strip off some unsuspecting human.

"How did you sleep? I slept great. Your sofa is more comfortable than my bed."

"I need coffee before I can deal with you."

Instead of offending her, his surly response elicited a laugh. It was surprisingly husky, not the high-pitched, shrill giggle he had expected ... and dreaded.

"I'll get you some." She jumped down from the stool and headed for the kitchen. "How do you like it?"

If she wanted to serve him like a waitress in a diner, he wasn't going to argue. "Black," he answered as he settled himself on a barstool.

Moments later, she handed him a mug of steaming coffee and then hopped back on her barstool. He muttered thank you before taking a sip. It scalded his tongue, but he didn't care. He needed the jolt of caffeine.

"I'm guessing you're not a morning person," she said, laughter coloring her voice.

He grunted.

"Why are you up so early?"

He took another sip of coffee before answering. "I spent a dozen years in the Army. It's a habit."

He was lying to her. But she didn't need to know about the nightmares that made it difficult for him to sleep more than a few hours at a time.

He doubted she ever suffered from nightmares. She definitely didn't look sleep-deprived. Her reddish-gold hair was in a loose bun on top of her head, and a black fabric headband held back the shiny strands around her face.

Her blue eyes were so bright they seemed to sparkle. And her skin ... God, her skin ... It reminded him of a cultured pearl—luminous and creamy with tints of peach. Not a single wrinkle or blemish marred it.

Had he ever been so fresh-faced? So eager to welcome a new day?

He didn't need a mirror to know that he looked older than thirty-six. It wasn't just the strands of gray in his hair or the patches of silver in his stubble. It wasn't just the wrinkles from the harsh Iraqi sun or the puffy skin under his eyes.

It was the way he felt ... the things he had seen ... the things he had done.

Once the caffeine had worked its magic, he asked her, "Why are *you* up so early?"

"I'm still on East Coast time. It's nine o'clock in Ithaca." Her mouth curved in a small smile. "And I'm a morning person."

This time he didn't bother holding back the groan. She laughed again, a light, happy sound—one that made him want to smile.

"I'm starving," she announced. "I peeked into your fridge, and it looks like you have everything I need to make breakfast. If you're willing to share your food, I'll do all the work."

"I'm not a two-year-old. I know how to share."

"I plan to go grocery shopping later today," she added.

He wondered if she had enough money for groceries. She'd been upfront about her current financial situation, admitting that she was "poorer than a church mouse" until she started her new job.

That was why she'd opted to move into the apartment immediately. She had told him that she couldn't afford to waste any more money on a hotel.

"I'll help with breakfast," he said.

He stood slowly, worried that he would go down when he put pressure on his prosthetic limb. That hadn't happened in months, not since he'd moved to San Francisco, but it was something he always feared.

By the time he'd reached the kitchen, Margo had already pulled the eggs and bacon out of the fridge. "I'm in the mood for an omelet. Sound good to you?"

"Yeah."

He kept his fridge well-stocked, and he grabbed a block of cheddar cheese, a tomato, and a bag of spinach and placed them on the island. She must have conducted a thorough investigation of his kitchen before he'd woken up, because she easily found the grater. She passed it to him, and he got to work shredding the cheese.

"Do you have a baking sheet? I couldn't find it."

"No. Why do you need one?"

"For the bacon." She sighed. "I'm going to have to add a baking sheet to my shopping list. I can't go for very long without freshly baked chocolate chip cookies."

"If you'll share your cookies, I'll buy the baking sheet."

She looked at him, a mischievous smile on her face. "I'm not a two-year-old," she pointed out, mimicking his earlier comment. "I know how to share."

To his surprise, they successfully accomplished the task of making breakfast with very little talking. They worked remarkably well together, especially since they had known each other for less than twenty-four hours. In his experience, it took a while before people developed the kind of teamwork he and Margo seemed to instinctively have.

He handled the prep work, and she cooked. Roby helped, too, hoovering the pieces of food they accidentally dropped on the floor.

After plating both omelets, she added a couple of strips of bacon and passed him a plate and fork. He started for the dining room, but stopped when she picked up her plate and fork, leaned back against the countertop, and dug into her omelet.

For a moment, he was nonplused, recalling innumerable times when his mother chastised him for eating while standing in the kitchen. With a shrug, he propped his ass on the edge of the counter and lifted a piece of bacon to his mouth.

"I got an email notification that the movers will be here tomorrow morning between ten and noon," she told him.

"Do I need to move some things around so your stuff will fit?"

She glanced at him, surprise etched on her face. "You don't have to do that. This is *your* apartment."

"It's *our* apartment now."

He didn't mind making room for Margo's belongings. Although he'd told her that he didn't want a roommate, that wasn't entirely true. Because of his time in the military, he was used to sharing his space.

He had never lived alone, and the past two months without a roommate had been kind of lonely. While he'd made a few friends at work, he didn't have any close friends nearby. His best friends were halfway around the world, wearing fatigues and driving Humvees, and most of his family lived in North Carolina.

Margo shook her head slowly. "I left most of my stuff in Ithaca. My furniture was old and cheap, and I thought it would be smarter to just replace it than ship it across the country. I only shipped my mattress, bedroom furniture, clothes, and a few boxes. I donated the rest."

"Did you grow up in Reno, too?" he asked before taking a bite of omelet.

Margo looked at him blankly. "Reno?"

"Yeah. Your uncle is from Reno. Is that where you grew up?"

She laughed. "I hate to be the one to break it to you, but Uncle Dave isn't from Reno. If you pick nicknames based on hometowns, his should be Wyandotte."

"Where's Wyandotte?"

"Just south of Detroit. A lot of auto and steel workers live there."

Zeke had never been to Detroit, so he wasn't familiar with the surrounding suburbs. "Is that where you grew up?"

She nodded. "My mom was a third-generation auto worker. Uncle Dave didn't want to work in the auto plants, so he joined the Army."

"What about your dad?"

"He died when I was three. I don't remember him. It was always just me and my mom."

"Does your mom still live in Wyandotte?"

"No." Her glow seemed to dim a little. "She died when I was a sophomore at Michigan State."

A fierce yet unexpected feeling of protectiveness surged through Zeke. Except for her uncle, Margo had no family. But she wasn't alone anymore. She had Zeke to watch out for her now.

"What about you?" she asked. "Where did you grow up?"

"Asheville, North Carolina."

"I've never been there. What's it like?"

"It's pretty. It's right in the middle of the Blue Ridge Mountains." He didn't want to talk about himself or his hometown; he was more interested in her. "How did you end up in San Francisco?"

"I've always wanted to live here."

"Why?"

"I usually tell people that I just had a feeling that I belong here." A tinge of peach stained her cheeks. "But that's not the truth. It's because of *The Wedding Planner*."

"What wedding planner?" He frowned in confusion, glancing at her bare ring finger. "You're engaged?"

She laughed lightly. "No. I don't even have a boyfriend. I'm talking about the movie with Jennifer Lopez and Matthew McConaughey. It's one of my favorites. I saw it for the first time when I was eleven, and from that moment on, I wanted to live here."

"Yeah, I remember that movie. I was in college when it came out. I took Andrea to see it."

"Who's Andrea?"

He blinked, unaware that he'd uttered that last sentence out loud. When he didn't answer her question, Margo repeated it.

Reluctantly, he said, "Andrea is my ex-wife."

Margo froze with her fork halfway to her mouth, a hunk of omelet dangling from it. "You're divorced?"

He nodded curtly.

"Oh." After a beat of silence, she asked, "How long were you married?"

"Almost twelve years."

He glanced down at his plate, his stomach turning over at the sight of the congealed cheese. The omelet had tasted pretty good until he'd opened his big mouth and mentioned Andrea.

He hated to talk about his ex-wife. She was just another one of his mistakes … another one of his failures.

"How long have you been divorced?" Margo prodded, setting her plate down on the counter.

Jesus, she's nosy.

Choosing to ignore her question, he moved to the trash can and scraped the remainder of his omelet into it, his fork making an ugly screeching noise against the porcelain. He hoped his silence gave her a clue that he didn't want to discuss Andrea.

"How did you end up in San Francisco?" Margo asked.

Zeke gave an internal sigh of relief that she had dropped the subject of his failed marriage. He was so relieved he happily answered her question.

"After I left the Army, Riley O'Brien & Co. offered me a job I couldn't turn down."

The company, which was headquartered in downtown San

Francisco, was the oldest manufacturer of blue jeans in the United States. People around the world wore their signature blue jeans, known as Rileys.

Margo held out her hand for his empty plate. "What kind of job?"

"The company has a hiring program specifically for veterans," he said as he relinquished his plate to her. "And I have a special skill set that it needs."

She looked up at him, the smooth skin between her eyebrows furrowing. "A special skill set?"

He could tell by the tone of her voice what she was thinking. It was what everybody thought: the only skill a soldier possessed was the ability to kill. But that was a fallacy. Soldiers, even the lowest-ranking ones, had a lot of skills, and smart companies like Riley O'Brien & Co. realized that fact.

"I'm an expert in supply chain and logistics," he explained.

Seeing the blank look on her face, he added, "Supply chain and logistics involves moving goods and materials from one place to another as quickly and efficiently as possible. It's what I did in the Army."

"Oh, like FedEx or UPS?"

He nodded. "They're logistics providers that work in partnership with other companies. Most big corporations have entire departments dedicated to managing their supply chain. It's a really big deal right now, especially for retailers that are trying to fine-tune their omnichannel strategy."

He found his job fascinating and could talk about it for hours. But most people thought it was boring. They only cared about free shipping.

"I have no idea what omnichannel is," she said wryly. "But I don't feel bad because I doubt you know what pyuria is."

"You're right. I have no idea what pyuria is. What is it?"

"The presence of pus in the urine, usually caused by a bacterial infection. It's often a sign of a urinary tract infection in humans and animals."

Her answer was so unexpected a surprised chuckle escaped him. The same thing had happened yesterday when she'd told him that hippos were the dirtiest animals. She delivered bizarre information so matter-of-factly that he couldn't help but laugh.

"Well, I guess I should tuck that piece of information away in case I'm selected to compete on *Jeopardy!*"

She smiled widely. "Is that one of your life goals?"

"What?"

"Is competing on *Jeopardy!* one of your life goals?" she asked, clarifying her question.

"No."

At this point, he had only a few life goals. He wanted to sleep through the night without any nightmares. He wanted to run in marathons again. He wanted to end his three-year dry spell and fuck a soft, sexy woman until he came so hard he passed out.

But all those things required him to do one thing: deal with the toxic emotions he had from getting his leg blown off in an IED attack.

The clink of dishes caught his attention. Margo was loading their plates and utensils into the dishwasher, her movements fast and economical.

"As soon as I'm finished cleaning up, I'm going to get ready and head to the grocery store." She glanced at him, the bottle of dishwashing liquid clasped in her hand. "Do you want to come with me?"

A trip to the local Safeway would give him an opportunity to get to know her better. And more important, it would give him the opportunity to pay for her groceries. If she protested, which she probably would, he'd just tell her to add the cost of her food to next month's rent.

"I'll be ready in fifteen minutes," he said.

CHAPTER THREE

There were fat cats. And then there were *fat* cats.

Margo rubbed the round belly of the feline stretched out on the exam room table. Adele, an eight-year-old tabby, tipped the scales at nineteen pounds.

Margo glanced at Adele's adoring owner, who stood on the other side of the table. If she had to guess, she'd estimate that Greg McNeil was about her age.

Tall and lanky, he wore his light brown hair in a man bun—a look she did not endorse for any guy except Charlie Hunnam. Silver hoops pierced his left eyebrow and nostril, as well as his lower lip.

"Mr. McNeil, I think it's time to change Adele's diet. She weighs almost double what she should. That extra weight puts her at risk for diabetes, and it will eventually cause problems with her joints."

"What do you suggest?"

"First, you need to reduce the amount of food you're feeding her, and I recommend buying food that is specifically formulated for indoor cats, which are less active than outdoor cats."

Shifting her attention to Adele's head, Margo scratched

gently behind one of the cat's ears. She began to purr, arching her neck in pleasure.

Greg sighed gustily. "Adele spends most of her day in the studio with me, either sleeping or sunning herself on the windowsill."

"That's a hard life," Margo deadpanned before asking, "Studio? Are you an artist?"

"A tattoo artist, although I prefer to be called a tattooist."

That explained the colorful tattoos that wrapped around his arms and crawled up his neck. She didn't mind a little body art, but Greg McNeil was a walking advertisement for his profession.

Returning to the subject of Adele's sedentary lifestyle, she said, "You might want to buy a laser pointer. The red dot is irresistible to cats. It will definitely get her moving."

He nodded in agreement. "That's a good idea."

"Other than her weight, Adele seems to be in perfect health."

Beaming, he said, "That's my girl."

"If we find any abnormalities with her blood work or urine, we'll give you a call." She gave the plump feline one final stroke. "Did you name her?"

He nodded. "After Adele. She's my favorite singer."

Margo barely managed to hold in her laughter. Based on his appearance, she would have bet that he listened to heavy metal or alternative rock. She would have lost that bet.

But then again, Greg McNeil already defied a big stereotype: he had a cat. Typically, most guys preferred canine companions.

Grabbing a note pad, she made a list of food brands that she thought would work for his pet. "Here are some suggestions for Adele." She handed the paper to him. "Give me a call or shoot me an email if you have any questions or concerns."

He folded the list in half and shoved it in his T-shirt pocket. "Thanks, Dr. Lange." He picked up Adele's carrier and set it on the exam table. "How long have you worked here? We saw a different vet last time."

"Today is my one-month anniversary with Bay Area Animal Care."

This morning, her co-workers had surprised her with balloons and a big box of cupcakes to celebrate the occasion. The sweet treats had been decorated with a variety of animal faces including a hippo.

She had saved that one for Zeke, hoping it would garner a chuckle or two. He didn't laugh enough, and she found herself saying and doing things just so she could hear the deep rumble of his laughter.

Noticing that Greg was having a hard time maneuvering his pet into the carrier, Margo hurried to help him. As she held the carrier steady, he gently shoved Adele into it. The chubby cat let out a mournful meow that clearly conveyed her displeasure.

As Greg latched the carrier, he asked, "How do you like working here? I took Adele to another clinic closer to my place, but I didn't like it."

"I love working here," she answered honestly.

So far, her new job was working out even better than she'd hoped. She had been worried about fitting in with the existing veterinarians and support staff, but everyone had welcomed her and gone out of their way to be helpful.

The two other veterinarians on staff, Jon and Tricia, had invited Margo to their favorite bar for cocktails last week. She'd had a good time, and afterward, Tricia had suggested that the three of them should have a "vets only" happy hour every Wednesday.

Jenny, the vet tech, had persuaded Margo to attend a Pure Romance party at her apartment in The Haight-Asbury neighborhood. She had never attended a sex toy party before, and she'd figured it was something she needed to experience at least once.

She hadn't purchased anything at the party. What was the fun in buying flavored massage oil when you had to massage yourself? And she already had a vibrator that worked just fine on the rare occasions she used it.

She walked Greg and Adele to the reception area. They were her last appointment of the day, and after she said good-bye, she went to check on her overnight patients.

The clinic was designed in a big rectangle, and the space was divided into three distinct areas. The lab, surgery suites, break room, and stainless steel cages were in the back, the reception and waiting area were in the front, and a row of five exam rooms were sandwiched between them.

After confirming that the overnight staff had clear instructions for the badly-behaved beagle who'd eaten more than a pound of dark chocolate, Margo hung up her white doctor's coat and pulled on the North Face fleece over her navy blue scrubs. She'd found the hot pink jacket at the Goodwill store on Fillmore Street, and she'd paid only ten dollars for it.

So what if it clashed with her hair? It would have cost at least a hundred bucks brand-new.

Now that she was bringing in a regular paycheck, her financial situation was more stable. But she would need several months to rebuild her savings account to a level where she felt comfortable enough to splurge on little luxuries.

Fortunately, Zeke had allowed her to pay a reduced rental rate for the first couple of months and make up the difference once she wasn't so cash-strapped. She was grateful that he was so flexible. In fact, he'd been the one to suggest it.

Margo draped her messenger bag across her body, grabbed

the box with Zeke's hippo cupcake, and left the clinic. Her commute consisted of a short bus ride and a fifteen-minute walk.

Usually, she enjoyed the trek from Pacific Heights to the Marina District, but last week, it had rained every day. The monsoon-like weather was an anomaly for mid-April, according to Jenny, who was a San Francisco native. It rarely rained so heavily in the Bay Area, and the rainy season normally ended in March.

Zeke, once again displaying his chivalrous streak, had offered to drive Margo to work so she wouldn't get soaked. But she had declined, not wanting to inconvenience him. The animal clinic was on the opposite side of the city from his office, which was located downtown, near the Financial District.

Zeke May was exactly what her uncle Dave had promised—a decent, honorable man. She couldn't imagine a better roommate, male or female. He was tidy, considerate, and surprisingly generous.

Despite her initial trepidation about having a roommate, she really liked living with Zeke. He usually got home before she did, and she liked knowing he would be there when she walked in.

She liked the sound of his voice, the smell of his shower gel, and the sight of him lounging on the leather sofa. She liked everything about him ... a little too much. In fact, she was starting to compare every man she met to Zeke.

Yesterday, a guy had asked her out after she had examined his black Labrador. She had turned him down, not only because she thought dating a client was a bad idea, but also because he hadn't appealed to her on any level.

She hadn't liked his perfectly styled blond hair or his clean-shaven face—so unlike Zeke's modified crew cut and perpetual scruff. She hadn't liked his pale eyes, narrow shoulders, or soft, manicured hands—so different from Zeke's chocolaty gaze, broad shoulders, and callused hands.

And she'd *hated* the way the guy jerked on his dog's leash and snapped at the beautiful animal. His actions were a complete contrast to Zeke's treatment of Roby—the tender way he stroked the Doberman's back and the gentle, quiet tone he used when he spoke to him.

More than once, she'd come home from work to find Zeke and Roby playing fetch in the backyard or snuggling on the sofa. And without her mentioning it, Zeke had offered to install a doggy door. Now, Roby could come and go as he desired while she was at the clinic.

As she exited the Muni bus, she sent a quick text to Zeke to let him know when she'd be home. He'd never asked her to do so, but she thought it was the considerate thing to do when it was his night to make dinner.

Minutes later, she entered the apartment. A deliciously spicy aroma saturated the air. Her stomach growled in anticipation, even though Zeke's version of a home-cooked meal involved opening packages, cartons, and bags, and heating up the contents.

Roby dashed into the living room to greet her. She knelt and let him sniff her scrubs to his heart's content, knowing that he smelled the scent of other animals on her.

Holding the cupcake box out of his reach, she rubbed behind his ears. "How's my sweet boy?" she crooned. "Did you have a good day?"

Zeke stepped out of the kitchen. He wore a plaid button-down shirt in shades of blue and brown, open over a dark brown T-shirt, and a pair of dark-washed Rileys. He gave her a small smile, revealing a flash of straight, white teeth.

God, he was gorgeous. And somehow, he seemed to get

better-looking as the days passed.

"Yeah, I had a good day," he said, answering the question that she'd posed to Roby. "Thanks for asking."

With a laugh, she stood. No one would ever mistake Zeke for a sweet boy.

"Hey, Zeke."

"Hey, Go-go. How was your day?"

Nicknames were a part of military life, based on familiarity and friendship. When Zeke had first called her Go-go, she had been on the fence about it. But now she liked it.

"I had a fantastic day," she answered. "I *love* my job."

She toed off her tennis shoes and used her foot to push them toward the wall. Zeke met her in the dining room, and the urge to stand on her tiptoes and kiss him hello was so strong that she had to put the table between them to stop herself.

He glanced down. "What's that?"

"What?"

He pointed toward her hand, where the pink bakery box nestled. "That."

Her fantasy of kissing Zeke had erased the hippo cupcake from her mind. "Give me a minute to change, and then I'll show you."

She placed the box on the concrete tabletop before heading to her bedroom. After shedding her messenger bag and fleece, she stripped out of her scrubs and replaced them with a long-sleeved Michigan State tee and black leggings.

Knowing her feet would get cold, she pulled on a pair of tan UGG boots that she'd discovered at the Salvation Army in Ithaca. They'd been almost brand-new when she'd bought them, probably discarded by a spoiled Cornell student.

She took a moment to toss her dirty scrubs in the hamper,

wash her hands, and remove her makeup. After working around animals all day and dealing with a variety of bodily fluids, she always felt grungy.

As she left the bathroom, she heard Zeke's phone ring. His deep voice floated from the kitchen. "Hello, Andrea."

Zeke's ex-wife called at least a couple of times a week. Sometimes the conversations lasted a few minutes, and sometimes they lasted an hour.

Margo felt her lips curl in disgust. *Andrea.*

A few days after Margo had moved into the apartment, she'd discovered a box of pictures in the hall closet. She had given in to the temptation to snoop and spent a few minutes flipping through the stack of photos before guilt had set in. That was how she knew what Zeke's ex-wife looked like.

Andrea May wasn't cute. She wasn't pretty.

She was beautiful.

Tall and willowy like a supermodel, with thick, coffee-colored hair that waved down her back. Her smooth, olive complexion emphasized her light green eyes, and her lips were a perfect, plump bow.

Realizing that she was lurking in the hallway, Margo returned to her bedroom and curled up in the armchair situated in the corner. She told herself to think about the surgery scheduled early tomorrow morning, but she couldn't stop thinking about Zeke and his ex-wife.

He never talked about Andrea, and Margo was intensely curious about her. She wanted to know how long Zeke had been divorced. She wanted to know why his marriage had ended. And most important, she wanted to know if he was still in love with his ex-wife.

Why else would he continue to stay in touch with her? Why

else would he take her phone calls and spend hours on the phone talking with her? Why else would he—

A hard knock on her door interrupted her list of unanswered questions.

"Dinner's ready," Zeke said.

By the time she reached the door, he'd already left. She slowly made her way to the dining room, wishing that Andrea would accidentally drop her phone into the toilet and be unable to recover any of her contacts.

Climbing onto the barstool, she asked, "What are we having?"

"Tortilla soup and salad with chipotle ranch dressing," he answered curtly.

Regardless of how much time Zeke spent talking with his ex-wife, when the call ended, his mood was always darker than the sky during a thunderstorm. Margo briefly considered hijacking his phone and blocking Andrea's number.

He stomped into the dining room with a bowl of soup in each hand and set them down with an angry-sounding bang. Turning on his heel, he headed back to the kitchen and returned a moment later with salad plates and a big wooden bowl overflowing with greens.

After dumping everything on the table, he slid onto the barstool across from her and reached for the salad tongs. She stopped him by placing her hand over his.

"Wait," she ordered softly. "I want to show you what's in the box."

He met her gaze, his mouth tight with anger and impatience. "Show me, then."

Leaning over, she nabbed the box. "The people at work gave me balloons and cupcakes to celebrate my one-month anniversary. I saved one for you."

She opened the lid and turned the box so he could see it. He stared down at the hippo cupcake for a moment. Slowly, his lips turned upward until finally, his mouth stretched into a grin.

He looked up at her, his dark eyes shining with amusement. "Thanks, Go-go."

Grabbing her fork, she cut a piece of cupcake and held it up in front of him. "Life is short. Eat dessert first."

For a long moment, he just looked at her, unblinking. Then he laughed, that deep rumble that warmed her insides every time she heard it.

"You're right. Life *is* short."

With his gaze holding hers, he grasped her wrist and brought the cupcake-loaded fork to his mouth. His lips closed over it, devouring the moist cake and creamy frosting in one big bite.

"That's all sugar," he said, his fingers still wrapped around her wrist. "Maybe it will sweeten me up."

CHAPTER FOUR

Neat and orderly. That was how Zeke preferred things.

He liked everything to be in its place, and his workstation at Riley O'Brien & Co. reflected his predilection for organization. He tried to minimize the use of paper, and when he couldn't avoid it, he employed a color-coded system that allowed him to find the information he needed in seconds.

Everyone in Zeke's department was borderline obsessive-compulsive about organization. You couldn't be disorganized or scatterbrained if you wanted to excel in supply chain and logistics.

When Zeke had been in the Army, he had been part of the elite Logistics branch. The sheer size of military operations provided logisticians with a level of experience not found anywhere else.

Military logisticians accomplished the same five Rs of supply chain management that civilian logisticians did—getting the right product to the right place, at the right time, at the right price, and the right quantity—but they did it in environments where failure meant the difference between life and death.

Zeke had loved his job as a military logistician—the

challenge, the people, the travel. If not for the IED attack, he would have happily stayed in the Army. But that attack had changed everything.

Fortunately, several people who worked in Riley O'Brien & Co.'s supply chain and logistics department had military backgrounds, so Zeke had immediately felt comfortable in his new position. The company also recruited graduates from Zeke's alma mater, the University of Tennessee, which had one of the best supply chain management programs in the world. He was older than the other UT alums, but they still bonded over Vols football.

Over the past several months, Riley O'Brien & Co.'s supply chain and logistics department had been reorganized to support the new business goals outlined by CEO Quinn O'Brien. Zeke had been hired to direct a new group that focused exclusively on company-owned stores.

Part of the department's reorganization had included a redesign of the workspace. Because communication and collaboration were so critical, the company had done away with the traditional cubicle environment.

The new design included open layout workstations with short, glass partitions and a few lounge areas for quick conversations. Zeke liked his current work environment a hell of a lot more than he'd liked the chaos of a combat tent or the isolation of a closet-sized office.

Despite the lack of walls, the workspace wasn't noisy or distracting; it had a vibrant buzz of energy. And if you needed privacy, you could use one of the huddle rooms, places where employees gathered to work on team projects.

Zeke's laptop dinged, warning him that he had a meeting in thirty minutes. Grabbing a stack of red folders, he flipped through them. As he searched for the ones he would need for the meeting, he heard Justin's voice float from the adjacent workspace.

"Dude, you're killing me with the humming."

Ignoring Justin's complaint, Zeke continued to sort through his folders. He knew the younger guy wasn't talking to him.

"Zeke!"

Startled, Zeke vaulted to his feet and looked over at Justin. "What?"

"You're humming is driving me *crazy*," he griped.

"I'm not humming." Zeke frowned. "I don't hum."

Shaking his head, Justin insisted, "You've been humming for the last hour."

With a glower, Zeke dropped down into his office chair. He hadn't realized it until Justin pointed it out, but he *had* been humming.

Justin stood and leaned his elbows on the low partition separating their workstations. His dark brown hair brushed the collar of his flannel shirt. He'd buttoned it all the way to the neck, where a black bow tie nestled, and striped suspenders stretched over his shoulders.

Yep, Justin was one-hundred-percent hipster. The only thing missing was a fedora.

"I'm pretty sure you were humming 'Can't Feel My Face,'" Justin added.

Zeke definitely could feel his face, and it was growing hot with embarrassment. This was all Margo's fault.

Justin smirked. "I didn't know you liked The Weeknd."

"I don't," Zeke muttered.

He'd never even heard of The Weeknd until Margo had moved in two months ago, and he wasn't a fan. Zeke didn't understand why she loved the singer so much. Even if you could endure the guy's annoying falsetto, his hair looked like a pineapple sprouting from his head, and his name was just plain stupid.

Zeke had grown up listening to Soundgarden, Guns N' Roses, Red Hot Chili Peppers, and Metallica. That was real music.

He was convinced that no man over the age of thirty, except for him, listened to The Weeknd, Taylor Swift, Demi Lovato, or Bruno Mars. But Margo constantly had some pop tune playing on the sound system, and she sang along with it, usually at the top of her lungs.

At least she wasn't tone deaf. To be fair, her singing voice was nice … better than nice. He liked it, even when she belted out "Shake It Off."

"You haven't been your typical grumpy self lately," Justin continued. "Did you finally get laid?"

Zeke glared at him. When he'd been Major May, he hadn't had to deal with smartass remarks from his subordinates. It was times like these when he really missed the Army.

"I am your boss," he pointed out. "Maybe you should show me some respect."

Justin, the little shit, just laughed. "I respect you, Z. That's why I suffered through an hour of your humming before I said anything." His expression turned thoughtful. "Seriously, you seem a lot happier lately. What's the deal?"

Zeke shook his head. "Nothing," he denied.

Yet deep inside, he admitted that Justin was right. He was happier.

He didn't know why. Maybe it was because he was finally settling into his new life.

Or maybe it was because of Margo. Except for her deplorable taste in music, she was damn near the perfect roommate.

She wasn't as neat as he was. Then again, few people were. She left her shoes all over the apartment, like little obstacle courses for him to trip over. But so what? He just picked them— and himself—off the floor and tossed the footwear into her bedroom.

He liked living with her. He liked her calm temperament. She wasn't a drama queen, unlike Andrea, who had regularly thrown tantrums like a nap-deprived toddler.

He liked Margo's intelligence and her sense of humor—never mean-spirited or snarky. She laughed a lot, and he liked the sound of it, echoing throughout the apartment—a reminder that she was there, with him.

He even liked the way she teased him, calling him "Crankenstein" in the morning when he growled at her. She wasn't just a morning person; she was an all-day person. She seemed to have a perpetual smile on her face, and he looked forward to seeing it—and her—when she walked through the door after work.

He spent more time with Margo than he did alone. After work, they hung out, talking or watching TV. And on the weekends, they shopped and ran errands together because he had a car, and she didn't. They'd even gone sightseeing together, visiting Fisherman's Wharf, touring the Cable Car Museum on Nob Hill, and walking through Golden Gate Park with Roby.

Justin tapped out a beat on the partition's glass pane. "Did you sign up for the company softball team?" he asked. "I don't really want to. I'm not into sports."

Yeah, like that's a news flash.

Zeke didn't want to sign up for Riley O'Brien & Co.'s team,

either. He liked sports just fine, but his prosthetic leg prevented him from sliding into the bases. Of course, he wasn't playing for the Giants; this was just a corporate softball league. He doubted there would be much sliding required.

"Brent said it wasn't mandatory," Justin added.

Brent Knowles had overseen the supply chain and logistics department for ten years. Prior to joining Riley O'Brien & Co., he'd worked at UPS for twenty-five years. He knew the industry inside and out.

"He also said that he would prefer our participation," Zeke reminded Justin. "So, yes, I'm going to sign up for the team." He pointed his forefinger at him. "And so are you, hipster."

Justin sighed. "*Damn.* I knew you were going to say that."

"Suck it up. There are only eight games including the tournament."

"Plus weekly practice," Justin said glumly, a whine threading through his voice.

Before Zeke could reply, his cell phone rang. Justin dropped back into his chair, giving him some privacy. Glancing at the screen, Zeke saw his ex-wife's name. He pushed the ignore button, having no desire to talk to Andrea.

When he'd first moved to San Francisco, she had called every couple of weeks, just to check in. Now, she called him every day, sometimes more than once. And lately, she had been dropping hints that she wanted to reconcile.

I think we made a mistake. I miss you. I want to try again. I love you.

He didn't know how to respond when she said those things. He didn't agree. And more important, he didn't feel the same way.

They'd been together for sixteen years, a relationship that had begun their senior year of high school and ended almost three years ago. Their divorce had been finalized just a few months before he'd been injured in the IED attack.

After spending several weeks in the ICU at Ramstein in Germany, he'd returned to the States to finish his recovery at Walter Reed Army Medical Center in Maryland. His parents had been there when he'd arrived.

Much to his surprise, Andrea had been there, too. She had insisted that he move back into the townhome they'd shared as husband and wife to recuperate.

His ex-wife had taken care of him while he learned how to live with one healthy leg and a stump that ended just above his knee. She had taken a leave of absence from her job as a pharmaceutical sales rep and willingly ferried him to doctor appointments and physical therapy sessions. More important, she had encouraged him when he'd been discouraged and depressed.

She'd stood by him when he couldn't stand on his own, even though she had been the one who'd wanted the divorce. She had been unhappy for a long time, and he'd known it.

He had assumed that his military career was the root of her unhappiness. Still, he hadn't wanted to give it up.

Eventually, Andrea had explained that the Army had nothing to do with it. She just wanted more—to love intensely and passionately and to be loved the same way.

She had been determined to get a divorce. She had been so resolute that he hadn't fought for her or their marriage.

If they'd had children, he wouldn't have given up so easily. But they had never been able to agree on timing. When she'd wanted to try, he hadn't been ready. And when he'd been ready, she hadn't wanted to try.

They had rarely been on the same page, and when they had

gone their separate ways, he'd been disappointed rather than devastated. In retrospect, he'd describe the whole experience as painless.

Almost losing his life in Iraq had given Zeke even more clarity about Andrea. He had loved her, but not the way she wanted to be loved … not the intense, passionate love that she craved.

She had supported his decision to take the job with Riley O'Brien & Co. and relocate to the West Coast. After he'd moved, she had dated a cardiologist whom she'd met at a medical conference. That relationship had lasted only a couple of months.

Then she'd dated a landscape architect who had lived a few doors down. That hadn't worked out, either, and after they'd stopped seeing each other, she had started calling Zeke more frequently.

He felt obligated to take her calls. She had helped him through the worst time in his life, and he owed her. In fact, he could never repay her for what she'd done for him.

But talking to her always put him in a bad mood. Marrying Andrea had been a mistake, and he didn't like to make mistakes. Nor did he like to fail.

His phone chimed, signaling a text. It was from Andrea: "Thinking about you."

She had ended the message with a red heart emoji. He grimaced. Eventually, he was going to have to be straight with her: there was no chance of them getting back together.

She had been right about their marriage. She deserved more, and he … well, he didn't know what he deserved. But he knew that his future did *not* include a reconciliation with his ex-wife.

They'd been so young—only twenty-two—when they had

married. He had never dated anyone else. She had been his first serious girlfriend and his first lover. They had been together for nearly five years, and marriage had been the next step on the path to adulthood. At the time, getting married had seemed like the right thing to do.

But he was older now. Smarter, too. And he realized that he had married Andrea because everyone had expected them to tie the knot, not because he'd wanted to spend his life with her.

That realization, that truth, made him feel like shit. It made him ashamed and angry, and every time he talked to her, all those ugly emotions boiled to the surface. And he found it difficult to keep a lid on them.

He responded to Andrea's text: "Busy day. Thanks for checking in."

After shoving his phone in his jeans pocket, he picked up the folders he needed for the meeting. As he headed to the assigned huddle room, his phone chimed with another text.

Clenching his teeth in aggravation, he silently castigated himself for responding to Andrea's text. He never should have engaged. Now she would text him all afternoon.

As usual, he was the first person to show up for the meeting. Thanks to the Army, he was a little anal-retentive about being on time. He dropped the folders on the frosted glass conference table and pulled his phone out of his pocket, intending to put it in silent mode.

He paused when he saw the text was from Margo: "How's your day going?"

And just like that, his bad mood disappeared, and he felt like smiling. He replied to her message: "Good. How's your day go-going?"

She responded with a happy face emoji and followed with

several dog face emojis and a single cat face emoji. His smile turned into a grin. Apparently, she'd had more canine patients today than feline patients.

"What do you want for dinner?" she asked. "Tacos? Spaghetti?"

"Whatever you want." He started to hit send but decided to add another sentence: "I'll stop at the bakery on the way home and get a chocolate meringue pie. Let's eat dessert first."

CHAPTER FIVE

Roby's high-pitched whine startled Margo out of a deep slumber. She wasn't a light sleeper; it took a lot to wake her. She had lived in some very noisy places, including a studio apartment above a dive bar, and she could snooze through almost anything.

Struggling to orient herself, she checked the alarm clock on her nightstand. It was almost two a.m., and she'd climbed into bed around ten thirty. Earlier in the evening, she and Zeke had devoured tiny slices of chocolate meringue pie before enjoying a dinner of soft chicken tacos, Spanish rice, and refried beans.

Roby nudged her hand with his wet nose. Then he licked it with short, quick swipes.

"Do you need to potty?" she asked, thinking he might have an upset belly.

Before she could move, he nipped her fingers, not hard enough to hurt, but hard enough to shock her. He didn't bite unless someone was in immediate danger, and he'd *never* bitten her.

Alarmed, she switched on the lamp on her nightstand. "What's wrong, Roby?"

The Doberman ran to the bedroom door, scratched at it, and

then came back to her. He sat beside her bed, whimpering, his black eyes begging her to get up.

Something had to be terribly wrong for Roby to be so agitated. With her heart pounding in fear, she tossed back her down comforter and surged to her feet. She slept in a cami, cotton boy-short panties, and fuzzy socks, so she spared a moment to don her long terrycloth robe and knot the belt before grabbing her phone.

Remembering the home invasion that had occurred in her apartment in Ithaca, she turned off the lamp. She didn't want to alert an intruder to her location or let him know she was awake and aware.

She made her way to the door as quietly as possible and pressed her ear against it. She couldn't hear anything. No footsteps, no breaking glass, nothing.

Clutching her phone, she dialed Zeke. It rang and rang and rang before going to voice mail. She cursed under her breath. He probably had put his phone on silent when he went to bed. And she'd left her messenger bag—the one that contained her pepper spray and Taser—in the living area.

Idiot!

She stood there, unsure of what to do next. The apartment was in a very safe neighborhood, and break-ins—home invasions, especially—weren't common. She didn't want to call 9-1-1 and alert the police if there was no real danger.

If there was an intruder, he would probably still be in the living area. If she was quiet, she should be able to get to Zeke's room without attracting notice. Plus, Roby was with her, and he would attack if she gave the order. But her beloved dog wouldn't be able to protect her against a gun.

She shoved her phone in the pocket of her robe and grabbed

the aluminum baseball bat she kept beside the door, specifically for this reason. Her hands were damp with nervous sweat, making the bat's grip slippery.

"Shhh," she warned Roby.

Grasping the doorknob, she opened the bedroom door as quietly as she could, wincing when it emitted a little creak. An LED night-light illuminated the hallway, placed there by Zeke so she would be able to see if she got up in the middle of the night to go to the bathroom.

Before she could take one step, Roby sprinted down the hallway. To her surprise, he skidded to a stop in front of Zeke's door instead of continuing into the living area.

That allayed her biggest fear—there was no intruder. But what was going on?

Worried that something was wrong with Zeke, she left the bat behind and rushed down the corridor, her feet sliding on the hardwood floors. As she neared his room, she could hear his voice.

She came to a stop beside her dog, wondering if Zeke was on the phone. But who would he be talking to at this odd hour? Andrea?

A low moan drifted through the wooden door. Maybe he and his ex-wife were enjoying some stimulating phone sex. She scowled at the thought, grinding her teeth together. She was insanely jealous of a man who wasn't hers and a woman she'd never met.

Just as she started to return to her room, Zeke spoke again. She couldn't make out the words, but he sounded agitated, almost panicked. She had never heard him sound that way before, and her stomach turned over.

Roby started scratching on the door, his paws moving

frantically. There was no way he would act like that if Zeke were just talking on the phone.

The volume of Zeke's voice increased—loud enough for her to hear what he was saying through the door. Leaning closer, she realized he was crying out "no" over and over.

Zeke was having a nightmare—a bad one from the sound of it—but he wasn't in any danger, and neither was she. The tension drained out of her body, and she slumped wearily, resting her forehead against the door.

She wanted to comfort Zeke. She wanted to crawl into bed with him, wrap her body around his bigger one, and hold him until his nightmare ended.

Instead, she patted the side of her thigh to get Roby's attention. He stopped scratching at the door, his head cocked toward her.

"Come on, boy, let's go back to bed."

Roby ignored her. He rarely disobeyed her, yet Zeke had captured his canine heart. Grabbing his collar, she tried to pull him away. But he was too strong, and she couldn't get him to budge.

The Doberman obviously didn't want to leave Zeke while he was tormented by a horrible nightmare. And she didn't want to leave him, either.

She knocked softly on the door, hoping it would wake him. But it had no impact. She repeated the motion, louder this time. Unfortunately, that seemed to intensify his nightmare.

Hesitantly, she reached for the doorknob. With her hand hovering above it, she debated whether she should open the door. Roby made the decision for her when he began to repeatedly ram his head into it, a determined doggy head butt.

She opened the door just a crack, and Roby immediately

squeezed through it. The mouth-watering scent that she had come to associate with Zeke wafted over her—a woodsy, tangy combination of sandalwood and citrus.

She'd never been inside Zeke's bedroom. He always kept the door closed, and she had respected his privacy—until now. A tendril of guilt squeezed her conscience, but she reminded herself that she wasn't just being nosy.

Poking her head into the room, she tried to ascertain the layout. No light permeated the space, and she couldn't see a thing. She had no idea where his bed was situated.

With no alternative, she turned on the flashlight app on her phone and pointed it into Zeke's bedroom. Shining the light around, she discovered that his room was much larger than hers. He had enough space to accommodate a full suite of dark, sleek furniture including a dresser, matching chest of drawers, and tall armoire.

She focused the light on the king-size headboard and moved it lower, slowly exposing Zeke to her gaze. He lay on his back, shirtless, with his left arm curved above his head. Dark hair shadowed his armpit and the wide expanse of his chest.

Her conscience scolded her for being voyeuristic, but she gave it the finger. She had spent hours wondering what this man looked like naked, and right or wrong, she was going to take the opportunity to assuage her curiosity.

Sweeping the light downward, she eyed the toned muscles of his stomach, the silky-looking trail of hair that disappeared into the waistband of his gray underwear, and the sizable bulge of his sex. He was *de-luscious*, to quote her man-eating co-worker, Jenny.

As Margo continued her inspection, several things registered simultaneously: Roby had jumped on the bed and curled up near Zeke's left hip; Zeke had pushed the tangled sheet and comforter toward the footboard; and his left leg ended a few inches below the edge of his boxer briefs in a rounded stump.

All the breath in her lungs left in a *whoosh*. Zeke was an amputee, and she'd been completely ignorant of that fact.

Questions floated through her mind. How and when had Zeke lost his leg? Had it occurred while he'd been in the military, serving his country? That seemed likely.

Was his nightmare related to his missing limb? Did he have nightmares regularly? And were they a symptom of a larger problem, perhaps post-traumatic stress disorder?

Roby shifted closer to Zeke and exhaled a contented sigh. Zeke was no longer moaning or talking in his sleep. He seemed to be resting peacefully, his face relaxed.

She turned off the flashlight app, plunging the room into darkness. She didn't know if Zeke's nightmare had ended on its own or if Roby's presence had something to do with it, but she decided to let the Doberman stay where he was … where she wanted to be.

Lucky dog.

She stood there for a moment before returning to her room. She left her door open in case Roby wanted to return to her bed, but she doubted he would move until Zeke forced him to.

Of course, Zeke would be shocked when he woke up with Roby in bed with him. He would wonder how the dog had gotten into his room.

She rarely lied, believing the old adage "Honesty is the best policy," but she was going to lie to Zeke. She would tell him that Roby had wanted to go out during the night, and that she'd fallen asleep before he'd come back in. She would insinuate that her dog had found his own way into Zeke's bedroom by opening the door.

Zeke would buy that story. Dobermans were one of the smartest dog breeds, and they could be trained to do almost anything, including open doors.

After removing her robe, she slid back into bed. Lying on her side, she stared at the open doorway, where the night-light glowed faintly. Her thoughts were spinning, faster than a Tilt-a-Whirl.

Zeke had mentioned during their first meeting that he had served in both Afghanistan and Iraq. With an uncle in the Army, she had always held servicemen and women in high esteem, appreciating their dedication and sacrifice. They made it possible for her to live her life the way she wanted to, and she was grateful.

Was Zeke one of the thousands of soldiers who had lost a limb in combat in the Middle East? Or had the injury occurred in a more innocuous setting here in the U.S.—a car accident on the way to the grocery store or a hit-and-run while he crossed a busy street?

She didn't know the answer because he'd never mentioned that he was an amputee. He'd never even hinted at it, and she'd never guessed, even though they'd lived together for more than two months.

He always wore clothes that covered his lower body—jeans, cargo pants, pajamas, sweats—so she had never seen his legs. And while she had occasionally noticed that he limped, it was so slight she had never imagined anything more than an achy ankle or a bum knee. No one would ever guess that he had a prosthetic leg.

She had never known anyone who'd lost a limb. Her expertise was limited to quadrupeds; several patients at Bay Area Animal Care were missing a limb.

Animals lost limbs in a variety of ways—usually an accident—and most could function with only three legs. Losing a limb didn't prevent them from living full lives, and she believed the same was true for humans.

She thought about getting up and researching amputation online, but decided against it. She had an early-morning surgery scheduled, and she owed it to her patient to be alert. She would conduct her research during her lunch break.

Her heart ached when she thought about Zeke and the pain he must have endured, both physically and emotionally. First, the trauma of the injury, and then the trauma of having to relearn how to do everything. Moreover, losing his leg meant the end of his military career, which he'd obviously loved.

And what about Andrea? Had she abandoned Zeke when he'd needed her the most?

Marriage was sacred, especially the part about "in sickness and in health." If you couldn't rely on your spouse, who could you rely on?

Margo clenched her fingers into her plush down comforter. Her jealousy was clouding her judgment; she wasn't being fair. She was assuming the worst about Zeke's ex-wife, with no proof that Andrea was a heartless bitch.

Tears burned the backs of her eyes. Zeke had suffered a tremendous loss, yet he had somehow found the courage to start over in a new city with a new job.

She had respected and admired him before she'd known about his leg. But now, those feelings were amplified. His determination and strength awed her. She doubted she would have the resilience he'd demonstrated.

She imagined that it must have been particularly difficult for Zeke to adjust to life as an amputee. She wouldn't be surprised if he thought his missing limb meant that he was lacking in some way.

Maybe some women would find an amputee unattractive. But she wasn't one of them. For her, Zeke as a whole, was greater than the sum of his parts.

Her feelings for him were completely different from any she had felt before. She'd had only one serious relationship, and that had been years ago, when she had attended Michigan State. During veterinary school, she'd dated sporadically, but no one had interested her more than her studies and her future career as a veterinarian.

She had never felt this strongly about a man. And her feelings for Zeke were growing stronger by the day.

She was falling for him.

Margo wished Zeke had told her about his leg. His silence on the subject—his secrecy—hurt her feelings. But knowing Zeke, she doubted that he discussed his condition with anyone.

Nonetheless, she wanted him to *want* to tell her what had happened to him. She wanted him to trust her enough to share the most painful parts of his past.

She felt closer to him than she'd ever felt to anyone. She told him everything … well, almost everything. She didn't tell him that she thought of him as more than a roommate and more than a good friend.

She didn't tell him that she wanted to go down on him while he sat on the sofa in the living room. And she didn't tell him that she fantasized about him picking her up, holding her against the wall, and loving her until they were all sweaty and sticky and satisfied.

Hmm.

Was that kind of sex even possible with a prosthetic leg? She wondered how much weight it could bear. It would probably depend on the model of the device, as well as material and age.

What sexual positions were best for lower-limb amputees? Were some more comfortable than others?

Hmm.

That was something she was going to have to research ... just in case.

CHAPTER SIX

Every Tuesday, Zeke had softball practice at Lindley Meadow in Golden Gate Park from seven to eight o'clock. This evening was the first time his team would meet, and Zeke had just enough time to stop by the apartment to scarf down a snack and change clothes.

Roby was waiting at the front door to greet him, and Zeke spared a moment to sit on the sofa and rub the Doberman's belly. It was their evening routine.

Zeke had grown up in a pet-free home because his mother was allergic to all furry beasts. To his surprise, he really liked having Roby around. He didn't even mind when the dog snuck into his bedroom and crawled into bed with him.

But he did mind Roby's enthusiastic wake-up kisses. Those he could do without.

He gave the canine one final pat and hurried to his bedroom. After removing his brown lace-up boots, he shed his jeans and button-down shirt and donned a white long-sleeved thermal tee, a pair of gray sweat pants, and tennis shoes.

Riley O'Brien & Co. had provided its players with practice T-shirts stamped with the team logo, as well as a full uniform consisting of a team jersey, full-length pants, and cap. Zeke was relieved that they would be wearing full-length pants instead of knee-length pants so he could hide his prosthetic limb.

No one at Riley O'Brien & Co. knew he was missing half a leg. Hell, only two people in the entire Bay Area knew: Zeke's primary care physician and his prosthetist, the guy who made sure his prosthetic limb fit correctly and performed as it was supposed to.

Zeke wasn't ashamed of being an amputee, but he didn't advertise the fact, either. He wanted people to view him as a regular guy—one with two legs. He'd seen it happen too many times with other veterans: once people knew you were an amputee, they treated you differently.

But he had to acknowledge the fact that he *was* different from other men. His lack of a limb prevented him from doing certain things and performing certain activities. He couldn't run or shower without the right kind of prosthetic. And he couldn't have sex, either, unless the woman was on top or they were positioned on their sides.

That was one of the reasons he had avoided sex altogether. Being with someone new was awkward enough with two legs.

He wasn't sure how a woman would respond to his stump and prosthetic limb. Would she be repulsed? Or worse, would she find it sexy?

He hated to admit it, but he was afraid to find out. And that fear was compounded by the fact that he'd had sex with only one woman: Andrea. All his sexual experience was limited to his ex-wife and what she had preferred.

After pulling the practice T-shirt over his thermal, Zeke headed to the kitchen. On the way through the living room, he caught sight of Roby. The dog was lying on his belly on the

Afghan rug with a scrap of purple material tucked between his front paws.

Knowing that it wasn't one of the dog's squeaky toys, Zeke distracted the animal by scratching behind his pointy ears. With his other hand, he snatched the unknown item from the Doberman's paws. That was when he realized that Roby's misappropriated plaything was a pair of bikini panties.

Margo's panties.

Tiny. Lacy. Delicate.

Sexy.

And then his brain disobeyed a direct order from its commanding officer. It conjured up an image of Margo wearing these panties and nothing else.

The color would glow vibrantly against her creamy skin. The miniscule triangle would barely hide her pussy; it might even reveal some strawberry-blond curls. And the stretchy lace would lovingly hug the round curve of her ass.

Oh, yeah, Margo had a great ass. He'd noticed it before. He was a man, and he wasn't blind.

But she was his roommate. And more important, she was way too young and too full of joy for someone like him.

He shouldn't be thinking about her in her underwear. He shouldn't be wondering if the pair he held were fresh out of the laundry or if she'd already worn them. And he sure as hell shouldn't be getting hard just by thinking about how she'd smell, especially when his dick hadn't been interested in any woman since he'd lost his leg.

His insubordinate brain needed to be court-martialed, found guilty, and sentenced to life in Leavenworth.

Zeke stalked to Margo's bathroom, tossed the panties inside, and slammed the door shut, though he didn't know what good that would do since Roby could open doors. Her dog wasn't nearly as well-behaved as she thought he was.

With that taken care of, Zeke grabbed a granola bar from the pantry. As he bit into the chewy snack, he warned his brain to never again think about Margo naked.

She wasn't naked, his brain countered belligerently. *She was wearing panties.*

He groaned under his breath. This wasn't good. He couldn't lust after his roommate. It would ruin everything.

On the way out the door, he grabbed his fleece jacket. Although it was still light outside, the temperature had started to fall, and it was a little chilly.

As he made the trip to Lindley Meadow, he forced himself to think about softball instead of Margo and her sexy underwear. So many Riley O'Brien & Co. employees had signed up for the late-spring/early-summer league, the company had formed multiple teams to compete and coordinated the practice times and locations for each team.

Because they were playing slow-pitch softball, ten players were on each team. All the teams had jeans-related names, like Pockets and Zippers. Zeke couldn't decide if the names were inventive or idiotic.

His team—the Rivets—consisted of six men and four women. Prior to practice, everyone on the team had received an email with the practice schedule, game schedule, and assigned equipment manager. Fortunately, Zeke wasn't responsible for that onerous task.

Based on Zeke's initial assessment, his teammates ranged in age from early twenties to late sixties. He seemed to fall somewhere in between.

Did that make him middle-aged? Probably so.

Zeke and his teammates stood in a circle near the edge of the softball diamond. He didn't know any of them personally, but he knew *of* one of them: Cal O'Brien, the great-great-grandson of the company's founder. He headed up Riley O'Brien & Co.'s global marketing and communications department, managing a massive group of people.

The dark-haired man appeared to be just a few years younger than Zeke, in his early thirties. His tall, lean frame hinted at an active lifestyle.

Cal spoke first. "Hi, everyone. Let's start by introducing ourselves. For those of you who don't know me, I'm Cal O'Brien." He pointed at the twenty-something Asian guy standing next to Zeke. "Bohai, why don't you go first ... tell us your name and what you do for Riley O'Brien & Co."

After everyone had introduced themselves, Cal said, "We need a team captain—someone who can represent the team during the games, assign fielding positions, and create the lineup." His light blue eyes skimmed over the group. "Anyone want to volunteer?"

Silence greeted Cal's question, and he chuckled. "I feel like that teacher in *Ferris Bueller's Day Off* ... Anyone? Anyone?"

It was physically painful for Zeke to just stand there. The military had conditioned him to step up.

He waited, counting off the seconds in his head. *One. Two. Three. Four. Five.* No one raised their hand.

With an internal sigh of resignation, he said, "I'll do it. I'll be the team captain."

Cal's eyebrows arched. "Yeah?"

Zeke nodded. "I played baseball in high school, and I also played on the intramural softball team in college."

"Sounds like we're in good hands, then."

Being the team captain wouldn't be all that terrible. At least it would allow Zeke to decide what position he played. And he would be able to substitute other players in the lineup so he wouldn't have to run bases.

"Let's go sit down and decide who's going to do what," Cal suggested, tilting his head toward the bench inside the chain-link dugout.

As the group started toward the dugout, the O'Brien heir fell into step beside Zeke. "This is a first," the younger man said.

Glancing sideways, Zeke asked, "What's a first?"

"Usually, I get stuck being the team captain. I think it's because no one wants to step on my toes."

Zeke stopped mid-stride. Everyone except for Cal continued. They turned to face each other.

"Am I stepping on your toes?"

"Hell, no! I'm glad someone had the balls to volunteer. I'm tired of always being the team captain. It's a pain in the ass."

Cal's candor made Zeke laugh. "I knew I should have kept my mouth shut."

"Why didn't you?"

Zeke shrugged. "It's not the first time I've volunteered to do something unpleasant."

The other man stared at Zeke, his gaze assessing. "You're one of the veterans we hired through our new program, aren't you?"

"Yeah."

"I thought so." When Zeke arched his eyebrow in a silent question, Cal explained, "It's the way you stand." He held out his right hand. "Thank you for your service to our country."

It made Zeke uncomfortable when people thanked him for his military service. He had always felt fortunate that he could serve. But he was glad people recognized the sacrifice that servicemen and women made every day.

Shaking Cal's hand, Zeke said, "It was an honor."

"How do you like working for us?" Cal asked as they resumed the trek toward the dugout. Before Zeke could answer, the other man snorted derisively. "I doubt you'd tell me if you *didn't* like it … since I'm one of *the* O'Briens."

"You're right." Zeke admitted, nodding his head. "But I wouldn't lie and tell you that I liked it, either."

Cal laughed, clearly delighted by his answer. "I think Riley O'Brien & Co. is lucky to have you, Zeke," he said, slapping him on the back.

Zeke spent the next thirty minutes assessing his team's batting and fielding abilities. The level of skill surprised him. Apparently, Riley O'Brien & Co. employees took their softball seriously.

With Cal's help, Zeke assigned positions and created a lineup. It had been a no-brainer to assign the pitcher position to Norah Williams, a young black woman who worked in the company's e-commerce department. She had played softball at the University of North Carolina and had a fluid underhand toss.

No one had wanted the catcher position, so Zeke had forced his teammates to draw straws. The loser was Jake Lilliard, a vice president in the finance department who had roared into the parking lot on a black Triumph motorcycle.

Jake looked way too young to hold such a high-ranking position with one of the biggest apparel companies in the world. Zeke would guess the tall, auburn-haired man was thirty years old, max. But Jake was supposedly a genius with numbers, and Quinn O'Brien had recruited him directly from Stanford's MBA program.

Grumbling, Jake donned the catcher's protective equipment and took up his position. Everyone had a turn at bat, and by the end of the hour-long practice, the team was playing well.

"Good job, everyone," Zeke praised his teammates as they shoved their equipment into the mesh bag. "See you at the game."

The violet of twilight had given way to an indigo night sky. Zeke shrugged on his fleece jacket, grateful for its warmth. As he began the walk back to his Jeep Cherokee, Cal and Jake flanked him.

"Want to grab a beer?" Cal asked.

"Magnolia Brewery is pretty close," Jake said. "Have you ever been there? They make their own beer."

"Sure," he answered, partly because it had been a long, long time since he'd grabbed a beer with anyone, and partly because he had no desire to commit career suicide and ignore an invitation from an O'Brien.

"It's too far to walk, though," Cal added. "Do you mind driving, Zeke? My Caddy is a bitch to park, and Jake only has his bike."

Zeke readily agreed, privately relieved by Cal's suggestion. Since the IED attack, he had a hard time being a passenger in any vehicle. He preferred to be in the driver's seat—literally and figuratively.

During the short drive to Magnolia Brewery, Cal and Jake talked about the monthly poker game that Quinn hosted at his house in Laurel Heights. Apparently, it was a tradition that had started when Quinn and Cal lived together, and invitations to the game were highly coveted.

A memory of playing poker with his buddies in Iraq floated through Zeke's mind. He missed the camaraderie ... the good-natured ribbing that always occurred when a group of men got together to play a card game.

"Do you play poker?" Cal asked Zeke from his place in the backseat.

"Yes. Badly."

Jake laughed. "Then you and Cal have something in common."

"Asshole," Cal muttered. "I'm a fucking awesome poker player."

Looking over his shoulder at Cal, the young VP smirked. "Keep telling yourself that."

The brewery was what Zeke had expected. A big bar, lots of dark wood, long tables with benches, and an old-fashioned tile floor. For a Tuesday night at eight thirty, it was quite crowded, but they managed to find some space on one end of a table near the back.

Once Zeke was settled on the bench, he asked, "So what do you recommend?"

"If you like IPAs, you should try the Proving Ground IPA," Cal suggested. "It's won a lot of awards."

"I like dark beers," Jake added. "I always get the Lightning Imperial Stout when it's on tap."

"Or you could get a beer flight," Cal said. "Then you could try several different brews."

Zeke took Cal's suggestion, ordering a three-beer flight when the server came by. It didn't take long for her to return with their beers.

Cal held up his pilsner glass of blond ale. "Here's to not being the worst team in the softball league."

Laughing, Zeke and Jake tapped their own glasses against Cal's. "Hear, hear," they chimed.

Zeke took a sip of his wheat beer. He'd already forgotten its name, but he liked it. It left a tangy, citrusy aftertaste.

"What branch of the military were you in?" Cal asked Zeke.

"Army."

"Did you join right out of high school?"

Zeke shook his head. "After college. I was part of the ROTC program."

Reserve Officers' Training Corps had paid for his college education. In return, he had been required to commit to five years in the Army.

"How long did you serve?" Jake asked.

"Twelve years."

Zeke took another sip of his beer, wondering if a casual outing with colleagues was going to morph into the Spanish Inquisition. He sure as hell hoped not.

"How long have you worked at Riley O'Brien & Co.?" he asked Jake.

"Almost five years."

"Why did you leave the Army?" Cal asked.

Obviously, Zeke's efforts to redirect the conversation hadn't worked.

"I was injured."

He could tell Cal and Jake wanted to follow up with more questions, but his tone made it clear that they wouldn't be answered. He didn't talk about the IED attack, and he wasn't going to start now.

It was bad enough that he had to relive it in his nightmares. He didn't want to spend his waking hours talking about it. In fact, he'd never talked about the IED attack with anyone except the counselor in Maryland who had specialized in combat injuries and PTSD.

A lot of soldiers refused to acknowledge that they needed help to deal with their emotions, but Zeke wasn't one of them.

He'd known that he needed help, and he'd gotten it.

The counselor had assured him that the attack hadn't been Zeke's fault. But the fact was, it had been his decision that put the supply convoy in harm's way. He was the one who had insisted that they take that specific route, believing it to be safer and faster.

Sometimes Zeke wished he couldn't remember the attack. Most people who experienced traumatic injuries like his had no memories of what happened immediately before, during, or after.

But his memories were so clear they were like a movie playing in IMAX—a loud, violent, stomach-churning movie.

He remembered the lead Humvee exploding first, creating a cloud of smoke and dust. He remembered the IED hitting his vehicle with an ear-deafening boom and a bone-jarring quake.

He remembered seeing his best friend with half his face blown off. And he remembered looking down and seeing nothing but bone and blood and charred flesh where his left leg had been.

He carried the memory of the attack with him—emotionally and physically. It would always be with him.

But he was alive, and he was grateful that his life had been spared when so many of his buddies lay in a grave. He hadn't always felt that way, but he did now.

His phone vibrated in the pocket of his sweat pants, startling him. He reached for it reflexively.

The screen displayed a text from Margo: "How was practice? I made spinach lasagna for dinner. Have you eaten?"

Glancing up from his phone, he asked the guys, "Are we just drinking or are we eating, too?"

"Eating," Cal and Jake answered simultaneously.

Zeke replied to Margo's text: "Practice was good. I'm the team captain. Having dinner with a couple of co-workers. Home around eleven."

She responded with two emojis: a baseball bat and a smiley face.

He placed his phone on the table, facedown, and met the curious gazes of the men across from him. Cal cocked his head toward Zeke's phone.

"Wife?" he asked.

Zeke shook his head. "No. I'm not married. It was my roommate. She was just checking in."

He realized his mistake immediately. The military had taught him to answer only the question asked and then to shut up. But he had just over-shared in a big way.

"*She?*" Jake repeated. "You have a female roommate?"

"Yeah."

Zeke could tell by the looks on their faces what they were thinking. For some unknown reason, he felt compelled to set the record straight.

"She's *just* my roommate. It's completely platonic. I don't think about her that way. She's attractive, but I'm not attracted to her. Not even a little."

Cal smiled slowly, his eyes glinting with amusement. "Not even a little?" He glanced sideways at Jake. "Our man Zeke doth protest too much, methinks."

Jake nodded. "Methinks, too."

"It's not like that," Zeke protested.

But then he realized that maybe, just maybe, it *was* like that.

CHAPTER SEVEN

Margo had paid only a hundred dollars for her evening gown, but she felt like a million bucks in it. After weeks of searching consignment boutiques around the city for the perfect dress for the Pictures & Paws Gala, she'd finally found it.

The art auction and gala benefited the Fog City Animal Shelter, a nonprofit, no-kill shelter that served greater Marin County. Every year, the event was held at the Four Seasons San Francisco on the third Saturday in May and featured an art auction consisting of pictures by famous photographers followed by dinner and dancing.

Margo's veterinary clinic had sponsored two tables at the gala, and all employees had been invited to attend and bring a guest. Zeke was the only person she'd wanted to go with, and a few days ago, she had finally worked up enough courage to ask him. She'd lied and told him that her date had canceled because of a business trip.

She was turning into quite a liar when it came to Zeke. But she'd instinctively known that he wouldn't have agreed to go with her unless he'd thought that she had been deserted.

He had agreed to escort her, albeit reluctantly, and not before expressing his displeasure about wearing a tux. Apparently, he'd never worn one. In the past, he'd always worn his formal Army uniform, which he called his "mess dress."

She, meanwhile, had never spent so much money on a single piece of clothing. But this dress ... Oh, it was totally worth it. She had immediately fallen in love with the mermaid gown, with its navy-blue lace and nude underlay.

The cap sleeves and plunging illusion V-neck kept it modest. But it was sexy, too—snug and formfitting, especially around her hips and butt. Plus, the underlay gave the impression that she was nude under the lace, and the curves of her breasts were visible through the nude material of the V-neck.

The dark-colored lace sparkled with tiny beads, making the dress shimmer when she moved, and her back was completely exposed from her nape to her waist. Her nude satin sandals— another consignment store find—added three inches to her height.

She'd curled her hair into loose waves and pulled it up on one side with the crystal hair comb she'd splurged on. Smoky gray eyeshadow and mascara emphasized her blue eyes, and peachy-nude gloss shimmered on her lips.

Turning to Roby, she asked, "So what do you think?"

The Doberman, who was curled up on top of her paisley duvet cover, didn't even open his eyes. She hoped Zeke's response would be more encouraging.

She wanted to make a good impression with her colleagues, but more important, she wanted Zeke to notice her. She desperately wanted him to *see* her ... to *desire* her.

Although she and Zeke had planned to drive to the Four Seasons together, he'd texted her about an hour ago, to let her know that his softball game was running long. She could tell from his message that he was upset by the delay. He had apologized profusely and promised to get to the gala as soon as possible.

She knew most women would be incensed about the change in plans, but she wasn't. These things happened. She was just happy that Zeke was going to be at the gala with her, even for a limited time.

Since his company softball league had started three weeks ago, they hadn't spent much time together. She got the sense that he was avoiding her, but she didn't know if that was reality or her overactive imagination.

Her phone chimed with a text notifying her that the cab was waiting out front. Contrary to the rest of the world, she didn't use ride-sharing services like Uber. Call her paranoid, but she thought they weren't as safe as a cab.

After grabbing her diaphanous midnight-blue wrap and satin clutch, she left the apartment and carefully descended the front steps in her heels. The cab driver didn't bother to open the car door for her, but she still felt like a princess … a very uncomfortable princess. Apparently, evening gowns were designed for standing, not sitting.

To her relief, the drive to the Four Seasons didn't take long. Located in the heart of the SoMa district, the luxury hotel was right across the street from Yerba Buena Gardens, an eighty-seven-acre urban garden.

The Pictures & Paws event was being held in the Veranda Ballroom and Terrace. When she arrived on the fifth floor, the space was already packed with people, all of them garbed in colorful evening gowns or sleek tuxedos.

She had never attended an event like this, but she squared her shoulders and reminded herself that she had just as much right to be here as anyone else, maybe more. She was educated and licensed to care for the animals everyone professed to love so much.

Hundreds of pictures decorated the walls, a mixture of black-and-white and color images hanging from metal rods. Most of the photos featured animals. She wished she had the money to bid on and win a couple of the pictures, but she was still trying to rebuild her rainy-day fund.

She took her time getting to the tables reserved for Bay Area Animal Care, enjoying the lively atmosphere. She had just removed her wrap and dropped it on one of the chairs when she heard her name.

Turning, she spotted Jenny hurrying across the room, as fast as her tight red dress would allow. Her shiny black hair swung around her face, revealing glimpses of sparkly, dangly earrings.

Jenny hugged her. "You look gorgeous," the petite woman gushed, her almond-shaped eyes wide with obvious admiration. "Where did you get your dress?"

"At this tiny consignment shop on Sacramento Street. I can't remember the name of it."

"I can never find anything good at those kinds of shops."

Margo smiled wryly. She doubted Jenny had ever stepped into a consignment shop or thrift store. Her family was extremely wealthy, and her father spoiled his only daughter shamelessly. She worked at the clinic because she loved animals, not because she needed the money.

"And I love your hair," Jenny added. "I never see it in anything but a ponytail."

"That's not true. Sometimes I wear it in a braid."

Her friend laughed. "I like it better this way. It's so glamorous … like the hairstyles in the 1940s. Very Agent Carter."

"Thank you." Margo frowned. "Who's Agent Carter?"

"You know, from the Marvel comics. World-class spy. Captain America's girlfriend."

Margo nodded. "Oh, right."

"So, where's your roomie? I can't wait to meet him."

Margo had mentioned Zeke to Jenny a couple of times. Okay, more than a couple of times. She talked about him incessantly.

Suddenly, a horrifying thought occurred to her. She'd never told Jenny that she had feelings for Zeke.

What if Jenny flirted with Zeke? What if he liked it? What if her co-worker and her roommate clicked?

Margo lightly touched the other woman's forearm. "Jenny…" she began, but stopped when she couldn't figure out the best way to articulate her feelings. She really wanted to say: *Hands off. He's mine.*

Jenny met Margo's gaze, her face openly curious. After a moment, her glossy red lips curled into a smile.

"Don't worry, Margo. I'm not going to poach on your territory."

"He's not my territory," she admitted reluctantly.

"But you want him to be." Jenny smiled knowingly. "Isn't that why you invited him tonight and wore a dress like that?"

She nodded. "I want him to notice me as a woman, not just an androgynous roommate," she confided.

"Oh, he'll definitely notice you. And he won't be the only one, either. No guy could overlook you in that dress." She laughed, the husky sound edged with wickedness. "This should be a very entertaining evening."

*****

A third person in the Bay Area now knew that Zeke had a prosthetic limb—the tailor at Saks Fifth Avenue who had fitted him for his tuxedo. The gruff older man had felt the edges of Zeke's molded plastic socket through the expensive wool-blend of the trousers, but he hadn't seemed to care much. He'd been more interested in whether Zeke dressed left or right.

As Zeke stood in the elevator in the Four Seasons, he ran his hand over his hair, searching for any unruly strands. Satisfied that everything was in order, he adjusted the French cuffs of his bright white tuxedo shirt and furtively checked his fly to make sure it was zipped.

Never in his life had he showered, shaved, and dressed as quickly as he had tonight. He was surprised he'd nicked himself only once.

Even though he'd driven like a maniac to get to the hotel as fast as humanly possible, he was still forty-five minutes late. He hated being late, regardless of the circumstances. But his tardiness tonight was even more unacceptable because Margo had been counting on him.

Because of a stupid softball game, she'd had to take a taxi in an evening gown. She was probably livid, and he couldn't blame her.

Why hadn't he just left the game early? Better yet, why hadn't he declined Margo's invitation to attend Pictures & Paws?

He should have. But he'd hated the thought of her going to this type of event alone. And, if he were honest with himself, he would admit that he'd wanted to go with her, even if it was a monumentally bad idea.

Being around her was *torture*. A couple of days ago, he'd accidentally bumped into her in the kitchen, his front grazing her back. That small touch had created a big problem ... behind his zipper.

Ever since that day when he had retrieved Margo's panties

from Roby's paws, Zeke had tried—and failed—to push her back into the roommate-only zone. But those tiny panties had already done their damage.

Whenever they were together, he constantly thought about what she wore underneath her clothes. He even thought about it when they weren't together.

His dormant libido had awakened, and now the damn thing was boiling like an active volcano. It could erupt at any time.

Zeke should be happy that his penis had returned to its normal operations. But he wasn't. Instead, he was frustrated and edgy and hard all the fucking time.

He didn't understand why this was happening now. And he sure as hell didn't understand why it was happening with Margo.

It didn't happen with anyone else.

Today, during the softball game, a pretty woman on the opposing team had run into him. The force of the impact had knocked them to the ground, with her sprawled on top.

She'd been a sweet-smelling, curvy armful. And his penis had been uninterested.

If it could talk, it would have said, *I'm bored.* But around Margo, it said, *Mmm, I want some of that.*

Of course, his dick didn't care about the eleven-year age gap between them. And it didn't care that she had her whole life ahead of her, while he had already lived a big portion of his.

Finally, the elevator reached the fifth floor. When he stepped out, he immediately began to look for Margo. No matter where they were, her bright hair made it easy to spot her.

After searching the area where the pictures were displayed and the ballroom where dinner would be served, he wandered onto the terrace. The huge space overlooked Yerba Buena Gardens, and the surrounding buildings provided plenty of light.

He surveyed the small group of people on the terrace. His gaze landed on a woman with vibrant reddish-gold hair. She was a little taller than Margo, and her hair was wavy instead of straight. Her back was to him, the flawless skin exposed by her formfitting dress.

Damn, that dress is something else.

The dress's lace overlay gave the impression that she was naked underneath. And the way it hugged her curvy hips and cupped her round ass … that should be prohibited in public venues to prevent riots.

Wait … he recognized that ass. He saw it—stared at it—every day.

The woman in the sexy dress was Margo. And the moment his dick realized that fact, it woke up from its nap and did a couple of stretches in preparation for vigorous exercise.

Zeke took a deep breath and exhaled slowly. For a moment, he thought about turning around, going back home, and locking himself in his bedroom until this insanity passed.

But then Margo glanced in his direction. And he knew, without a doubt, that he wasn't going anywhere.

He could tell the moment she saw him because her lips tilted in a delighted, welcoming smile. Shock sizzled through him. Every other woman he knew would have given him an icy glare for being so late. Andrea would have harangued him for being selfish and inconsiderate, and she would have been right.

But Margo wasn't angry. She was happy to see him, and that made him feel even guiltier for being late.

She gave him a little wave before beckoning him with a flutter of her fingers. He moved toward her, trying not to limp as he crossed the terrace. The fall during the softball game had aggravated his leg.

When he reached her, she leaned up and gave him a hug. The first time she'd hugged him, months ago, he had just stood there like a giant oak tree, uncomfortable with her affectionate nature. But he was used to it now, and he hugged her back.

As he wrapped his arms around her, his palm grazed the bare skin of her back. How could anyone's skin be so soft? Was she this soft everywhere?

He moved his hand a little lower, and his fingers encountered the lace of her dress. He wondered if she was wearing panties underneath, and if so, what color they were.

"I'm so glad you're here," she murmured. "Thank you for coming."

"I'm sorry I'm late, Go-go."

"It's okay," she replied, waving off his apology.

She stepped back and assessed his appearance. "You look very good in a tux, Zeke. But your bow tie is crooked. Lean down a little so I can fix it."

He complied, bending down until his nose was almost buried in her fragrant hair. It smelled like cherries and vanilla.

As she fiddled with his bow tie, she asked, "Did you win the game?"

"Yes. Six to four."

"Yay! Good job, team captain!"

The sound of a man clearing his throat drew Margo's attention. As she turned, the decorative comb in her hair sparkled. "I'm so sorry for being rude, Derek. Let me introduce you."

Suddenly, Zeke realized Margo wasn't alone. He had been so dazzled by her that he hadn't even noticed the guy standing in front of her.

"Zeke, this is Derek Symons. He's one of my clients."

Zeke eyed the other man, cataloguing his Armani tuxedo—

the same one that Zeke had deemed too expensive when he'd gone shopping at Saks. They were about the same height and build, but the similarities ended there.

Derek was just as young and fresh-faced as Margo. Unlike Zeke, he didn't have any gray strands threading through his dark brown hair, nor did he have any lines radiating outward from his hazel eyes.

Margo continued with her introduction. "Derek recently joined Abbott, Seligman…" She smiled ruefully. "What was the rest of it?"

"Abbott, Seligman & Rodarte," Derek supplied. "It's one of the largest law firms on the West Coast. So far, it's going well. I'm really happy there."

Zeke could feel Derek's eyes on him, sizing him up, wondering who he was. He extended his right hand to the younger man, who gripped it strongly.

"Zeke May."

"It's a pleasure to meet you, Zeke. How do you know Margo?"

Margo laughed lightly. "Oops, I left that part out! Zeke is my roommate. I had a hard time finding a place to live when I moved here, and he had an extra bedroom to rent. He and my uncle are old Army buddies."

Margo's explanation was completely accurate. Yet it made Zeke irrationally angry, especially the "old" part and the way she minimized their relationship.

"Roommate," Derek repeated, visibly perking up. He was obviously interested in more than Margo's stellar skills as a veterinarian.

The two of them had a lot in common. They were at the same point in their lives, their careers taking off.

Both were hopeful and optimistic. They oozed enthusiasm and eagerness.

Margo and Derek made sense. Margo and Zeke did *not* make sense.

"Yeah, I'm her roommate," Zeke confirmed, giving Derek the green light to make his move.

But he really wanted to say: *Hands off. She's mine.*

CHAPTER EIGHT

"Are you okay?" Jenny asked, placing her hand atop Margo's.

Margo stared out the windshield of Jenny's sporty BMW. It was late, past eleven o'clock, and the residential street was quiet.

When Margo didn't reply, the other woman sighed. "You did everything you could to save that dog."

Margo knew the vet tech was right. She'd spent five hours in the operating room with Jon and Jenny, trying to repair the injuries the golden retriever had sustained in a car accident while riding with its owner. But they hadn't been able to save the canine.

"Do you need anything?" Jenny asked softly, sympathy shading her voice. "Wine? Ice cream? A Ghirardelli chocolate bar?"

"No."

The only thing Margo needed was already in the apartment: Zeke.

"You did a good job tonight," Margo told Jenny, knowing the younger woman was upset, too. "Thank you for staying late. And thank you for giving me a ride home."

"Any time."

She scooped her messenger bag from the floorboard, opened the door, and climbed out. "I'll see you on Monday," she said before pushing the door shut.

Looking up at the Victorian, she noticed the lights were on in the apartment. She doubted Zeke was still up, though. He usually went to bed around ten, even on non-work nights. When she teased him about it, he told her that old men go to bed early.

But he'd stayed up late for the Pictures & Paws gala last weekend. They hadn't returned home until nearly midnight.

The evening hadn't turned out as she'd hoped. He had treated her the same way he always treated her. And at one point, he'd disappeared to take a phone call from Andrea, leaving Margo alone with Derek.

Zeke's indifference had badly bruised her ego, and when Derek had asked her out, she had impulsively accepted his invitation. Of course, she regretted that decision now, and she needed to find a way to gracefully get out of the date.

Pausing at the base of the steps, she tried to muster the energy to mount them. Just then, they seemed as overwhelming as the Rocky Steps at the Philadelphia Museum of Art.

Her entire body ached from the arduous, lengthy surgery. Mercifully, she'd been able to shower at the clinic, washing the stench of antiseptic and death from her skin. She would be able to immediately climb into bed and put this horrible day behind her.

She trudged up the steps and let herself into the apartment. Roby met her at the door, and the sight of him almost brought her to tears. She dropped her messenger bag by the door and knelt to hug her canine best friend.

Hearing footsteps, she glanced up to find Zeke towering over her. He wore a long-sleeved, heather gray T-shirt, a pair of blue-

and-gray-striped pajama pants, and his favorite shearling slippers.

The expression on his face was one she'd never seen before. He looked like he wanted to kill someone.

Shocked, she lurched to her feet. "I didn't think you'd still be up."

"Where the hell have you been?" he thundered, his voice vibrating with fury. "You said you were going to be home at six. I've been calling and texting you for hours." He moved closer, bending down until their faces were only inches apart. "What were you doing that was so damn important you couldn't spare three seconds to let me know you were okay? Are you so immature and inconsiderate that you can't think of anybody but yourself?"

His anger, coupled with the stress of losing a patient, was too much for her. A low cry burst from her throat, followed by a flood of tears that trickled down her cheeks.

Zeke froze. "*Fuck me,*" he swore viciously.

The vulgar word surprised her. He had never said *fuck* in her presence.

Through blurry eyes, she saw his face contort with a grimace. He reached for her, pulling her into his arms and hugging her tightly.

"I'm sorry," he murmured. "I shouldn't have yelled at you like that."

Burrowing closer to his body, she tried to muffle her sobs. He pressed a kiss to the top of her head and then gently nuzzled her hair.

"I'm sorry," he repeated softly. "Please don't cry, Go-go. I promise I won't ever yell at you again."

She looked up into his face, a little exasperated by his assumption. "I'm not crying because you yelled at me. I've been yelled at before, and I can handle it. I can handle *you*."

"Then why are you crying?" he asked, using his thumb to brush tears from the corner of her mouth.

"One of my patients died today. A golden retriever. They brought him in just before the clinic usually closes. That's where I've been."

Zeke's face softened with sympathy. "I'm sorry to hear that." He loosened his arms and ushered her into the living room. "Sit down. I'll get you some Kleenex."

She kicked off her tennis shoes and settled on the sofa with her knees drawn to her chest. Roby started to jump up next to her, but she pointed toward his red corduroy bed, and he curled up there instead.

Zeke returned a moment later, a box of tissues in his hand. After passing it to her, he sat down and draped his arm around her shoulders.

"What happened to your patient?" he asked.

"He was in a car accident with his owner. I tried to save him, but I couldn't." She sucked in a breath, trying not to cry. "His injuries were too extensive."

"I'm sorry." Zeke clasped her hand. "Violent death takes a toll on everyone, but I think it's worse for people like you … the people who heal … the people who repair the damage that others have created." He rubbed his thumb over her knuckles. "I've seen some horrible things. Men blown apart in front of me. Women who've been gang-raped and beaten to death. Kids with their throats slit."

She had been waiting for him to open up … to share his pain with her, but the thought of him seeing those things made her sick with sorrow. She tried to hold it in, but she couldn't. It overflowed, and she started crying again.

He pulled her closer, tucking her smaller body against his side. "Shh," he murmured. "It's going to be okay."

The fact that he was comforting *her* when she was upset about something that had happened to *him* ... well, that just made her cry harder. He was the best person she'd ever known—innately kind, quietly compassionate, and surprisingly thoughtful.

"Have you ever lost a patient before?" he asked.

"Yes. It always makes me sad, but this time it was so much worse. I don't know why. Maybe because he fought so hard. We worked on him for five hours. I really thought he was going to make it." Grief clogged her throat, and she cleared it roughly. "When he was gone, I didn't bother to check my phone. I had it on silent, so I didn't hear your calls or texts."

He leaned his head against hers. "I am *such* an asshole. *Jesus.*"

She giggled soggily. "You are not." She plucked a tissue from the box and wiped her eyes. "You were right. I *should* have let you know where I was."

"I called the clinic a few times and got the answering service," he said. "When I couldn't reach anyone, I drove over to check. But all the lights were off, and the door was locked."

She immediately felt guilty for being so wrapped up in her own misery that she hadn't considered him or his feelings. If the situation had been reversed, she would have been frantic. She would have yelled at him until she was mute and he was deaf.

"I'm the asshole in this situation, Zeke, not you. I would have been worried, too."

"I wasn't worried." He sighed tiredly. "I was scared to death. I thought something had happened to you."

Stunned by his comments, she turned her head to look at him. He did the same, and she stared into his dark eyes for a long moment.

"I'm sorry," she apologized, her voice almost a whisper.

"I have never been so scared in my life, Margo."

"Never?"

"Never."

Zeke had deployed to two of the most dangerous places on earth, and he'd lost a leg. But the thought of something happening to her had scared him more than combat and amputation.

The urge to touch him overwhelmed her, and she tentatively placed her hand against his cheek. Holding her breath, she waited … praying that he wouldn't jerk away.

Her prayers were answered.

As he sat beside her, motionless, she traced the strong line of his jaw. His stubble was prickly against her fingers, and she lightly scratched her nails through it, making a circle around his mouth.

When she grazed his bottom lip with her fingertips, he swallowed audibly. She removed her hand and shifted on the sofa until she knelt beside him.

"Zeke…"

His gaze fell to her mouth and lingered there. "What?" he asked huskily.

Leaning forward, she curved her hands over his shoulders and pressed her lips against his. He gasped, obviously surprised by the kiss, but didn't pull away.

She was so elated, so relieved, she almost laughed. Instead, she took advantage of his surprise, darting her tongue inside his open mouth. He tasted so good, an exotic spice that set her taste buds on fire.

She delicately touched her tongue to his before withdrawing it. A growling sound rumbled deep in his throat, the noise heating her insides and creating an ache between her thighs.

Suddenly, he moved, palming the back of her head and forcing their mouths together. This time, she was the one who gasped in surprise... He had turned into the aggressor.

Sinking into his kiss, she opened for him and let him have what he wanted. He took control, driving his tongue inside her mouth. He licked deeply, sweeping it across the interior of her cheeks and along the edge of her teeth.

He sucked on her tongue, drawing it into his mouth, over and over. When he finally lifted his lips from hers and dropped his hands from her head, she was breathless. Her nipples were hard under the lace cups of her bra, and the flesh between her legs was drenched and aching for him.

Was Zeke as aroused as she was? God, she hoped so.

She leaned back to look at him. His face was flushed, his mouth was damp and puffy from their kisses, and his eyes were hazy, the dark irises barely distinguishable from the pupils.

The leather cushions made it easy for her to slide backward on her knees. She glanced at Zeke's lap. His cotton pajama pants couldn't hide his erection.

She wanted to be with him ... to feel him inside her. But she knew that wasn't going to happen tonight. He hadn't told her about his leg yet, and until he'd shared that information with her, she knew he wouldn't feel comfortable enough to have sex.

But she wasn't going to leave him like this—hard and wanting.

Sliding from the sofa, she scooted between his knees. He tensed visibly, and she knew why: he was worried she would touch his prosthetic leg.

He started to straighten from his relaxed position, but she stopped him by placing her palm on his flat stomach and pushing gently. He opened his mouth, ready to protest, but she stopped him again, this time by cupping her hand over his erection and squeezing lightly.

With a moan, he dropped his head back against the sofa cushion and closed his eyes. She lifted the hem of his T-shirt and unbuttoned the fly of his pajamas.

"Lift your hips," she murmured.

He complied, and she began to tug down his pajamas and boxer briefs. The moment she freed his hard-on, he immediately dropped his hips. It took her a moment to realize he was afraid she would expose the socket of his prosthetic limb, which probably began mid-thigh.

She hated the fact that he was self-conscious about something that showed how brave he was. She desperately wanted to make him forget about his missing leg, just for a little bit.

She focused her attention on his erection. Longer and thicker than she had expected, it jutted out from a cluster of dark hair. The plump, fleshy head glistened with fluid that seeped from the tiny slit, and her mouth literally watered with the desire to taste him.

Feeling his eyes on her, she impulsively decided to give him a better view than her forest-green scrubs. With no ceremony, she whipped the top over her head, tossed it behind her, and unhooked the bra clasp between her breasts.

As she slowly pulled apart the blue lace cups, his gaze avidly tracked her hands. His breath hissed between his teeth when she revealed her nipples.

She moved deeper into the space between his knees. Gripping his hips, she exerted gentle pressure to bring him toward her.

"Closer," she urged.

He widened his legs and slid forward until his erection almost touched her chest. She swiped her forefinger across the tip, gathering pre-cum. His gasp quickly turned into a groan when she smeared the pearly cream on her pebbled nipples. They were so hard they hurt.

Taking Zeke's hands, she placed them on her breasts and held them there. His dark skin was a dramatic contrast to her pale flesh.

"Touch me," she implored.

He shaped the mounds with his warm palms, massaging gently before brushing his thumbs back and forth over the puckered tips. When he rolled the peaks between his callused fingers in a delicate pinch, pleasure-pain streaked through her.

While he continued to play with her breasts, she grasped the base of his erection and wrapped her lips around the rounded head. The musky smell of his arousal surrounded her.

"Oh, Jesus," Zeke groaned. "I can't believe this is happening."

She sucked lightly before tonguing the tiny slit and tasting him. His flavor filled her mouth, salty and tangy.

Widening her mouth, she took him deeper, letting her teeth graze the thick veins along his penis. She alternated between sucking his hard-on like a lollipop and licking it like an ice cream cone.

Lifting her head, she asked, "Do you like this? Does it feel good?"

He nodded, his jaw clenched so tightly she could see the muscle ticking. When she enveloped his erection again, he flexed his hips, slowly and repeatedly thrusting into her mouth. His breathing changed, becoming choppy and labored.

"Your mouth," Zeke gasped. "Jesus Christ, Margo. Your mouth."

She lifted her head again. "What?"

"Don't stop," he begged, pushing her head back down. "Please don't stop."

As soon as she sucked him back into her mouth, he began to thrust faster than before. Using her ponytail, he gently moved her head up and down on his erection.

With her mouth full of him, she cupped his testicles. They were drawn up tight, and she knew he wouldn't last much longer. She gently squeezed his sac, and his rhythm faltered.

"Oh, Jesus, that feels good."

He tugged on her ponytail, pulling her away from him. She looked up, wondering why he had stopped her.

"I'm about to come," he warned her gruffly.

"That's the point." She licked her lips, tasting him on them. "I'm ready when you are."

His eyes widened. "Do you want me to... Are you going to..."

She answered his question by guiding his erection back into her mouth. Yes, she wanted him to come in her mouth, and yes, she was going to swallow.

When she sucked hard on the head, his body bucked and he cried out. Semen spurted into her mouth, and she gladly took everything he gave her.

His big body was shaking with his orgasm, his penis still pulsing in her mouth. Slowly, she let it slip from her lips, swiping her tongue over the slit one last time.

Sitting back on her heels, she evaluated the result of her efforts. Zeke's eyes were wet-looking, like he was on the verge of tears, and it suddenly occurred to her that this might be the first time he had been intimate with someone since his injury.

He exhaled a shaky breath before tucking his spent penis

back into his underwear. As he pulled up his pajama bottoms, she stood, found her scrubs top, and pulled it over her head.

She curled up next to him on the sofa. He settled his arm around her shoulders and rubbed the side of her neck with his knuckles. The events of the day caught up with her, and she closed her eyes. The last thing she heard before she fell asleep was Zeke's voice.

"Jesus. I can't believe that actually happened."

CHAPTER NINE

In Zeke's experience, bad decisions fell into two categories: they either fucked up your life or they barely made a blip in it. He wasn't sure which category last night fell into, but he suspected that kissing Margo, touching her breasts, and coming in her mouth was going to result in more than a blip.

His morning snack popped out of the toaster, and he placed the wheat bread on a plate. As he spread peanut butter over the slices, he wondered if maybe he'd dreamed the whole damn thing.

He still didn't know how he and Margo had gone from talking about a dead dog to her giving him a blow job. If he were drawing a flowchart at work, he wouldn't see any possible way to get from point A to point B.

After screwing the lid back on the peanut butter, he opened the strawberry jam and smeared it on his toast. He took a big bite, careful not to drop any food on his softball uniform.

He wasn't hungry. In fact, he felt a little queasy. He dreaded the moment when Margo would emerge from her bedroom.

It was eleven o'clock, and he was surprised she was still asleep. Of course, yesterday had been a hellish, exhausting day for her, and she probably needed the rest.

She had fallen asleep on the sofa, snuggled up against him. And even though he'd told himself to go to his bedroom, he had fallen asleep beside her.

When he'd woken up in the middle of the night, his arm had been numb from the weight of her soft body. He had left her sleeping on the sofa, part of him wishing that he could have carried her to bed.

As he chewed, he thought about what he was going to say to her. He couldn't just pretend last night had never happened, no matter how much he wanted to.

The memory of what they had done was burned into his brain. All he could see was Margo on her knees in front of him, his dick sliding in and out of her lush mouth.

Jesus.

Without question, last night had been the single most erotic experience of his life. Now he understood why the entire male population was obsessed with blow jobs.

Since he'd never had one before, he hadn't been aware of what he'd been missing. But Margo had shown him how mind-blowing it really was.

It was an understatement to say that Andrea hadn't been sexually adventurous. She had liked the missionary position and that was it. She hadn't been willing to try any others, and at some point, he'd stopped trying to convince her.

And forget about oral sex. She thought fellatio and cunnilingus were "yucky" and "unsanitary."

Andrea was no longer hinting that they should reconcile. Whenever they spoke, which was way too often, she acted like getting back together was a foregone conclusion. She had even mentioned coming to San Francisco to visit.

Her presumption was his fault. He had been avoiding the much-needed conversation that would clarify his feelings on the subject.

Faintly, Zeke heard the squeak of Margo's bedroom door—he really needed to put some WD-40 on the hinges—and wiped his mouth. He didn't want to have peanut butter and strawberry jam all over his face when he talked to her.

She rounded the corner from the hallway, and he took in her appearance in one swift glance. A gray camo-patterned bandana covered her hair, and she wore a teal T-shirt and black yoga pants.

As she came closer, he noticed that she looked tired, almost fragile. Her face lacked its usual glow, and the skin under her eyes looked bruised.

She stopped in the dining room, and they stared at each other across the granite bar. He had been afraid that she would try to kiss him good morning, and even more afraid of how he would respond.

But she was keeping her distance. And unlike every other morning, she wasn't smiling and chirping at him. She probably regretted what had happened on the sofa as much as he did.

The tense, uncomfortable silence pissed him off. This was exactly what he *hadn't* wanted … what he had been trying to prevent.

An ember of anger smoldered inside him. He was angry with Margo, but he was even angrier with himself.

When he'd been in the Army, he had preached accountability and responsibility to the men and women in his command. Now it was time for him to practice what he'd preached. He had to accept the consequences from last night and try to minimize the blowback.

With that in mind, he said, "Good morning."

"Good morning," she replied as she joined him in the kitchen.

"Listen, I know this is awkward, but we need to talk about last night."

"I was just thinking the same thing." She grabbed the teakettle and brought it to the sink. "Why don't you start?"

"It never should have happened," he stated flatly.

When she finished filling the kettle with water and turned off the faucet, she said, "You think it was a mistake."

"Not a mistake, exactly. More of a…" He hesitated, struggling to find the right word. "An aberration."

"An aberration," she echoed.

"Yeah. We were both upset, and neither one of us was thinking clearly. We just got caught up in the moment."

In the cold light of day, he wondered if he'd taken advantage of her, even though she had been the initiator. She had been vulnerable, grieving the loss of her patient. He wasn't sure if she had wanted him or if he had just been a convenient outlet for her pain.

She nodded thoughtfully. "Are you attracted to me, Zeke?"

He didn't know how to answer her question. Should he admit that he lusted after her or should he lie and tell her that she didn't flip his switch?

"Yes, I'm attracted to you," he answered honestly. "I thought that was pretty obvious last night."

She brought the teakettle to the stove and turned on the gas heat. "So where do we go from here?"

"I want to keep things platonic. I don't want last night to ruin things between us."

"So, we're just going to pretend it never happened?" she

asked as she retrieved her favorite mug from the dishwasher.

"No. But it can never happen again."

You want it to, a voice inside him whispered. *You want it to happen again and again and again.*

He told the voice to shut the fuck up. It was just his deprived dick talking, anyway.

"If we weren't roommates, would you feel differently?"

"No. I'm not the kind of guy you need."

"What kind of guy do you think I need, Zeke?"

"Someone..."

She turned to face him. "Someone ... what?"

"Someone other than me. I'm not the right man for you."

She stared at him, her face unreadable. "It sounds like you've given this a lot of thought."

A lot of thought? It's all I've been able to think about.

"I have," he confirmed. "I know we can move past this."

He couldn't lose her. She was the best roommate he'd ever had. And somehow, she'd become his best friend, too.

He told Margo things that he'd never told anyone else. There had even been a few times when he'd been tempted to tell her about the IED attack and his leg. But he'd held back because he didn't want her to pity him or see him as weak.

After several moments of silence, Margo finally said, "I don't want this to ruin things between us, either." She tilted her head toward the clock hanging beside the pantry door. "You're going to be late for your softball game."

He glanced at the clock before bringing his gaze back to her. "Are you still coming to the game?"

She hesitated. "I haven't decided yet."

The anger inside him flared. If last night hadn't happened, she wouldn't have any qualms about coming. In fact, she would have bounced out of her room this morning, excited and eager to attend the game.

The teakettle whistled shrilly, and she turned off the burner with a flip of her wrist. He stood there, watching as she opened the little canister of tea she preferred in the morning.

"I'd like for you to come," he said.

For some reason, his comment made her laugh. She mumbled something, but he couldn't hear it.

"What?"

She popped the tea bag into her mug and lifted the kettle from the stove. "I just said, 'Good luck.'"

"Thanks." He tossed the remains of his snack in the trash and put the empty plate in the sink. "I'll see you later."

"Uh-huh."

He left the apartment without another word. During the drive to Lindley Meadow, he thought about the conversation with Margo. She had agreed with him, and he should feel relieved. Instead, he felt like a black cloud had settled over him.

When he arrived at the softball field, most of his teammates were already there, including Cal and Jake. Over the past several weeks, he and the two men had become friends. He liked Cal's raunchy, juvenile sense of humor and Jake's win-some-lose-some attitude.

Zeke greeted everyone before directing them to the field to warm up. Today, the Rivets were playing a team with a truly cringe-worthy name: We Byte. Unsurprisingly, the players worked for a tech start-up.

Ten minutes before the game was scheduled to begin, Zeke called his teammates back to the bench and ran through the lineup. When he finished, he set his clipboard down on the bench and looked beyond the chain-link fence to the line of bleachers.

He scanned the crowd, but didn't see Margo. Disappointment swamped him, making his shoulders slump.

"Looking for someone?"

Glancing sideways, Zeke found Cal standing next to him. "What?"

"Are you looking for someone?" Cal asked, tilting his head toward the bleachers.

"Yeah."

The younger man focused on Zeke, his eyes shaded by a navy-blue ball cap. "Who?"

"Margo."

"Ah, the mysterious Margo." Cal pursed his lips. "You talk about her all the time, but I'm beginning to think she's a figment of your imagination."

Jake joined their conversation. "What are we talking about?"

"Margo," Cal answered. "I was questioning whether she really exists."

"She exists," Zeke snapped. "She's just not here."

After checking the field to make sure the umpires had arrived, Zeke clapped his hands together. "It's go time, people!"

To Zeke's surprise and consternation, We Byte was a formidable competitor. Despite Norah's masterful pitches and the team's excellent fielding, the score was tied at the top of the seventh and final inning.

The Rivets batted first, and Cal managed to score a single run, putting their team ahead. Then it was We Byte's turn. With two outs, and two strikes, Norah tossed the pitch.

The batter got a piece of it, sending the ball into the infield between second and third base. As she took off, running for first base, Bohai jumped for the ball and missed.

From his position in the outfield, Zeke watched the batter

pass second base and sprint for third base. With the ball heading his way, he had no choice but to try to field it.

Praying his prosthetic could handle it, he jogged backward, his eyes on the ball. When he realized it was slightly over his head, he jumped with his glove outstretched behind him.

The ball dropped into it just as he landed hard and fell backward onto the grass. He sat up and lifted his arm in victory.

A cacophony of cheers erupted. He pulled off his glove, and seconds later, his teammates surrounded him, shouting out congratulations.

In his peripheral vision, he glimpsed a long, pink tongue coming toward him. Before he could dodge it, the tongue landed on his face, sweeping across his cheek. As he pushed the dog's snout away, he realized the slobbery lick had come from Roby.

His presence could mean only one thing: Margo was here. She had come to the game after all. Suddenly, the gloominess that had shadowed him disappeared.

"Nice catch," Cal said, extending his hand to Zeke.

Once Zeke was on his feet, he immediately scoured the small group of people for Margo. It didn't take long to find her.

She had changed into a gauzy shirt that was dark blue on top and lighter blue on the bottom, dark-washed skinny jeans that ended above her ankles, and a pair of beige flats. A floppy straw hat sat on her head, and a huge smile curved her mouth.

He headed straight for her, Roby loping alongside him. When he reached her, she stood on her tiptoes and threw her arms around his neck in a big hug.

Her floppy hat slapped his nose, and he pulled it off her head. A mass of strawberry-blond hair cascaded past her shoulders, releasing a sweet fragrance.

She gave him a loud smacking kiss on his cheek. "That was a

crazy awesome catch!" she exclaimed.

He grinned at her exuberance. "Crazy awesome?"

She nodded emphatically. "We Byte should change their name to We Suck."

Laughing, he plopped the hat back on her head. Her gaze darted to something behind him. Looking over his shoulder, he saw Cal and Jake lurking a few feet away.

"Hey, Zeke, are you going to introduce us?" Cal asked with a smile.

Zeke shifted so he could stand beside Margo. As he made the introductions, he saw his buddies through her eyes. Jake and Cal were young, good-looking, and successful. Plus, Cal was loaded with a capital L.

Zeke wondered if she found them attractive. The thought created an unpleasant burn in his chest.

"Zeke mentioned that you started a new job a few months ago," Jake said. "How's it going?"

Margo smiled wryly. "Well, if you had asked me that question yesterday, I would have burst into tears."

"So, it's not going well?"

"No, it is," she replied. "I just had a bad day yesterday. I lost a patient—a golden retriever. He was riding in the car with his owner, and they got into a bad accident. People don't realize they're putting their pets in danger if they don't restrain them properly."

"So dogs need to wear seat belts?" Cal asked, his tone completely serious.

Margo laughed. "Kind of. They need to wear a safety harness, which hooks into a seat belt buckle."

"I didn't know that," Jake said.

"Neither did I," Cal admitted. "But I don't have any pets."

Zeke couldn't help but smile. Poor Cal. He had no idea what he was in for now.

"You really should think about adopting a pet," she told Cal. "Did you know that nearly three million cats and dogs are killed each year because shelters don't have enough room?"

Jake winced. "That's horrible."

She glanced at Roby, who had been walking in circles around them. "I'm sorry, but my dog is getting restless. He sat for the whole game, and I need to take him for a walk." She smiled at Cal and Jake. "It was a pleasure to meet you both."

Leaning down, she clipped Roby's leash on his collar. As she rose, she said, "Zeke, I'll see you later."

"Don't you want to ride home together?" he asked.

She shook her head. "Go out and celebrate your win."

He watched her as she walked off the field, Roby trotting beside her. A gust of wind almost blew off her hat, and she slapped her hand on top of her head to keep it in place. She laughed, and the sound of it made him smile.

"*So,*" Cal said, drawing out the word, "that was Margo. Your roommate. The one you're not attracted to. The one you don't think about 'that way'."

Jake snorted. "He thinks about her 'that way' and a thousand other ways, too, I'll bet."

"At least a thousand," Cal agreed. "In the car. On a bar. Against a door. On the floor. In the shower. In a tower." He paused. "I'm channeling Dr. Seuss."

Jake snickered. "On a bed. In a shed. In a tent. Under a vent. On a slope. With some rope."

"Rope is too rough. It chafes delicate skin," Cal noted. "I prefer to use one of my ties."

Zeke crossed his arms over his chest. "Are you done yet?"

"Why are you still here? Don't you have anything better to do?" Cal asked. "Yes, you do. Her name is Margo."

Tired of their bullshit, Zeke said, "Margo and I agreed to keep things platonic, not that it's any of your business."

"Why?" Jake asked.

"Because we don't make sense."

Jake's eyebrows arched. "From what I just saw, it seems like you and Margo make a lot of sense."

"No, we don't," Zeke insisted.

"Why not?" Cal asked.

"I'm eleven years older than she is. I've seen too much, and she hasn't seen enough."

"Okay, so there's an age difference," Cal acknowledged. "What else?"

"There are too many reasons to list."

"Then just give me one."

"Fine!" Zeke exclaimed, goaded into explaining. "If she were a color, she'd be yellow. Not an obnoxious, overwhelming yellow, but an optimistic, cheerful yellow."

Cal blinked slowly. "And what color are you?"

"I'm not a color." Zeke shrugged. "Just a shadow."

"I don't understand what you're saying, man," Jake said.

"Okay, how about this: if she were food, she'd be a muffin, fresh out of the oven. Warm and sweet and soft. The kind that tastes so good, when you take the first bite, you just have to close your eyes and savor it."

Jake and Cal were silent, their eyes steady on him. He could tell he had surprised them. Hell, he had surprised himself. He wasn't the kind of guy who spilled his guts.

"I understand what you're saying." Cal took off his baseball cap and shoved it in his back pocket. "But hearing how you described her ... you're in love with this woman, Zeke. You're just too stupid to realize it." He rubbed his hand over his sweat-dampened hair. "Instead of thinking about all the reasons you and Margo don't make sense, you should start thinking about all the reasons the two of you *do* make sense."

CHAPTER TEN

The red numbers on Margo's alarm clock stared back at her. It was just after two a.m., and she was wide awake.

She groaned in frustration. She had to get up early for the clinic's staff meeting, which occurred every other Friday, and afterward, she had a full day of appointments. She needed to go to sleep or else she would be a zombie.

Roby had woken her up around midnight, desperate to get to his favorite human. Zeke had nightmares at least twice a week, and she was used to the Doberman interrupting her beauty sleep.

After dragging herself out of bed and letting Roby into Zeke's room, she had returned to her room. She'd tried counting sheep, but her thoughts had drifted to the man who slept down the hall.

It had been a month since Zeke had stood in the kitchen, dressed in his softball uniform, and told her that he wanted to keep things platonic. She had replayed their conversation over and over in her head, and she was still astounded that she had managed to keep her emotions under control.

When she had woken up alone on the sofa that morning, she had warned herself to prepare for the worst. Although she had expected to hear that he viewed that night very differently than she did, hearing him describe it as an aberration had hurt her badly.

And his insistence that neither of them had been thinking clearly had made her angry. She'd needed to know if he had been turned on because of her or because he'd been "caught up in the moment."

When he'd admitted that he was attracted to her, she had been overjoyed and relieved. She'd already known that he cared about her. Otherwise, he wouldn't have been scared when he'd thought something had happened to her.

Those two things combined—mutual attraction and care—had convinced her that she had a shot with Zeke. That was why she had attended his softball game. But later, when he'd arrived home, the affection he had shown at the park had been replaced by aloofness.

At that point, the voice of reason had piped up, pointing out that Zeke could be attracted to her without having feelings for her or wanting to be with her. Caring didn't always translate into love.

And that was what she wanted from Zeke: she wanted him to love her as much as she loved him. She was madly, completely, head-over-heels in love with the man, and he acted as if he wanted nothing more than to avoid her.

They didn't spend much time with each other anymore. Although they still ate dinner together most nights, Zeke immediately retreated to his bedroom afterward. On the weekends, they did their own thing. They didn't even run errands together.

Although both had agreed they didn't want that night to ruin things between them, it had. Sexual tension spiced every interaction. They were too aware of each other now to be comfortable as platonic roommates.

She couldn't forget how good it had felt to take him into her mouth, and she knew he couldn't forget it, either. It was in his eyes when he accidentally touched her hand or brushed up against her in the kitchen.

Several times over the past few weeks, she'd caught him staring at her, a frown on his face. His expression hadn't been angry, but perplexed. And when she had asked him if everything was okay, he had answered, "I'm not sure."

Distantly, she heard Roby's nails clicking on the wood floors. A few seconds later, he entered her bedroom and made his way over to her.

Instead of jumping on the bed to join her, he sat down beside it. Nudging her hand, he let out a high-pitched whimper.

"What's going on, Roby?"

He whimpered again. Sighing, she rolled over and turned on the lamp on her nightstand.

"Why aren't you with Zeke?"

He reared up and placed his front paws on the side of the bed, clearly wanting something. It was times like these when she wished she could talk to animals, like Eddie Murphy's character in the Dr. Doolittle movies. Those films were one of the reasons she was a veterinarian today.

She patted the mattress. "Come to bed."

He dropped his front paws to the floor and trotted to the doorway. He stood there, whimpering. With a huff of exasperation, she tossed back the covers and got out of bed for the second time.

After sliding her feet into her fuzzy slippers, she joined Roby. "What is your problem tonight?" she groused, the lack of sleep making her irritable.

Roby took off down the hall, toward Zeke's room. She could

hear his moans and cries now, tormented sounds that indicated he was having another nightmare.

She hurried behind the Doberman, a little worried. Zeke usually calmed down when Roby was with him.

Thanks to the night-light, she could see Roby sitting in the hall near Zeke's open door. The dog was shivering with fear, and she could understand why.

This nightmare wasn't like the others. It was a thousand times worse. Zeke was sobbing in his sleep, a deep, wrenching sound that made her throat tight and her chest ache. She had read a couple of memoirs written by soldiers who had served on the front lines in Afghanistan and Iraq, so she had a better idea of what Zeke had experienced.

Rubbing Roby's pointy ears, she said, "It's okay, puppy. I'll take it from here."

She entered Zeke's room and closed the door behind her. A little bit of light filtered into the room from a small gap between the curtains, and she could see the shape of Zeke's big body in bed.

He was lying on his back on the side of the mattress closest to the door. He was naked except for a pair of boxer briefs, and the sheet and comforter were tangled around his right foot.

Nightmares were a common symptom of PTSD, according to the book she'd read about the disorder. It had offered several suggestions to help someone suffering from nightmares. Ending the nightmare, either by waking him up or substituting another scenario, was the ultimate objective.

Moving deeper into the room, she said, "Zeke, it's Margo. You're safe. You're in your bed in our apartment in San Francisco. You're safe."

She repeated the sentences over and over, but they seemed

to have no impact. Deciding to try a different tactic, she said, "I've always wanted to go to Hawaii. I think it's because I've spent so much of my life in cold climates. I want to lie on the beach and listen to the waves while the sun warms my skin."

Rounding the footboard, she moved to the other side of the mattress. She untangled the sheet and comforter and pulled them up on her side of the bed. She left him uncovered because she didn't know if the weight of the material would intensify his nightmares.

After propping a pillow against the headboard, she kicked off her slippers and crawled onto the bed. As she reclined against the pillow, she asked, "Have you ever been to Hawaii, Zeke? I would love to go there with you."

Her strategy seemed to be working. He was no longer sobbing or moaning, and he had stopped thrashing around.

"We could stay at one of those fancy resorts with a balcony that overlooks the ocean. We could walk on the beach and swim in the ocean. I burn easily, so you'd have to rub a lot of sunscreen on me. I would like that … your hands on me."

Hesitantly, she touched his hair. It was silky soft, like baby duck down.

"We could drink Mai Tais at sunset. I've never had a Mai Tai. I bet they're delicious. But you'd probably choose beer over a fruity drink."

His breathing had evened out. He was no longer trapped in a nightmare. There was no reason for her to stay, but she didn't want to go.

"We could go to a luau and see hula dancers and stuff ourselves on Polynesian food. I've never eaten anything Polynesian except for Polynesian sauce at Chick-Fil-A, and I doubt that counts."

Pulling the covers over him, she whispered, "I would love to go to Hawaii on our honeymoon. I would love to lie next to you in a big bed with smooth white sheets and a fluffy white comforter. We could open the balcony doors so we could hear the ocean while we made love."

She wanted forever with him. She wanted to marry him, bear his children, and grow old with him.

But she doubted Zeke would ever get married again. He had admitted to her that he hated to fail, and his attitude about marriage was probably "lesson learned."

Of course, the biggest obstacle was the fact that Zeke didn't think he was the "right man" for her. When he'd said that, she had been speechless with shock. Otherwise, she would have demanded to know why.

Did he believe that being an amputee made it impossible for him to be a good partner? Did he feel inadequate and defective?

Many men who had lost limbs in combat felt that way, according to the research she'd done online. But she didn't think Zeke was one of them.

Then again, if the loss of his limb didn't bother him, he would have told her about it. She was starting to think he was never going to tell her.

Perhaps his situation as an amputee contributed to his belief that he wasn't the right man for her. But she suspected the main reason was that he was still in love with Andrea.

A couple of weeks ago, Margo had mustered the courage to ask Zeke about his ex-wife. She had asked why he and Andrea talked so frequently when they had nothing connecting them any longer—no marriage certificate, no children, nothing.

To Margo's surprise, he had answered her question. He'd said his relationship with his ex-wife was "complicated." Margo knew what that really meant—his feelings for Andrea were complicated.

He'd said that he and Andrea had a lot of history—sixteen years, to be specific. And then he'd pointed out that he and his ex-wife had started dating when Margo was seven years old. She had no idea why that thought had crossed his mind.

It wasn't just the constant phone calls that made Margo wonder if Zeke was still in love with his ex-wife, although she had noticed that he no longer talked to Andrea in front of her. Now, he excused himself and retreated to his bedroom. He clearly wanted his conversations to be private.

A couple of days ago, Margo had come home from work to find him sitting at the dining room table with the box of pictures from the storage closet on the barstool next to him. He had been looking through the photos, an expression on his face that Margo could only describe as wistful.

When he had noticed Margo, he'd immediately tossed the pictures back into the box and closed the cardboard flaps. Pretending not to know what was inside the box, she had asked him what he was doing. He hadn't answered. He'd just picked up the box and carried it to his bedroom.

That incident had made Margo question her intelligence. A smart woman would start looking for another place to live.

Even if Zeke wasn't in love with Andrea, that didn't mean he would fall in love with Margo and want to share his life with her. Could she change his mind?

She wasn't sure she wanted to try. She didn't want to have to convince him to be with her. She wanted him to come to her with an open heart, wanting to be with her as much as she wanted to be with him.

As she sat in the dark, listening to his breathing, she

wondered how much longer she would be able to share an apartment with Zeke. Only a masochist would continue to live with him, unwilling to give up on the dream of them being together.

She scooted down in the bed until her head rested on the pillow. Turning onto her side, she gazed at Zeke's shadowed profile.

Last week, he'd flown to Las Vegas for a supply chain and logistics conference. It had been the first time he'd gone out of town since she'd moved in, and she had been alarmed by how lonely she'd felt.

When he had called unexpectedly, just to say hi, she had been so excited that she'd blurted out, "I miss you so much!" After a long, awkward pause, he'd said, "I need to run, Go-go. I'll text you later."

Lying beside him, she was more afraid than she had ever been. She was afraid she wouldn't be happy with anyone but Zeke. And she was afraid he would never feel the same way about her.

Lightly, she placed her hand on his chest. His skin was hot, and the springy hair on his chest tickled her fingers. She could feel the thump of his heart under her palm, strong and steady, just like him.

He had said he wasn't the right man for her. But that was only true if she wasn't the right woman for him.

She thought they were the perfect fit.

CHAPTER ELEVEN

Roby had slept with him again last night. Through the covers, Zeke could feel the dog's warmth against his side. Fortunately, he had woken up before the Doberman. Otherwise, his face would be covered in dog slobber.

The scent of cherries and vanilla lingered in the air, and Zeke inhaled greedily. He loved the smell of Margo's shampoo. It literally made his mouth water.

She makes your mouth water, a voice inside him whispered.

He silently acknowledged that the voice was right. The proof was in his boxer briefs. The thought of Margo made his morning wood more like morning iron.

As he took another breath of deliciously fragrant air, he wondered why he smelled Margo instead of Roby. That was weird. Had she used her shampoo to bathe her dog?

Opening his eyes, he turned his head toward the wall of windows. Grayish-white light brightened the room, enough for him to see that Roby wasn't in bed with him ... Margo was.

He blinked slowly, sure he was imagining her. But she was still there when he opened his eyes. She was sound asleep, lying on her side on top of the covers. Her face was only inches away from his, her skin luminous in the morning light.

Why is she here, in bed with me?

Carefully, he rolled onto his right side, trying not to wake her. Her peachy-pink lips parted slightly, and he barely suppressed the urge to lean forward and taste them.

Her eyelids fluttered before lifting slowly. He stared into her sleepy eyes, a gorgeous color that reminded him of the Blue Star hyacinths his mother had planted in her garden.

Margo's eyes widened. "Oh, no," she breathed.

She jerked backward, and he clamped his forearm over her waist to keep her from escaping. He splayed his hand over her lower back, letting his fingers graze the waistband of her panties.

"What are you doing in my bed, Go-go?"

"Umm ..." She licked her lips. "Umm ..."

He waited for a few seconds before saying, "Umm is not an answer."

"I'm sorry. I didn't mean to fall asleep here. I planned to go back to my room."

He rubbed his fingertips over the lace of her panties. "That still doesn't answer my question."

Just as she opened her mouth to provide an answer, he realized the covers were bunched between them. His entire body was exposed ... including his stump. Horrified, he grabbed for the sheet, desperate to cover his lower body.

"Zeke, stop," she ordered softly, wrapping her hand over his. "You don't have to hide from me. I know about your leg. I've known about it for months."

Stunned, he brought his gaze to hers. "You have?"

She nodded. "A few weeks after I moved in, Roby woke me up in the middle of the night. I thought someone had broken in, but it was because you were having a nightmare. He wouldn't leave you. He kept scratching at the door, so finally, I let him in. That's when I saw your leg."

He couldn't believe what she was telling him. Questions ping-ponged inside his head.

Lightly caressing his fingers with hers, she said, "Whenever you have a nightmare, he wakes me up, and I let him into your room so he can sleep with you. Last night, he couldn't calm you down, so I stayed with you instead."

She had known about his leg all this time? She knew about his nightmares? Roby couldn't open doors on his own?

"If you knew about my leg, why didn't you say something about it?"

"Why didn't you?" she countered.

"Because I want you to treat me like a normal guy. I don't want you to feel sorry for me."

"You are a normal guy."

Oh, shit. He hadn't meant to say those things out loud.

"And I don't feel sorry for you." Under her breath, she mumbled, "Right now, I feel sorry for myself."

Baffled by her comment, he asked, "Why do you feel sorry for yourself?"

She huffed in obvious frustration. "Because I'm in your bed, Zeke, and you haven't even noticed that I'm almost naked."

Glancing down, he eyed her breasts. Her tight black camisole barely contained the plump mounds.

"I noticed," he assured her.

She slid her hand between their bodies. "I noticed something, too," she murmured, brushing her knuckles against his cotton-covered erection.

Jesus.

All the blood rushed from his head and pooled in his groin.

A half-naked woman was in bed with him—a woman he wanted desperately. Before he'd met her, he hadn't known what it was like to feel this way.

She knew about his leg. She knew about his nightmares. And she still wanted to have sex with him.

He wasn't going to waste any more time talking. He could think of a lot of other things he'd rather do with his mouth.

He rolled onto his back, hooked an arm around her hips, and pulled her on top of him. Her full breasts flattened against his chest, and his hard-on nestled into the notch of her thighs.

Reaching up, he tugged the elastic band from her ponytail. Shiny, fragrant strands created a curtain around their faces. He threaded his fingers through her hair and brought her mouth to his. She sighed when their lips touched, a tiny exhale that sounded like pleasure and relief combined.

He'd been fantasizing about her mouth for weeks now. The taste of it. The feel of it. The wet heat of it as she sucked on his tongue and his dick.

And now, he devoured it, biting and licking her lips until she pulled her head back, gasping for air. He gave her a moment before diving back in.

Her lips fell open, and he dipped his tongue inside, moaning as he got a taste of her … sweet and earthy, like maple syrup. He licked and savored, touching his tongue to hers, sliding it against hers, sucking hers into his mouth.

Releasing her lips, he trailed his mouth across her jaw toward her neck. She tilted her head back, giving him access to the sensitive skin. With his tongue, he found the frantic flutter of her pulse. It seemed to match his own.

"Sit up," he ordered hoarsely.

She immediately did as he asked, placing her palms on his

shoulders and using them for leverage. Finding the hem of her top, he said, "This needs to go."

She raised her arms. He ripped the camisole over her head, revealing her breasts.

Jesus.

He'd seen them before, touched them, too. But his memory wasn't anywhere close to the reality—firm, perky mounds tipped with dainty apricot-colored nipples.

He wanted those nipples in his mouth. He wanted to feel them against his tongue.

Now.

She must have been a mind reader, because she leaned forward, letting her breasts swing over his mouth. He caught one of her nipples between his lips and sucked it deep. While he laved the hard nub with his tongue, he massaged her other breast with his hand, shaping and molding it to fit his palm.

The contrasting textures intrigued him: the silky plumpness of her breasts and the pebbled velvet of her nipples. He swirled his tongue around the peak before giving it a hard nip.

She gasped. "Zeke, oh, my God. Do that again."

He obliged her before shifting his mouth to her other breast and giving it the same attention. As the rich, sweet taste of her skin filled his mouth, he wondered what she would taste like between her legs.

Jesus.

He wanted to shove his face between Margo's legs. Would she let him?

Skimming his hands over her rib cage, he traced the line of her spine until he reached the waistband of her panties. He slid both hands under the lace and cupped her ass cheeks in his palms.

As he kneaded her ass, she nuzzled her face into his chest. She found his nipple and flicked it with her tongue. When her teeth grazed it, a spark zipped down his nerve endings, making his dick even harder.

She rocked her hips a little, grinding on him, and for a moment, he was afraid he was going to shoot off in his underwear like a teenage boy. Gripping her waist, he lifted her off him, reducing the delicious pressure on his dick.

"Zeke, no," she protested. "I don't want to stop."

Before he could tell her that he had no intention of stopping—that he just needed a little time to regain some self-control—she wriggled out of her panties. The moment he stripped off his underwear, she climbed back on top of him.

She sat up with her knees bracketing his torso. Like a heat-guided missile, his eyes found the apex of her thighs.

Jesus.

The hair covering her pussy was a little darker than the strawberry-blond strands on her head. He wanted to nuzzle his face into that tiny tuft and let her smell fill his nose before spreading the lips of her pussy and licking her plump pink flesh.

And the only way he was going to get what he wanted was to ask for it.

"Margo…" He paused, surprised by how raspy his voice sounded. He cleared his throat roughly. "I want to…"

He hesitated, unsure of how to phrase it. *Perform cunnilingus?* That sounded like a surgical procedure. *Go downtown?* She might give him bus fare.

Fuck it.

He wasn't going to ask. He was just going to do it, and if she didn't like it, he would stop.

Clasping her waist with both hands, he slid down the bed a

few inches. Then he lifted her up and placed her pussy right on his face.

Margo's squeal of surprise barely registered because his senses were on overload. He was lost in her.

Her private curls tickled his mouth, and her smell intoxicated him. She was so wet her juice had glazed his lips. He licked at it, and the taste of her almost made him lose it. No wonder guys talked about pussy as if it were a gourmet meal.

Gently, he eased his tongue between the folds of her sex, stroking the delicate tissue. He delved deeper, finding the opening to her body. He lapped up her juice before pushing his tongue inside her.

Above him, Margo moaned softly. Suddenly, a stab of apprehension dampened his excitement.

He had never done this before. He was just going on instinct and what he'd heard over the years.

What if he wasn't good at it? What if he disappointed her?

Margo's voice floated from above. "Again, Zeke. Do it again."

Wanting to please her, he darted his tongue inside her again. Then he swept it upward until he reached her clitoris. It was smooth and hard, like a pearl, and he rolled his tongue over it.

She cried out in unmistakable pleasure, so he did it again and again until the little nub throbbed against his tongue. Switching things up, he licked circles around her clit, occasionally swiping his tongue over it.

He could tell she liked that because she began to move against his mouth, little moans drifting from her with every rock of her pelvis. Digging his fingers into the cheeks of her ass, he pulled her tighter against his face and sucked on her clit.

She froze with her thighs trembling around his head. She

screamed his name, her voice echoing in the room as her juice flooded his mouth. He couldn't be one hundred percent certain, but he was pretty sure he'd just made her come.

She lifted herself off his face. He glanced up, past the vibrant curls on her pussy and the sinuous curve of breasts. Her hands were clenched on the headboard, and she was looking down at him.

This woman turned him on like no one else. His ears roared with the sound of his blood rushing through his veins, and his dick throbbed with every beat of his heart.

"Have you been with anyone since you lost your leg?"

He shook his head, and a small, pleased smile curved her mouth. Dropping her hands from the headboard, she scooted down his body until his hard-on was snug against her ass and her knees hugged his hips. With just a little nudge, he would be pressed up against her asshole.

Jesus.

He'd never been one of those guys who got turned on by backdoor sex, but the thought of taking Margo's ass made his balls draw up tight. Maybe he was one of those guys after all.

She rose onto her knees, positioning herself over his erection. "Zeke."

Reluctantly, he dragged his gaze from where their bodies touched. "What?"

"Do you want me?"

"Yes," he answered hoarsely.

She wiggled a little. The tip of his hard-on nudged her slick opening, and her juice trickled over him. She lowered herself in a slow, torturous slide, her internal muscles tightly clasping his dick. Widening her legs, she took him deeper ... deeper ... ah, deeper.

Jesus.

With his balls flush against her, she braced her hand in the middle of his chest and began to ride him slowly. He wanted to be patient, to let her set the pace. But she was tight and hot, and he couldn't stop himself from clenching his hands on her hips and taking over.

He worked her over his dick, lifting her up and thrusting deep when he brought her down. He knew he was taking her too hard and too fast, and he told himself to slow down, to be gentle with her. But his control was unraveling, like a spool of thread.

It wasn't because he hadn't had sex in nearly three years. It wasn't because this was a new position for him.

It was because of Margo. *She* made him lose control.

He lifted her again, and when he drove deep this time, his control snapped. With a roar, he came, harder than he ever had. As he flooded her with his seed, he heard her cry out. Her pussy clenched around his dick, the powerful spasms wringing him dry.

She fell forward, tucking her face into the side of his neck. She was shaking, and he ran his hand up and down her back, trying to soothe her.

His vision was blurry, and when he blinked, he realized tears were leaking from his eyes. He had no idea why he was crying. He'd never cried after sex before.

But this wasn't just sex. It was a hell of a lot more.

"I'm sorry." His voice sounded like he'd swallowed gravel. "I know I was too rough. Did I hurt you?"

Turning her head, she kissed his jaw. "No."

She lifted her hips, and he pulled out as carefully as he could. She climbed off him and rolled onto her back.

He glanced down at his dick, which was still semi-erect. It glistened with their combined fluids, visible proof of how irresponsible they'd been.

"We didn't use a condom."

"I know," she replied. "But we're both clean, and I'm on birth control pills, so there's nothing to worry about."

Her calm response told him that she'd known there was no risk. He was the one who had been careless.

Suddenly, she jumped off the bed and pointed to the clock that sat on his nightstand. "Is that right?"

"Of course."

He wouldn't have a clock in his room set to the wrong time. That would defeat the purpose, wouldn't it?

Her eyes widened in obvious dismay. Then she darted for the door and flung it open.

"Stop right there," he barked, sitting up in bed.

She froze, standing in his open doorway, stark naked. "What?"

"We have to talk about this."

"Not now, Zeke. I'm late for work."

And then she disappeared in a flash of smooth, white skin and tousled, reddish-gold hair. He flopped back on the mattress, wondering if he'd just been a hit-it-and-run victim.

CHAPTER TWELVE

When it came to wine, Margo had low standards. She drank it to relax, not as a sign of her socio-economic status.

As she took a sip of the pinot noir she'd bought at Trader Joe's, she prayed the vintage would loosen the tension that knotted her entire body. She wasn't looking forward to talking with Zeke about what had happened in his bed this morning.

She had used work as an excuse to hightail it out of his room. She could have missed the meeting and talked with him. But she hadn't been ready to hear him say that they'd made a mistake.

Leaning against the kitchen counter, she took another sip of wine. It tasted good, but then again, she couldn't tell the difference between a five-dollar bottle and a fifty-dollar bottle.

For once, she had beaten Zeke home from work. Her days were usually crazy, full of sick animals and worried owners. But today had been surprisingly low-key and peaceful, and she'd been able to leave an hour earlier than usual.

Zeke had sent her a text, warning her that he would be late because he was dealing with a supply chain emergency. That was the only communication they'd had all day … except for the nonverbal communication in his bed.

Closing her eyes, she massaged her forehead with her fingertips. She didn't have a lot of sexual experience—she'd only been with three guys, including Zeke—but this morning had rocked her world off its axis.

He had sent her spinning with two luscious orgasms. It made sense that he was good in bed; he was a classic overachiever.

Her feelings for him had intensified her physical response ... that, and the knowledge that she was the only one he'd been with since he had lost his leg. She hoped that meant something—that this morning had been more than just sex for him.

She absently lifted the wineglass to her mouth. To her surprise, it was empty. She debated whether to have a second glass.

Oh, what the hell. Why not?

As she poured another serving of pinot noir, she asked herself what she wanted from Zeke ... assuming he didn't come home from work and insist that they forget this morning ever happened.

She knew what she didn't want: a roommate-with-benefits arrangement. But what if that was all he was willing to offer her? She could never be satisfied with that, not when she wanted an exclusive relationship that would eventually lead to marriage and children.

A buzzing sound echoed in the apartment. After placing her wineglass on the counter, she headed toward the intercom near the front door. She wasn't expecting anyone, but sometimes delivery people left packages with other residents when they couldn't reach the recipient.

Pressing the intercom button, she said, "Can I help you?"

"Yes," a woman's voice answered. "I'm here to see Zeke May."

Huh?

The woman spoke again. "Are you Zeke's roommate? I'm Andrea May."

For a moment, Margo was frozen in disbelief. Zeke's ex-wife was in San Francisco?

"Can you let me in?" Andrea requested.

Like an automaton, Margo pressed the button to allow Andrea inside. Then she leaned against the wall and took several deep breaths. This was the last thing she had expected to deal with tonight.

Just then, a knock sounded on the apartment door. She took one more deep breath and exhaled before opening the door.

"Hello," Andrea said, extending her hand. "You must be Margo. I'm Andrea May."

Margo took the other woman's hand, noting the perfect French manicure on her nails. "Yes, I'm Margo."

The photos of Andrea didn't do her justice. Zeke's ex-wife was even more beautiful in person.

Margo would have killed to have the other woman's long, feathery eyelashes. They had to be fake, right? And her long, wavy hair had to be extensions. No one's hair could be that thick without the help of a salon.

Andrea knew how to dress to accentuate her tall, willowy figure. She wore a pair of cream-colored trousers that made her legs look a mile long, a silky black shirt with a draped neckline, and red patent leather stilettos.

Next to Andrea, Margo felt like a troll. She was at least six inches shorter than the other woman.

Margo had planned to shower and change before Zeke got home. She was still wearing her maroon scrubs from work, her makeup had worn off, and her hair was twisted into a messy bun on top of her head.

"It's so nice to meet you," Andrea said before releasing Margo's hand.

The taller woman moved forward, as if she had every right to be there, forcing Margo to scoot to the side of the entryway. And that was when she noticed the black suitcase Andrea pulled behind her.

Slowly, Margo closed the door and followed Andrea into the living room. Zeke had neglected to mention that his ex-wife was coming for a visit.

Where had he planned for her to sleep? Somehow, she doubted Andrea would be bedding down on the sofa.

"This is a nice apartment," Andrea noted. "It's bigger than I thought it would be." She glanced down, her scarlet lips pursed in visible distaste. "I always hated this rug."

Pushing down the telescoping handle of her suitcase, Andrea asked, "Where's Zeke? He's usually home by now, isn't he?"

"He had to work late. He didn't mention that you were coming."

Andrea sat down on the sofa and crossed her long legs. "We've talked for months about me visiting, and I decided to surprise him."

"Oh," Margo replied lamely, wondering if Andrea's presence would be a good surprise or a bad surprise.

"I thought it would be a good idea to come out since I'll probably end up relocating here. Zeke loves his job at Riley O'Brien & Co., and I don't think he'll be willing to move back to Maryland."

What?

"It's probably better that we start over in a new city, anyway," Andrea continued.

Margo stared at Andrea, unable to believe what she was

hearing. "Start over? Are you and Zeke getting back together?"

Andrea nodded. "We made a mistake when we got divorced. *I* made a mistake. Zeke didn't want the divorce. I did." She smiled wryly. "What's that saying ... 'You don't know what you've got 'til it's gone' ... That was me. I didn't realize how lucky I was to have Zeke."

Margo couldn't help but think that Andrea was a *very* stupid woman. If he were Margo's husband, she would never let him go.

Andrea eyed Margo thoughtfully. "You probably aren't old enough to have the kind of regrets that I do."

You're wrong about that. I have a lot of regrets ... like letting you into the building.

Andrea smiled wistfully. "Zeke and I always planned to have kids. It's not too late for us. We still have time."

The thought of Andrea having Zeke's babies made Margo feel physically ill. *She* wanted to be the mother of his children.

Andrea had already had her chance with Zeke, and she'd blown it. It was Margo's turn now.

For a moment, Margo thought about telling Andrea exactly where she had been this morning and what she'd been doing. But she swallowed the words.

She loved Zeke with her whole heart. He had suffered too much, and she wanted him to be happy, even if that meant he was happy with someone else.

"Did Zeke say when he'd be home?" Andrea asked.

"No, but I'm sure he'll be here soon." Margo snapped her fingers to get Roby's attention. "I'm going to take my dog for a walk so you and Zeke can talk privately."

Andrea smiled. "I'm hoping we'll do more than talk."

She looked away from Andrea's smug face. She couldn't bear

the thought of Zeke and his ex-wife together … couldn't bear the thought of him kissing and touching Andrea less than twelve hours after he'd been buried inside Margo.

Desperate to escape, Margo hurriedly clipped the leash to Roby's collar and pulled on a lightweight sweater. "Please tell Zeke that I'll be back in a couple of hours … around eight o'clock."

She grabbed her keys from the metal hook next to the door and rushed out of the apartment. It wasn't until she was halfway down the block that she realized she'd left her phone and wallet at home.

She had no money for dinner or even a cup of coffee. But that was okay because she wasn't hungry. The conversation with Andrea had obliterated her appetite.

Margo wandered through Pacific Heights with no destination in mind. Summer in the Bay Area wasn't like summer in other places. It wasn't warm and sunny; it was chilly and cloudy. This evening was no different, and it fit her mood perfectly.

Zeke had screwed Margo even though he was working things out with his ex-wife. *What a jerk!*

As she walked, she silently berated herself for falling in love with him. Not only was he a jerk, he was emotionally unavailable.

Any man who talked to his ex-wife every day clearly hadn't moved on. Any man who wanted his ex-wife to visit wasn't ready for a relationship with someone else.

And any woman who ignored those red flags deserved to be miserable.

With no way to keep track of time, Margo relied on the sun to let her know when it was time to head home. When the sky darkened to twilight, she reluctantly led Roby back to the Victorian.

There was no way she was going to stay there with Zeke and his ex-wife, not even for one night. As soon as she found her phone, Margo planned to call Jenny and ask if she could stay with her. And if she couldn't reach her friend, she'd book a cheap hotel room and stay there until Andrea left.

As Margo stood on the sidewalk in front of the house, she recalled the day she'd met Zeke. She never could have predicted that she would fall in love with her roommate, who also happened to be a big jerk.

After letting herself into the apartment, she released Roby from his leash and hung up her sweater. The Doberman immediately dashed off, probably heading for his food bowl.

She stood in the small foyer for a moment, listening for voices. When she heard nothing, she exhaled a relieved breath. Zeke and Andrea had either retreated to his bedroom or gone out, and she was glad she wouldn't have to see them together.

The living area was empty and dark, but the dining room wasn't. Zeke was there, sitting on a barstool. He wore a plain black T-shirt that revealed his muscular biceps and sinewy forearms and a pair of faded jeans. A bottle of beer was on the table in front of him.

She moved deeper into the room, and he shifted on the barstool, turning his body toward her. His expression was impassive, and she couldn't read his mood.

Reaching the table, she curled her hands over the back of the barstool adjacent to where Zeke sat. She needed something to hold on to because her knees were shaking with a combination of anger and anxiety.

"Where's Andrea?"

"I don't know," he answered, his monotone voice giving nothing away.

He picked up the beer and took a big swallow of the brew, his dark eyes surveying her over the lip of the bottle. He returned it to the table with a soft *clink*.

"If I had to guess, I'd say that she's probably at the airport, trying to get a flight back to BWI. Or she could be at a hotel." He shrugged. "I don't really care where she is, as long as she's not here."

"I don't understand. She said that you discussed her coming out to visit."

"Yeah, we discussed it. And I told her not to." He tilted his head. "What else did she say?"

"She said that you were getting back together."

He stared at her for a long moment before asking, "You think I would have sex with you when I'm planning to reconcile with my ex-wife?"

"I don't know," she retorted. "Would you?"

"No, I wouldn't." His shoulders seemed to droop a little. "Is that the kind of man you think I am?"

She heard the disappointment in his voice … the accusation threaded through it. It made her defensive.

"What am I supposed to think?" she demanded. "You talk to Andrea every day. *Every day.*"

"So?"

"So?" she repeated, aware that her voice was dangerously close to a shout. "No man talks to his ex that much unless he's still in love with her … unless he wants another chance."

"You think that I'm still in love with Andrea? *Jesus.*" He shook his head. "I talk to her because I owe her. She took care of me after I lost my leg, and I can't ever repay her for that."

He sighed. "I know it's not a good idea for us to talk so often, and I told her that a couple of days ago. I also told her that there was no chance of us getting back together. That's why she flew out here—she thought she could change my mind."

Lifting the beer, he drained the rest of it in one gulp. After depositing the bottle on the table, he stood.

"Andrea thinks it was a mistake for us to get a divorce, but I know it was the right decision. She wasn't happy, and neither was I, although I didn't realize it at the time."

He came to stand beside her. Dropping her hands from the barstool, she turned to face him. She had to tilt her head back to meet his eyes.

"Andrea divorced me because she wanted to be loved passionately. I didn't love her like that. I couldn't love her like that even if I tried."

He tucked a loose strand of Margo's hair behind her ear. "But that's how I love you, Go-go."

She was afraid she'd heard him wrong—afraid that she was imagining this whole conversation. "You love me?"

"Yeah, I do." His deep voice softened. "Passionately. Endlessly. Without reason. Without limits."

Cupping her cheek in his palm, he rubbed his thumb over her lower lip. "You light up all the dark places inside me. You brighten my world. When I'm with you, I feel alive and hopeful and excited. You make me happy."

Her emotions overwhelmed her, and tears welled in her eyes. "You make me happy too."

"I kept telling myself that we didn't make sense." He caught one of her tears on his fingertip. "But we do."

She nodded. "Yes, we do."

"I kept telling myself that I wasn't the right man for you..."

"You are," she insisted. "You're the right man for me because I love you."

"Why don't you say that last part again," he suggested.

"I love you, Zeke."

"I love you too." A slow smile curved his mouth. "I think we need to modify our sleeping arrangements. I want you in my bed every night, and I want to wake up with you every morning." He bent down and pressed a gentle kiss to her lips. "Roby can't sleep with us, though."

"Why not?"

"Because my bed isn't big enough for all of us." He wrapped his arms around her waist and pulled her closer. "And we're going to be doing things that an innocent dog shouldn't see."

She laughed, happiness bubbling up inside her like hot springs. "Your bed isn't the only place we're going to do those things."

Zeke's eyes darkened with unmistakable desire. Suddenly, he picked her up and set her on top of the dining room table. As he untied the drawstring of her pants, he said, "You're right. We need to get him a blindfold."

EPILOGUE

One year later

The lobby of the Hudson San Francisco was much busier than Margo had expected. The historic hotel must be hosting a conference today.

As she crossed the marble floor to the elevators, her phone vibrated in the back pocket of her jeans. She reached for it, knowing she'd see a text from Zeke.

His message read: "I'm here. Where are you?"

She typed a reply: "Almost there. Just getting into the elevator." She added a heart emoji before sending the text.

Once she was inside the elevator, she pressed the button for the second floor and shoved her phone into her messenger bag. She wasn't running late, but Zeke was always early, and he usually ended up waiting on her. Fortunately, the man had the patience of a saint—when it came to her, anyway.

The elevator dinged, and the doors slid open. Stepping out, she hooked a left toward the catering office. Menu tasting was one wedding-related task that she didn't mind.

She and Zeke were getting married in less than a month, and

they had to make their final food selections today. Her fiancé's aptitude for organization and attention to detail had come in very handy over the past few months as they'd planned the ceremony and reception.

Zeke's family had been astounded when he and Margo had gotten engaged. No one had expected him to remarry.

When they had flown to Asheville so she could meet his family, his mother had welcomed her with open arms. She'd confessed to Margo that she had been afraid her oldest son would die alone.

Margo had assured her future mother-in-law that Zeke would never be alone again. And she'd promised to make her a grandmother, several times over.

Because this was Zeke's second marriage, Margo had been willing to have a small ceremony at the courthouse. But he'd insisted that they have a traditional wedding. When she'd asked why, he had said, "Because I'm never going to do this again. And neither are you."

She had planned to scour consignment boutiques for a wedding dress. A lot of women gave their dresses away, especially if their marriages didn't work out.

When Zeke had found out that she was going to wear a "tainted" dress—his words, not hers—he'd called Jenny. They had ganged up on her, and somehow, she'd ended up with a brand-new wedding dress that cost more than the monthly rent on their apartment.

As Margo walked down the carpeted corridor, she heard instrumental music drifting from the speakers in the ceiling. Listening closely, she identified the tune as "Ex's and Oh's" by Elle King.

The song made Margo think of Zeke's ex, and she couldn't

help but smile. Zeke and Andrea talked infrequently, maybe once a month, and Margo had no problem with it. During their most recent call, Andrea had revealed that she was pregnant, even though she wasn't in a relationship.

Margo had been sitting next to Zeke on the sofa when Andrea had made her announcement, and his response had been hilarious. He'd said, "How the hell did that happen?"

When he'd ended the call, Margo had offered to show him how babies were made. He had taken her up on the offer, and she'd introduced him to the reverse chair position. Afterward, he'd proclaimed it to be his favorite position, which was what he said every time they tried something new.

As Margo reached the catering office, she took a moment to comb her fingers through her hair and straighten her floral peplum blouse. She'd found the top in a thrift store near the Art Institute and had paid five bucks for it. The Anthropologie label inside told her that it had probably cost at least a hundred dollars brand-new.

She pulled open the glass door and immediately spotted Zeke. He was sitting at a round table with the hotel's wedding coordinator, Heidi Lynch, a petite brunette in her mid-thirties.

Zeke and Heidi were looking at the binder he had put together to keep track of wedding details. When he glanced up and saw her, a sexy smile curved his mouth.

It was a special smile—one that he gave only to her. It made butterflies take flight in her stomach every time she saw it.

He stood, and she let her gaze travel the length of her hot husband-to-be. He'd dressed up a little for their appointment.

He wore a cream-colored button-down shirt with a red-and-blue Tattersall pattern, dark-washed Rileys, and brown leather lace-up boots. He looked so delicious she wanted to gobble him up in one bite.

Leaning down, he pressed a light kiss on her lips. "Hey, Go-go."

"Hi."

He turned toward Heidi. "I need to talk with Margo for a moment. Is there someplace private we can go?"

"Sure," Heidi replied. "There's an empty office down the hall, second door on the right."

Weaving his fingers through Margo's, he tugged her down the hall to the vacant office. The door was open, and he flipped on the overhead light before ushering her inside.

As Zeke closed the door, she asked, "What's up?"

"That's a good question." He took her hand and pressed it against his zipper. "Here's your answer."

She stroked his erection through his jeans. "Does looking at your color-coded wedding binder turn you on?"

He chuckled. "The thought of marrying you turns me on."

"Is this ..." she lightly squeezed his hard-on "... what you wanted to talk about?"

"No."

Before she could ask another question, he slid his hands into her hair and cupped her head in his palms. He maneuvered her back against the door, and then he kissed her as if he hadn't seen or touched her in years. When he finally lifted his head, her mouth felt bruised and puffy, her legs felt like overcooked spaghetti, and her panties were more than a little damp.

"How was your day?" he asked huskily, dropping his hands to her hips.

"Same stuff, different day."

"So, you had a great day."

She nodded. She loved working at Bay Area Animal Care, and Jon and Tricia had mentioned that they'd like for Margo to become a partner in the business.

"What about you?" she asked. "Did anything exciting happen at Riley O'Brien & Co. today?"

"That's what I wanted to talk to you about." He smiled. "Brent pulled me into his office today and told me that he wants to retire in eight to twelve months. He's going to recommend that I take over the entire supply chain and logistics department."

"Oh, my God, Zeke!" She lunged up on her tiptoes and threw her arms around his neck. "That's crazy awesome! I'm so proud of you!"

He hugged her to him. "I love you, Go-go."

"I love you too."

"I wish you were naked right now," he added.

She couldn't help but laugh. "As soon as we finish with the wedding tasting, we can go home and—"

"I can taste you," he said, waggling his eyebrows.

"You took the words right out of my mouth."

And then he took every thought from her head by kissing her senseless. When they returned to the catering office, Heidi was waiting for them near the glass door.

"Ready for the tasting?" the wedding coordinator asked.

Margo and Zeke nodded their assent. As the three of them made the trek from the catering office, Heidi asked if Margo and Zeke were going to honeymoon after the wedding.

Zeke looked at her as if she had spouted horns and turned into the Minotaur. "Hell, yes, we are."

"Where are you going?" Heidi asked.

"Hawaii."

Zeke had picked their honeymoon destination without any input from Margo. She had been stunned when he'd told her where they were going. She wondered if his subconscious had heard her when she'd talked about her dream of going to Hawaii with him.

"Which island?" Heidi asked.

"Maui," Margo said.

"Have you ever been there? It's beautiful."

Margo shook her head. "Neither one of us has been there."

"I know I'll enjoy the scenery," Zeke said, winking at Margo.

As Heidi pushed through a swinging door, she said, "Our kitchen is busy today because of the conference, and our executive chef isn't available to meet with you. But the sous chef and pastry chef will join us after you've had a chance to taste everything."

The wedding coordinator led them to a small tasting room attached to the kitchen. A rectangular table filled the space, covered with a crisp white tablecloth.

Heidi gestured to the chairs grouped around the table. "Please have a seat." She turned to a young man dressed in a black chef's smock and matching baggy pants. "Bring out the hors d'oeuvres."

As Zeke pulled out a chair for Margo, he said, "Wait."

The young man froze, and everyone's attention swung to Zeke, Margo's included. He glanced down at her, his eyes lit with love and his mouth tilted in a smile.

"Life is short," he said. "Let's eat dessert first."

A Kick in the Pants

CHAPTER ONE

Wager. Bet. Chance. Stake. Risk. Most people made decisions by considering pros and cons. But Jake Lilliard was a gambling man, and he evaluated opportunities a little differently.

Instead of listing the pros and cons of a situation, he weighed the risks and rewards and calculated the odds of getting what he wanted. And he always factored in luck, something that other people overlooked.

Lady Luck was a fickle bitch, and she could screw up everything, no matter how much you planned and prepared. But she'd always had a soft spot for Jake, and he hoped she wouldn't abandon him when he needed her the most.

After five torturous months of wanting Kyla Andrews, Jake was finally—*finally*—going to be able to do something about it. In less than two weeks, she would graduate from Riley O'Brien & Co.'s management trainee program, and he would no longer be her boss. The moment he relinquished that title, he was going to make his move.

It might sound dramatic, but pursuing Kyla would be the biggest risk Jake had ever taken. He'd never wanted a woman the way he wanted her.

Hell, he'd never wanted *anything* the way he wanted Kyla. What had started out as a spark of interest had escalated into a soul-deep craving he could barely control. He burned to know the textures and tastes of her body ... to tangle his hands in her honey-blond hair ... to make her silvery-gray eyes turn hazy with desire.

Jake was always careful about his interactions with female colleagues, mindful of any behavior that could be considered sexual harassment. But everything was different with Kyla.

A couple of times he'd allowed his hand to linger on her shoulder. And more than once he'd let himself get close enough to smell her perfume. He knew it wasn't smart, but sometimes his desire for her overwhelmed his common sense.

For the most part, though, he had maintained his professionalism with Kyla. His poker face rarely cracked, and only the people who knew him best would ever guess that he'd spent hours imagining her naked and spread out on his desk.

Something banged against the door to Jake's condo, and he jerked in surprise. The stack of poker chips in his hand spilled onto the slate tile floor.

"Dude!" The exclamation filtered through the wooden barrier. "I could use some help!"

Kicking colorful poker chips out of his path, Jake hurried to open the door. His roommate and best friend, Charlie Shipley, stood in the hallway, awkwardly holding a portable poker table.

"Thank you so much," Charlie said sarcastically.

Jake flattened himself against the wall to let the other man pass. "You're welcome."

Charlie hefted the table higher, until it covered the scarlet UNLV printed on his gray T-shirt. Both he and Jake had obtained undergrad degrees from their hometown college.

When Charlie had decided to go to medical school at Stanford University, Jake had applied to the school's MBA program. They both had been accepted into their respective programs, and they'd moved to Northern California together. That had been nearly eight years ago.

"I hate going to the basement," Charlie grumbled

"Was it dark down there?" Jake gibed. "Were you scared?"

"I'd flip you off if my hands were free," Charlie replied sourly, his brown eyes narrowed behind the thick black frames of his glasses.

"You could just say the words."

Charlie shook his head, his dark hair drooping untidily over his forehead. "Nah. If I curse at home, I might slip up at work."

Charlie was a pediatrician, part of a multi-physician practice near Saint Philomena Children's Hospital. For the past three years, a local parenting magazine had named him "Best Pediatrician in the Bay Area".

Jake was convinced that Charlie excelled at his profession not only because he loved kids, but also because he loved the same things that kids loved: video games, animated movies, pizza, and chocolate milk. He was a ten-year-old boy hiding out in a man's body.

"The next time we host poker night, you're going down to the basement to get the table," Charlie said.

"Fine." Jake closed the door behind the other man. "I'll get the table if you'll deal all the hands so I don't have to."

Charlie shuffled forward into the living room. "The guys won't agree to that. You're a much better dealer than I am. You learned to deal before you learned to walk."

"You know that's not true. I was in kindergarten when my dad taught me to deal."

Jake's dad, Ralph, was a professional poker player. After he'd won his fourth World Series of Poker bracelet four years ago, he had retired. But it hadn't stuck. He couldn't stay away from the table for too long.

Charlie shot Jake a questioning glance. "Should we set up the table on the balcony?"

They lived in a three-bedroom penthouse unit in a residential high-rise. The steel-and-glass cylinder towered over the SoMa area, giving them unparalleled views of the city's skyline.

Jake opened the sliding glass doors and stepped out onto the balcony. Behind him, Charlie flipped the switch for the wall sconces and the mini bulbs strung under the overhang and along the railing.

A gentle breeze teased Jake's hair. It was a perfect night to sit on the balcony with friends, play Texas Hold'em, and drink beer.

"It feels good out here," Charlie noted.

The rainy season had ended in late April, and the Bay Area had enjoyed decent weather for the past two weeks. But by the time Memorial Day rolled around in a couple of weeks, the weather would likely be chilly and foggy.

With the two of them working as a team, it didn't take long to set up the poker table. Once they'd dragged four chairs outside, Jake scooped up the poker chips he'd dropped earlier and returned them to their aluminum case.

When Jake finished fastening the latches, Charlie passed him a Blue Moon. He took a pull on the bottle, relishing the beer's strong wheat taste.

Charlie tipped his bottle toward Jake. "So how was your day, dear?" he quipped.

"Eh, it was okay," Jake answered with a shrug.

As a vice president in Riley O'Brien & Co.'s finance department,

Jake spent a lot of time with the company's CFO Diana Stanton. Today, he'd been stuck in a seven-hour meeting with her. She had been even more irritable than usual, complaining about everything from the temperature in her office to the taste of her coffee.

Jake couldn't deny that Diana was a Grade A pain in the ass, but he didn't have a problem with her. While her abrasive attitude rubbed almost everyone else the wrong way, he had figured out how to work with her, and if necessary, how to work around her.

Usually he tried to charm the cantankerous CFO out of her bad moods, but today he had lacked the patience to flatter and cajole. He hadn't been sleeping well, and he doubted that he would until Kyla was lying next to him. Unfortunately, he had no idea when—or if—that would happen.

Charlie chuckled. "Another day, another hard-on for Kyla."

A couple of months ago, everyone from the finance department had decided to go to a new restaurant for happy hour, and Jake had invited Charlie along. His best friend knew him better than anyone in the world, and when Jake had introduced Charlie to Kyla, it hadn't taken Charlie more than two minutes to realize Jake wanted her.

Ignoring the taunt, Jake took another swallow of his beer. Charlie shot him an amused glance.

"How many days?" Charlie asked.

When Jake didn't answer, Charlie asked him again. And again. And again.

"Eleven," Jake finally shouted.

Eleven days until he could taste Kyla's plump lips and touch her smooth skin. Eleven days until he could hear the sounds she made when she came.

Whoa, chief. You're getting a little ahead of yourself.

"T-minus eleven days and counting 'til lift-off," Charlie said, a smirk appearing on his face. "Or maybe I should say blast-off since you've already had lift-off."

"You're a real fucking comedian."

"Dude, you've totally lost your sense of humor," the other man lamented. "This chick has you twisted tighter than barbed wire."

Growing up, Charlie had spent his summers on his grandfather's huge ranch in northern Nevada. As a result, he often thought about things in ranching terms.

Although Jake wasn't fond of the term 'chick', he supposed he should be relieved that his best friend hadn't called Kyla a heifer. That would have necessitated a little chat about acceptable nouns to use when referring to her. He really hoped "girlfriend" would be one of them in the future.

"I know she's pretty," Charlie continued, "but you've been with women a lot hotter than Kyla Andrews."

At this exact moment, standing in his condo and drinking beer with his best friend, Jake couldn't think of any woman hotter than Kyla. And he had a hard time remembering any of the women he'd had sex with, too, anyone except for Hannah, his high school girlfriend and first lover.

"Seriously, Jake. I've never seen you act like this about a woman. Why is Kyla so special?"

Jake rolled his shoulders, uncomfortable with the direction of the conversation. He didn't want to talk about his *feelings*, for fuck's sake.

Then he abruptly realized how embarrassed Charlie must have been when he'd fallen apart after his long-time girlfriend and fiancée had left him standing at the altar with no explanation. There had been several occasions when Charlie had sobbed like a baby. Of course, he'd also been shitfaced at the time.

Taking another swig of beer, Jake pondered Charlie's question. Finally, he figured out the best way to explain his fascination with Kyla.

"She's earnest."

Charlie's dark eyebrows crawled up his forehead. "Earnest?" he echoed.

Jake nodded. "Yes, earnest. Everything she does, everything she says, it's so earnest. There's no selfishness, no self-absorption. When I talk to her, she listens with this expression that's so intent—so focused. And she's the same way with other people. They can be talking about their cat, and she listens with the same attention. She's genuinely and sincerely interested. She's just so..." he searched his head for the right word, "...sweet. She's sweet."

Charlie's brown eyes widened. "*Oh, man,*" he breathed, "you're in—"

Just then, a hard knock sounded on the door. Jake glanced at his watch. It was exactly seven o'clock. He didn't need a peephole to know that Zeke May stood on the other side.

Zeke had served in the Army for more than a decade, and he was always on time, unless his fiancée was with him. Margo wasn't quite as punctual as her husband-to-be. But who cared about punctuality when her smile was brighter than the Vegas strip and sweeter than late-summer strawberries?

Charlie beat Jake to the door, welcoming Zeke inside with a slap on the back. The tall veteran held a stack of cardboard pizza boxes.

As Zeke deposited the boxes on the gray granite island, he said, "Hey, guys. How's it going?"

When Jake had met Zeke a little over a year ago, the dark-haired man had been taciturn and rarely smiled. But being with Margo had changed him. She made him happy, and his ready smiles and frequent laughter proved it.

Zeke and Margo were getting married in a few weeks, and he had asked Jake to be a groomsman. Jake had been honored, but unsurprised. Over the past several months, he and Zeke had become close friends, almost as close as he and Charlie.

"Beer?" Charlie offered Zeke. "We've got Sierra Nevada," he added, knowing that the other man preferred pale ales.

Zeke nodded, and after Charlie snagged a bottle from the fridge for him, Zeke popped the top and leaned back against the island. "Cal just texted me. He's going to be about an hour late."

Cal O'Brien was the fourth poker player in their little group. He was one of *the* O'Briens—the great-great-grandson of the man who had started Riley O'Brien & Co. back in the mid-1800s. Cal headed up the company's global marketing and communications department.

Jake had interacted with Cal a few times over the past six years for work-related projects. But he hadn't gotten to know the other man on a personal level until they'd played on the same company softball team last spring.

Cal was a good softball player, but he wasn't much of a card player … despite his insistence that he was awesome. While his poker face was decent, his pale blue eyes gave everything away.

Charlie opened the lid of the pizza box on top of the stack, and the enticing aroma of pepperoni saturated the air. A second later, he shut the lid and shoved the box aside.

Glancing at Jake, Charlie said, "Zeke got your favorite pizza: pepperoni and jalapenos. So disgusting."

"Thanks, man." Jake handed Zeke a paper plate and a stack of napkins. "We're eating and playing on the balcony."

The three of them loaded their plates with pizza, exchanged their empties with full bottles, and headed out to the balcony. It wrapped around the condo in an L-shape and added about three hundred square feet of outdoor living space.

As they sat down at the rectangular patio table, Zeke said, "I've never been out here before. This is great."

Although Zeke had never asked how Jake and Charlie could afford a penthouse unit in one of the most expensive high-rises in the city, his curiosity was evident. It wasn't a secret that Jake's dad was a professional poker player, so Zeke probably assumed that gambling had paid for the condo.

His assumption wasn't incorrect. But the money hadn't come from Ralph's winnings; it had come from the sports book business that Jake had started when he was a freshman in high school. He still owned the business, but a local team managed the day-to-day operations.

Jake didn't make a habit of telling people about his side gig as a bookie. He'd realized it was better to keep that information to himself.

Everyone had an opinion about gambling, whether they admitted it or not, and most of them were opposed to it, even when they thought they weren't. And people really disapproved of bookies since they profited when a gambler lost.

Beyond Charlie, only one other person in the Bay Area knew about Jake's side gig: Quinn O'Brien, the CEO of Riley O'Brien & Co. and Cal's older brother.

Quinn also had attended Stanford's MBA program, and Jake had met the young executive during an alumni event. They had formed a casual friendship over mediocre hors d'oeuvres and cheap wine.

When Quinn had suggested that Jake join Riley O'Brien & Co., he had felt compelled to disclose that he was a bookie. To his surprise, Quinn hadn't been bothered by it. In fact, the young

CEO had been impressed by Jake's ability to run such a large operation.

Jake had come up with the sports book scheme while participating in an after-school math club. He'd started out taking bets on college football games, and by the time he'd moved to Northern California, the business had grown into one of the largest independent sports book operations in Vegas. It had an annual handle of nearly fifty million dollars.

Jake's earnings had paid for his and Charlie's education at UNLV and Stanford. In exchange, Charlie had agreed to provide free and unlimited medical care to Jake's future children, whenever they arrived.

"Why is Cal late?" Charlie asked before taking a huge bite of pizza.

Zeke shrugged. "He said he had something important to do."

"Something important?" Jake repeated. "More like *someone* important."

"Bebe," they chorused.

Cal had recently asked his girlfriend, Bebe Banerjee, to marry him. She had accepted his proposal, probably because he'd bribed her with cream-cheese brownies. Either that, or she'd been blinded and disoriented by the obscenely large yellow diamond that Cal had picked out for her engagement ring.

"When Cal gets here, I'm going to give him shit for blowing us off," Jake vowed.

Charlie snorted. "Like you wouldn't do the same thing for Kyla."

"I wouldn't..." Jake denied, but stopped when Zeke shot him a knowing look.

"You would," Charlie insisted.

Jake gave a self-deprecating laugh. "Yeah, you're right."

"I know."

Charlie and Zeke were the only people who knew about Jake's interest in Kyla. It wasn't something he wanted to advertise until it no longer violated Riley O'Brien & Co.'s employee policies.

"Speaking of Kyla..." Zeke began. "Have you talked to her about her plans after she graduates from the management trainee program? I'd love to have her back in the supply chain and logistics department."

"No." Jake shook his head. "I don't know which positions she's interested in."

After a beat of silence, Charlie began to guffaw. "Why don't you just ask?" he suggested through his laughter. "Hey, Kyla, what's your favorite position?"

Jake narrowed his eyes. "Charlie..." he warned, but his best friend just rolled his eyes and took another bite of pizza.

"Are you still going to ask her out when she's finished with the program?" Zeke inquired.

"Yes."

Jake wasn't sure how Kyla would react to his interest. His dad had taught him to read people ... to scrutinize their expressions, to study their body language, to listen to what they did and did not say. Unfortunately, Jake's feelings for Kyla hindered his ability to read her.

He knew she liked working with him, but that was only because she'd told him so. He knew he could make her laugh until she cried. He also knew that she blushed a lot when she was around him. But pink cheeks did not necessarily mean she felt the same way about him that he felt about her.

Zeke's phone buzzed, and he immediately picked it up. A smile curved his lips—one that only his fiancée could elicit—

before he returned the phone to the table.

"Margo wants to know if you've decided on what we're doing for my bachelor party," Zeke said.

Because Jake was the only local groomsman (the other two were Zeke's brothers, and they lived in North Carolina), he had been tasked with planning the bachelor party. Zeke had been very vocal about the activities he considered unacceptable. The list was extensive. No strip clubs, no surfing, and no bars-on-wheels, just to name a few.

Jake had considered paintball, but had decided against it after weighing the risk of injury against the reward of male bonding in an outdoor environment. He had also factored in Zeke's history as a soldier who'd completed tours in Afghanistan and Iraq. There was a risk that paintball could stir up bad memories of being in combat.

After a lot of research, Jake had finally decided on skydiving. It was a little risky, but the reward was worth it.

From Jake's perspective, jumping out of a plane wasn't nearly as risky as asking Kyla out on a date. At least he'd be wearing a parachute when he went skydiving. Nothing would soften his fall if she turned him down.

CHAPTER TWO

After spending the entire morning hurrying from one overlong meeting to another, Kyla wished she could wave a magic wand and eliminate meetings. And if she couldn't eliminate them, she would use that magic wand to ensure that her meetings ended on time.

She'd just suffered through a meeting that had finally wrapped up thirty minutes after it was supposed to. And because it had run over, she was going to be late for lunch with her older sister. Fortunately, Vanessa's schedule today wasn't as crazy as it usually was, and she was still able to meet Kyla at their favorite café.

Despite the protracted meetings, Kyla loved working for Riley O'Brien & Co., the nation's oldest designer and manufacturer of blue jeans. It was part of the very fabric of America, no pun intended. Its signature blue jeans, known as Rileys, were a staple in nearly every closet across the country, and under Quinn O'Brien's leadership, the company was thriving.

Shifting her leather bag to her other shoulder, she stabbed the down elevator button again. She knew pushing the button more than once didn't make the elevator arrive any faster, but it made her feel better to do something. She tapped her foot impatiently, the sound of her high-heeled boots making a sharp staccato on the stained concrete floor.

Kyla really hated being late. She hated feeling rushed and frazzled, and she hated the impact of her tardiness on other people. She didn't want them to be inconvenienced or think that she didn't value and respect their time.

A loud ding announced the elevator's arrival, and the doors right in front of her opened with a *swoosh*. The cab was empty, and just as she pressed the button to take her to Riley Plaza's second floor reception area, she heard a male voice call out, "Hold the elevator!"

She stuck her hand between the closing doors, and a big foot covered in a black motorcycle boot slipped through the crack. As the metal panels retreated, a jeans-clad leg joined the boot, followed by the rest of a body ... one belonging to Jake Lilliard.

She and her deliciously hot boss were alone in an elevator, a setting seemingly designed for passionate encounters. She'd had more than one fantasy that involved him backing her against the wall of the cab and kissing her until she clenched her fingers in his whiskey-colored hair and moaned against his mouth.

Yes, she was a cliché: the foolish woman who had fallen for her boss. And yes, she knew how pathetic that was.

When Jake spotted her, his lips lifted in a smile. It was so warm and engaging that she found herself returning his smile without even thinking about it.

His eyes swept over her, glimmering with shades of green and gold. The color made her think of hiking through the forest on a sunny spring day.

"Thanks for holding the elevator."

"Sure," she replied, pleased to hear that she sounded completely normal despite the butterflies flitting around her stomach.

She stepped backward to make room for him. As he entered the elevator cab, his arm grazed hers, hard and warm through his black-and-gray San Francisco Giants T-shirt.

He was a big guy, probably close to six-three, and even with the four-inch boost from her boots, he was several inches taller than she was. His broad shoulders made the elevator seem even smaller.

His voice rumbled near her ear. "Where are you headed?"

"To lunch," she muttered, trying to ignore the way her spine tingled.

She kept her eyes straight ahead, irrationally annoyed with him. It wasn't his fault that she was a walking, talking cliché.

She knew it was stupid and unprofessional to crush on her boss, but she couldn't help it. Jake was just so funny. So smart. So kind. So interesting. So handsome.

And so off-limits.

Only for ten more days, a voice inside her whispered.

She ignored the voice. It didn't matter if Jake was her boss or not in ten days. He had shown zero interest in her as anything but a colleague.

Much to her disappointment, he was friendly, but nothing more. He'd never done anything to indicate he even recognized she was female, let alone that he was attracted to her.

She, meanwhile, was deathly afraid she would slip up and let him know how much she wanted him. The thought made her mouth go dry and her stomach churn. She would be absolutely mortified if he had an inkling of how she felt about him.

Out of the corner of her eye, she saw him lean back against the side of the elevator and brace his hands on the metal railing. She'd wasted a few hours fantasizing about those big hands and how they'd feel on her—

"Want some company for lunch?" he asked.

She took a deep breath, trying to dispel the image of Jake's hands on her breasts. Would he be gentle with her nipples, playing and teasing them? Or would he be rough, pinching and pulling them? Both techniques sounded good to her, as long as Jake was the one practicing them.

She took another deep breath, and the scent of his cologne filled her nose, woodsy and crisp. *Damn it!* Now little whiffs of him would distract her all afternoon. She probably wouldn't get anything done.

"Did you hear me, Kyla? Do you want to grab some lunch together?"

"I'm meeting my sister. No boys allowed."

His lips quirked at her answer. "Maybe tomorrow then."

"Maybe," she replied noncommittally.

Jake was a great supervisor, and she'd learned a lot from him. But every moment she spent with Jake was dangerous, and it was prudent to limit her exposure to him. So far, she had managed to maintain her professionalism with him ... just barely.

Kyla knew it was only a matter of time before her willpower collapsed under the constant pressure of her desire for Jake. She prayed she could make it through the end of the trainee program without embarrassing herself.

Except for Jake, she rarely had trouble resisting temptation. She could walk past her favorite boutique, see a fabulous dress on display, and not give in to the desire to go inside and whip out her credit card. She could eat at five-star restaurants and manage not to stuff her face with thousands of calories.

But Jake was more tempting than a Stella McCartney frock or a gourmet meal, and every second she spent with him made the cracks in her willpower widen. In fact, if her willpower were the

Hoover Dam, everyone should be worried about an epic flood.

She sighed, silently begging the elevator to move faster. If she spent much more time alone with Jake in this tiny space, she might throw herself at him.

To her relief, the elevator dinged just then, and the doors slid open. She exited the cab, aware that Jake was right behind her.

"Have fun at your girls-only lunch," Jake said, a trace of laughter in his deep voice. "I'll see you later."

Before she could reply, he strode off. She watched him as he moved toward the executive wing, wishing that he was the cliché: the hot guy who falls for the trainee.

With Jake occupying her thoughts, she turned toward the escalator and immediately slammed into someone who smelled like plums. As she stumbled back, she glimpsed startled green eyes set in a face surrounded by short, chocolaty ringlets.

Recognizing the other woman, Kyla exclaimed, "Phoebe! I'm sorry! Are you okay?"

Phoebe Werner waved away her concern. "I'm fine. It takes more than a blond pixie to bring me down."

Like Kyla, Phoebe was one of Riley O'Brien & Co.'s management trainees. But unlike Kyla, who was close to completing the twelve-month program, Phoebe was just now finishing the first of four rotations. Each rotation consisted of three months in a department of the trainee's choosing.

Kyla had met Phoebe on the first day of their new rotations. It usually took her a while to get comfortable with new people, but she had immediately felt at ease with Phoebe. Maybe it was the petite brunette's warm smile and melodic laugh. Or maybe it was her calm strength and infinite patience.

Whatever the reason, Kyla liked Phoebe a lot, and she'd been one of the handful of people with whom Kyla had recently celebrated her twenty-seventh birthday. After dinner and drinks, the group had gone to Kiln or Be Kiln, a paint your own pottery studio, and Kyla had confirmed that she lacked artistic talent.

Although they hadn't known each other very long, Kyla considered Phoebe a good friend. She hoped that they would become even closer, if given the opportunity.

The two women had already bonded over the fact that they were both Bay Area transplants. Kyla had grown up in Boston and gone to college in Ohio. Phoebe, meanwhile, was a native Idahoan, and she had moved to San Francisco from Boise.

"I'm meeting Vanessa for lunch at Remy's," Kyla told Phoebe. "Do you want to join us?"

Phoebe smiled. "I would love to, but I can't. I have a doctor's appointment." She tilted her head toward the escalator. "We're going the same direction, though. We can walk together."

Moments later, Kyla and Phoebe were on the sidewalk, heading south toward Remy's. The country French café had opened a little over three months ago, and it had immediately become one of Kyla's favorite places for lunch.

Glancing sideways, Kyla studied the merlot-colored sweater that Phoebe wore. It crisscrossed over her torso, and a charcoal cami peeked out from the deep V-neckline. A pair of dark-washed skinny jeans and gray suede booties with a wedge heel completed her outfit.

"I love your sweater. Did you make it?"

Phoebe nodded. "I knitted it on Sunday while I binge watched *Black Mirror*."

"I don't even know where to start with that statement."

"What?" Phoebe giggled. "What was wrong with it?"

"You knitted an *entire* sweater in one day? And what is *Black Mirror?* I've never heard of it."

Phoebe smoothed her fingers over the soft-looking yarn covering her forearm. "This is really just a scarf with sleeves. It's not a challenging pattern at all."

"It's really pretty. The color looks great with your hair."

Phoebe's "scarf with sleeves" wasn't the only thing that was pretty. The woman wearing it was pretty, too.

Kyla was sure more than one guy had fixated on the tiny brown freckle just to the side of Phoebe's upper lip. It was Mother Nature's finishing touch, like chocolate flakes on top of whipped cream.

"*Black Mirror* is a British TV show," Phoebe explained. "It's kind of like *The Twilight Zone* in the sense that episodes aren't connected, and each one features different characters."

"What's it about?"

Phoebe's lips turned down in a frown. "It's about the consequences of technology on modern society. It's dark satire."

"So, what you're really saying is that it's depressing."

"Oh, yeah. Even the most optimistic person would probably feel like crying after watching it."

"Speaking of crying, did you get everything worked out for your next rotation?" Kyla asked. "Did you get a place in the e-commerce group like you wanted?"

"Yes. And there was no crying involved. Just a lengthy conversation with Miranda."

Miranda Hoyt was the HR manager who handled the trainee program. It was just one of her many responsibilities, and it always ended up being a low priority.

"I know Miranda is doing her best, but I think the management trainee program needs a dedicated manager," Kyla said.

"I agree. It's too much work for someone with so much on her plate."

"I think I'm going to mention it to Teagan," Kyla said. "She needs to know that the program could be improved."

Teagan O'Brien-Priest was the reason Kyla had joined Riley O'Brien & Co. When she had graduated with her MBA from Miami University in Ohio, her mom had begged her to look for a job in the Bay Area. Unfortunately, she'd struck out.

Kyla had been ready to accept a job in Minneapolis when she got an unexpected phone call from Teagan offering her a position in the management trainee program. She knew the O'Brien heiress had offered her the position because of Kyla's mom, Letty. She worked for Teagan and her husband, Nick.

Letty's official title was live-in housekeeper and chef. Her unofficial title was surrogate mother.

"Why don't you put together a report outlining the changes you'd make if you ran the management trainee program and then float it to Teagan?" Phoebe said. "Maybe that will make a lightbulb go off."

Kyla considered Phoebe's suggestion. "That's a good idea. All the trainees get a week of vacation after graduation. I could work on the report then."

They passed Remy's charming patio, which was enclosed by a decorative wrought iron gate, and stopped near the front door. Kyla gave the shorter woman a quick hug.

"I'll see you later. Good luck at your doctor's appointment."

Phoebe's face went blank. "It's just a routine checkup." As she walked away, she called out over her shoulder, "Let me know if you need any help with the report."

Kyla waved her thanks before entering the café. Her gaze skipped over the rustic brick floors, mahogany wood paneling, and gas-burning sconces before landing on her older sister. Vanessa stood at the long wooden bar, looking down at her phone with her glossy pink lips pursed.

The two of them were almost identical except for the fact that Vanessa was nearly seven inches taller than Kyla—the quintessential statuesque blonde. And she had bigger boobs, damn her.

As usual, Vanessa wore all black. A conservative black pencil skirt, a black silk blouse, and a thin black snakeskin belt. Her red patent leather heels added some color to the otherwise monochromatic outfit.

Kyla stared at the bright shoes for a moment, a conflicting mix of relief and despair swirling inside her. Those heels proved that Vanessa hadn't completely lost herself—that Alan Toft hadn't managed to completely eradicate her true personality.

Years ago, Vanessa had gravitated to bright, vibrant hues. But since she'd become involved with Alan, she had adopted his minimalistic style. At his urging, she had removed all color from her wardrobe. For a while, she had worn black and white but now wore black almost exclusively.

Kyla was afraid it wouldn't be too much longer before her sister's collection of bright, sexy shoes disappeared. And at that point, Alan will have succeeded in making Vanessa's life completely colorless.

Kyla wished her sister would find a guy who didn't want to change her … a guy who made her want to wear a rainbow of colors. And while she was wasting her time and making wishes, Kyla figured she might as well wish that she could find a guy like that for herself.

Vanessa was so absorbed in whatever was on her phone that she didn't even notice when Kyla came to a stop next to her. She waited a moment before waving her hand in front of Vanessa's phone. That got her attention.

"Hey, Sass," she said, using her special nickname for her sister. "Thanks for waiting on me."

Kyla and Vanessa shared a two-bedroom apartment in a contemporary duplex in Russian Hills, a small neighborhood on one of San Francisco's highest hills. They hadn't seen each other in a few days, though, because Vanessa had been in Los Angeles, pitching a new client for her architectural design firm.

To Kyla's surprise, she had missed Vanessa quite a bit. She liked living with her sister.

When they'd been young girls, they had shared a bedroom, and they hadn't liked it.

They had lived apart for several years, but it hadn't taken long for them to fall back into their familiar patterns from childhood. They still argued about Kyla's messiness, but nowadays, their disagreements were settled peacefully, probably because they drank wine.

After giving her big sister a hug, Kyla asked, "Why didn't you get a booth?"

"I've been sitting all day. It felt good to stand for a while." She grabbed her black patent leather tote from the bar stool and slung it over her shoulder. "But I'm ready to sit now. I'm starving."

In less than a minute, the hostess had shown them to a cozy booth in the back. The banquet seat was upholstered in taupe linen with French words written in black cursive. Kyla spotted *bon appétit* and cuisine before she tossed her fuchsia biker's jacket onto the cushion.

Vanessa picked up the menu. "Lunch is my treat today."

"Why? What do you want in return?" Kyla teased.

"The toilets at home could use a good scrubbing," Vanessa answered, her gray eyes sparkling with mischief.

"Who do you think I am? Cinderella?"

"You say that like it would be a bad thing."

Vanessa tilted her head, the blunt ends of her glossy hair falling past her shoulders. She only wore it down when Alan wasn't around because he preferred it slicked back in a tight bun. Whenever he saw it down, he complained that it looked too unkempt.

"I don't understand why everyone feels sorry for Cinderella," Vanessa continued. "She had to clean a few chamber pots before she got her happily ever after. Boohoo. We all have to put up with a little shit before we find a prince."

Kyla stared at her sister. Did Vanessa actually think Alan was her prince? If anything, he was the evil villain … or the village idiot, depending on the situation.

They abandoned the subject of Cinderella and spent the next couple of minutes reviewing the menu. It didn't take Kyla long. She could almost recite it word-for-word since she'd been to Remy's so many times. After the server delivered glasses of water and described the daily specials, they placed their orders.

Vanessa took a sip of her blood orange sparkling water. "Have you talked to Miranda yet about where you're going to be placed permanently after you graduate from the trainee program?"

"No, she canceled our meeting yesterday. Honestly, I was relieved. I can't make up my mind."

Since Riley O'Brien & Co. was expanding, a lot of departments were eager to fill empty positions with qualified candidates. Kyla had several options including positions in every department in which she'd done a rotation.

"Since you're such a little math geek, you should stay in the finance department," Vanessa suggested.

"You've always been jealous that I love numbers, and they love me back."

Vanessa's lips twitched. "Do all numbers love you or just six and nine?"

It took Kyla a moment to get the joke, and when she finally did, she rolled her eyes. Vanessa burst out laughing. "It took you long enough to get it," she noted through her giggles.

When Kyla didn't join in, Vanessa sighed dramatically. "Oh, come on, Ky. You know that was funny. You've completely lost your sense of humor. Maybe it's because sixty-nine doesn't love you as much as you thought."

Ignoring her sister's gibes, Kyla said, "I'm not sure it would be a good idea to take a permanent position in the finance department. Even if I reported to someone other than Jake, we would still work together on a few projects."

"I don't understand why you think there's a problem." Vanessa lifted her shoulder in a dismissive shrug. "So what if you want to do him. That's what happens when people work closely together."

"*Shh.* Don't be so loud."

Kyla looked around the café, hoping no other Riley O'Brien & Co. employees were close by. Fortunately, she didn't recognize any of the other diners.

"Seriously, Ky. Do you know how many women have crushes on their co-workers or their bosses? Thousands. Maybe even millions."

"There are a lot of stupid women in the world," Kyla noted wryly.

Vanessa frowned. "You're not stupid for having a crush on Jake, but you *are* stupid for letting it impact your career. I didn't think twice about joining Alan's firm even though we're together.

It was a good career move."

Kyla bit her lip to stop herself from blurting out that Vanessa *should* have thought twice about it. It was bad enough that she had sex with such an ass. Did she have to work for him, too?

The arrival of their food paused their conversation. Kyla had ordered the daily special: a mixed greens salad with grilled chicken, roasted beets, goat cheese, and walnuts.

Délicieux!

Kyla was so hungry, she devoured half of her salad before she came up for air. Returning to the topic of their previous discussion, she said, "Whenever I'm with Jake, I constantly have to remind myself to be professional. We always end up having these really personal conversations … the kind of conversations people have on dates."

"Maybe you should try going on an actual date with him. You only have a few days left in the finance department. You should ask him out when your rotation is over."

Kyla blanched at the thought. "*No way.*"

"Why not? Does he have a girlfriend?"

"I have no idea. But even if he doesn't, I am *not* going to ask him out."

"I know you're shy, and I know how hard it is for you to talk to guys in social situations, but you just said that you and Jake have already had those awkward getting-to-know-you conversations." Vanessa rolled the stem of the water goblet between her fingers. "There's no harm in asking him out once he's no longer your boss."

"No harm?" Kyla repeated, her voice nearly a screech. "I would be humiliated if he said no! Or what if he said yes because he was too nice to say no? Or what if he thought I was just asking him out to network? Or what if—"

Vanessa set her goblet down on the table with a sharp click. "Kyla Genevieve Andrews! Do you like him or not?"

"Yes! But I think it's better to end my rotation on a professional note."

"And then what? Wave whenever you run into him in the elevator?"

Kyla fell silent. Her throat got tight when she thought about not seeing Jake every day. He was the best part of her day … and night.

"I don't know," Kyla finally answered.

"Here's the way I see it: since you don't have any plans to hook up with him after your rotation is over, you might as well stay in the finance group. More than likely, your crush will run its natural course over the next couple of months, and you'll find someone more interesting or good-looking than Jake to fixate on."

Kyla eyed her sister. She couldn't deny that Vanessa made a lot of sense except for one tiny thing: there was no one more interesting or good-looking than Jake. And Kyla greatly feared her feelings for him went well beyond the typical short-lived crush.

CHAPTER THREE

"You're going to feel a little prick."

Kyla looked away from her arm as the phlebotomist positioned the needle in the crook of her elbow. She wasn't afraid of needles, but she got a little queasy if she watched the stainless-steel tube pierce her skin.

"The hypodermic is in." The phlebotomist, an older black woman with a short, silver afro, patted Kyla's shoulder. "We like to get a least a pint of blood, and it should take about ten minutes for the bag to fill. Once it's full, I'll send you to the recovery station where you need to have a drink and a snack to replenish the lost fluid. You can leave the recovery station after fifteen minutes."

"Okay," Kyla replied.

"I'll be back to check on you in a few minutes," the woman promised before hurrying away.

Relaxing in the portable blood donation chair, Kyla glanced around the spacious conference room where Riley O'Brien & Co. hosted its annual blood drive for the American Red Cross. The nonprofit organization had split the space into three areas for donor registration, donation, and recovery.

Tall soundproof panels separated the registration area into small intake rooms. Donors had to provide sensitive information, so privacy was important, especially for work-related blood drives. In the middle of the room, ten mesh-backed donation chairs were grouped in a circle so employees could socialize while they gave blood.

Except for Kyla, the donation chairs were empty. It was just after eight o'clock, and she assumed most people needed at least a couple of cups of coffee before they opened their veins. She, meanwhile, had been at work for more than an hour. She had only eight days left in her finance rotation, and she had a lot of projects to complete before she graduated.

Hearing footsteps behind her, Kyla looked over her shoulder and caught sight of Jake as he walked toward the donation area. He wore a pair of dark-washed Rileys and an olive-colored thermal tee that outlined his broad chest and flat stomach and showed off his muscular arms.

Except for his attire, he looked like a prisoner heading to the gallows, his jaw clenched and his shoulders stiff. When he saw Kyla, his greenish-gold eyes widened, and a look of profound relief crossed his face. He hurried toward her, and as he reached her side, he said her name like a prayer, his voice barely audible.

"Good morning," she replied.

He stared down at her, still and silent as his gaze trailed over her face. His scrutiny made her terribly self-conscious, and she raised her hand to smooth her hair, forgetting for a moment she was tethered to plastic tubing. His eyes fell to the needle and the blood-filled tubing, and his face paled until it was nearly the color of milk.

Fearing that he might faint, she grabbed his hand and tugged him toward the donation chair next to her. "Sit down," she ordered.

He obeyed her immediately, dropping heavily into it. He leaned back and closed his eyes, his lashes long and spiky against his ashen cheeks.

"Okay?" she asked softly, rubbing his knuckles with her thumb.

Her voice was calm, but her chest felt tight with worry. He squeezed her hand, his long fingers weaving with hers as he pulled in several shaky breaths. After a long moment, he opened his eyes and met her gaze.

"Trypanophobia," he muttered, color filling his face.

"What?"

"Fear of needles."

"Oh, I thought you might be afraid of the sight of blood."

He grimaced. "That too. Hemophobia."

"Ridiculous man," she scolded. "Why are you here if you're afraid of needles *and* blood?"

His burnished eyebrows arched. "Because I need to set a good example. I can't expect the people in my group to do something I'm not willing to do. Plus, giving blood saves lives. Haven't you seen the TV commercials—one blood donation saves *three* lives?"

She was torn between exasperation and admiration. "So, I should force myself to kill huge, hairy spiders even though I have arachnophobia?"

"No," he answered, his eyes lit with amusement. "I'd be happy to kill them for you."

As they stared at each other, Kyla realized Jake's phobias had the surprising result of making him even more attractive to her. He always seemed so in control, almost invincible, and the fact that he had admitted his weakness made her feel closer to him.

The phlebotomist returned, pushing a metal cart filled with supplies. She stopped next to Kyla and fiddled with the tubing that ran from Kyla's arm to the plastic collection bag.

"Looking good, girl." She turned to Jake. "Don't tell me a big, strong man like you is afraid of a tiny piece of metal?"

"Are they mutually exclusive?" Jake asked with a rueful smile.

The phlebotomist chuckled. "In your case, they're not." She eyed Jake and Kyla's entwined hands. "I take it you two know each other."

Embarrassed, Kyla tried to jerk her hand away. Jake's fingers tightened for a split second before he let go.

"He's my boss," Kyla explained, tucking her hand between her denim-clad thighs.

The phlebotomist's lips twitched. "Don't worry, honey, I won't tell anyone that you and Mr. Afraid of Needles are having one of those steamy office romances."

"We're not," Kyla protested emphatically.

Too emphatically.

Jake glanced at her alertly. She could feel her face growing hot, and she looked away from his penetrating gaze.

The phlebotomist picked up a purple tourniquet and stretched it between her hands. "Are you ready, tough guy?" she asked Jake.

He glanced at Kyla, his gaze panicked. "Please distract me," he begged. "Tell me what you did last night."

"I went to an art exhibition with my mom, and after that I hung out with her while she made cookies."

The phlebotomist snapped on a pair of blue latex gloves, and Jake jerked in surprise when she began to palpate his arm, searching for a viable vein. Apparently, she found one quickly because she reached for a foil square containing an alcohol pad and tore it open.

Jake took a deep breath. "Keep talking, sweetness."

The endearment surprised Kyla. She glanced at the phlebotomist, and the older woman winked before she cleansed the skin of Jake's inner elbow and forearm.

"Where was the exhibition?" Jake asked.

"The San Francisco Public Library."

Jake stared at her, his eyes locked on her face like a nuclear missile locked on its target. "What was it about?"

"The history of wedding cakes."

"And why are you interested in the history of wedding cakes?"

She laughed at his obvious bafflement. "I'm not. But my mom is. Lately she's been obsessed with baking cakes."

Kyla briefly broke eye contact with Jake. The phlebotomist had removed a butterfly needle from its sterile packaging and was attaching it to the tubing.

"The exhibition was based on a book called *Wedding Cakes: A Slice of History*," Kyla continued. "Did you know that there are a lot of superstitions associated with wedding cakes?"

Jake slowly shook his head. "No, I didn't know that. But I have a feeling you're going to tell me about them now."

"Apparently, if the bride tastes the wedding cake before the ceremony, she will lose her husband's love."

"That makes sense. Tasting the cake before the ceremony means she's impulsive and impatient."

Kyla's mouth fell open. "Are you being serious?"

Jake chuckled softly. "What do you think?"

She shot a surreptitious glance at the phlebotomist to check her progress. She was preparing to insert the needle into Jake's vein, so Kyla rushed to turn the conversation to him.

"What did you do last night?" she asked. "Did you hang out with Charlie?"

A weird expression chased over Jake's face. "He was on call. He had to go check on a patient who was admitted to Saint Philomena."

Saint Philomena Children's Hospital was the only healthcare facility in the Bay Area that exclusively treated children. It was renowned for its neonatal intensive care and its burn unit.

"The needle is in," the phlebotomist announced.

Jake shifted his gaze toward his arm, but Kyla stopped him by saying, "Don't look!"

The phlebotomist pushed a red squishy ball into his palm. "Just focus on squeezing the ball. I'll be back to check on you in ten minutes."

"I can do that," Jake agreed before returning his attention to Kyla. "Thank you for distracting me."

"You're welcome."

Jake's eyes drifted away from hers. She could tell the moment he saw the needle in his vein because he tensed up, and his breathing turned erratic.

"Look at me, Jake." She had to repeat his name three more times before he brought his gaze back to her. "I told you what I did last night. Now you tell me."

He turned his face away and muttered something she couldn't make out. She thought she heard the word "cuddle" but that didn't make sense.

"What did you do?"

Looking down at his lap, Jake said, "Cuddled babies at Saint Philomena."

His answer was so unexpected ... so bizarre ... she didn't know how to respond for several seconds. Finally, she said, "Hospitals allow people to cuddle babies that aren't theirs? Don't parents have a problem with that? I wouldn't want some strange guy coming in off the street and holding my newborn."

He looked up and caught her eyes. "Saint Philomena has a volunteer cuddle program for babies who were born addicted to opioids. They don't have anyone to hold them. Whenever Charlie goes to the hospital, I tag along, and while he takes care of his patients, I cuddle the babies."

His face had regained all the color it had lost earlier. In fact, now it was bright red. Was he embarrassed to admit that he cuddled newborns? She couldn't imagine why he would be. It made him even sexier in her eyes.

"Cuddling helps them." Defiance underscored his voice. "There are a lot of studies that prove that cuddling reduces the amount of time babies with NAS spend in the hospital and the amount of medication they need to get better."

"What's NAS?"

"Neonatal abstinence syndrome. Babies with NAS have a hard time digesting breast milk, and they vomit excessively. They also suffer a lot of pain from muscle stiffness and spasms. And their skin gets irritated easily. Cuddling soothes them and allows them to sleep."

"When did you start cuddling?" she asked.

"A few years ago."

"So how did you get started? Did you just feel the need to cuddle one day, so you stopped by the hospital?"

The side of Jake's mouth hitched up. "Not exactly. One night after work, Charlie asked me to pick him up at Saint Phil's. I couldn't reach him on his phone when I got there, so I went inside. While I was looking for him, I walked by the nursery. It was full of babies, and all of them were screaming at the top of their lungs."

He shook his head. "They were so loud, I could hear them

through the glass. There were only a couple of nurses in there, and even if they'd held a baby in each arm, they couldn't have held them all."

Jake shifted restlessly, crossing his ankles and then uncrossing them. "Charlie found me standing in front of the nursery. He used his badge to get us inside. Before I knew what was happening, I was wearing a paper hospital gown over my clothes and holding a baby that had been born to a fifteen-year-old heroin addict. He had a bad case of NAS. I mean *bad*. I cuddled him for hours before Charlie dragged me home."

The image of a big, strong guy like Jake cuddling a tiny, helpless baby as it went through withdrawal made Kyla's heart feel swollen and raw. She didn't have a crush on this man. She was halfway in love with him.

"What was the baby's name?" she asked, knowing that Jake wouldn't have forgotten, no matter how many years had passed.

"Jesse." He smiled wistfully. "He was lucky. A couple from Sausalito adopted him."

The arrival of the phlebotomist ended their conversation about cuddling. "How's it going?" She checked Jake's bag first before turning her attention to Kyla. "Looks like you're done." She winked at Kyla. "That was fast. Something got your blood flowing."

After expertly removing the needle and bandaging Kyla's arm, the phlebotomist said, "One full glass of apple juice or lemonade and at least two cookies. Don't leave until I give you my blessing." When Kyla hesitated, not wanting to abandon Jake, the phlebotomist made a shooing motion with her hands. "Go. You need to replenish your fluids and stabilize your blood sugar."

Following orders, Kyla rose from the donation chair. As she

reached for her phone, Jake's fingers tangled with hers. The feel of them, warm and slightly rough, sent a tiny tremble through her stomach.

"Grab a drink and a snack and then come back to me." When she hesitated, his fingers tightened. "Please."

*****

Jake was doing his best to ignore the huge-ass needle protruding from his median cubital vein, but it wasn't easy. At least Kyla was there to distract him. She sat sideways on the chair next to him, sipping lemonade and nibbling cookies.

He always dreaded the annual blood drives. In the past, he'd made a point of being the first person to give blood so no one would witness it when he got sweaty and shaky. He had never come close to fainting, but seeing Kyla with a needle stuck in the smooth white skin of her arm had turned him inside out.

After taking a sip of her lemonade, Kyla said, "I did a lot of volunteer work in college through my sorority, but I haven't done anything here. I think it's time."

"There's always a need for cuddlers." He shot her a questioning glance. "Do you like babies?"

He wasn't asking out of idle curiosity. Her answer was important, and he hoped her dreams aligned with his.

"I've never been around any babies, so I can't say for sure. But I know I want to have children someday. How about you?"

"Yeah, I want a big family."

"How big?" she asked warily.

"Four or five kids. I'm an only child, and I think only children are lonely children."

"I can't imagine being an only child, although I'm sure my mom fantasized about it frequently," she said wryly.

He laughed. "I doubt that. Probably she only fantasized about it occasionally."

She rose abruptly and leaned across his torso. She was so close he could smell the citrusy fragrance of her shampoo.

"What are you doing?" he asked, unable to hide his accelerated breathing.

"Checking your output. Your bag is halfway full." Turning her head, she smiled into his eyes. "You're doing great."

Kyla nabbed a cookie from the stack beside her and took a bite. Several cookie crumbs clung to her lower lip, drawing his attention.

"These are wicked delicious."

"Wicked, huh?" Jake smiled. "You can take the girl out of Boston, but you can't take Boston out of the girl."

"It just slips out," she admitted with a grimace. "I've tried to break myself of the habit, but it's too ingrained."

"I think it's cute. There's nothing about you that needs to change, Kyla."

"You are *wicked* wrong about that," she quipped, making him chuckle.

Her pink tongue darted out to gather the cookie crumbs, and a moan built in his throat. He tried to silence it, but he wasn't entirely successful. A muffled growl escaped his mouth, and Kyla's eyes shot to his face.

"Are you in pain?" she asked, her face etched with concern.

"I'm fine," he lied.

He couldn't believe it, but he was getting hard, even with blood trickling out of his arm. His zipper was smashing his burgeoning erection, and there was nothing he could do about it unless he ripped the needle from his arm and sprinted to the privacy of his office.

She sighed gustily. "You shouldn't force yourself to give blood when you have phobias about it."

"Stop talking about my phobias."

"It's nothing to be embarrassed about," Kyla said soothingly.

He grunted. Embarrassed didn't come close to describing the depths of his humiliation. He wasn't thrilled that he had acted like a wimp in front of Kyla. At the same time, however, he was glad it had happened in front of her instead of someone else. He knew she would keep his secret.

Trying to change the subject, he asked, "What do you think merits embarrassment?"

"Getting your prom dress caught in the elevator doors and having it torn off you in front of your classmates," she answered promptly.

"*Damn.* That is embarrassing. Please tell me that didn't happen to you."

She laughed, and the husky sound wrapped around him, warming him like a fluffy goose down comforter. She had a great laugh, sexy and sweet, just like her.

"It happened to the reigning mean girl in my high school."

"Karma," he replied succinctly. "What did she do when the elevator ripped off her dress?"

Kyla stared into space, obviously back at her high school prom. "She just stood there in her underwear, screaming at the top of her lungs while everyone circled around her, laughing and hooting."

"You weren't one of them."

She jerked her head toward him. Her gray eyes, so much like the fog that swirled around the Bay, met his.

"No, I wasn't part of their group."

"That's not what I meant. You didn't laugh and hoot."

She blinked slowly, her long lashes feathering outward. "No."

"What did you do?"

"I pulled a tablecloth off one of the nearby tables and covered her with it."

He nodded, unsurprised by her answer. She would never stand around and take pleasure from someone's misfortune, regardless of how mean-spirited they were.

"Was the mean girl mean to you?"

"Her name was Megan." Kyla smiled wryly. "And yes, she was mean to me."

"What did she do?"

"Just the typical mean girl stuff," she answered with a shrug.

"Like what?"

"Like bumping into me in the cafeteria."

It took him a moment to figure out why that was mean. "*Oh.* She made you drop your tray."

Kyla shook her head. "No. She made sure I didn't drop it. She pushed it toward me so my lunch ended up all over me."

What a bitch. The thought of anyone abusing Kyla, emotionally or physically, made him want to smash something.

"Why did she target you?" He answered his own question because Kyla had just taken a drink. "I'm sure she was jealous. You were probably hotter than she was."

Kyla choked on her lemonade. He tried to lean over so he could thump her on the back, but the plastic tubing stopped him. She held up a hand to let him know she was okay, and after a moment, she stopped coughing.

"You think I'm hot?" she whispered.

"Uh…" he stammered, cursing himself for his verbal blunder.

His comment about Kyla being hotter than the mean girl had

just slipped out. He sure as hell couldn't tell her the truth.

Fuck, yeah, I think you're hot. You're so hot I can barely keep my hands off you. And I'm counting the days until I don't have to.

She stood abruptly, putting her chest even with his face. He got a glimpse of something lacy between the buttons of her lavender shirt, and his mouth tingled. He wanted to pop open those buttons, pull down the cups of her bra, and find out if her nipples were as pink as her lips.

"Your bag is almost full," she noted. "I'll get you some lemonade and cookies."

He watched her as she walked over to the refreshments, her round ass perfectly outlined by a pair of Rileys. He silently thanked Amelia O'Brien for making over the women's division and redesigning the women's jeans. She had done a great service to all mankind.

Quinn had initially hired Amelia to design a line of accessories for the company. Apparently, he had liked the designs so much he'd asked her to head up the women's division. And he must have liked more than just her designs since he had married her a few months later.

Over the past year or so, Amelia had completely transformed the women's division. When she had taken over, it had been nothing more than an afterthought. Today, it generated more than a third of the company's annual revenue.

The phlebotomist arrived beside him, pulling his attention from Kyla's mouthwatering posterior. She nodded toward Kyla.

"She's so sweet I just wanna eat her with a spoon."

"You're not the only one," he admitted as she slid the needle from his arm and dropped it in the red plastic container next to his chair.

"She obviously feels the same way about you."

He looked up into her dark eyes, his heart thudding heavily. "She does?"

She snorted. "So, you're one of those—cute but clueless."

He laughed. "Most people think I'm pretty sharp."

She pressed a piece of gauze against the puncture and folded his forearm up to hold the cotton in place. Deftly unwinding a length of stretchy blue tape, she bandaged his arm.

He looked around her, tracking Kyla's progress as she came toward him, her hands filled with a plastic cup and cookies. She sat down sideways in the donation chair and held out the refreshments.

"I got you some snickerdoodles."

He swung his legs to the floor so they faced each other. Plucking a cookie from her hand, he took a bite. It melted on his tongue, a sweet, buttery treat spiced with cinnamon and nutmeg.

"Damn, this is good. Much better than the cookies we had at the last blood drive."

The nurse pointed at Kyla. "This sweet thing brought them with her." She winked at him. "Make sure you enjoy *all* those sweets, Mr. Afraid of Needles."

Trying not to think about all the ways he wanted to enjoy Kyla, he held up the cookie and asked, "You made these?"

"No, my mom made them last night after the exhibition." Her lips turned down at the corners. "I'm a terrible cook. If I had made them, you might have ended up in the ER needing your stomach pumped."

He chuckled at the glum expression on her face. "I'm sure you're not that bad."

She shook her head. Shiny hair waved over her shoulder, glinting with shades of pale amber, gold, and honey.

"No, I really am. Even though my mom is a world-class chef,

every time I cook, something bad happens." She sighed. "I made a romantic dinner for my boyfriend—"

"*What?* You have a *boyfriend?*"

She flinched a little, probably because he'd almost shouted the question. He had wondered about her sex life, but she had never, ever mentioned a goddamn boyfriend. He held his breath while he waited for her answer.

"No, I don't have a boyfriend. I was talking about the guy I dated in college."

He exhaled loudly, almost light-headed with relief. He didn't know what he would have done if she had told him that she had a boyfriend. He scrambled to gather his thoughts. They had been talking about her cooking skills, or lack thereof...

"So, you poisoned your college boyfriend?"

She flushed. "Not on purpose."

"Are you wanted for attempted murder?" he asked with a laugh.

She scowled. "It's not funny."

"What happened?"

"He never told me that he was allergic to cinnamon, and I made this pasta dish with butternut squash. It had cinnamon in it, and he ended up in the ER."

She looked so miserable he felt compelled to comfort her. "That wasn't your fault. You were trying to do something nice for him. He should have warned you."

"The next time I cooked for him, I made shrimp scampi. It was my mom's recipe, and she promised me it was easy. She said it was impossible to mess up."

"And?"

"That time we both ended up in the ER with food poisoning."

He grimaced. "I'm sure that was awful."

"He broke up with me a few days later," she said flatly.

He could tell by the lack of emotion in her voice that her ex-boyfriend had hurt her badly. What a stupid dickhead, to give up a woman like Kyla over something so ridiculous.

Jake would eat beef jerky for every fucking meal if it meant he could be with her. He wasn't sure there was anything he *wouldn't* do to be with her.

CHAPTER FOUR

Public speaking made most people anxious, but Kyla preferred it over casual chitchat. At least she could prepare for speeches and presentations, which reduced the risk of her looking and sounding like an idiot.

Several hundred Riley O'Brien & Co. store managers had flown into San Francisco for their annual meeting. Although a presentation from the finance department hadn't originally been part of the meeting schedule, the head of store operations, Mateo Morales, had squeezed Kyla and Jake in right before drinks and dinner.

Kyla glanced out across the ballroom in the Hudson San Francisco. This was the first time she had visited the historic hotel, and even though she had grown up in a city rich with history, the building still impressed her.

It recently had received a sixty million dollar makeover, according to the hotel events manager. Although the renovation had preserved the hotel's historic character, it also had included a twenty-first-century update.

The ballroom and other meeting spaces featured the latest audio-visual technology, and Kyla had already uploaded her presentation slides to the hotel's system. Currently, the cover slide filled the huge screen at the front of the room.

She and Jake had spent hours preparing for this presentation, creating slides and outlining talking points. They had worked over the weekend to get it ready, and she hoped their hard work would impress at least a few people. Unfortunately, Kyla doubted their audience would be very engaged. Everyone would be tired after a long day of seminars and ready for a glass of wine.

After checking and double-checking everything in the ballroom, Kyla grabbed her bag and headed for the coffee shop she'd noticed when she had entered the hotel. The presentation wasn't scheduled to begin for more than an hour, so she had time to enjoy a cup of tea and review her notes.

As she walked down the deserted corridor, she texted Jake to let him know where she'd be. She didn't want him to have to search for her when he arrived. He replied immediately, promising to meet her there with time to spare before the presentation began.

She smiled down at her phone. That was one of the things she liked best about Jake—he always did what he said he would do. He had never let her down.

She started to drop her phone into her bag when it chimed. The text was from Vanessa. "Good luck on your presentation! Don't forget to take off your mic if you go to the bathroom."

Laughing under her breath, Kyla wondered if Vanessa's warning came from experience. She gave a lot of client presentations, and she'd had more than a few tech mishaps and wardrobe malfunctions.

A few moments later, Kyla reached the double doors that led to the lobby. Before she could grab the handle, the door flew open. She lurched backward, trying to avoid being hit by the ornate wood, and stumbled on her tall, chunky heels.

Big hands gripped her upper arms and stopped her from falling. She looked up, an apology on her lips, but it died in her throat when she got a look at the man towering over her. He was a fine male specimen. More than fine, to be honest.

A navy blue pinstriped suit stretched over his broad shoulders, and the bright white of his shirt contrasted with his bronzed skin and glossy black hair. Except for his ocean-blue eyes, he looked as if he had Mediterranean ancestry, Greek or Italian, maybe.

"Steady," the hottie murmured before slowly releasing her arms.

His voice was deep but lacked any foreign accent. Despite his exotic looks, he was as American as baseball and apple pie.

She sucked in a breath, and the spicy scent of his cologne filled her lungs. He didn't smell as good as Jake, but almost.

He smiled slowly, showing off his white teeth and a dimple in his right cheek. "Hello."

"Hello."

Hearing how breathy her voice sounded, she cringed. As her cheeks heated, she realized only an inch or two separated them. As she put some space between them, he held out his right hand.

"Garrett Gale."

"Kyla Andrews," she replied, giving his hand a perfunctory shake.

"I'm sorry I almost knocked you down. I had my nose stuck in my phone, and I wasn't paying attention to where I was going."

"Don't worry about it." She adjusted her bag more securely on her shoulder. "It was nice to meet you, Garrett. Have a great day."

"Let me get the door for you," he offered, pulling it open and holding it for her.

"Thanks."

To her surprise, he followed her and fell into step beside her.

"Are you a guest at the hotel, Kyla?"

"No," she answered curtly.

She wasn't interested in making idle chitchat with a stranger, no matter how good-looking he was. She picked up her pace, and he lengthened his stride to keep up with her.

"Then why are you here? Drinks at the bar? A spa day with the girls?"

She thought about ignoring him, but then her good manners prevailed. "I'm giving a presentation later today."

"Since Riley O'Brien & Co. is using every inch of our meeting space, I assume you're with them?"

Something he'd said snagged her attention. "*Our* meeting space?" she repeated. "Do you work for the hotel?"

"No. I own it."

His answer surprised her. When she had run into him, she'd assumed he was just a guest at the hotel.

"You own the Hudson San Francisco?"

"My company does," he clarified. "GHG. Gale Hotel Group."

"It's beautiful. You did an amazing job with the renovation."

"It is beautiful," he agreed. "But I can't take any credit for the renovation. My design team deserves all of it."

"The events manager told me that you hired a historian to find old photos so the design would be authentic."

"I do that for all historic projects." He gestured to the floor. "Based on the old photos we were able to find, this was the original pattern. We had to guess the colors, though."

She glanced down at the carpet. With its rows of interlocking olive-colored diamonds outlined in thin bands of cream and navy blue, it wasn't the most attractive carpet she'd ever seen. But then again, she preferred more contemporary design.

They reached the lobby, and a group of people swarmed around them. He gently grasped her elbow and turned to face her.

"Can I buy you a cup of coffee or tea before your presentation?" he asked.

She hesitated but then told herself not to be an idiot. Jake had shown no interest in her, and a man who was obviously interested stood in front of her—a man who was not only incredibly handsome but also incredibly successful if this five-star hotel was anything to go by.

"That sounds good," she said.

With a hand on her lower back, Garrett ushered her into the coffee shop. After they placed their orders, he led her to a small round café table in the back. Someone had obviously taught him old-fashioned manners because he pulled out her chair and waited for her to get settled before he unbuttoned his suit jacket and sat down.

"Is your company based in San Francisco?" she asked.

Garrett shook his head. "Seattle. This is the only asset we own in the Bay Area, but I'd like to acquire more."

Before Kyla could pepper him with questions, a young woman with waist-length blue hair arrived with their drinks. He thanked her with a smile, and when he brought his attention back to Kyla, he amped up the wattage of his smile. If she weren't head over heels for Jake, she would be a puddle of goo right now.

"What is your presentation about?" he asked.

She wrinkled her nose. "It's not a particularly sexy or exciting topic."

He laughed softly. "Now I'm really curious."

"Riley O'Brien & Co.'s unprecedented growth is making it difficult to accurately forecast revenue and expenses on a corporate basis. I'm giving a presentation to the store operations group to introduce them to ways they can make their projections more accurate."

Kyla had tried to make the presentation fun and interesting. Jake had given her creative license with the slides, and she had chosen a carnival theme. After all, forecasting revenue was kind of like being a fortune-teller. She had even brought a prop with her, a crystal ball she'd bought in a metaphysical shop.

"Every company has trouble with forecasting," Garrett said. "It's a little easier for the hospitality business because our rooms and conference facilities book months in advance, but I would think that forecasting customer demand for apparel is next to impossible."

They spent the next twenty minutes discussing the similarities and differences between the hospitality and retail business. By the time her phone buzzed to let her know she needed to return to the conference room, she was thoroughly impressed with Garrett's intellect and business acumen and charmed by his teasing flirtatiousness.

"Thank you for the tea," she said. "This was fun."

"You're welcome."

He rose from his seat and hurried around the table to pull out her chair. "I'm going to be in town for a few days. Would you like to go to dinner tomorrow night at The Ellington Club?"

Garrett's invitation surprised Kyla, and she couldn't help but feel flattered. She had been approached by good-looking guys before, but it didn't happen very often. And she hadn't gone on more than a couple of dates since she'd moved to the Bay Area twelve months ago.

Even though her heart belonged to Jake, she had to accept Garrett's invitation. She owed it to all the single girls in the world who would kill to go out with him

"I'd love to have dinner with you," she said, aware that *love* was a bit of an exaggeration.

He smiled, obviously pleased with her consent. "Do you want to meet me or do you want me to pick you up?"

She appreciated his sensitivity to the fact that they didn't know each other well enough for him to come to her home. "I'll meet you."

He nodded. "Seven o'clock?"

"Yes."

Holding out his right hand, he said, "It was a pleasure to make your acquaintance, Kyla. I'm looking forward to dinner."

Just then, she heard her name. Glancing around for the source, she saw Jake at the entrance of the coffee shop. The fierce expression on his face was one she'd never seen before, his mouth tight and his brows lowered. He was obviously upset, and she wondered if something had happened at work.

Jake stalked forward, reaching them in seconds. As he looked back and forth between her and Garrett, she couldn't help but notice the two men had similar builds—the same height, the same broad shoulders, and the same muscular physiques.

But beyond that, they didn't look anything alike, especially with Garrett dressed in an expensive suit and shiny dress shoes and Jake sporting a black leather motorcycle jacket, faded Rileys, and his favorite black motorcycle boots. Garrett looked polished and urbane, while Jake looked like every good girl's bad-boy fantasy.

Jake faced Garrett. "Who are you?"

*****

Jake knew he had some rough edges, yet he had always believed that he was too evolved to turn into a Neanderthal when another man touched his woman. But he didn't know himself as well as he'd thought.

The moment he had seen Kyla with the dark-haired douche, Jake had been overwhelmed with the primal urge to find a club and beat the shit out of him. It was an urge he'd never felt before, and it was made worse by the fact that Kyla wasn't really his woman ... not yet.

He'd never been even slightly jealous over a woman, but he knew that what he felt right now could not be described as simple jealousy. It went far deeper than that, edging toward possessiveness.

Jake kept his eyes locked on Kyla's face. If he got another glimpse of the douche's hand holding hers, he might actually lose it. Every beat of his heart thumped with the rhythm of rage, making his pulse pound in his ears and his blood sizzle.

"Who are you?" he asked again when neither Kyla nor the douche answered his previous question. Her eyes widened, and he realized his voice had sounded like the growl of a wounded bear.

"This is Garrett," she said. "He owns the Hudson San Francisco."

Jake clenched his teeth when she smiled up at the douche. Irrationally, he was pissed that she had given one of her gorgeous smiles to someone other than him. Jake wanted all her smiles.

He wanted *everything* she had to give.

The douche stuck out his hand, eying Jake with an assessing head-to-toe look. "Garrett Gale."

Jake gave him the briefest handshake in the history of handshakes. Then he shoved his hands in the pockets of his motorcycle jacket to stop himself from ramming his fist into the douche's face.

"Garrett, this is Jake Lilliard," Kyla added. "He's the vice president of finance at Riley O'Brien & Co. and my boss."

Garrett's dark-as-sin eyebrows shot up. "Your boss?" he echoed without looking away from Jake.

"Yes," Kyla confirmed.

Jake knew that his feelings for Kyla were obvious to the other man, but to his surprise, Garrett's gaze momentarily glinted with sympathy. Maybe the guy wasn't such a douche after all.

Jake shifted his attention to Kyla. Despite his anger, his cock twitched when his gaze touched on her short denim skirt, shapely legs, and tan open-toed heels.

She had pulled her long hair into a loose bun, and the shiny gold strands were an exact match for her cropped jacket. Under it, she wore a silky red shirt that matched her lips and her toenails.

A delicate gold necklace with an open circle in the middle glinted against her upper chest, and he wanted to trace it with his tongue. When he finished with that, he wanted to lick a trail down to her nipples and suckle them through her shirt. Then he wanted to slide his hands under her tiny skirt, pull off her panties, and work his cock into her over and over until she screamed his name.

He was sure Garrett the Douche wanted to do the same damn thing.

Determined to get her away from the other man, Jake said, "The presentation starts in ten minutes. We should probably get going."

"I'm ready."

He tilted his head toward the front of the café. "Why don't you go ahead? I need to take care of something first."

She glanced toward Garrett. "Thanks again. I'll see you tomorrow night."

"Count on it," Garrett replied with a smile.

Jake stiffened. There was no way in hell he was going to stand by and let another guy have a go at Kyla. He was only *two fucking days* away from being able to make his move.

With a small wave, Kyla left them. Jake knew her mind had already moved on to the presentation notes she needed to review, so it didn't even register with her that Jake had stayed behind with Garrett.

Both Jake and Garrett watched as Kyla made her way out of the coffee shop, her round hips swaying under her skirt and her calf muscles flexing with every step. Once she was out of sight, Jake brought his attention back to Garrett.

"Stay away from Kyla," he ordered flatly, his tone giving no hint to the jealousy swirling inside him.

Garrett casually pushed his suit coat apart and tucked his hands into his trouser pockets. Rocking back on his heels, he said, "It must suck to be you ... to be interested in Kyla but not be able to do anything about it because of your professional relationship." He shook his head. "I'm not sure I could withstand the temptation. I admire your restraint."

Jake stepped closer to Garrett. He stared into the other man's eyes, not bothering to hide anything from him.

"I'm only going to say this one more time: stay away from her."

Garrett's eyes narrowed. "And what if I don't stay away from her, *boss*?"

"I'm only her boss for two more fucking days," he bit out.

Garrett barked out a laugh. "Oh, it *definitely* sucks to be you." He pointed at Jake. "*You* have to wait two days, but *I* don't." He moved the tip of his thumb to the middle of his chest. "I'm going to have dinner with her tomorrow night. Two days from now, it won't matter that you're not her boss anymore. *You* won't matter."

Jake took a deep breath and counted to ten instead of throwing a punch. He'd been in plenty of fistfights. In fact, he'd started a few himself. But he wasn't going to start one in a five-star hotel. Kyla was worth fighting over, but he wasn't going to do it when she was nearby.

"She's more than just a fuck," Jake said. "She's ... she's ..."

"She's what? Your first-grade teacher's illegitimate daughter? Your dog walker's long-lost cousin? Your proctologist's younger sister?" Garrett held out his hands. "Tell me, *boss*, who is she?" He smirked. "Oh, wait, I know ... she's the love of your life."

Jake stared at the other man, his heart thudding heavily. He'd known for a while that his feelings for Kyla were more than lust, but he hadn't wanted to put a name to them. They hadn't even gone on a date, for fuck's sake. But that hadn't stopped him from falling.

"Yes," he admitted quietly. "Kyla is the love of my life."

Garrett's eyes widened. "Are you serious?"

"Yes."

"You should have led with that, boss." Garrett gave Jake a friendly slap on the back. "Then you could have prevented all this macho posturing."

"Macho posturing?" Jake repeated in disbelief.

Garrett grinned. "What would you call it? Chest thumping? Territorial marking?"

Jake jerked away from the douche and his friendly back-slapping. "You're going to stay away from Kyla? You're going to cancel your date?"

Garrett guffawed. "Hell, no, I'm not going to stay away from her. And I'm not going to cancel my date with her, either."

"*You motherfucker.*"

Garrett lightly punched Jake in the shoulder. "Cheer up. I'll say something nice about you during dinner."

Jake didn't bother to reply. It had just occurred to him that he was still Kyla's boss, and one of the perks of that position was his ability to require her to work late. Spinning on his heel, he walked away.

"Good luck, *boss*," the douche called out.

Jake smiled. Lady Luck was a fickle bitch, but she'd always had a soft spot for him.

CHAPTER FIVE

According to the Hudson San Francisco's website, The Ellington Club was a retro supper club that offered gourmet dining, live music, and dancing. Kyla scrolled down to read more about the restaurant where she had agreed to meet Garrett.

Named after jazz great Duke Ellington, it was located on the top floor of the historic hotel and offered panoramic views of the Bay. Several local magazines had voted it as one of the best date spots in the city.

"Sounds nice," Kyla murmured to herself.

When she realized that she was more excited about the location of her date rather than the date itself, she scowled. She should be ecstatic about the opportunity to enjoy a romantic evening of dinner and dancing with Garrett Gale.

Unfortunately, he didn't do anything for her. She appreciated his good looks, but she wasn't attracted to him. When he had touched her hand, her stomach hadn't gone all warm and liquid, her skin hadn't tingled, and her heart hadn't pounded with excitement. Her body only responded that way to Jake.

She sighed, wishing that she were spending the evening with Jake instead of Garrett. She would love to spend a romantic evening with him, snuggled up in a dark booth with his hand on her thigh or swaying to a sultry song with their bodies touching from neck to knees.

She gave herself a mental kick. She refused to be one of those women who thought about one man while she was out with another one.

Glancing at her tablet, she checked the time. It was a little before five o'clock, but since she had been at work since seven this morning, she decided to go ahead and pack up for the day. She needed at least an hour to get ready for her date, and even though the Hudson San Francisco wasn't too far from her apartment, traffic could be iffy.

After straightening her workstation, she tucked her tablet into her bag and slung it over her shoulder. She headed out of her cubicle, intending to take the fastest route to the elevators.

As she rounded the corner, she ran into Jake. He seemed to materialize out of the air, like a genie from an old oil lamp.

He glanced at her bag before meeting her eyes. He looked a little frazzled, his thick hair sticking up in a couple of places as if he'd run his fingers through it a few times.

"Are you leaving already?" He shot a quick look at the silver watch on his left wrist. "What time is it?" Before she could answer, he said, "It doesn't matter. I'm just glad I caught you before you left."

He shook his head, a mix of exasperation and irritation on his handsome face. "Diana just ambushed me. Somehow, she missed the fact that one of our lines of credit is up for review, and the bank requested updated financial documentation by tomorrow at nine a.m. Eastern. I started to panic because there's no way I could get the whole package done by then, but then I remembered that you helped me with the one for Union Bank a couple of months ago. If you help me, I might be able to get the package done by the deadline."

She hesitated, because even though she didn't really want to go out with Garrett, she didn't want to be rude and cancel on such short notice. But she knew how bad it would look if Jake missed the deadline, and she couldn't let him down.

Jake gave her a beseeching look. "I know you worked all weekend on the store managers' presentation, but I'm desperate." He held up his hands and curled his fingers over to mimic a dog begging for a treat. "Please, Kyla, I'm begging you."

Charmed by his teasing, she laughed. "You don't have to beg. I'm happy to help." She patted his upper arm, letting her hand linger for a moment on the sleek muscles covered by his sweater. "I'll meet you in your office in a few minutes. I need to make a quick phone call."

He grinned. "You're a sweetheart." He immediately turned and began the walk back to the elevators. Looking over his shoulder, he called out, "I owe you."

She waved away his thanks before returning to her cube. She needed to let Garrett know she couldn't meet him, but they hadn't exchanged contact information. She hoped the hotel would know how to reach him.

After tracking down the main number to the Hudson San Francisco, she placed the call and asked the woman who answered the phone to ring Garrett's room. He didn't answer, so she pressed zero and got bounced back to the attendant.

Kyla knew the hotel wouldn't give out Garrett's number, but she didn't want to break their date via voice mail or leave a message with one of his employees. Instead, she told the woman on the phone that she needed to talk to him as soon as possible and asked her to track him down.

Disconnecting the call, she leaned back in her office chair to wait for Garrett's call. She hated to admit it, but she was more excited about working late with Jake than she had been about going on a date with Garrett.

Kyla Genevieve Andrews, you are pathetic.

Moments later, her phone rang. She checked the caller ID, noting that the number had a Seattle area code. Pressing the button to accept the call, she said, "Kyla Andrews."

"Did you call because you wanted my opinion on what to wear on our date?" Garrett asked without bothering to greet her. His deep baritone resonated through her earbud as he continued, "If so, might I suggest something sheer, short, and easy to remove?"

She couldn't help but laugh. "Hi, Garrett."

"Hi," he replied before saying, "What did you need, cupcake?"

His endearment threw her for a second. "Uh…" she stuttered before blurting out, "I can't go to dinner with you tonight. Jake needs my help with a last-minute project."

"A last-minute project, huh?"

"Yes. I'm sorry. I was almost out the door when he caught me. He was desperate for my help."

To her surprise, Garrett chuckled. She frowned, a little offended that he wasn't more disappointed that she had canceled their date.

"I'm sure he was desperate," Garrett replied, his voice tinged with amusement.

"I'm sorry," she repeated, unsure how else to respond.

"That's okay. I understand."

In fact, Garrett was so *understanding* that Kyla wondered if he was even bothered that he wouldn't see her tonight. Suddenly, her pride demanded that she reschedule their date.

"Maybe we can go to dinner another night," she suggested.

"I'd like that."

Just then, her phone vibrated in her hand, and a text popped up from Jake: "Where are you? We need to get busy."

"Garrett, I need to run. Jake's waiting on me."

"I want you to give Jake a message," Garrett requested.

"What kind of message?" she asked warily. "You barely know him."

"We had an interesting conversation yesterday after you introduced us."

Her eyebrows arched in surprise. "You did? About what?"

"Ask Jake," he suggested.

After Garrett dictated his message for Jake, she ended the call and headed to Jake's office. When she got there, she found him reclining in his office chair with his feet propped on the frosted glass surface of his desk.

Instead of his black motorcycle boots, he wore a pair of brown leather lace-up boots. Those scuffed boots had some serious mileage on them.

He was completely absorbed in the papers he held in his hand, and she took a moment to study him. He must not have shaved this morning because dark auburn stubble shadowed his jaw. She wondered what it felt like … prickly and coarse, most likely. But his thick hair looked soft and touchable.

After knocking lightly on the doorjamb, she entered Jake's kingdom. His office was one of the few that was carpeted, and her silver metallic flats barely made a sound as she walked toward him.

"There you are," Jake said, a smile tilting his lips.

"Here I am."

She dumped her bag on one of the chairs in front of his desk and rummaged inside for her tablet. With it in hand, she sat down in the other chair, tucking one leg under her.

His eyes swept over her, seeming to linger on her dangly earrings before returning to her face. "Thank you for staying late." He smiled slowly. "This is the second time that you've rescued me this week."

"Maybe I should start wearing a cape and red boots like Supergirl."

Jake dropped his feet to the floor, muttering under his breath. She couldn't make out a single word.

"What?"

"Nothing," he barked.

She blinked in surprise. She had never heard him use such a harsh tone before—not with her, not with anyone. His mood had gone from good to growl.

Deciding to get down to business, she asked, "Where do you want to start?"

Three hours later, they had finished ninety percent of the loan package. Jake rose from his office chair with a groan.

"I can't sit here any longer," he announced.

Kyla glanced toward the floor-to-ceiling windows in Jake's office. It was past eight o'clock, and the sky had darkened to a deep indigo.

Jake lifted his arms over his head in a big stretch. His navy-blue sweater rose enough for her to see the plaid button-down shirt he wore underneath it. She sighed inwardly, disappointed that she hadn't been able to catch a glimpse of his abs.

"I know we still have work to do," he continued, "but I need a break."

Rounding his desk, he stopped in front of her. He took her tablet and placed it on top of the desk before grabbing one of her hands and pulling her to her feet.

"Let's go up to the roof and take a walk around the garden." He stepped back and eyed her. "Do you have a jacket? It might be chilly."

"No. But I'm sure I'll be fine."

She was wearing a long-sleeved, salmon pink chiffon blouse with a pussy-bow and charcoal wide-legged pants with matching salmon pink polka dots. She'd bought the outfit last month during a shopping trip with Vanessa.

The moment she'd spotted it, she had fallen in love, but her older sister had pretended to stick her finger down her throat. What did Vanessa know? She dressed like the angel of death, assuming the angel of death wore all black.

Jake ushered her out of his office. They navigated the maze of cubicles in silence to reach the elevator. Seconds later, they were on the roof.

Turning in a circle, Kyla took in the view. The city of San Francisco spread out before them, nothing but a sea of twinkling lights. They were up high enough that she could barely hear the traffic below.

"I've never been up here this late," she said. "It's beautiful."

Jake placed his hand on her lower back, his palm heating her through her silk blouse. His touch made her breath fracture, and she focused on pulling some much-needed air into her lungs.

He gently guided her toward one of the stone walking paths before removing his hand. Cool air rushed over the spot he had warmed, and she shivered visibly.

"You're cold," he noted. "We should go back inside."

"Let's stay a few minutes."

They ventured farther along the path, passing a redwood pergola and a stone bench. A strong breeze blew across the roof, bringing the heady aroma of roses with it. Her nipples pebbled from the chill, and she crossed her arms over her chest. She didn't want Jake to see the hard nubs.

Jake grasped her elbow and pulled her to a stop. "If we're going to stay up here, I want you to wear my sweater."

Before she could protest, he whipped the garment over his head and handed it to her. "Put it on," he directed, his tone indicating that he would accept no argument.

She clenched her hands in the sweater, the soft cashmere warm from the heat of his body. As she pulled it over her head, Jake's scent wafted over her, a mouthwatering combination of musk and spice.

She looked up at him, and he grinned. "My sweater gave you a serious case of flyaway hair."

As he placed his hand on her head, static electricity crackled between them. He laughed softly before smoothing her wild hair. It felt so good she had to lock her knees to keep from leaning into him and nuzzling her head against his hand.

"I think I'm making it worse," he said.

She almost moaned in disappointment when he dropped his hand. Resolutely, she resumed their walk, and he fell into step beside her, his hands tucked in the front pockets of his Rileys.

"I've lived in the Bay Area for eight years, and I still can't get used to the summers here," Jake said. "I'm used to sunshine and triple-degree heat."

Kyla abruptly realized that she had no idea where Jake had grown up. She couldn't believe the subject had never arisen. She talked about her childhood in Boston all the time.

She wanted to know more about Jake's life before he'd moved to the Bay Area and started working for Riley O'Brien & Co. The more she learned about him, the more she wanted to know.

"Where did you grow up?" she asked.

"Las Vegas."

She hadn't expected that answer. Her surprise must have been evident on her face because he grinned.

"Everyone has that reaction when I tell them Vegas is my hometown," he said. "I think it's because most people think it's a place to visit instead of a place to live."

"I don't know anything about Las Vegas other than the fact that gambling and prostitution are legal there."

Jake vigorously shook his head. "Prostitution is *not* legal in Las Vegas. It's legal in some parts of Nevada, but not in Clark County, which is where Las Vegas is located."

"Hmm."

"You might like Vegas," Jake murmured. "It's a place for people who love numbers."

"I thought it was a place for people who love to gamble."

"It is. It's also a place for people who love to visit strip clubs, eat at buffets, and attend musicals."

"I don't like to do any of those things."

Kyla didn't want to have anything to do with gambling, legal or illegal. Her father had been a compulsive gambler, and his addiction had nearly bankrupted their family.

He had gambled away the money he and her mother had saved for retirement. And he probably would have gambled away his kids' college funds if they'd had any.

Her father's death certificate listed homicide as Russell Andrews's official cause of death. But gambling was the real reason her father wasn't alive today.

*****

The end justified the means. That was what Jake had told himself while he lurked around Kyla's cubicle, waiting for her to go home to get ready for her date. He had been worried she might slip out before he could stop her.

His conscience twinged at the fact that he had manufactured an urgent project that required her to stay late. But he soothed it by reminding himself that he had no choice. He couldn't let her go on that date with Garrett the Douche. Surely any guy in his position would do the same thing?

He just hoped she never found out that the deadline for the financial documentation was six months away. He grimaced when he realized he was going to have to update the numbers for the real deadline, but then he shrugged.

The end justifies the means.

A gust of wind carried the sweet smell of rosemary to Jake. It mixed with the pungent odor of basil and the bright scent of citrus from the potted lemon and key lime trees in Riley Plaza's rooftop garden.

They strolled past a fountain shaped like huge metal scissors, and Kyla stopped in front of it. Water made a tinkling sound as it bubbled over the blades and trickled into to the basin below. She leaned down and trailed her fingers through the water.

He took a moment to snap a mental photo of her. His girl definitely liked color. Her sexy blouse was the same color as the peonies that bloomed in the sky-high garden.

He wondered what Kyla had planned to wear on her date with Garrett. Most of Jake's first dates had worn little black dresses, but knowing Kyla, she would have opted for something brighter.

She flicked her fingers toward him, and droplets of water flew, catching the light like liquid diamonds. She laughed, and just like always, his heart got a jolt when a smile curved her plump lips. He wondered if heart attack victims felt the same way when they received four hundred joules from a defibrillator.

She tilted her head, and the end of her ponytail swept over her shoulder. A couple of wispy tendrils framed her face, tangling with the delicate silver earrings hanging from her lobes. He had a momentary fantasy of sucking her earlobe into his mouth, jewelry and all.

"I think I've found a place I want to volunteer," she said.

Forcing himself to focus on her words, he said, "Oh, yeah? Where?"

"The Bay Area Women's Center. I read an article about it a couple of days ago. It sounds like it could use my help."

Jake frowned. "I'm not familiar with it. What does it do?"

"The Center's primary mission is to provide shelter for women and children who are victims of sexual assault and domestic violence, but it also provides counseling and offers life skills classes."

Domestic abuse was one of those topics that made Jake want to hit someone. And yes, he recognized the heartbreaking irony of his feelings. He just couldn't imagine hurting someone he loved, physically or emotionally. For Jake, loving someone meant cherishing them.

"I could teach a class at the Center," Kyla continued.

"What kind of class?"

"Money management." She bent down and shoved her nose in the creamy white center of a gardenia. "Oh, that smells *divine*."

She rubbed the petals between her thumb and forefinger and then brought her fingers to the spot behind her ear. At that moment, Jake would have given one of his own fingers to nuzzle his nose into that spot. Not his thumb ... maybe his pinkie.

"According to the article," Kyla continued, "a lot of the women who end up at the Bay Area Women's Center are trapped in their current situation because of money. Their partners use money to control them. They give them an allowance and make them account for every penny. When these women try to save money to escape, their partners find it and beat them for hiding cash."

"*Assholes*. If you can help these women get away from their abusive boyfriends and husbands, you should."

"It's not just men," Kyla countered. "Women abuse their partners, too. The percentage of lesbians who have been abused by their partner is actually higher than the percentage of heterosexual women."

Surprised by that bit of information, he asked, "Are you sure about that?"

"I'm quoting the article, which referenced a CDC study."

His stomach growled, and he realized that they hadn't eaten dinner. When he'd concocted this *distraction*, he hadn't planned to starve Kyla of food, only Garrett's douchebag company.

He wouldn't have been surprised to find out that Garrett had talked Kyla into a late date. Jake needed to keep Kyla at work late enough that she went home and went to bed.

Alone.

"When we get back to my office, we can order some takeout from that Thai place you like," he suggested.

"I actually had dinner plans tonight," she said.

He feigned surprise, hoping he was a good enough actor to fool her. "You did?"

She nodded. "I had a date with Garrett Gale at The Ellington Club."

Now that he knew the douche had planned to take Kyla to the most romantic restaurant in the city, Jake didn't feel one ounce of guilt about lying to her. If anyone was going to take her to The Ellington Club, it was going to be him.

"Garrett asked me to give you a message," Kyla continued.

Jake tensed. What the fuck had Garrett said to her? He was almost afraid to ask, but when she didn't elaborate, he prodded her, "What's the message?"

"Well played."

"What?"

"That's his message: well played."

Jake absorbed her answer. "And that's all he said?"

She nodded. "That's it. He said you'd know exactly what he meant."

Jake laughed, long and loud. If not for the fact that Garrett was a rival for Kyla, he might even like the douche.

"Were you disappointed that you had to cancel your date to help me?" he asked, even though he wasn't sure he wanted to hear the answer.

Kyla's cheeks turned the same shade as her shirt. She licked her lips, and he tracked the movement with his eyes. For months, he had dreamed about that pink tongue licking the tip of his cock before those sweet lips sucked him deep.

"I wanted to help you," she finally replied.

"But were you disappointed about not seeing Garrett?" he persisted.

She looked away from his penetrating gaze, her eyes darting around the garden. He waited patiently, and finally she answered with a softly spoken no.

Satisfaction flooded Jake, along with a healthy dose of relief. If she had been disappointed, he would have been tempted to let her go.

His conscience chimed in: *Who are you kidding? It wouldn't have made a goddamn difference. You want a chance with her ... a chance to show her that you're the one.*

He sighed, silently acknowledging that his conscience was right.

"Did you have plans tonight?"

Kyla's question interrupted Jake's discussion with his conscience.

"No. Charlie's on call."

Her lips twitched. "I meant plans with a woman."

He eyed her, wondering if her question was casual or if she was really interested in his answer. He hadn't gone on a date in several months. Not since he had realized Kyla was the only one he wanted.

"I'm not dating anyone."

"Oh," she murmured. "That's surprising."

"Why?"

"Because you're ... I just thought ..."

"What?"

She bit her lip, the blush on her cheeks deepening. He smiled, ridiculously pleased with her discomfiture. He liked making her a little off balance. It seemed only fair since she had upended his happy-to-be-a-bachelor existence.

"Nothing."

Snapping off a sprig of peppermint, she rubbed it between her fingers. The frosty scent of the herb perfumed the air and stung the delicate tissue of his nostrils.

"My dad loved anything and everything peppermint," she said. "He was a smoker for a long time, and peppermint candy helped him kick the habit."

Jake knew Kyla's dad was no longer living, but he didn't know any details. Maybe her dad had died of lung cancer.

She had never alluded to what had happened to him. Jake was curious, but he was hesitant to pursue the subject because he didn't know if she still grieved over her father.

Some people never stopped grieving, and if Kyla started to cry, he wouldn't be able to stop himself from holding her. And once he had her in his arms, he was afraid he'd violate every professional and personal boundary that existed.

"Were you close to your dad?" he asked.

"If you had known Russell Andrews, you wouldn't have asked that question. I'm sure he loved us, but he didn't love us *enough*."

Jake wondered what she meant by that statement. He wanted to know what she considered *enough*.

"I think that's why his death hurt so much," she continued. "We grieved the loss of possibility—the possibility of being close to him—more than we grieved him."

"I can understand that."

"You know what's interesting? Even though none of us was close to my dad, we all fell apart after he died. My mom stopped cooking. I dropped out of college and moved home. Vanessa missed so many deadlines at work that she was fired from a job she loved. And Ben's grades slipped so much he lost his scholarship."

Kyla tossed the peppermint into a clump of bright red geraniums. "We were really struggling, emotionally and financially. When my dad died, my mom was clueless about their finances. She didn't know how much money he made or how much they had. She didn't know what their monthly expenses were or how to create a budget and stick to it."

"Is that why you majored in finance?"

She tilted her head, obviously considering his question. "Before I dropped out of college, I was majoring in psychology. I wanted to specialize in adolescent counseling. I changed my major to finance when I went back. I've always loved math, but yeah, maybe what happened after my dad died is the reason I chose finance." A pleased smile lifted her lips. "And speaking of finance … I've decided to take the position that reports to Sam."

"That's great!"

In his enthusiasm, he opened his arms to hug her, and she stepped into them. She wrapped her arms around his waist and tucked her head under his chin. He squeezed her tightly, loving the way she felt against him.

"I'm so glad you're staying in the finance department." Her hair muffled his words. "You are a huge, huge asset to our group."

He wasn't blowing smoke up her skirt just because he wanted to get under her skirt. She honestly was a rock star with numbers.

He reluctantly loosened his arms, letting them fall to his sides. She stayed where she was, but tilted her head back to look at him. The lights from nearby skyscrapers turned her silvery gaze to molten gray.

"We can celebrate your new job tomorrow night at your graduation party," he said. "The whole department will be there."

She clapped her hands. "I'm so excited."

He couldn't help but laugh. There was no way Kyla was as excited as he was. In less than twenty hours, he would no longer be her boss.

CHAPTER SIX

Yellow sugar sprinkles shimmered along the rim of the cocktail glass, and bright red cherries floated in the chilled liquid. The pineapple martini was almost too pretty to drink, but Kyla took a sip anyway.

As she enjoyed the tasty mix of vodka, rum, and fruit juice, she glanced around the private dining area at The Deep End. Located on the second floor of the restaurant, the space was large enough to accommodate at least eighty people. With its moveable frosted glass panels, the area could be used as one big space or divided into several smaller spaces.

The Deep End was Andre Shiroc's newest restaurant. Kyla had heard her mom talk about the celebrity chef in reverent tones. That was how she knew it was impossible to get a table at The Deep End. But nothing was impossible for Cal O'Brien, it seemed. Jake had told her that Cal and Andre Shiroc were good friends, and Cal had pulled some strings to secure a private room for the party.

Tonight, Kyla and her fellow Riley O'Brien & Co. employees were the only ones in the private dining area. Most of the finance department was here, about fifty people, and everyone was mingling and enjoying cocktails before dinner.

Kyla took another sip of her martini, swiping her tongue along the rim to gather some sugar. Like the drink, the granules tasted like pineapple.

"Kyla, you're my favorite trainee," Sam Ferron said, throwing his arm around her shoulders and squeezing her close to his side.

"Thanks, Sam. You're my favorite accounting director."

Over the past several months, she and Sam had formed a close friendship. Although he was only a few years older than she was, he had five daughters.

Sam had married his high school sweetheart, Tracie, the day after they had graduated. He'd told Kyla that both of their families had been opposed to the marriage. Nonetheless, he claimed it was the best decision he'd ever made.

"I prayed every night that you would take the open position that reported to me," Sam added.

She eyed him skeptically. "You prayed every night?"

Placing his palm on his chest, Sam said, "I swear. Ask Tracie if you don't believe me."

"I'm glad you're happy, Sam, because I can't imagine a better job or a better boss for me."

Tonight kicked off the long Memorial Day weekend, and all recent management trainee graduates had the rest of the week off. Kyla would start her new job the following Monday.

One of the servers returned with another tray of drinks and announced that dinner was on its way. Deciding that now was the perfect time to make a trip to the ladies' room, Kyla drained her martini and excused herself.

Following the signs, she headed toward the other side of the warehouse. After passing a wood-and-steel staircase that separated the dining area from the restrooms, she spotted a single elevator tucked into the corner. Next to it was a frosted glass door etched with the word "Relief."

Someone had a quirky sense of humor. Kyla laughed to herself as she pulled open the door.

Metal wall sconces illuminated the corridor, throwing pools of golden light on the dark wood plank floors. A door opened a few feet ahead of her, and Jake emerged from it. He froze when he saw her, his eyes widening before he ambled toward her.

The narrow corridor made her even more aware of his height and muscular physique, and her body reacted the way it always did when he got close. Her heart began to pound, and her breathing grew shallow. Suddenly, her throat was dry, and she swallowed thickly.

Stopping right in front of her, he looked down into her face. His eyes caught the light from the sconces, glinting with a swirl of green and gold. They dropped to her mouth before jumping back to hers.

"You've got sugar on your lips," he notified her, his voice low and gravelly.

She licked her upper lip. "Did I get it?"

He moved closer, the front of his long-sleeved dress shirt brushing against her chest. She sucked in a shaky breath, trying not to let him see how much his nearness affected her. But she didn't think she was successful in hiding her desire.

"Not there." He touched his thumb to her lower lip, toward the corner. "Here."

Dropping his head, he licked the spot where his thumb had been. She gasped, certain that she was having yet another X-rated dream starring Jake. When his tongue flicked along the outer edge of her upper lip, she realized it wasn't a dream.

"And you've got some here," he murmured, tracing her lower lip with his tongue.

She gripped his upper arms, his biceps rock hard under her fingers. "What are you doing?" she breathed against his mouth.

He drew back to stare into her eyes. "I'm not your boss anymore, Kyla. I'm just a guy who works for the same company you do, and lucky for me, that company doesn't have any rules against co-workers dating, even if they're in the same department."

She barely heard a word he said because her ears were roaring with her pulse. "What?"

He smiled slowly, and she couldn't tear her eyes from his mouth. She clutched his arms tighter, wanting those lips on every part of her body.

"I'm not your boss anymore," he repeated. "I have been counting the days until … until I could …"

"Until you could what?" she whispered.

"Until I could be with you," he answered hoarsely. "That's all I want … a chance to be with you."

Be with you.

She let go of his arms, fisted his shirt in her hands, and pulled him forward at the same time lunging up on her tiptoes. She pressed her mouth against his, and his hands fell to her hips, his fingers digging into the upper curves of her rear.

His stubble was scratchy, but his lips were soft and warm. Tilting his head, he aligned their mouths and took control of their kiss. He nipped her lower lip, demanding entrance, and she opened for him. His tongue swept inside, and she couldn't hold back a moan when she tasted him.

Nothing—no one—had ever tasted so good. Jake tasted better than her mom's devil's food cake with cherry-vanilla icing, better than a hot fudge sundae with marshmallow topping, better than…

She twirled her tongue around his, and their kiss grew hotter … wetter. She locked her hands around his neck to hold him tighter, and he delved deeper into the interior of her mouth, forcing her to open even more.

Greedily, she sucked on his tongue, and he pulled her closer, nudging his erection into her stomach. Arousal flooded her panties, and every thought flew from her head except one: how soon could she get him inside her?

Desperate to soothe the ache between her thighs, she raised her leg and hooked it around his. He moaned deep in his throat before palming her butt and lifting her until his erection nestled against her crotch.

"Oh!"

The exclamation came from behind them, and Jake jerked away from her, breathing hard. Glancing over her shoulder, Kyla glimpsed Sam's startled face.

"I'm really sorry," Sam said, his face redder than cinnamon candy. "I didn't expect … I was just …"

After an awkward pause, Jake cleared his throat. "Sam, can you give us a second?"

Sam hesitated before saying, "They served dinner a few minutes ago. Everyone was asking where Kyla was, so I volunteered to find her."

A laugh rumbled in Jake's chest. "You found her. Go tell everyone she'll be there shortly."

Sam nodded before clumsily backing out the door. It banged shut behind him, and Kyla brought her attention back to Jake. He slowly dropped his hands from her hips, almost as if he couldn't stand not to touch her.

Kyla took a steadying breath. Her former boss had just kissed her, and her current boss had witnessed it.

"Sam won't tell anyone," she said.

"I don't give a fuck if he tells the whole world," Jake shot back, his tone low and intense.

She had never heard him say the F-word before, and her mouth fell open in surprise. His eyebrows arched as if daring her to comment on his bad language, and she snapped her mouth shut.

"Kyla, I'm done hiding my feelings for you."

He gazed at her intently, obviously waiting for her to respond. But she just stood there, her throat too tight to speak. She couldn't believe this was happening.

Jake had feelings for her.

Feelings!

She wanted him so much, and miraculously, it seemed that he felt the same way. She had never guessed. He had done a great job hiding how he really felt.

After a moment, he sighed and tilted his head toward the door. "Let's go have some dinner."

Placing a big hand on her waist, he turned her and ushered her forward. Suddenly she remembered why she had been in the corridor in the first place: she needed to go to the bathroom. She stopped, and he glanced down at her, his eyebrows arched in silent query.

"I need a second. You go ahead."

He studied her for a moment, his eyes lit with concern. "Are you okay?" He stroked her cheek with the back of his fingers. "Are *we* okay?"

She was too overwhelmed to do anything but nod. He sighed again, his breath stirring her hair. "I didn't plan to kiss you in a dark hallway, but…"

She finally found her voice. "But what?"

"But I'm glad I did." His firm lips quirked in a satisfied smile. "Especially since you kissed me back."

*****

As Kyla's celebration wound down, Jake stationed himself beside the staircase so he could check in with everyone who had come. Since Diana had already left the party, he was the next-highest-ranking person in the group. As such, he felt responsible for the employees who were here, even if they didn't report directly to him.

One by one, his colleagues trickled out of the dining area, and he thanked them for attending. At the same time, he assessed whether they were sober enough to drive home. He didn't want anyone in his group to hurt themselves or others by driving drunk, and he offered to pick up the tab if they needed a ride.

He, meanwhile, hadn't had more than a few sips of beer. And he'd barely eaten anything, either. His appetite for food and drink had been overtaken by a far more powerful hunger for Kyla. Now that he'd had a taste of her, he wanted her even more. He'd wanted her forever, and he sensed that he was *this close* to getting exactly what he wanted.

Finally, Kyla and Sam were the only people remaining upstairs. They'd sat next to each other during dinner, and more than once, Jake had noticed them whispering to each other, their heads close together.

When Sam hadn't been busy whispering to Kyla, he'd been studying Jake with an unreadable expression. Sam was happily married, so Jake doubted the other man was jealous. If anything, he was probably concerned that Jake was playing games with Kyla.

Leaning against the banister, Jake waited for them to make

JENNA SUTTON

their way to the stairs. Not for the first time this evening, he let his gaze wander up and down Kyla's body.

Although she usually wore Rileys, tonight she had dressed in a pair of black trousers that showed off her slender waist and round hips. He especially liked her silky shirt, which was the color of dark cherries. With its row of tiny ruffles running down the front, it accentuated her full breasts.

Since he had a predilection for that particular part of a woman's body, he had spent a fair amount of time furtively eyeing Kyla's. From what he could tell, they were bigger than average, and he was desperate to touch and taste them.

When Kyla and Sam reached his side, Jake held out his right hand to the older man. "Thanks for coming tonight, Sam," he said as they shook hands. "I hope you enjoyed yourself."

Sam arched an eyebrow. "I doubt that I enjoyed myself as much as you and Kyla."

Kyla made a funny sound, something between a gasp and a giggle. She glanced at Jake, her face bright pink, and he smiled down at her.

"You may be right, Sam," he agreed without taking his eyes off the gorgeous blonde in front of him. "I know I've never *enjoyed* myself quite so much."

Sam snorted. "That was fairly obvious."

Kyla's cheeks got even pinker, and when she dropped her gaze to her feet, Jake brought his attention back to Sam. "Did you drive here or did you take a taxi?"

"I took a taxi from work with Kyla, and we were just talking about how to get home."

"I thought we were going to share a taxi," Kyla interjected.

Jake caught her gaze. "I'll give you a ride."

Before she could reply, Sam dropped a kiss on her cheek. "I'll see you later." Gripping the railing, he started down the stairs but only took a couple of steps before he stopped and looked over his shoulder. "Enjoy that ride, Jake," he said with an exaggerated wink.

Jake waved good-bye to Sam before turning back to Kyla. She was gripping her big purse in front of her like a shield, and he held out his hand to her. "Let's get out of here."

She stared down at his palm, motionless, and pressure built inside his chest—something far worse than panic. But then she placed her slender hand in his, and the pressure dissolved like a spoonful of sugar in hot tea.

Moments later, they reached his motorcycle, which he'd parked near the restaurant's side entrance. Kyla looked down at his primary mode of transportation and then looked up at him, her face etched with a mix of shock and trepidation.

"You ride a motorcycle?" She slowly shook her head. "How did I *not* know that about you?"

Raising the Triumph's seat, he pulled out two black helmets. He held one out to her, but she didn't take it. He hung his helmet on the handlebars and placed hers on top of her shiny hair. After fastening the strap, he tugged on it to make sure it was tight enough.

She nervously grasped his hand and tilted her head back until she could meet his eyes. "Jake, I'm risk-averse, and riding a motorcycle ranks pretty high on my risk continuum."

The earnest expression on her face was just so damn cute he couldn't help but drop his head and touch his mouth to hers in a brief kiss. Wrapping his hand around the back of her neck, he said, "You're safe with me. I promise."

He wasn't irresponsible, impulsive, or reckless. And he would be extra careful with Kyla because, although she didn't know it, his future happiness completely depended on her.

Taking her bag, he stowed it under the seat before shrugging off his jacket and draping it over her shoulders. A weird thrill shot through him when he saw her small frame enveloped in it.

Maybe it was something left over from high school when a jock gave his girl his letterman's jacket. Did teenagers even do that anymore? She made him feel like a teenager—anxious, eager to please, and most of all … horny.

As Kyla eased her arms into his jacket and zipped up the front, he climbed onto the bike. Once she finished, he held out his hand to her, and this time she took it without hesitation, swinging her leg over the seat and wrapping her arms around his waist.

The supple muscles of her thighs cradled his legs, making his cock throb. The throbbing intensified when she shifted forward and her firm breasts pressed against his back.

Glancing over his shoulder, he asked where she lived. Once she had provided her address and he had confirmed the best route to her apartment, he placed his hands over hers.

"Don't let go," he directed, emphasizing his command with a gentle squeeze.

"I won't."

After donning his night glasses, he started his motorcycle and kicked it in gear. "Here we go."

Her arms tightened, and he eased away from the curb. He picked up speed but stayed well below the speed limit. He didn't want to scare her or give her any reason to regret trusting him.

As the city streamed by them in a blur of colorful lights, cool air rushed against his face. This was the first time he'd ever ridden his bike with a woman, and he was glad it was with Kyla.

It didn't take long for them to reach her place, a mid-century modern structure perched on the side of the hill. With its flat roof, rectangular glass panels, and straight lines, it looked out of place among the Victorian homes that filled the rest of the neighborhood.

He parked along the curb, switched off the engine, and kicked down the stand. She slowly removed her arms, and he swiveled his head to look behind him.

"We're here. Safe and sound, as promised."

With a bright smile, she alighted from the bike. "That's the first time I've ever been on a motorcycle," she said as she unbuckled her helmet.

He chuckled. "I kind of figured that, sweetness."

He swung off the bike, removed his helmet, and opened the seat to grab her purse. He handed it to her before stowing both helmets.

He turned to face her, and though she stood motionless in front of him, he could sense her tension. His own muscles were tight with a mix of arousal and nerves.

Before he had kissed her in that dark hallway, he had planned to casually ask her out to dinner. He hadn't wanted to come on too strong and scare her off. But he had blown that plan out of the water when he had backed her against the wall and devoured her mouth like a tasty cream puff.

Now he didn't know what to say or do. He knew what he *wanted* to do....

Tilting his head toward the duplex, he said, "Let me walk you to your door."

She spun around and hurried up the stairs to her front door. He followed behind her at a slower pace, his mind working feverishly.

He reached her side, and she looked up at him, her eyes flashing like lightning in the glow of the porch light. Stalling, he reached for the zipper pull on his jacket and tugged it down until the leather panels fell apart. He gently removed the jacket and let it hang from his hand.

His mouth was so dry he felt as if he'd drunk an entire bottle of whiskey the night before, and he swallowed noisily. "Kyla…"

"Jake…"

They had spoken at the same time. Both stopped abruptly, their gazes locked together. She giggled, but the sound was unlike her typical husky laughter. Instead, it was high-pitched and edged with nerves.

"Would you…"

"Would you…"

Again, they had spoken at the same time, and now Jake was the one who laughed nervously. If Charlie could see him now, he'd fall to the floor in hysterics.

Stepping forward, Kyla rested her hands on his chest. They heated him through his cotton shirt, and involuntarily, his pectoral muscles jumped, eager to feel her touch.

"Jake, did you mean what you said earlier?"

"I always mean what I say," he quipped before asking, "When?"

"When you said, you weren't going to hide your feelings for me anymore."

He nodded emphatically. "*Hell, yes*, I meant that."

Her eyes grew brighter. "You have feelings for me?"

He hesitated, unsure of how to answer her question. He didn't think it was a good idea to blurt out that he was in love with her when they hadn't even gone on a date.

"Yes, I have feelings for you," he confirmed, hoping she wouldn't ask him to expand on what he meant by *feelings*.

Clasping his free hand with hers, she wove her fingers between his and tugged lightly. "Come inside."

CHAPTER SEVEN

The apartment was dark, and Kyla flipped on the foyer light as she entered. Jake followed behind her, closing the door and locking it with a loud *snick*. She barely heard it over the pounding of her heart, and she silently willed herself to calm down.

She led the way into the small living room, which Vanessa had furnished with a black leather sofa, matching chair, and glass occasional tables. A cream-colored rug patterned with big black blocks covered the hardwood floors.

After dropping her bag beside the sofa, she switched on the sculpted metal lamps, illuminating the stark white walls. She turned to face Jake, who stood just inside the room, his hands in the front pockets of his dark-washed Rileys. His gaze swept the room before landing on her.

"This room is—"

"Cold," she interjected. "Lifeless. *Boring.*"

"Nothing like where I imagined you would live," he finished.

She smiled. "So, you don't think I'm cold, lifeless, or boring?"

His lips twitched. "No, those aren't the adjectives I'd use to describe you."

She really wanted to know which adjectives he'd use. At the

same time, she was afraid to ask. Instead, she said, "I moved in with my sister when I got the job at Riley O'Brien & Co. I had nothing to do with the décor."

"You and your sister must not be anything alike."

"This apartment isn't her, either. It's just the person she's trying to be."

His eyes narrowed. "Is she going to be home soon?"

Vanessa had sent a text earlier today letting Kyla know that she planned to go directly to Alan's house after work. He rarely came here.

"No, she's spending the weekend with her boyfriend."

He didn't reply, and after an awkward moment, she remembered her manners enough to ask, "Would you like a drink? Beer? Wine?"

He shook his head before walking toward her. When he stood in front of her, he caught a loose strand of her hair and rubbed it between his thumb and forefinger. "You have no idea how many times I've imagined being here … alone with you…" He stared down at her, his gaze trailing over her face. "I have wanted you every minute of every day since we first met."

"You have?" she asked, her voice shaded with disbelief.

He nodded solemnly. "Every minute of every day."

She had suffered for months, believing that he wasn't interested. She had almost killed herself trying to remain professional, and now she didn't have to. She could just…

She threw herself at him. Literally threw herself at him.

As her body slammed into his, she wrapped her arms around his neck. He staggered backward with a loud grunt, his arms locked around her waist. His knees caught the edge of the sofa, and he fell onto the leather cushions, taking her with him.

Before she could blink, he rolled her under him and covered

her mouth with his. Sensation bombarded her—the heavy weight of his body, the hard press of his erection, the soft brush of his lips.

This kiss wasn't as wild as their first one. He seemed more in control, lightly sucking on her lower lip before dusting little kisses over her face.

"You are so sweet," he murmured against her cheek. "Everything about you is so damn sweet."

He placed open-mouthed kisses down the side of her throat, and she arched her neck to give him better access. As she caressed the hard muscles of his shoulders and back, he licked tiny circles on the fragile skin, slowly working his way to the spot where her pulse thrummed.

He swirled his tongue over it before sucking it into his mouth. She felt the deep pull at her core, a fast, relentless rhythm, and she widened her legs so he could settle deeper between her thighs.

Abandoning her exploration of his upper body, she slipped her hands between them and began to unbutton her shirt. Once it was open, she unsnapped the front clasp of her bra and pulled the lace cups away from her breasts. Her nipples were already puckered, the sensitive tips flushed with arousal.

Jake levered up on his forearms, and she held her breath as his gaze roamed over her chest. When his eyes met hers, hot with hunger, all her breath whooshed out. He *definitely* liked what he saw.

"So sweet," he whispered.

Dropping his head, he circled her nipple with his tongue but didn't pull the taut peak into his mouth. After several torturous swirls, he switched his attention to her other nipple and treated it to the same attention. The ache between her legs grew sharper, almost painful, and she whimpered.

"Jake…"

He made a low noise, an unspoken question. Threading her fingers through his thick hair, she pushed her chest toward his mouth and moaned, "Please. Please."

In reply, he wrapped his lips around her nipple and sucked deeply. The hard pull sent waves of pleasure through her. As her vaginal muscles rippled, she gasped, stunned by how close she was to climaxing when he'd barely touched her.

He used his teeth on her, lightly scraping her nipple before biting gently. She couldn't hold back a moan as a tingle shot down her spine, pleasure and pain merging into a liquid rush between her thighs. Clenching her fingers in his hair, she tugged until he grunted and raised his head to meet her gaze. His eyes were heavy-lidded and hazy with lust.

"Touch me," she demanded, raising her hips in a not-so-subtle message. "Please, Jake, I need you to touch me."

She could see the exact moment when he understood exactly what she was asking for—his pupils dilated until they nearly obliterated the green-gold irises, and a swath of red settled high on his cheekbones.

Bracing himself on his arms, he knelt and raised her leg before tugging off her black high heel. He did the same with her other shoe, wobbling on the sofa cushions, and she giggled at the awkwardness of their position.

Jake obviously didn't share her mirth. His expression was austere in the glow of the lamps. Watching his face, she unfastened her pants and bared her lower stomach. His jaw clenched, and his eyes narrowed as she slowly pulled down her zipper until her panties were visible. He swallowed noticeably, his Adam's apple bobbing in his throat.

To her surprise, he backed away from her, sliding to the floor and sitting back on his heels. Grasping her legs, he repositioned her until she reclined against the cushions with her butt almost hanging off the sofa and her thighs bracketing his upper body.

When he hooked his long fingers into her waistband, she raised her hips to help him. He jerked her pants and underwear down over her legs and flung them across the floor, his gaze focused on the place between her thighs. She was too aroused to be embarrassed by his scrutiny.

Leaning forward until his face hovered above the hair covering her mound, he breathed deeply. "You even smell sweet." Gripping her knees, he pushed her thighs apart. "I have to taste you, Kyla. I can't wait any longer. I have to know how sweet your pussy is."

Before she could voice her hearty agreement, Jake ran his hands up her thighs until his fingers grazed the folds of her sex. He spread her open, and without any delay, he bent his head and gave a slow, luscious lick, starting at the place where arousal trickled from her body and ending at her clitoris.

He growled in his throat, the low sound rumbling across her delicate tissue. "Delicious," he breathed. "The sweetest thing I've ever tasted." Black spots danced in front of her eyes as he sucked on her sensitive nub. "I could eat your pussy for hours … licking your juice and sucking on your clit."

He ran his tongue over her clitoris, tiny little strokes that made her legs tremble, before trailing lower. He circled the entrance of her body, lapping hungrily at the plentiful wetness before driving his tongue into her opening. With each forceful dart, he made a deep sound in his throat, the kind of noise people made when they enjoyed a particularly tasty dessert.

He replaced his clever tongue with his fingers and returned it to her clit. Back and forth, he stroked it across the knot of nerves until she panted and clenched her fingers in his hair.

She had never felt anything like the pleasure Jake was giving her. Every muscle, every nerve, every cell of her body zinged, electrified by the feel of his mouth.

"Yes, yes, yes," she chanted, unable to form any other words.

Her control began to unravel as her orgasm built. Looking down, she saw his tousled head working between her legs, a sight so erotic ... so exciting ... that she couldn't help but rock frantically against his mouth.

He slid one hand under her butt and held her against his mouth while he continued to devour her. With one more deep plunge of his fingers inside her and one more hard pull of his mouth on her clit, she rocketed to a place she had never been before. She called his name over and over as pleasure raced through her, her vaginal muscles pulsing and clenching so powerfully she felt the tremors in her womb.

He didn't stop until she whimpered and begged and writhed against his mouth. Finally, he drew back and dropped a soft kiss to the inside of her thigh. As she unclenched her fingers from his hair, he raised his head and met her eyes.

After clearing his throat, he said, "Thank you."

"Thank *you*," she replied huskily before blurting out, "I don't think I've ever come that hard."

As she cringed in embarrassment, he stroked her thigh. "Don't be embarrassed, sweetness. It makes me feel pretty damn great to know it was good for you." The corner of his mouth edged up. "I've fantasized about going down on you ... how you'd smell, how you'd taste, the sounds you'd make when you came. That was better than anything I ever imagined."

She returned his smile. She had some fantasies of her own, and she had every intention of making them reality.

*****

The scent of Kyla's arousal perfumed the air, musky and sweet and delicious. Jake took another deep breath, and his cock twitched eagerly, demanding attention. Somehow, he managed to ignore the greedy fiend inside his jeans and instead searched the rug for Kyla's panties. His control was shredded, and if he didn't get her covered up…

Spotting the scrap of lavender lace out of the corner of his eye, he stretched and nabbed it with the tip of his forefinger. He turned back toward Kyla just as she slid from the sofa to the rug. She knelt in front of him and shrugged her silky shirt and bra from her shoulders.

He couldn't help but ogle her naked body: her creamy, smooth skin; her plump breasts tipped with large, berry-colored nipples; and the fluff of golden hair covering her pussy.

Before he could tell her how gorgeous she was, she reached out and began to unbuckle his belt, her hands steady and agile. Her gaze was focused on the task, her eyelashes curling against her cheeks and her lush lower lip caught between her teeth.

He stared down at her sweet face until the clink of his belt caught his attention. As she unbuttoned his jeans, he caught her hands in his and brought them to his chest.

"No," he murmured.

She looked up, her eyes wide. "No?"

He shook his head even as his erection throbbed. He wasn't sure he'd ever been this hard before, and he wouldn't be surprised if the buttons on his fly left a permanent imprint on his dick.

"Why not?" Kyla asked. "I'm completely naked, but you're completely clothed."

"Sweetness, I haven't even taken you on a date yet."

She blinked owlishly. "What?"

"I didn't plan to strip you naked before we'd even gone on a date."

She laughed softly. "Maybe you should tell me your plan."

He caressed her fingers. "I want to take you to dinner, somewhere nice. I want you to dress up, I'll come to your door like a gentleman, and then we'll enjoy a bottle of wine with dinner and maybe some dancing afterward. Then I'll take you home, give you a good-night kiss, and call you the next day."

Her lower lip pushed out in a tiny pout. "I don't like your plan." She shifted closer until her nipples brushed the backs of his hands. He exhaled loudly as a bead of sweat rolled down his back. "My plan is better."

"What's your plan?" he asked.

"It starts with you taking off your pants."

"No," he replied, his voice resolute. "We are not going to go any further until we've gone on a date."

Without any warning, she used her forearms to shove him backward. He lost his balance and ended up sprawled on his back on the rug. She crawled between his legs and palmed his erection through his jeans. She squeezed lightly, and all the blood drained from his head.

"We can go on a date later." She deftly unbuttoned his fly. "Right now, I'm implementing my plan."

"Kyla … oh, *fuck*," he moaned as she slid her hand inside his boxer briefs.

Fisting his cock, she squeezed with just the right amount of pressure to make his vision blur. She gently freed his erection from his underwear.

"You need to make a decision, Jake. Do you want our first time to be on the living room floor or in my bed?" She rubbed her thumb over the tip of his cock, gathering the creamy fluid that had leaked out. "I'll be happy either way, just as long as you're inside me."

Looking him straight in the eyes, she brought her thumb to her mouth and licked it clean with little darts of her tongue. A shock of energy shot down his spine into his balls, and he almost came right then. He hissed as his cock pulsed, and she gave a little smile, a satisfied curve of her plump lips.

"Do you have a condom?" she asked.

He nodded. "In my wallet."

"Get it," she ordered.

Raising his hips, he fished his wallet from his back pocket and pulled out a condom packet. She snatched it from his hand and held it up in front of him.

"So …" she said, waving the little square around, "bed or floor?"

Her eyes sparkled with a mix of mischief and happiness, and pure joy filled him. He had waited his entire life for her, and she more than made up for every boring day and lonely night he'd endured.

"You have three seconds to decide before I tear this open and climb on top of you," she warned.

He knew a bluff when he saw one. She wouldn't go through with her threat.

"Can I at least take off my boots?" he teased.

Shaking her head, she methodically tore open the condom wrapper. "One…" she said, starting her countdown.

"This rug is kind of scratchy. You're going to get rug burn on your knees."

She smiled crookedly. "That's okay. You're going to get rug burn on your butt." She waggled her eyebrows. "Two …"

Deciding to call her bluff, he wrestled his underwear and

jeans past his hips, more aroused and amused than he had ever been in his entire life. To his surprise, she pulled the condom from its wrapper.

"Two-and-a-half…"

He placed his hands behind his head in a relaxed pose. He waited, sure she would stop now.

"Three," she said before leaning over him and rolling the condom over his erection.

Shocked, he grabbed her wrist. "I thought you were bluffing."

She shook off his hold. Before he could sit up, she swung her leg over him until she perched on his thighs. He steadied her by gripping her hips, and she rose on her knees, the lean muscles of her thighs flexing. He watched mutely as she positioned herself over his erection, her breasts thrust forward.

"I don't gamble," she said breathlessly, slowly lowering herself until the head of his cock was wedged inside her. "And I never bluff."

He barely heard her. A loud roar filled his ears from the blood racing through his body. She rocked a bit, but her tight little pussy resisted the intrusion of his erection.

"You're going to have to help me," she gasped. "I haven't done this in a while."

Releasing her hips, he eased his hand between her slippery folds. He gathered some of her juice on his fingers and massaged her clit with gentle circles. She moaned and arched her back just enough for him to slide a little deeper.

She sucked in a deep breath. "Oh, God, Jake. You're big. Much bigger than—"

He shushed her with a finger over her lips. He didn't want to hear or think about her being with another man.

Not now. Not ever.

"Relax against me," he rasped, bringing his knees up to support her, "and widen your legs."

She followed his directions, and he pumped his hips in shallow thrusts. "Take me," he crooned, stroking her clit and working his cock into her. "Deeper. Yes, that's it. You can do it, sweetness. Take all of me. Yes, *yes*."

He slowly rooted deeper, making sure not to hurt her, and she moaned. "Just a little more," he panted.

When he finally bottomed out inside her, she was trembling against him. "Good?" he asked hoarsely. "Please, God, let it be good for you because I'm not sure I can stop now."

"Yes, it's good," she breathed. "So good."

She swiveled her hips, and the supple muscles of her pussy clenched around him. Closing his eyes, he gritted his teeth to stop himself from shooting off.

"Wait," he ordered, clamping his fingers into her ass cheeks to keep her still. "Give me a minute."

"I can't," she gasped, wriggling against his hold. "I need … please …"

Every inch of his body was on fire, and he could feel his orgasm boiling inside him. Keeping one hand on her ass, he sat up and shoved his other hand into her hair. He cupped the back of her head and brought her face to his.

"I wanted to go slow, but I can't." He licked her bottom lip. "Give it to me hard and fast."

Wrapping her arms around his shoulders, she rested her forehead against his and began to move. Despite his demand, she started off slowly, grinding her pussy on his cock. With each downward thrust, she let out a breathy little moan that made his balls tighten.

"Faster," he urged, rolling his hips and pressing her down on him.

She responded with a sharp nip on his lower lip and a swivel of her hips that made his eyes roll back in his head. Her rhythm quickened until she rode him frantically. With his hands gripping her waist, he met her thrusts.

He tried to hold back his climax until she came again, but the burn moved from his balls to his cock. When it raced to the tip, he buried his face in her throat and exploded inside her.

The force of his orgasm tore a loud, guttural groan from his throat. At the same time, she arched against him with a loud cry, her pussy rippling around his cock. The rhythmic clenches wrung another burst from him. He stiffened, and his cock jerked again and again until his vision went dark.

After a moment, he fell backward with Kyla slumped over him. He felt like his soul had left his body when he had emptied himself inside her. Everything he had was hers.

She nuzzled her face into his neck and said something that he couldn't hear. "Hmm?" he asked, rubbing big circles on the smooth skin of her back.

"What do you think of my plan now?"

"You were right." He let loose with a raspy chuckle. "Your plan was better. *A lot* better."

She licked the side of his throat. "Would you like to hear about phase two of my plan?"

CHAPTER EIGHT

Kyla's stomach woke her. Empty and aching with hunger, it wouldn't allow her to sleep any longer, regardless of how exhausted she was. She checked the bedside clock. It was after noon, which explained why she was so ravenous.

She carefully lifted Jake's arm from her waist and slid from the bed. After pulling a nightgown over her head, she took a moment to enjoy the sight of him wrapped in her vibrantly colored paisley comforter. The poor guy was passed out, nearly comatose. She had kept him up until early morning after they had returned from their Saturday night date.

His face was buried in her pillow, his hair tousled from her fingers. The sheet had dipped below his waist, leaving his torso bare. He had mentioned that he swam laps every morning, which explained his muscular arms and toned abdomen.

The man not only had a six-pack, but a well-defined V-cut, something she had only seen on male models, pro athletes, and actors. She had spent more than a few minutes last night licking that enticing ridge of muscle.

She left the room as quietly as possible, carefully closing the door before hurrying down the hall to the bathroom. Once inside, she brushed her teeth and debated whether to take a quick shower. She was sore and sticky from sex, and eventually she decided to ignore her growling stomach. She took her time in the shower, letting the hot water soothe her achy body.

She'd had more sex in the past thirty-six hours than she'd had in her entire life. She didn't know whether that spoke to how desperate she was for Jake or how pathetic her sex life had been before him.

After finishing her shower, she dried off and smoothed on some tangerine-scented lotion. She pulled on her yellow robe and padded barefoot to the kitchen, eager to fill her empty belly.

As she rounded the corner, she spotted Vanessa sitting at the kitchen table. Kyla came to an abrupt halt in the doorway, and her sister looked up from her tablet.

"Good afternoon," Vanessa chirped.

Smiling, Kyla entered the kitchen. "I thought you were spending the weekend with Alan." Opening the door to the fridge, she perused the contents. "I didn't expect to see you until later tonight. When did you get home?"

"Last night."

Kyla snapped her head toward Vanessa. She really hoped she had misunderstood what her sister had said.

"Last night?" she repeated.

Vanessa nodded, her eyes sparkling with amusement. "Yes. I was snug in my bed when you got home last night."

Kyla could feel her face turning red. "I didn't know you were here."

"Obviously." Her sister snickered. "I had to put in my earbuds to fall asleep."

Kyla grabbed a carton of strawberry yogurt from the fridge and slammed the door shut. "I'm sorry," she said, unable to look Vanessa in the eye.

"I'm not. I'm happy for you. I know how much you like Jake."

"How do you know I was with Jake?" Kyla asked as she opened a drawer and grabbed a spoon.

Vanessa laughed. "Because you screamed his name at least fifty times."

Kyla bobbled the spoon, dropping it back into the drawer. It made a loud clang as it hit the other silverware.

"Oh, my God!" she exclaimed. "Shut up!"

Vanessa snorted. "That's what I thought when you guys woke me up at three in the morning."

"You're killing me," Kyla muttered.

After retrieving the dropped spoon, Kyla joined her sister at the table. Vanessa turned sideways in her chair and crossed her legs. Kyla couldn't help but smile when she saw the sparkly teal polish on her sister's toenails.

"You have to give me the details," Vanessa demanded. "How did you end up in bed with Jake?"

Kyla wasn't surprised by Vanessa's question. She and her older sister were very close, and she probably would have disclosed the details to Vanessa even if she hadn't asked for them. She shot a quick glance toward the doorway to make sure Jake wasn't close by before telling Vanessa what had happened at the celebration dinner on Friday night and the ride home.

"And?" Vanessa prompted when Kyla fell silent.

Kyla took a moment to peel back the top on her yogurt. As she stirred it, she said, "I invited him in and then I threw myself at him."

Vanessa giggled. "Subtle."

Kyla took a bite of yogurt, savoring the creamy snack. "He was insistent that we go on a date before we had sex but—"

"You persuaded him otherwise," Vanessa chimed in.

"Exactly." Kyla grinned. "He stayed the night, and we spent most of yesterday in bed."

Vanessa eyed her with approval. "I'm proud of you, Ky. I didn't think you'd go for it." She nodded toward the spoon, which held a dollop of strawberry-studded yogurt. "That looks good," she said as Kyla took a bite. "I'd ask for a taste but I have a pretty good idea where your mouth has been."

Kyla choked on the yogurt. She gave Vanessa a baleful glance, but her sister only laughed.

"So where were you when I got home?" Vanessa asked.

"Jake insisted that we go out. He was obsessed with the idea of taking me on a date. He wanted it to be a *real date*. He wouldn't tell me where we were going, only that I needed to dress up."

Jake had reassured her that he would pick her up in his car rather than on his motorcycle. She hadn't cared what kind of car he drove until she saw it—a vintage cherry-red Ford mustang. When she'd told him that the car was gorgeous, he had winked and said, "Not nearly as gorgeous as you are."

"What did you wear?" Vanessa asked.

Kyla took another spoonful of yogurt before answering. "The dress I bought at Lulu's."

A few weeks ago, Kyla and Vanessa had spent a Saturday afternoon browsing the shops on Fillmore Street, a trendy shopping district packed with boutiques and restaurants. Kyla had found a metallic gold lace dress with cap sleeves and a full skirt, and she had bought it despite the outrageous price. She had dreamed of wearing it for Jake, but she'd never thought she would get the chance to do so.

Vanessa smiled. "You look gorgeous in that dress. Shoes?"

"My beaded gold sandals—the really tall ones with the strap around the ankle."

"Nice," Vanessa said, nodding approvingly. "Hair? Up or down?"

"Up with dangly gold earrings."

"Did Jake swallow his tongue when he saw you all dressed up?"

"No, he swallowed mine," Kyla quipped.

Vanessa laughed. "Even better."

"He brought me those." Kyla pointed to the flower-filled vase on the kitchen counter. The bouquet featured a fragrant mix of bright pink roses, yellow lilies, orange gerbera daisies, and deep purple sweet peas.

Vanessa studied the bouquet. "Alan never buys me flowers." Her voice held a note of wistfulness. "I love them, but he says they're distracting and smelly."

Kyla bit her lip to stop herself from yelling at Vanessa: *"Alan is a selfish jerk. Dump him and find a good guy like Jake ... a guy who will buy you flowers just because."*

Vanessa brought her attention back to Kyla. "Where did you go on your date?" she asked.

"Destello."

"The Cuban place? The one with the salsa dancing?"

Kyla nodded. "It was *awesome*. The food was incredible. And the dancing... it was so fun and sexy."

Vanessa's eyebrows arched in surprise. "You danced? You don't know how to salsa."

"I do now. Every thirty minutes, they give a short lesson on Cuban salsa dancing. Did you know the dance is called Casino?"

At first, she'd been too embarrassed to go out on the dance floor, but Jake had convinced her to give it a try. To her relief, she'd picked up the dance quickly.

"Jake is a *fabulous* dancer," she added. "I was so surprised."

"I've heard that men who are good dancers are good lovers." Vanessa waggled her eyebrows. "I guess Jake proves it."

Kyla placed the spoon on the table and leaned forward. "Sass, it's never been like this for me." Lowering her voice, she said, "I never knew the difference between sex and lovemaking, but there *is* a difference. Every time I'm with Jake, I feel it."

"Oh," Vanessa breathed, clasping Kyla's hand, "you're in love with him."

She nodded, and her sister's hand tightened. "Be careful, Ky. Don't get in too deep. You don't know how he feels about you. You don't want to make the mistake of wanting him more than he wants you."

*****

When Jake opened the door to Kyla's bedroom, he could hear her voice drifting from the kitchen. He couldn't ascertain what she said, but he assumed she was on the phone.

He made the short trip to the bathroom and took care of his morning business before rummaging around in the vanity for a spare toothbrush. Luckily, he found one.

As he brushed his teeth, he glimpsed himself in the mirror. His hair was so wild he looked like a member of a 1980s hair band. Or maybe not. He didn't have a mullet, and he pitied the men who did.

After rinsing his mouth, he wet his hands and tried to smooth the unruly strands. When it became obvious that only a shower would fix them, he decided to convince Kyla to take one with him. His penis twitched at the thought of seeing her creamy skin all soapy and wet. He'd spent hours inside her, but he and his insatiable cock still wanted more.

Exiting the bathroom, he listened for Kyla. He couldn't hear her, so he called her name.

"I'm in the kitchen," she answered.

He followed her voice and found her leaning against the counter, wrapped in a yellow robe that reminded him of a fluffy toy duck. Her long hair was loose around her shoulders, and her cheeks were pink.

"Hey, sweetness."

In their bare feet, he was a foot taller than she was so he grabbed her around the waist and lifted her so he could drop a kiss on her luscious lips. He got a whiff of something citrusy and nuzzled his nose into her neck.

"You smell good," he murmured.

"It's my tangerine body lotion. I put some on after I showered."

"Does it taste as good as it smells?" Deciding to find out, he let her slide down his body and dropped his hands to the belt at her waist. "Maybe I should check to see if you missed any spots. I'd be happy to help you with any hard-to-reach places."

She grasped his hands before he could untie her belt. "Jake, I'd like you to meet my sister."

The words had barely left her mouth when he saw something move out of the corner of his eye. Snapping his head toward it, he was shocked to see a tall blonde rise from a chair at the small table. She gracefully made her way to him and held out a slender hand.

"Hello. I'm Vanessa Andrews."

He took her hand instinctively. "Jake Lilliard."

"Kyla has told me a lot about you," she replied, her lips tipped up in a small smile.

Releasing Vanessa's hand, he looked back and forth between the two sisters. Vanessa was a taller, harder version of Kyla. She lacked Kyla's softness … her sweetness.

Vanessa's smile wasn't as warm as Kyla's, and her eyes didn't sparkle like her younger sister's. He noticed that her shirt and cropped pants were both black, a jarring contrast to Kyla's brightly colored robe.

Jake's dad was the poker player, reading people for a living, but Jake had picked up some of his skill. And that was why it only took him a few moments to discern that Vanessa Andrews was a deeply unhappy woman.

Before he could ponder that mystery, Vanessa's eyes dropped to his chest, and her smile widened. "It's definitely a pleasure to meet you."

Glancing down, he was reminded that he was only half-clothed. He hadn't bothered to don his shirt, and he wore only his charcoal dress pants ... zipped but not buttoned. Even his feet were bare.

Vanessa's frank perusal of his nudity made his face hot. His embarrassment must have been obvious because Kyla giggled. When he glared at her, her giggles turned into full-fledged laughter.

Glancing sideways at her sister, Kyla said, "I told you that he was hot."

Vanessa laughed softly. "And you weren't exaggerating." She gave Kyla a meaningful look. "About anything." She collected a black bag from the counter. "I have some work to do, so I'm going into the office. I'll be back around six so we can drive together to Mom's." She nodded toward him. "I'm sure I'll see you again, Jake. Thanks for the show."

He watched Vanessa as she left the kitchen, and when she was gone, he brought his attention back to Kyla. "You have plans for tonight?"

She nodded. "My mom is making dinner, and then we'll probably watch a movie."

Disappointment flooded him. He had hoped they would be able to have dinner together.

He waited, hoping Kyla would invite him to her mother's home for dinner and a movie. He'd met Letty when she had stopped by the office to have lunch with her daughter, and he had immediately liked her. She would be a good mother-in-law.

When he became conscious of the drift of his thoughts, he got a little light-headed. He abruptly realized that he wasn't just in love with Kyla. He wanted to build a life with her.

Marriage. Children. Pets. Minivans ... okay, maybe not minivans. Maybe a mid-size SUV.

"Are you okay?" Kyla asked. "You have a weird look on your face."

His mind was filled with a slideshow of Kyla—naked in his bed, wearing a wedding dress, pregnant with his baby, surrounded by kids who were just as smart and sweet as their mother, growing old with him.

"Jake?" Kyla asked, her voice shaded with concern.

He focused on her face, and she frowned. "Are you upset that I talked with Vanessa about you?"

Shaking his head, he asked, "Did you talk about me a lot?"

"Yes."

His question was his best attempt to ascertain how she felt about him without being too obvious. He needed to know where she was emotionally so he could plan his next move.

He was in love with Kyla. He wanted them to be exclusive. Hell, he wanted to put a ring on it.

But he had to be realistic about the whole situation. Although he didn't think she considered him as a weekend fling, he had no way of knowing. He was probably far more emotionally invested than she was, and he needed to be patient. Every gambler knew that you couldn't show your hand too early, or you'd risk losing the game.

He crowded her against the counter until their bodies were pressed together. She tipped her head back and met his eyes.

"What did you talk about?"

She licked her lips before saying, "We talked about a lot of things."

Grasping her waist, he boosted her onto the countertop and stepped between her knees. "Like what?"

"At first I just talked about the projects we worked on together."

He brushed his mouth against hers. "That's boring."

She smiled, and he felt the movement against his lips. "I'm never bored when I'm with you."

That made *him* smile. "I'm glad I can entertain you. What else did you talk about?"

"One day Vanessa asked how old you were, and when I told her that you were thirty-one, she asked what you looked like." She smoothed a hand over his hair. "So, I described you."

She slid her fingers into his hair and lightly ran her fingernails over his scalp. The gentle scratch made him break into goose bumps.

"What did you say?" he asked as he skimmed his hands under her robe.

"I said that you were handsome. That you were tall and had beautiful eyes. And that you were sexy and had a great butt."

He cupped his hands around the smooth globes of her ass. "You have a great butt, too." He squeezed lightly. "There were a few times when I had to put my hands in my pockets so I wouldn't grab it."

She laughed. "Really?"

"Really," he confirmed.

Stroking his hand over her hip, he found the springy hair at the juncture of her thighs. She widened her legs, and he eased his fingers between the folds of her pussy. She was soft and hot and so fucking wet he almost came right then and there.

As he circled the entrance to her body with his forefinger, he wondered if she was too sore for this. He'd taken her so many times they had used all the condoms he'd brought with him and all of hers, too.

He dipped the tip of his finger into her, and when she let out a little moan of pleasure, he withdrew and slowly pushed two fingers inside. "Every time we were together, I thought about this. I had a constant hard-on."

She clutched his shoulders. "Every time we were together, I was afraid that you'd guess how I felt about you."

"How *do* you feel about me?" he asked, pumping his fingers in and out of her.

She rocked against his hand, panting softly. He flicked her clit with his thumb, back and forth, back and forth, and she whimpered.

"How do you feel about me, Kyla?" he persisted.

She looked at him, her eyes hazy with lust. "I want you."

Before he could formulate another question, she pushed her hand between them and cupped it over his, forcing his fingers deeper. She cried out, and her pussy clamped down on his fingers, almost vibrating with the intensity of her orgasm. He stayed with her until the last pulses had faded. Her hand fell away from his, and she slumped against him.

"It's different with you," she whispered. "It's not just sex. It means something."

And that was enough. *For now.*

CHAPTER NINE

A loud knock on Jake's partially open office door pulled his attention from the oversized computer monitor where he was reviewing a spreadsheet. He glanced up just as Quinn O'Brien stuck his head around the door.

"Hey, there."

Surprised, Jake vaulted to his feet. "Good morning."

"I thought you might already be here," Quinn said.

Jake darted a glance at his watch, wondering why the president and CEO of Riley O'Brien & Co. stood in his office at seven-thirty on a Monday morning. Quinn rarely dropped by unannounced, and even though Jake didn't think he had any reason to worry about his job, an arrow of anxiety shot through him.

If Quinn had come by fifteen minutes earlier, he would have found the office empty. At approximately seven-fifteen, Jake had been in his Mustang on the deserted lower level of Riley Plaza's underground parking garage. He hadn't been alone.

Kyla had been with him, sitting on his lap with her skirt hiked up to her waist and his cock lodged deep inside her. It had only taken a few thrusts and a couple of strokes across her clit for them both to go off like rockets.

The sex had been fast and rough, and it had barely taken the edge off his hunger for her. Since the party eleven days ago, Jake and Kyla had spent every night together. And every morning, he'd woken up wanting her more than he had night before.

Quinn cleared his throat. "Do you have some time to talk?"

"Of course," Jake replied, rounding his desk.

At thirty-five, Quinn controlled a multi-billion-dollar company, and he did a damn fine job of it. Jake wasn't the only one who thought so, either. Two well-known business magazines had named Quinn as one of the nation's top CEOs.

"A new smoothie bar just opened down the block," Quinn said. "Let's take a walk."

They took the escalator to the ground floor of Riley Plaza and exited the building. Since it was so early in the morning, the sidewalk was almost empty, and they could stroll along side by side.

"So…" Quinn said, drawing out the word, "Amelia told me that you played referee when she met with Diana to go over the annual budget for the women's division."

Jake glanced sideways. "Were those her words?"

Quinn met his eyes. "No. But you and I both know that's what you were doing."

A smart man went out of his way to avoid getting caught between two strong-willed women who disliked one another. Unfortunately, Jake didn't have that option when it came to Amelia and Diana. So, he slipped a whistle between his teeth, metaphorically at least, and called personal fouls when necessary.

Quinn stopped in front of a storefront with a bright orange awning. "This is it. Smoothie Criminal."

"What's their tagline? Our smoothies are so good they should be illegal?"

Quinn grinned as he pulled open the door. Jake followed him into the store and looked around. Other than a couple of people occupying the barstools near the windows, it was empty.

"It's not very busy," he noted *sotto voce*. "I hope the product is better than the name."

"I think it's clever," Quinn countered. "Smooth Criminal is a great song." He hummed a few notes of the hit before asking, "Don't you like Michael Jackson?"

"Of course I like Michael Jackson. Who doesn't like Michael Jackson?"

"Prove it," Quinn said, his dark blue eyes glinting with amusement. "Show me your moonwalk, Lilliard."

Jake glanced down at his feet. "Even Michael Jackson couldn't moonwalk in motorcycle boots."

Quinn made a rude noise. "Don't blame your boots. I'm wearing boots, and I can still do this…" He brought his arms close to his body and perfectly executed the spin move that the King of Pop had made famous.

The young guy behind the counter laughed. "Nice moves, dude. What can I get you?"

Jake looked at the menu hanging on the wall behind the counter. All the smoothies were named after illegal activities.

"I can't decide whether I want a 'Drunk & Disorderly' or a 'Public Lewdness,'" Quinn said, his voice threaded with laughter.

They placed their order. Quinn paid, joking that he was going to expense their smoothies since this was a business meeting.

As they waited for their smoothies, Quinn said, "Thank you for trying to ease the friction between Amelia and Diana."

"Somebody has to do it." Quinn's dark eyebrows arched, and Jake winced when he realized how rude his reply had sounded. "I'm sorry. I shouldn't have said that."

"Don't apologize. It's the truth. Somebody has to do it, and it can't be me." Quinn massaged his forehead. "If I interfered, Diana would accuse me of nepotism, and Amelia would accuse me of doubting her competence and her judgment. Either way, I'm fucked."

Suddenly, the loudspeaker blared throughout the small store. "Quinn O., you've been charged with public lewdness and petty theft."

Quinn snickered. "That's us."

They grabbed their smoothies and squeezed into a two-top in the corner. Jake lifted the plastic lid just enough to get a whiff of his smoothie.

Quinn took a big pull on his straw. "*Mmm*. This is good. You should try yours."

Jake tentatively took a sip of his smoothie. The sweetness of strawberries teased his taste buds, along with the complementary flavor of bananas. For a drink that was named after a criminal act, it tasted great.

Quinn slouched in his chair and studied Jake unblinkingly for several seconds. "I think Diana is the problem. What do you think?"

Jake took a moment to consider his response to Quinn's pointed question. It wouldn't reflect well on him to throw Diana under the bus, but it also wouldn't reflect well on him to be dishonest.

"I think Diana dislikes Amelia, and the feeling is mutual."

"Tell me something I don't know," Quinn said dryly.

"Okay. Amelia purposefully does things that she knows will annoy Diana."

Quinn narrowed his eyes. "Like what?"

"Like kicking Diana's desk non-stop during a meeting and

then pretending that she can't control herself because she suffers from restless legs syndrome. I'm sure it's just coincidence that she's always wearing pointy-toed cowboy boots on those days."

Quinn burst out laughing. "Damn, I love that woman."

"She's something, alright."

As Jake took a sip of his smoothie, one corner of Quinn's mouth lifted in an ornery smile. "I think I know a cure for her restless legs syndrome."

Jake choked a little on his fruity drink. He had a good idea of how Quinn planned to "cure" his wife's condition.

"Amelia isn't the only person who has a problem working with Diana," Quinn noted. "Most people think she's a huge pain in the ass. I've always been impressed that you work so well with her."

Jake laughed. "Compared to some of the people I encountered when I was a bookie, Diana is charming."

"I have a lot of respect for her. She's smart and loyal and a very hard worker."

"I have a lot of respect for her, too."

Quinn took another pull on his smoothie and shook the cup. "Diana has been with Riley O'Brien & Co. for more than thirty-five years, and it's time to make a change. She's done a good job for us, but I don't think she's the right person to lead the finance group moving forward. She's resistant to change, and she always thinks of why something can't be done instead of thinking of ways it can be done."

Unfortunately, Jake agreed with Quinn's assessment of the current CFO. Diana wasn't a problem solver. She was a finger pointer and a road blocker.

"I'm going to ask her to retire at the end of the second quarter," Quinn said.

Jake's stomach clenched, and he had to work hard to keep his poker face. He had never imagined that Quinn would demand Diana's retirement, and certainly not within the next four weeks.

"I think the company is ready for a new CFO," Quinn continued.

Jake placed his smoothie on the table, his gaze locked on Quinn. Ever since the day Jake had joined Riley O'Brien & Co., he'd been working toward one goal: to be the company's next CFO.

"I don't think you're ready to take on the CFO job," Quinn said.

Jake couldn't stop his shoulders from slumping in disappointment. He'd thought that he would have more time to show Quinn that he could handle the responsibility.

Once Quinn brought in a new CFO, it was unlikely that Jake would have an opportunity to move into that position any time soon. The average tenure for a CFO was more than ten years.

Quinn's eyes narrowed. "Do *you* think you're ready?"

Jake hesitated. He wanted to assure Quinn that he could perform the responsibilities of the CFO satisfactorily, but he didn't know if that was true.

Before Jake could answer Quinn, the chief executive spoke again. "You're not ready to be the CFO of a multi-billion-dollar company. You'll probably never be ready." Quinn smiled slowly. "I wasn't ready to take over a multi-billion-dollar company, but I did it anyway, and somehow I muddled through. So will you."

Jake shook his head uncomprehendingly. "What?"

"You're not ready to be the CFO, but you're the right person for the job."

"*Are you serious?*"

Quinn leaned forward and braced his forearms on the table. "Yeah, chief, I'm serious. Do you want the job?"

Jake exhaled roughly. "*Hell, yes*, I want it."

"Then it's yours. I've already cleared it with the Board. We'll announce it at the same time Diana's retirement is announced. I'm meeting with her later today." Quinn laughed dryly. "That's not a conversation I'm looking forward to."

They spent the next twenty minutes hashing out compensation including bonuses and profit sharing. Quinn was surprisingly generous. Jake would have taken far less than what the CEO had offered.

They made the trek back to Riley Plaza in silence. Quinn seemed to understand that Jake needed time to process his unexpected but much desired promotion.

When they reached the second-floor reception area, Quinn stopped and turned to face Jake. "You belong in the CFO office. Never doubt that."

"Thank you for the opportunity. I promise, Quinn, you won't regret giving me this shot."

"Lilliard, I knew that the moment I met you."

Quinn slapped him on the back and sauntered toward the elevators. Jake guessed that Quinn planned to stop by Amelia's workshop to discuss her restless legs syndrome.

For a moment, Jake stood in the reception area. Within a two-week period, everything he had wanted so desperately had fallen into his lap. First Kyla and now the CFO gig.

He laughed, almost giddy with happiness. The sound echoed off the stained concrete floors in the reception area.

He rushed to the elevator, eager to see Kyla and share the unbelievable news. As he entered the cab, he realized that in a few short weeks, he would move into the executive wing, and the nameplate next to his door would read: Jacob C. Lilliard, chief financial officer.

As CFO, he would supervise everything and everyone in the finance department. He stared at the metal panels in front of him, abruptly realizing how his promotion impacted his relationship with Kyla.

Everything and everyone.

Once he assumed his new role, he would be Kyla's boss again. The buzz of a million bees filled his ears, and only one thought came through clearly: Lady Luck is a fickle bitch.

*****

When Kyla arrived at Nick and Teagan's house in Pacific Heights, she bypassed the front door. She was, as her mom liked to say, "back door company", which meant that she could let herself in.

Nick and Teagan lived in an Italianate-Victorian mansion that had been built in the early 1910s. Before they had married, he had renovated the entire house. Vanessa had designed the new floorplan, even though her specialty was commercial design and not residential.

Teagan had asked Kyla to stop by so they could discuss the report she'd written about Riley O'Brien & Co.'s management trainee program. Originally, they had intended to meet at Riley Plaza, but Teagan had left work early because she'd been feeling under the weather.

Kyla hoped the conversation wouldn't take too long because she and Jake had plans for dinner. As soon as she finished with Teagan, Kyla planned to speed over to Jake's condo.

Fingers crossed he would be naked when he answered the door. She wanted a repeat of what they'd done this morning in his Mustang. Maybe they could find a deserted area in the parking garage under Jake's high-rise.

Kyla jogged up the stairs at the back of Nick and Teagan's house and opened the exterior door. It led to a spacious mudroom that was furnished with a massive steel blue hutch. After hanging her bag on one of the hutch's large bronze hooks, she pushed through the interior door and into the kitchen.

With its cream-colored, glass-fronted cabinets, natural stone backsplash, and commercial-grade appliances, the kitchen was elegant without being sterile. It was far nicer than the one she and Vanessa shared, but that was okay since neither of them could cook.

Teagan stood beside the huge granite island, drinking golden liquid from a clear glass bottle. She was dressed comfortably, clad in a gray Harvard sweatshirt, pink plaid pajama pants, and tan UGGs.

Her wavy, dark hair hung past her shoulders in tangled streamers, and her face was completely free of makeup, revealing her pallor. Her cobalt-blue eyes, framed by glasses with thick silver rims, lacked their usual sparkle.

"Hey, T," Kyla said. "Are you feeling better?"

"A little."

Moving farther into the kitchen, Kyla stopped next to the curvy brunette. She gently grasped Teagan's wrist so she could read the label on the bottle.

"Fever Tree Ginger Ale. Made with natural gingers." She glanced at Teagan. "Upset stomach?"

"Yes."

"Flu?"

"I'm not contagious, if that's what you're worried about," Teagan snapped.

Whoa. Cranky much?

"I'm worried about *you*, not catching something from you."

Teagan sighed softly. "I know. I'm sorry for snapping at you." She screwed the cap back on the bottle. "I'm pregnant."

"Pregnant!" Kyla squealed and threw her arms around Teagan. "That's wicked awesome! Does my mom know? She's going to be so excited!"

"It is wicked awesome. And yes, she knows. It's kind of hard to hide it from her when I throw up twenty times a day."

"Is the ginger ale helping?"

"Yes. And Letty found some recipes that are supposed to help with morning sickness."

"Where is my mom, by the way?"

Teagan grimaced. "I can't stand the smell of food cooking, especially vegetables, so she's making dinner in the carriage house and bringing it over here."

"How far along are you?"

"Only a few weeks." Teagan set the ginger ale on the island. "We aren't telling a lot of people, so please don't say anything, Kyla. It's still early, and something could happen ..."

Wrapping her arm around Teagan's shoulders, Kyla pressed her head against the other woman's. "Nothing is going to happen. You're going to have a healthy, beautiful baby, and my mom is going to spoil it rotten."

"Babies."

"What?" Kyla asked, drawing back so she could see Teagan's face.

Teagan held up two fingers. "Two heartbeats. Two babies."

"Twins!" Kyla screeched. "Oh, my God!"

Suddenly, Nick appeared in the doorway, dressed in a gray Under Armor long-sleeved tee that clung to his muscular chest and black track pants. Her screech must have activated his protective instincts. His light green eyes swept over the room, and his warrior stance relaxed when he saw that Kyla and Teagan were okay.

"I just told her about the babies," Teagan explained.

A huge smile transformed Nick's face. Kyla had known him for nearly six years, and she'd never seen him so happy, not even on his wedding day.

With his tawny hair, athlete's body, and eyes the same shade as the mineral olivine, Nick was extraordinarily good-looking. In fact, *People* magazine had named him one of the sexiest men alive. But that smile … it was breath-taking. He was obviously thrilled that he was going to be a daddy.

Kyla knew, without a doubt, that Nick Priest would be there for his children from their first breath to his last. And she was sure he'd do his best to make sure they were taken care of even after he was gone. Teagan was a lucky woman.

"Congratulations!" Kyla shouted.

She darted over to Nick, wrapped her arms around his waist, and squeezed him as tightly as she could. Grunting a little, he hugged her to him and dropped a kiss on top of her head.

Even though he was only eight years older than Kyla, he'd always had a fatherly demeanor with her. She was grateful for her relationship with Nick. It was a blessing.

Kyla doubted that Nick knew how much he'd changed her life and the lives of her immediate family. She would never admit it to anyone, but she secretly thought Nick was their guardian angel. He'd come along when they needed him most, hiring Letty to be his personal chef and part-time assistant while he'd played pro football for the Boston Colonials.

Kyla released Nick from her python-like squeeze and looked

up at him. "You know, my mom will think of your babies as her grandchildren."

If it were possible, Nick's smile grew even bigger. Teagan laughed before saying, "That's a win-win. Nick and I already think of Letty as their grandmother."

Kyla couldn't prevent the grin that took over her face. "Thanks for taking the pressure off me, T."

"If you think your mom is going to be satisfied with only two grandchildren, you're delusional," Teagan warned. "I don't think you realize how eager she is for you, or Vanessa, or Ben to make her a grandmother."

Teagan's face turned the color of skim milk, and her eyes widened behind her glasses. She lunged for the cabinet that hid the trash can at the same moment Nick did. He jerked it open just in time for his wife to puke up the ginger ale she'd just imbibed.

While Teagan heaved over the trash can, Nick held her hair away from her face. When she was finished, he moistened a paper towel with tap water and carefully wiped her cheeks and mouth.

"This sucks," Teagan muttered.

Pulling his wife into his arms, he murmured soothing noises and rubbed big circles on her back. Kyla felt as if she was intruding on a very private moment.

"Maybe I should come back later. This doesn't seem like a good time to talk about work."

Teagan chuckled weakly. "I'm not sure if or when there will be a good time in the next eight months."

Nick tossed the paper towel into the trash, pulled out the plastic bag, and efficiently tied it off. With the bag in hand, he exited the kitchen, leaving Kyla and Teagan alone.

After grabbing the ginger ale, Teagan slowly made her way to the kitchen table and plopped down on a chair upholstered in navy blue dupioni silk. "Let's talk about your report. Why did you write it?"

Familiar with the location of the kitchen supplies, Kyla opened the pantry and found a replacement trash bag. As she fitted it into the plastic can, she asked, "Do you know Phoebe Werner? She's also in the management trainee program. Relocated from Boise. Brunette. Short, curly hair. Big boobs. Little freckle above her lip."

"I don't think so."

"I guess it doesn't matter if you know her or not." Kyla pushed the cabinet door shut with her knee. "The report was her idea. We were talking about our experiences with the program, and we agreed that there were some aspects that could be a lot better."

"We don't solicit feedback from trainees, which is a problem because there's no way for us to know if it's a negative experience."

Shaking her head, Kyla slid into the chair diagonal to Teagan. "Don't misconstrue the report, T. My overall experience was positive. I'm appreciative that you worked behind the scenes to get me into the program, and I'm happy that I went through it."

"I shared your report with Winyu," Teagan said.

Winyu Parnthong served as the executive vice president of human resources for Riley O'Brien & Co. Kyla had seen him around the office, but she'd never spoken with him. The human resources department had not been one of her rotations during the management trainee program.

Teagan continued, "He was impressed with your analysis and your suggestions to improve the program."

"I'm glad my report was helpful. That's all I wanted to do … to improve the program."

Teagan picked at the label on the bottle of ginger ale. "Winyu agrees with you about the need for a dedicated manager for the trainee program."

It was important to Kyla that Teagan understood that Miranda wasn't incompetent, but simply overwhelmed. She didn't want to disparage or discount the other woman's hard work.

"I think Miranda is doing the best she can. But she has a lot on her plate, even without the additional responsibility of managing the trainee program."

Teagan nodded. "Winyu is aware of that. He's working to redistribute the workload in his department."

She stood abruptly, and Kyla jumped up from her chair, ready to help if Teagan needed her. The expectant mother waved her hand.

"Relax. I'm just hungry." She smiled wryly. "That's how I roll now. Either I'm barfing or I'm starving. There's no in between."

Kyla watched as Teagan rummaged through a wicker basket on the countertop. As she pulled out a plastic-wrapped brown loaf, she said, "Letty made banana bread this morning. Want a piece?"

"No, thanks."

Teagan unwrapped the bread, and to Kyla's amusement, she didn't bother to cut a slice. She just took a big bite off the end of the loaf.

Once Teagan had swallowed her mouthful of banana bread, she said, "After reading your report, I think the trainee program needs more than a dedicated manager. I think it needs to be completely revamped. I know we can do a better job recruiting people into the program and deploying them where they're needed most."

Her comments didn't surprise Kyla. Teagan had been the one

to push for a makeover of the entire women's division. She wasn't someone who would ever be content with the status quo. She was always looking for ways to improve the company.

"I know you really like working in the finance department, but would you be interested in managing the trainee program?"

Teagan's question came out of left field, and Kyla struggled to wrap her head around what the other woman was suggesting.

"I don't know. I've never considered doing something like that." She frowned. "Am I the right person to manage the program? Isn't there someone else who would be better?"

Teagan slowly wound the plastic wrap around the loaf of banana bread. "I think you're the perfect person to manage the program."

"You do? Why?"

"Because you're the person who recognized the flaws in the existing program. You're the person who took the initiative to write a report about it. You're the person who outlined a strategy to build on what we're doing right and fix what we're doing wrong."

"I'm not sure I'm qualified—"

"Don't be ridiculous," Teagan snapped. "You have an MBA from a top-rated university. So, that checks the box for education. As for experience, you've gone through the trainee program. You know what works and what doesn't. That experience is invaluable."

She considered what Teagan had said. The other woman had made some valid points. Maybe Kyla *was* the perfect person to manage the trainee program.

Teagan groaned pitifully and pressed her hand to her lower stomach. "Please, babies, give me a break."

Just then, Nick returned to the kitchen. He took one glance

at Teagan's waxen complexion and hurried to her side.

"Bed," he said. "Now."

Teagan tilted her head back until she could meet Nick's eyes. "This is your fault, you know."

His mouth quirked in a smile. "I know."

"Will you lie down with me?"

He nodded, and Teagan brought her attention back to Kyla. "Just think about what I said. Please. I think it would be a great opportunity for you."

Kyla nodded. "I will. I promise."

CHAPTER TEN

Unfortunately, Jake was fully clothed when he answered the door to his condo. Fortunately, he was shoeless. That meant Kyla could get his Rileys off in thirty seconds.

"Hi," she said, giving him a big smile.

He didn't respond to her greeting. Instead, his greenish-gold gaze roamed over her, seeming to catalog every distinct part, from her unbound hair and beaded tiered necklace to her emerald green V-necked sweater and floral print skirt and ending with her black Mary Jane heels.

He silently welcomed her into his condo by standing beside the door. Once she crossed the threshold, he closed the door with a soft *snick*.

His place had an open floorplan with a large bar splitting the kitchen from the dining and living areas. She stopped next to Jake's brown leather recliner, which was marred with several pieces of duct tape.

He still hadn't spoken. A knot formed in her stomach. Something was wrong.

After tossing her bag onto the recliner, she turned to face him. He stood about two feet away, his expression grave.

"We need to talk."

The tone of his voice, coupled with his foreboding expression, warned her that this was not going to be a pleasant conversation. It was quite possible that she would be in tears before it was over.

"I don't know where to start ..."

"I've heard the beginning is a good place."

"Right." A laugh rustled in his throat. "So, Quinn stopped by my office this morning. We went to a new smoothie bar called Smoothie Criminal."

"And?"

"And he gave me a promotion."

Relief flooded her. This was good news.

"That's great!" she exclaimed. "I'm so proud of you!"

She charged forward, intending to give him a hug, but he held out hands like a traffic cop. Confused, she stumbled to a stop.

"What's wrong? You should be happy that Quinn recognizes how hard you work. This promotion is a reward."

Jake looked down and rubbed the back of his neck. "Quinn offered me the CFO job, Kyla. He wants Diana to retire by the end of quarter."

"CFO?"

"CFO," he confirmed.

"Wow," she breathed. "That is a huge, huge deal."

He nodded. "It's my dream job. It's what I've been working toward since my first day at Riley O'Brien & Co. I just didn't think it would happen so soon. I didn't think Diana would retire for another five years. I never expected that Quinn would insist that she retire before she was ready. But he doesn't think she's the right person to do the job anymore. He's concerned about how difficult she is."

Kyla nodded. Difficult was one word to describe Diana. Bitch was another one.

"Jake, this is amazing. *You're* amazing. You'll probably be the youngest CFO of a *Fortune* 100 company." She waggled her eyebrows. "You'll definitely be the hottest."

He shook his head. "You're not getting it, sweetness."

"Getting what?"

"As chief financial officer, I will oversee everything related to the company's finances, from accounts receivable to payroll, and everything in between. I will also supervise everyone in the finance department. *Everyone.*"

"I understand that it's a big job," she conceded, "but I have no doubt that you can handle it. You need to have faith in yourself. I do."

He laughed, but the sound held little amusement. "You still don't get," he snapped. "I will be your boss, Kyla! I will be your boss's boss! And his boss's boss!"

Now she understood why he wasn't doing backflips. While she worked in the finance department, his dream job made it impossible for them to be together.

"I can't be in a relationship with someone whose boss reports to me," he continued. "It violates Riley O'Brien & Co.'s, code of professional conduct. It would be unethical and a conflict of interest because I will have the power to influence your career."

Kyla sat down on the curved arm of the oversized sofa. "That's a problem."

"A problem?" he repeated, his voice an octave higher than usual. "It's not a problem, Kyla! It's a fucking disaster!"

She'd seen Jake pissed off. She'd seen him angry. But she'd never seen him like this ... almost unhinged.

"I want the CFO job. And I want you. I don't want to give

up either one. I want it all, damn it!'"

And in that moment, she knew that she was going to give up her job in the finance department and take the one that Teagan had offered. On the drive to Jake's condo, Kyla had weighed the risks and rewards of managing the trainee program, but she hadn't been able to decide. Jake's promotion was the variable that tipped the scales.

Some people might think that she was sacrificing her career. But she didn't agree.

Her career path wasn't clearly marked. Unlike Jake, she hadn't been striving toward any particular job or goal. He had, and now that his dream job was within reach, she wasn't going to stand in his way.

While the finance job was safe and comfortable, the job managing the trainee program would probably be far more challenging. And potentially far more rewarding.

It was a risk that Kyla was willing to take to be with Jake. Even though their relationship was new, it was worth it.

Jake moved to stand in front of her. She looked up into his face, and he curved his hand around her jaw. "I can't give you up, Kyla. I *won't* give you up."

Turning her head, she placed a light kiss on his palm. "I can't give you up, either." She let him pull her to her feet. "I'll tell Sam tomorrow that I'm resigning my position."

He stared into her eyes. "I just want you to know … I don't think my career is more important than yours. And I know this isn't fair to you. If I could find any other solution, I would."

She nodded. "I know you would."

"What are you going to do?"

"I'm going to manage Riley O'Brien & Co.'s management trainee program."

The space between his eyebrows crinkled. "What?"

She spent the next several minutes telling him about the conversation she'd had with Teagan and her new job opportunity. When she finished, he picked her up by the waist and spun her around, sending her skirt belling out around her thighs.

"You're going to be perfect for that job, sweetness. I'm so proud of you." He set her back on her feet and pressed a kiss on her mouth. "That problem was a little too easy to solve. The next one won't be."

"Probably not," she agreed. "And that's why we need to celebrate this one."

"Hold on," he said before jogging into the kitchen.

He returned a moment later with a black champagne bottle and two crystal coupes. She took the bottle from him, wrapping her palm around the black foil on the neck.

"What kind of champagne is this?"

"Krug Clos d'Ambonnay 1995. It's made entirely from Pinot Noir."

He carefully placed the coupes on the small table next to the sofa, and she took the opportunity to link his hand with hers. Lacing their fingers together, she said, "Let's celebrate in the shower."

Jake smiled slowly. "That's a wicked awesome idea."

Minutes later, they stood in the bathroom, completely naked. The first time Kyla had seen Jake's bathroom, she had been speechless. Simply put, it was the largest, most luxurious bathroom she'd even seen anywhere—in person, on TV, online, or in a magazine.

Except for the large white rectangular tiles on the floor and the white sinks and toilet, aqua was the predominant color. Shimmery aqua mosaic tiles covered every inch of the walls and floor of the glassed-in shower. It was large enough to accommodate a basketball team. Twenty-plus shower heads and body jets sprayed temperature-controlled water.

Using the digital touchpad, Jake turned on the water. Steam immediately filled the shower, fogging the glass panels. He stepped inside first, carrying the champagne and a condom, and she followed.

As Jake placed the bottle on the shower seat in the corner, Kyla let her gaze wander over her guy. Against the vibrant aqua of the mosaic tiles, his skin looked darker than usual. His broad shoulders tapered into a lean waist, the muscles in his back and sides creating thick ridges under his skin.

His ass was so tight with muscle, a deep dimple sat high on each cheek. His legs were long and leanly muscled, and the backs of his thighs and calves were sprinkled with dark hair.

Jake turned and stepped under the rain shower head. Dropping his head back, he let the water pour over him. He lifted his arms to slick his hair away from his face, and the muscles in shoulders and arms bunched and shifted.

As she moved her gaze lower, over the defined muscles of his pecs and the hard sinew of his ribs, the flesh between her legs began to ache and swell. A line of silky hair created a swirl around his belly button before leading downward to a cluster of dark curls. He was already erect, his penis jutting toward her.

Jake wasn't hung like a porn star, and Kyla was glad about that. His penis was only a little longer than average, but it was wide and thick.

He caught her eyes and beckoned her to him with a curl of his finger. When she got within touching distance, he reached for her, pulling her under the spray with him.

Hot water trickled over her shoulders and breasts, stoking the fire already warming her skin. Jake's arms encircled her from behind, his erection pressing into her back.

He brought his hands to her breasts, lifting and shaping them with his palms. She arched against him, rubbing against his hard-on, as the water mingled with the slickness between her legs.

Using both hands, he lightly rolled her nipples between his thumbs and forefingers. He always started out that way, gentle and light. But slowly, he increased the pressure until he pinched the tight buds. Her pussy clenched each time he squeezed.

He maneuvered them away from the shower heads and jets until they faced the glass panels and water barely touched them. Reaching around her, he picked up the champagne bottle and poured the chilled liquid down the side of her neck.

The temperature differential made her gasp. He licked the champagne off her neck before gently biting and sucking the delicate skin.

Jake liked to mark her. He swore that he didn't, but he really did. And she liked it, too.

"Brace your hands on the glass and bend forward a little bit," he rasped.

He knelt behind her, his knees spread wide between her feet. She felt a trickle of chilled liquid on her back and knew he was pouring champagne down her spine.

His hot mouth sipped at the bubbly beverage, trailing from the middle of her back to the top of her butt crack. To her shock, he dipped his tongue between her butt cheeks.

She gasped his name and felt the hot kiss of his laughter on the sensitive skin of her rear. From behind, he slipped his hand between her thighs and stroked through the puff of hair. Finding her clit, he rubbed circles around it. Sensation gathered in that little collection of nerves, and her legs began to shake.

He moved his finger away from her clit and worked it inside

her. She moaned as her pussy clamped around his finger. Snaking his other arm around her, he palmed her mound in his big hand and squeezed. Then he slipped two fingers between her damp curls and began to massage her clit while he thrust his other finger into her in a slow, easy rhythm.

The steam created by the hot water made the air heavy. She gasped, trying to catch her breath, but Jake's hold never loosened, and his pace never faltered.

Desperate to come, she began to ride his hand, tightening her internal muscles whenever his finger slid inside. When Jake pressed his thumb against the tender rosette of her asshole, she came apart, screaming his name. The tile walls amplified her screams until her ears rang.

She collapsed against the glass panel, and Jake stood. His body surrounded her, tall and strong.

Cupping her hips in his hands, he placed his mouth against her ear. "Do you want me to pick you up and fuck you against the wall," he growled, "or do you want me to bend you over the seat and fuck you that way?"

His words sent a zing down her spine. It burst in her clit, and she quivered in his arms.

"I need to be inside you. Now. Tell me how you want it, or I'm going to decide for you."

She didn't bother to reply. She knew she would come either way.

Jake snatched the condom from the ledge, and she heard him rip it open with his teeth. He stepped back for a moment before he spun her around to face him. His eyes burned into her, no longer greenish-gold, but nearly black with arousal.

Gripping her waist with both hands, he lifted her. She spread her legs and hooked them over his hips. After centering himself against her opening, he slammed into her.

"Aw, fuck." He groaned deep in his throat. "I can't live without this." He pressed her back against the tile wall and began to pump into her. "I can't live without you."

She let her head fall back against the wall, her legs locked around his hips and her fingernails digging into his biceps. While he moved inside her with smooth, luscious drives, he spread kisses across her collarbone and the hollow of her throat.

Grunting, he hooked his forearm under her butt and held the back of her head in his palm. His fingers tangled in her hair, and he used the wet strands to pull her head back.

Their eyes met, and she could see her need reflected in his gaze. Pressure coiled low in her belly and spread to her womb.

"You're there," he panted. "Just let go. You're safe with me."

He shifted the angle of his pelvis, and his next thrust made fireworks erupt inside her. As her pussy rippled and clamped down on his erection, she cried out, "I love you. I love you. I love you."

He shuddered against her, and she watched him come. His entire body stiffened, and his lips pulled away from his teeth in a snarl. His penis jerked inside her, once, twice, three times, before he nuzzled his face into the valley between her breasts.

When their breathing slowed, he pulled out of her and let her legs drop to the floor. She was unsteady and trembling, and he secured her against the wall with his body.

"Kyla."

She looked up at him. He looked drugged, his pupils huge and his eyes unfocused.

"Did you mean it?" he asked.

"What?"

"You said you loved me. Did you mean it?"

*****

Jake was exhausted, mentally and physically, but he couldn't sleep. He rarely suffered from insomnia, and when he did, it was always because he was worried or unhappy.

But that wasn't the case tonight. He couldn't sleep because he was *too* happy. He had everything he'd ever wanted, including the love of the amazing woman lying next to him in bed.

He was one lucky bastard.

Earlier in the day, when he'd realized that he couldn't be Riley O'Brien & Co.'s CFO and be in a relationship with Kyla, he had felt angry and hopeless. He had been sure that lady luck had turned her back on him. But she hadn't.

Jake had never imagined that Kyla would make their relationship a priority over her career. If she hadn't agreed to resign from the finance department, he would have gone to Quinn and turned down the CFO gig. There were other CFO jobs with other companies, but there was only one Kyla Andrews.

After indulging in celebratory shower sex and take out from his favorite Greek restaurant, he and Kyla had talked about her decision. She had assured him that she had been intrigued by the idea of managing the trainee program, but had been afraid to take the risk.

Beside him, Kyla let out a little snore. He grinned into the darkness, grateful that he had the opportunity to learn all the quirks and conundrums and secrets that made Kyla the person she was.

Rolling over, he aligned his front to her back and began to count sheep. At sheep number fifteen, he noticed how good Kyla's face cream smelled. At sheep number twenty-two, he noticed that her nightgown had ridden up and exposed her thighs. At sheep number thirty-seven, he noticed how her ass perfectly nestled into the cradle of his pelvis. And at sheep number forty-four, he noticed that he had a hard-on that tented the front of his pajama pants.

He cursed under his breath. He knew she'd had a long day, too, and he wasn't going to wake her up just because he and his cock had insomnia.

He rolled over again, this time facing away from her and the temptation of her round ass. The down comforter felt heavy on his lower legs, so he kicked free of it and the top sheet. But once his feet were uncovered, the air circulating from the overhead ceiling fan turned his toes into ice cubes.

He shoved his feet back under the covers and flipped onto his back. He tried to fall asleep in that position, but his pillow, which had always been comfortable, made his neck ache.

And he still had a goddamn hard-on.

Desperate to get some sleep, he slid his hand under the drawstring waist of his pajamas and fisted his cock. He began to move his hand up and down, squeezing the head and shaft with every stroke.

Kyla stirred and rolled toward him. He froze, wondering if he'd disturbed her. When she didn't move again, he resumed his furtive fondling. With her lying right next to him, providing fodder for his masturbation reel, it wasn't long before he felt the familiar fiery burn at the base of his spine.

Suddenly, Kyla's hand covered his through his pajamas. "Need some help?" she whispered.

He couldn't help but laugh. Talk about getting caught red-handed.

"I couldn't sleep," he explained sheepishly. "I'm sorry I woke you up, sweetness."

Kyla didn't reply. She simply slipped her hand into his pajamas and nudged his hand away.

After rubbing her thumb over the tip of his cock and

spreading the pre-cum over the head and down the shaft, she picked up where he left off. Unsurprisingly, her soft hand felt a lot better than his callused mitt.

"I love your cock." Her sleep-husky voice raised goose bumps along his arms. "It's perfect. Not too big, not too small." The pace of her tugs increased. "It's nice and thick. I love the way it stretches me … the way it fills me."

Holy shit. Kyla is talking dirty to me.

Her words conjured an image of them in the shower, her head thrown back against the tile wall as he pounded into her. Blood rushed to his groin, hardening his cock even more.

"The next time you can't sleep, I'm going to use my mouth instead of my hand. I'm going to start off slowly, but then I'm going to put my tongue right here," —her thumb brushed over the slit crowning his cock— "and you're going to go crazy."

His breathing was erratic now, excited gusts and shallow pants. The burn had spread from his spine to his balls, and he knew he was close.

She traced the engorged vein running along the side of cock. "I'm going to suck you so deep. Would you like that?"

"God, yes," he gasped.

Rubbing the sensitive area on the underside of his cock just below the head, she said, "And I'm going to use my tongue on this spot right here. I'm going to play with you until you're pulling my hair and shoving your cock down my throat."

She moved her hand faster, her grip tightening on his shaft. "Will you come in my mouth or on my chest?"

And that was all it took. His orgasm slammed into him so hard, his back bowed off the bed. He erupted into her palm as she whispered a litany of praise, telling him how hot he was and how much she loved him.

"Kyla," he breathed.

She was sweet and dirty and perfect.

She laughed softly. "Sweet and dirty and perfect?"

He hadn't realized that he'd said any of that out loud, but he wasn't embarrassed that he had. He'd told her that he was done hiding his feelings for her, and he'd meant it.

"Yes. You're sweet and dirty and perfect. And you're *mine*."

"I don't know about the first part. But the last part is definitely true."

She pressed a chaste kiss on his mouth before bounding out of bed and padding to the bathroom. He checked the clock. They had gone to bed early, and it wasn't even midnight yet.

The bathroom door opened, and Kyla emerged. She'd pulled her hair into a ponytail, and without any make-up or jewelry, she looked like a sorority girl. She climbed into bed, settling on her side, and he rolled to face her.

Resting his hand on the curve of her hip, he said, "I love you, Kyla."

"I love you too."

"I know we haven't been seeing each other for very long, but I don't want to be with anyone else. I want us to be exclusive."

"So do I."

Thank God.

"Then it's settled. We're a couple. Jake and Kyla. Kyla and Jake."

She smiled. "My boyfriend is Riley O'Brien & Co.'s CFO."

"Not until July first."

Her smile faded. "July first," she repeated.

"What?" he asked, sensing that there was some significance with that date. "What's wrong?"

"July first is the day my dad died."

Stroking the blond wisps along her hairline, he asked, "How many years has he been gone?"

"Seven years." She shook her head. "Sometimes it feels like yesterday, and sometimes it feels like it never happened at all. Or it happened to another person ... another Kyla Andrews."

"How did he die?"

"Gunshot wound."

Jake hadn't expected that answer. "How did that happen?"

"My dad was a detective with the Massachusetts State Police. He was killed in the line of duty."

Because Kyla rarely spoke about her father, Jake hadn't known that the man had been a cop.

"Oh, sweetness. I'm so sorry you lost him that way."

"Me too."

"Law enforcement is dangerous work. I don't think people realize how dangerous."

"He got shot while investigating an illegal gambling ring based in Boston."

Holy shit. Was she kidding?

"Illegal gambling?" he croaked.

"You know, bookmaking."

Oh, yeah, Jake knew bookmaking. He was a fucking expert at it. He could teach a class on the subject.

"My dad and his partner, Brooks, were interviewing the leader of a huge bookmaking operation, a guy named Resene." Her lush mouth curled in disgust. "He didn't get his hands dirty. He had a network of people who did everything for him."

Bile rose in his throat. The only difference between Jake and Resene was that Jake's bookmaking operation was legal ... but only because it was based in Nevada. The exact same business was illegal in Massachusetts.

"My dad and Brooks went to the pub in South Boston where Resene ran his business. As you can imagine, it wasn't a safe place. One of Resene's guys had an itchy trigger finger. He shot first, and then everyone started shooting. My dad was hit six times. Five bullets hit his vest, but one hit about an inch below it. Right about here." She touched Jake low on his stomach. "It ricocheted inside him, damaging almost every major organ."

She sighed. "I didn't even know anything had happened to him. I had decided to stay in Ohio for the summer and take a couple of classes. I always turned my phone to silent when I was in class. When I saw a bunch of missed calls from my sister, I immediately knew something bad had happened to my dad. He died in surgery while I was standing in the Cincinnati airport waiting to catch a flight home."

Unshed tears pooled on her bottom eyelids. "There's actually more to the story, though."

Jesus, there's more?

"My dad was one of Resene's best clients. He had been for years. Somehow, he managed to keep the fact that he was a compulsive gambler a secret from everyone, even my mom. After he died, she found out that he'd opened more than twenty credit cards in her name. He'd also liquidated their retirement account. He trashed her credit and left her destitute."

Jake suddenly understood Kyla's desire to teach money management at the San Francisco Women's Center. Her mother had been a victim, not of physical abuse, but a victim nonetheless.

"Do you remember when the New England Patriots had an undefeated season, but lost to the Giants in the Super Bowl?" Kyla asked.

Jake remembered that football season vividly. Everyone had

thought the Patriots were a lock.

"Yeah. That was a bad beat."

She looked at him curiously. "What's a bad beat?"

"A wager that loses unexpectedly."

That Super Bowl game had ruined a lot of people financially. Too many people forgot that sports betting had nothing to do with skill, unlike other forms of gambling. Sports betting had everything to do with chance.

"Resene said my dad bet big on the Patriots, and when the Giants beat them, he didn't have the money to cover his losses."

"What was his figure?"

"Figure?"

"The amount he owed," Jake clarified.

"Two hundred thousand."

Jake winced. He didn't know how much a state police detective brought in annually, but it couldn't be more than sixty or seventy thousand. Paying off a debt more than three times that amount would be impossible.

"Did that include the vig?"

Her forehead furrowed. "What?"

Jake abruptly realized that he was giving himself away by asking such specific questions. A regular Joe wouldn't know sports betting terminology, even a well-used word like vig, which was the commission that bookies received on losing bets.

"When my dad couldn't cover his loses, Resene tried to blackmail him. But my dad decided to turn the tables. He tipped off the state police about Resene's operation. His plan was to take Resene down and wipe out his debt in one fell swoop."

Jake shook his head. "That plan never would have worked. When the police went through Resene's records, they would have found your dad's bets."

"Well, obviously, his plan didn't work because he's dead." She exhaled loudly. "My dad would still be alive today if not for gambling. I hate gambling. Cards, slot machines, tables. I hate it all. I don't even play the lottery. But sports betting is the worst. Bookies are like cockroaches. They should be exterminated."

CHAPTER ELEVEN

A couple of weeks after Kyla's dad had been murdered, she'd started having panic attacks. During the day, she'd been able to manage her grief. But at night, when her subconscious had taken over, her grief had broken free of the cage she'd shoved it in.

Her panic attacks had always struck while she slept, brought on by the same recurring nightmare. In the nightmare, Kyla was with her father at the pub when the shooting began. She stood by helplessly as bullets slammed into his body.

Night after night, she'd woken up drenched in sweat, her heart racing and her lungs laboring to pull in air. Finally, she had gone to the student health center on campus. The elderly doctor had prescribed medication taken before bed to prevent the panic attacks.

In less than a month, she'd been able to sleep through the night with no nightmares and no panic attacks. Shortly thereafter, she'd weaned herself off the medication.

But talking about her dad last night must have triggered something inside her brain because she'd just woken up in Jake's big bed, sweaty and breathless. She sat up with a hand pressed to her chest, her heartbeat thundering under her palm. It took her a moment to realize that Jake's side of the bed was empty.

She glanced at the alarm clock. It was a little after three o'clock in the morning. Where was her guy?

She slid out of bed and headed toward the bathroom. It was empty. She splashed cool water on her sweaty face and tidied her hair, which had slipped from its ponytail.

Deciding to look for Jake, she pulled one of his sweatshirts over her nightgown and wandered down the hall. Her fuzzy socks made it difficult to gain traction on the maple hardwood floors.

When she reached the living area, she spotted Jake and Charlie relaxing at the dining room table. Coffee mugs sat in front of them, along with a red Tupperware container. It was filled with a variety of cookies made by Kyla's mom.

Charlie saw her first. He nudged Jake's forearm to get his attention, and Jake glanced toward her. He looked like he'd aged ten years in less than five hours. His eyes were bloodshot, and deep grooves bracketed his mouth.

She ventured toward them, and Charlie rose from his seat and walked toward her. When they met in the middle of the room, he curled his hand over her shoulder.

"We can't change the past, Kyla. We can only change the course of our future."

She frowned. It was three in the morning, and he thought now was the time to channel Yoda? He squeezed her shoulder before disappearing down the hallway.

Jake stood as she approached the table. He was still wearing his version of sleep attire: a gray Stanford T-shirt and navy-blue and-white striped pajama pants.

He pulled out the chair that had become "Kyla's seat," and she sat down. After bringing her knees up to her chest, she tugged Jake's sweatshirt over her chilled legs.

"What's going on?" she asked. "I thought I took care of your insomnia earlier."

Her joke didn't garner a smile from Jake. If anything, it seemed to make him sad.

"What's going on?" she repeated, impatience underscoring her words.

He sighed. "I need to tell you something." His eyes met hers. "I'm afraid to tell you because I don't know how you're going to react, but I'm going to tell you anyway. I don't want to hide things from you. I don't want to hide the person I am or the things I've done."

Her mind galloped down a million different roads. Did he have an incurable disease? Did he have several children with multiple baby mamas? Did he have a criminal past?

"When I was a freshman in high school, I joined the math club."

Her breath whooshed out. "That's your big reveal?" she asked incredulously. "You were a nerd in high school?"

"Please, Kyla. Just listen."

Suitably chastised, she muttered, "Sorry."

"The club was unsupervised, and one day, some of the guys started making bets on the college football games that were scheduled that weekend. I didn't know enough about the teams to feel confident risking my money … my dad was stingy with my allowance. My friends got money for every A they received on their report card, but my dad refused to do that. He said knowledge was better than money."

"Your dad sounds like a smart guy," she said, wondering why Jake was sharing this information with her now.

"He has a genius IQ. It's helpful in his line of work."

A rogue thought skipped through Kyla's mind. If she and Jake had kids, there was a good chance they'd be ginger-haired geniuses who loved math.

"What does your dad do?"

"He's a professional poker player. Texas Hold'em is his game."

That took her by surprise. Last night, when they'd discussed gambling, would have been a perfect time for Jake to mention that his dad played poker for a living. But he hadn't.

She suspected Jake had kept quiet because she had been so vocal in her dislike of everything related to gambling. Although she had reserved her contempt for bookies, her disdain for all types of gambling had been evident. She'd flat out said that she hated everything about it. There wasn't a lot of room for misunderstanding there.

"I've never known anyone who plays poker professionally. That must have been interesting when you were growing up."

"He's one of the best, and for about a minute, I thought about becoming a professional poker player too."

"I'm glad you didn't. I wouldn't want to be with someone who gambles."

Jake rolled his lips inward. "Yeah, I got that message loud and clear last night when you told me about your dad."

"Gambling ruins peoples' lives."

"Sometimes. But sometimes it's just entertainment, like going to the movies. And sometimes it's an expensive hobby, like golf or skiing."

"I don't agree," she countered. "It's addictive, like drugs or alcohol."

He rubbed one of his hands over his face. "*Shit.*"

She picked up the Tupperware container and popped off the

top. After a brief review of the contents she nabbed an oatmeal raisin cookie and took a bite.

Once she'd swallowed, she asked, "Why are we having a philosophical discussion about gambling at three in the morning?"

"Because you have a real problem with it … with good reason." He swallowed audibly. "And because I own one of the largest independent sports books in Vegas."

She deconstructed Jake's sentences, trying to string his words together in a way that made sense. He watched her the whole time, waiting patiently for her to process what he had said.

"You're a bookie."

He nodded. "I started taking bets on college football games when I was fourteen. From there it just kept growing. I'm not involved in the day-to-day operations of the business anymore, but I'm still the majority owner. It has an annual handle of nearly fifty million dollars."

She'd heard his words. But more important, she'd heard the pride underlying them.

Jake was proud that he was a bookie. He was proud that he took money from desperate people … desperate people like her dad. He was proud that he ruined lives … the way her dad's life had been ruined.

Russell Andrews hadn't been the man she thought he was. And neither was Jake Lilliard.

She'd thought she had found a good man … a man who would love her and respect her … a man who would be the kind of father that she'd never had … a man she could trust.

She vaulted to her feet with such force that the chair toppled backward. The cookie she'd held in her hand was now crumbled at her feet.

"You're … you're just like Resene," she accused, her voice shaking with anger and disappointment and a million other horrible emotions.

Jake slowly rose from the table. "No, I am not," he denied, his voice harder and sharper than a diamond-bladed knife. "I own a business where people can *legally* bet on sports. I have *never* broken any laws related to gambling. And I have *never* been investigated by the police, the FBI, or the Nevada Gaming Control Board."

"It doesn't matter if it's legal or illegal!" She shoved her finger at him. "How many people have been bankrupted because of you? How many people have died because of you?"

She looked around at the luxurious penthouse. She had wondered how he could afford such a nice place. Now she knew that he'd paid for the condo with tainted money.

"I can't be here. I need to leave."

She spun around, and he caught her bicep in a tight grip. "It's not safe for you to be wandering around in the middle of the night," he growled. "If you want to go home, I'll drive you."

"In the car you bought with money you made from being a bookie?" She jerked her arm free. "No thanks."

He closed his eyes, took a deep breath, and slowly exhaled. Opening his eyes, he said, "I stayed up half the night talking to Charlie. He thought I shouldn't tell you about the sports book. He thought I should just sell the business with you none the wiser. Only a few people in San Francisco know about it, and odds are that you would never have found out. But I didn't want this to shadow our relationship."

He placed his hand on his chest, over his heart. "I want you to *know* me. I want you to accept the choices I've made in the past and love me anyway."

Her throat was too clogged with tears for her to reply. And even if she had been able to talk, she had nothing to say.

*****

"Come on! Open up!" Vanessa's bellow easily penetrated Kyla's bedroom door. "You've been in there for twelve hours straight. Don't you need to pee?"

Kyla ignored her. She didn't want to see or talk to anyone, not even her older sister.

Unfortunately, Vanessa kept talking. "You've been crying all day. You're probably dehydrated." Something hit the door. It sounded like her sister had kicked it. "Just tell me what happened? Did Jake hurt you?"

After a moment, Kyla heard her sister leave. The sharp click of her heels grew fainter as she moved down the hall.

Vanessa's question echoed in Kyla's head. *Did Jake hurt you?*

Hurt seemed like such an inadequate word for what Jake had done. He had devastated her. Destroyed her. Disillusioned her.

Rolling over, she pulled her knees to her chest. Her entire body ached, especially her heart.

She heard footsteps again, quieter than before. Vanessa must have slipped off her stilettos. The footsteps stopped at Kyla's door. A moment later, the door knob jiggled. Her older sister was nothing if not persistent.

Suddenly, the door knob fell to the floor. One of Vanessa's eyes appeared in the round hole, and then her hand wiggled through it. Somehow, she managed to rotate her wrist so her fingers could undo the lock.

"Abracadabra," Vanessa muttered.

Kyla jumped up from the bed just as the door swung open. Her sister stood framed in the opening with her feet spread wide and her hands on her hips in a stance reminiscent of Wonder Woman.

Her blond hair was in a ballerina bun, and she wore a tight black dress with long sleeves and a cowl neck. A wide black belt studded with vertical jet black beads cinched her slender waist, and a pair of pink pig slippers decorated her feet.

She strolled inside, kicking the door shut behind her. "Hey, Ky, how's your day going?" she asked casually, as if she hadn't just removed a door knob to break into Kyla's bedroom.

Kyla opened her mouth to tell Vanessa to get out, but a sob escaped instead. Her sister took two steps and enveloped her in a honeysuckle-scented embrace.

"Oh, baby sister," she crooned. "What am I going to do with you?"

Vanessa's concern stripped away Kyla's defenses, and she cried on her sister's shoulder until her eyes were nearly swollen shut. When her tears had mostly dried up, she left her bedroom without a word because Vanessa had been right—she did need to pee.

After taking care of that immediate need, Kyla wiped her face with a cold washcloth and brushed her hair and teeth. When she stepped out of the bathroom, she noticed Vanessa leaning against the wall, typing on her phone.

"I ordered your favorite orange peel shrimp before I let myself into your room. It'll be here in ten minutes." She looked up from her phone. "That gives you just enough time to take a quick shower. Then we're going to eat, and you're going to tell me what happened with Jake so we can fix this."

Kyla was too tired to argue with her steamroller ... oops ... her *sister* ... so she trudged back into the bathroom. Twelve minutes later, she stepped out of the shower. She made quick work of drying off and threw on a loose purple tunic, charcoal leggings, and her favorite stretchy ballet flats.

Feeling refreshed, she headed into the kitchen where she found Vanessa scooping brown rice from a white takeout container onto bright orange plates. At least Alan's influence hadn't extended to the china … yet.

As Kyla pulled open a drawer to gather the silverware, Vanessa said, "Okay, it's time for you to start talking."

"I don't know where to start."

"I'm more interested in the end." Vanessa carefully spooned orange peel shrimp on top of the rice. "What did you and Jake fight about?"

"He's a bookie."

Vanessa's head swung toward Kyla, her face etched with surprise. "What?"

"Jake is a bookie."

Her sister's eyebrows climbed up her forehead. "Sports betting is illegal in California. He could go to prison if he got caught." She methodically began to close the takeout containers. "Did you ask him why he was doing something so risky? Does he need to make extra money?"

"He started the business when he lived in Las Vegas. He's not involved in the day-to-day operations anymore."

"So, he's not doing anything illegal."

"Does it really matter if it's legal or illegal?"

Vanessa's eyes widened. "Are you being serious right now? Of course it matters. It's the difference between working in a high-rise office building or working out in a high-security prison yard."

"He's still profiting from someone's bad luck."

"So what?"

"He's taking advantage of desperate people. He's ruining their lives."

Vanessa turned and leaned against the countertop. She studied Kyla for a long moment before asking, "Is this about Dad?"

"Gambling ruined his life. It killed him, Sass."

Vanessa's expression softened. "Kyla. Think about what you're saying. Gambling didn't ruin Dad's life. He ruined it. Gambling didn't kill him. A guy with a gun killed him."

Kyla absorbed Vanessa's words. She let them sink into her mind and her heart, acknowledging the veracity of what her sister had said.

"Dad made his own choices, Ky, and he made the wrong ones." Vanessa slowly shook her head back and forth. "He made the choice to do something illegal. He made the choice to lie to Mom and steal from her. He made the choice to go after Resene instead of paying his debt." She exhaled noisily. "Those choices ruined his life. Those choices killed him. Not gambling."

Vanessa picked up the glass of chardonnay near her left hand and took a sip. "You're looking for someone or something to blame other than Dad, but he is the one who is responsible for the way his life turned out."

Kyla knew her sister was right. Their father had made the choice to lie, steal, and break the law. And when he had investigated Resene's illegal gambling organization, he hadn't done it because he wanted to uphold the law, he'd done it for selfish reasons.

"You took the negative emotions you had for Dad—all the rage and disappointment and sorrow—and transferred them to gambling."

Kyla met her sister's loving gaze. "And then I transferred them to Jake."

"Yes."

Kyla pressed her hands against her face. "How do I fix this? I said some hateful things to him—things he didn't deserve."

"You can fix it by saying some loving things to him—things he *does* deserve."

CHAPTER TWELVE

It took more than an hour of cuddling, but the newborn named Shea finally stopped crying and drifted to sleep.

Jake stared down at the baby girl tucked in the crook of his arm. She was only six days old, and her entire head fit in the palm of his hand.

Her mother was a thirteen-year-old girl who had been rescued from a trafficking ring that kept its sex slaves doped up on heroin. Her father was one of at least a thousand johns who'd paid for the pleasure of raping her mother.

Jake hoped that Baby Shea's life would be better than her mother's. No one should ever have to suffer the way that girl had suffered. And he hoped those johns found their way to hell sooner rather than later.

Careful not to jostle the baby, Jake stood and placed her in the neonatal crib. He lightly rested his hand on her chest for a minute to make sure that she didn't wake up.

Brenda, one of the older nurses in the neonatal department, came to stand beside him. "How's she doing?"

"Better. But still not good."

She patted his back. "I could say the same about you."

After Kyla had left his condo in the wee hours of the morning, Jake had dressed and driven to Saint Phil's. He'd taken a personal day from Riley O'Brien & Co., and he'd cuddled babies on and off for the past fourteen hours or so.

He was exhausted, and he really should go home. But he couldn't make himself leave the hospital. His condo was no longer a sanctuary. It was now a place that reminded him of the few brief days of happiness he'd experienced with Kyla.

Brenda lightly touched his forearm. "It looks like there's someone here to see you, Jake."

She pointed, and he followed the direction of her finger. Kyla stood in the hallway, visible through the wall of windows that fronted the nursery, and he swore his heart stopped for a moment.

"I'll see you later," he told Brenda.

As he headed toward the heavy double doors that secured the nursery from the rest of the hospital, he tore off the paper gown that he was required to wear when he cuddled the babies. Under the gown, he wore an old Red Hot Chili Peppers concert tee and faded Rileys.

He swiped his security badge over the reader, pumped some anti-bacterial foam onto his hands, and exited the nursery. Rubbing his hands together, he approached Kyla and stopped a couple of feet away from her.

She turned to face him, and he couldn't help but grimace. She looked like he felt. Her eyes were puffy and bloodshot, her usual creamy complexion was blotchy, and her lips were chapped. Even so, she was beautiful.

"Hi." She smiled tentatively, her apprehension obvious. "I hope you don't mind that I tracked you down here."

"It's fine. How did you know I was at Saint Phil's?"

"I stopped by the condo first. Charlie told me where to find you."

He wanted to touch her so badly his hands were shaking, so he shoved them into the front pockets of his Rileys. She tracked the movement with her eyes before bringing them back to his face.

"Why did you come here, Kyla?"

"I wanted to apologize to you"

Her answer absolutely floored him. He had never imagined that she would show up at Saint Phil's, intent on apologizing. He'd spent the entire day thinking that his luck had finally run out. But maybe it hadn't.

"I said some really hateful things to you this morning," she continued. "And you did nothing to deserve them. I'm sorry for that."

"It's okay."

And it really was. Kyla wasn't the only person on the planet who had a problem with gambling. He'd known that telling her about his sports book operation was extremely risky given what had happened to her father. But the reward was a relationship built on honesty, trust, and acceptance—a relationship that would last. And that was what he wanted with her.

"It's not okay," she countered fiercely. "I'm surprised you want to talk to me after the way I acted this morning."

"I really don't want to talk to you. I want to go home and sleep for ten hours straight."

"Oh." She nodded. "Okay."

As she turned away from him, he grasped her elbow. "Where are you going?" She looked up at him, and he was alarmed to see that her eyes glittered with tears. "What's wrong? What did I say?"

"I'm going home."

Abruptly realizing that she had misunderstood his earlier comment, he said, "No, you're not. You're coming with me." He stroked his fingers over the apple of her cheek. "When I said that I wanted to go home and sleep for ten hours straight, I meant that I wanted to go home *with you* and sleep for ten hours straight *with you*."

A huge smile lifted her luscious mouth. "Okay." Her smile faded. "We still need to talk, though. I want to explain some things to you."

"We can talk in the morning." He curved his hand around her nape. "You need to know that I will do anything to make things right between us. Anything. I'll shutter the business tomorrow and never take another bet. Or I'll sell it, and if you want me to, I'll donate the proceeds to Gamblers Anonymous. Just tell me what you want me to do, and I'll do it."

"No, Jake. I don't want you to do either of those things unless *you* want to do them." She gazed up at him. "I just want you to love me as much as I love you."

He leaned down and brushed his mouth over hers. "That's a sure bet."

EPILOGUE

Six months later

The cork made a loud pop as it exploded from the green champagne bottle. Golden liquid bubbled over Jake's fingers before he hastily filled the two crystal flutes.

After returning the bottle to the silver bucket, he picked up a flute in each hand and met Kyla in front of the floor-to-ceiling windows. The bright lights of Las Vegas glittered against the dark desert sky. She spun toward him, her periwinkle-shaded dress belling outward with the motion.

"What do you think of my hometown?" he asked as he passed her a flute.

"It's smaller than I thought it would be. And not as loud."

He chuckled. "Trust me, it's loud. We're just staying at one of the most exclusive hotels in the city, and we're in the penthouse suite. The whole place is probably soundproofed."

She licked her lush lower lip. "That's good since I can get a little noisy."

His cock twitched, and he gave himself a silent directive to stop thinking about the sweet sounds she made when he slid into her tight, wet pussy. He held up his flute for a toast, and she mimicked his movement.

"What are we toasting?" she asked.

"What do you think we should toast?"

"We could toast to professional success."

He laughed. "That's not very romantic, sweetness."

Her light laughter joined his. "Maybe not, but I'm thankful our jobs are going so well. You got through your first five months as CFO successfully, and the changes I've made to the management trainee program have been well received."

He nodded. "That's true. What else?"

She tilted her head, and a long strand of hair brushed her shoulder. The tendril was the exact same color as the bubbly liquid in her flute.

"We could toast Garrett for treating us to a mini-vacation in his hotel."

Somehow, Jake and Garrett had become friends. The hotelier had called Jake after his promotion had been announced and invited him out for drinks to celebrate his new gig. Although Jake had been surprised, he had accepted Garrett's offer, and now they hung out whenever Garrett was in town.

"We can thank him at the New Year's Eve party."

Kyla nodded. "Okay, how about a toast to Vanessa for finally kicking Alan to the curb?"

He couldn't stop his upper lip from curling in disgust. "*Asshole.*"

She giggled. "What do *you* think we should toast?"

"How about we toast to our sixth-month anniversary?"

"The best six months of my life."

"Mine too."

She smiled slowly, her pink lips tipping up at the corners. "How would you feel about this toast: to many more anniversaries?"

"I like that one."

They tapped their flutes together and chorused the toast. Kyla took a sip of champagne.

"*Mmm*, this is delicious."

A droplet of liquid shimmered on her lower lip, and he ignored his own champagne in favor of licking the curve of her mouth. The dry, crisp coolness of the alcohol mixed with Kyla's sweet taste. "*Mmm*, you're delicious."

She laughed softly before asking, "What's the plan for tonight?"

"We have a reservation in an hour for dinner followed by some dancing."

"Hmm," she murmured. "I have another plan."

She returned her champagne flute to the wood credenza and slowly, deliberately, untied the belt on her dress. Once it was loose, she flicked open the top button near her cleavage.

His cock thickened, and his heart began to pound like the furious beat of a rock anthem. He took a gulp of champagne, hoping to cool himself down.

"No," he countered. "We're going to stick to my plan."

She shook her head. "My plan is better."

She deftly opened the rest of her buttons, and the dress slid from her curvy body to pool at her feet. She stood before him in a lacy, cream-colored bra, and matching bikini panties. She turned, and he groaned when he saw the smooth globes of her ass and the narrow strip of lace nestled between them.

She made her way to the double doors leading to the bedroom, her round ass swaying. He followed silently, enjoying the view. Once inside the bedroom, she crawled onto the huge king bed on her hands and knees before rolling to her side and propping her head in her hand.

"My plan is *a lot* better," she purred.

He bypassed the bed in favor of the dresser. Opening the top drawer, he pulled out the leather case that held the engagement ring he'd picked out. He took a deep breath and then another when the first one didn't do anything to calm him.

He turned back toward her, the box in his palm. Her gaze locked on it, and she clambered to her knees.

"Jake," she gasped, "is that … are you … oh, my God …"

Reaching the edge of the bed, he opened the box and turned it so she could see the ring inside. She gasped again and placed her hands on her chest.

"Kyla, I want your face to be the first thing I see in the morning and the last thing I see at night." Emotion clogged his throat, making his voice hoarse. "I want you in my bed and in my heart and in my life forever."

Tears welled in her eyes. "Oh, Jake, I want the same thing."

"I want to hear your sweet voice say, 'This is my husband, Jake.' I want your children to be my children."

The tears spilled over her lashes and rolled down her cheeks. She roughly brushed them away with shaking fingers.

"There are so many things I want, and they all begin and end with you, Kyla. Will you marry me?"

She nodded, and he removed the ring from its velvet bed and slid the delicate platinum band onto her finger. Small white diamonds made a halo around the five-carat oval sapphire.

"Why did you pick a sapphire?" she asked.

"Because my girl likes color."

She threw herself at him, wrapping her arms around his neck and pressing her wet cheek against him. "I love you so much," she whispered.

"I love you, too, sweetness." He dusted kisses on her cheeks, forehead, and chin. "I planned to ask you to marry me after dinner, but…"

She drew back to stare into his eyes. "But what?"

"I just couldn't wait any longer."

She smiled. "Do you have any other plans I should know about?"

"I planned for us to have a short engagement and get married before Valentine's Day. And I've already contacted a realtor so we can start looking for houses."

Her smile widened. "I have a better plan."

"No," he countered. "I'm sure my plan is just about perfect."

She shook her head, and he sighed. He really hoped she didn't want a long engagement.

"What does your plan involve, exactly?" he asked warily.

"It involves us getting married here. Tonight."

His heart stuttered. "Tonight?"

"Yes. Tonight."

"You're right," he admitted. "Your plan is better. *A lot better.*"

Will Never Fade

CHAPTER ONE

Party. Get-together. Bash. Fete. Shindig. Celebrating New Year's Eve with a bunch of tipsy strangers wasn't Phoebe Werner's idea of a good time. She would much rather hang out with a small group of people at home.

But she hadn't lived in San Francisco long enough to make more than a handful of friends, and she refused to sit in her apartment alone on this special night, especially since there had been a time when she'd wondered if she would live to see the new year.

Pulling the glittery invitation from her beaded clutch, Phoebe double-checked the address for the party. She wasn't familiar with this part of the city, even though it was only a few blocks from Riley Plaza, the skyscraper in which she worked.

She didn't want to go to the wrong location and end up wandering around, alone and in the dark. Given the way she was dressed, someone might mistake her for a hooker.

She glanced at the oversized metal numbers hanging above the high-rise's sliding glass doors. This was the right place.

After tucking the invitation back into her clutch, Phoebe thanked the Uber driver. She opened the door and climbed out as gracefully as possible, tugging down her short skirt so she wouldn't flash anyone.

Once she was inside the building, she checked in with the security guard behind the reception desk and followed his directions to the elevator bank. As she waited, she evaluated her reflection in the mirrored surface of the elevator doors.

She barely recognized the woman staring back at her. She wasn't the same Phoebe she had been three years ago.

It wasn't just the sparkly silver tank top and tight black skirt, although she rarely wore such sexy or revealing clothes. And it wasn't the smoky eye shadow and bright red lipstick, although she couldn't remember the last time she'd worn this much makeup, if ever.

I'm different. Inside and out.

The elevator dinged, the mirrored panels opening with a *swoosh*. She followed a couple of people into the cab and pressed the button for the twenty-fourth floor.

Moments later she stood in front of a natural maple door. Music filtered from inside, a song she didn't recognize. As she lifted her fist to knock, she wondered if anyone would even hear her.

Her hand trembled just a little, and she clenched it into a tighter fist. She hadn't been to a party like this since ... *before* ... and she was nervous. For a moment she thought about turning around and going home. Would it really be so bad to welcome the new year wearing her favorite pajamas and eating a bowl of rocky road ice cream?

Her clutch vibrated in her other hand, signaling a text, and she fished out her phone to read it. The message was from Kyla Lilliard, her closest friend in San Francisco. Kyla and her new husband, Jake, were hosting the party.

"Where are you?" Kyla's text read.

Phoebe typed her reply, "At the door."

Before she could knock, the door flew open, revealing Kyla on the other side. The curvy blonde grasped Phoebe's hand and tugged her into the foyer.

"You're finally here!" Kyla squealed.

Phoebe couldn't help but smile at the other woman's exuberance. She probably had wondered if Phoebe was going to show up at all. It was late—only about forty minutes 'til midnight.

Phoebe had waffled about whether to attend the party. Eventually, though, she had decided to come. Kyla was one of the sweetest women Phoebe had ever known, and she hadn't wanted to hurt her feelings by snubbing her invitation.

"Thanks for inviting me," Phoebe said, brushing back one of the dark curls that had fallen into her face.

Kyla gave her a brief hug. "I'm so glad you came."

The two of them had known each other for less than a year, but it seemed as if they'd been friends forever. They both worked for Riley O'Brien & Co., the nation's oldest designer and manufacturer of blue jeans. People around the world wore its signature jeans, known as Rileys.

Draping her arm over Phoebe's shoulders, Kyla brought her deeper into the apartment before turning to face her. "Let me take your coat."

Kyla held out a hand tipped with raspberry-colored nails. They were a perfect match for her slinky, sleeveless dress, which sparkled with strategically placed sequins.

Phoebe unwound the soft red scarf from her neck. Made of cashmere, it was a favorite piece, one she'd knitted herself. After shoving it into her pocket along with her clutch and phone, she shrugged out of her coat and passed it to the other woman.

"Stay right here," Kyla ordered. "I'm going to put this in my bedroom. I'll be right back."

As Kyla headed down the corridor, her silver metallic stilettos clacking on the gray slate floor, Phoebe glanced around the spacious apartment. Housing in the Bay Area was outrageously expensive, especially compared to her hometown of Boise, Idaho. She could only imagine how high the monthly mortgage on a place like this would be.

Jake must be doing pretty well if he could afford this apartment. Of course, he had recently been promoted to CFO of Riley O'Brien & Co., and he'd probably received a significant raise.

The apartment had an open floorplan, and the kitchen, dining room, and living room flowed together. Floor-to-ceiling windows provided an amazing view of the San Francisco skyline.

Through the crowd, Phoebe could see several people mingling outside on the balcony. To her surprise, she recognized quite a few of the revelers. Maybe she wasn't going to welcome the new year surrounded by strangers after all.

As her gaze wandered, it landed on a tall guy across the room. His back was to her, but he reminded her of someone she used to know ... someone she had wanted from the first moment she had seen him smile.

His dark hair was short, and a black dress shirt stretched over his broad shoulders. A black leather belt cinched his lean waist, and his black trousers outlined his butt. It looked tight and squeezable even from twenty feet away.

"Do you want something to drink? Beer? Wine? Something non-alcoholic?"

Phoebe snapped her head toward Kyla, surprised her friend

had returned already. "I'll have some wine. Chardonnay if you have it."

With a nod, Kyla skirted the granite bar that separated the kitchen from the dining room and living area. She plucked a bottle from the counter and poured a splash of Napa Valley vintage into a plastic wine goblet.

Kyla's glossy lips tilted into a small smile. "Fancy, huh?" she asked, passing the wine to Phoebe.

She laughed. "Very. I should have worn a ball gown and a tiara."

"And we have champagne for later."

After pouring herself a glass of ruby red wine, Kyla tapped her goblet against Phoebe's and took a sip. Her silvery-gray gaze swept over Phoebe.

"I like that top," she said, gesturing toward Phoebe's tank with her wine goblet. "Your girls look good."

Phoebe looked down, grimacing a little when she saw the expanse of exposed cleavage. "Too much?"

"No." Kyla shook her head emphatically. "You look hot."

Surprised, but pleased, Phoebe said, "Thanks."

She'd had to buy a new outfit for the party because her old "going out" clothes had no longer fit. By habit, she'd started her search in the plus size section, as she'd done since she had been a pre-teen. But then she'd remembered that those sizes were now too large. Shopping in the regular section was just another reminder of the changes she'd experienced.

"It's so good to see you," Kyla said. "I missed you."

Phoebe had spent the weeks before and after Christmas in Boise. Her entire family lived there. She was the only Werner who had dared to leave the state.

"We texted every day while I was gone," Phoebe pointed out.

Shaking her head, Kyla said, "Texting is a poor substitute for meaningful conversation."

"Meaningful?" Phoebe repeated with a laugh. "When do we have meaningful conversations?"

Kyla giggled. "Good point."

Just then, Margo May appeared beside them. "Phoebe!" she exclaimed, her mouth lifting in a delighted smile. "I was hoping you would be here!"

Margo reminded Phoebe of sunshine. Just being in the other woman's presence warmed her up and brightened her day.

Margo gave Phoebe a careful hug, mindful of the wine she held. The younger woman wore a halter dress with a glittery lace bodice in a hue somewhere between emerald green and teal. It looked amazing with her strawberry blond hair, dark blue eyes, and creamy complexion.

"How was your visit to Asheville?" Phoebe asked Margo.

"Wonderful. I was so sad to leave."

Margo's husband, Zeke, had grown up in North Carolina. They had decided to spend their first Christmas as a married couple with his family.

"The Mays are the most incredible family," Margo added. "They're not dysfunctional at all."

Phoebe laughed. "*Every* family is dysfunctional."

"Is your family?" Kyla asked.

"They are if you consider nosy and overprotective to be dysfunctional."

"Okay, then the Mays are a bit dysfunctional." Margo's eyes narrowed speculatively as she gazed at Phoebe. "You know, Zeke's youngest brother, Noah, is single. He's a really nice guy. And good-looking, too … almost as good-looking as Zeke."

That comment gave Phoebe pause because Zeke was F-I-N-

E. If Noah was even half as good-looking as his older brother, then he was hot with a capital H.

Margo tipped her head toward Phoebe. "Noah's coming to visit next month. Maybe you and he could go out and do something fun." Her lips twitched. "Or stay in and do something fun."

Before Phoebe could express her lack of interest in either option, Zeke joined them. Like Phoebe and Kyla, he also worked for Riley O'Brien & Co. He'd joined the organization after serving in the Army for more than a decade. Supply chain and logistics was his forte.

Margo and Zeke had met when she'd moved to San Francisco to join a local veterinary practice. She had needed a place to live, and Zeke had needed someone to help with the rent.

It was easy to see why he had fallen head-over-heels for his roommate. Frankly, it was impossible not to love Margo. He hadn't stood a chance against her extreme lovability.

Zeke wrapped his arms around his wife from behind and nuzzled her ear. "I love you, Go-go." He must have been oblivious to the fact that his deep voice was audible over the music because he added, "You're the best thing that's ever happened to me. I don't know what I did to deserve you."

He also must have been oblivious to the fact that he had an audience in the form of Phoebe and Kyla because he nudged his wife's head to the side to give him access to her neck. As he lavished kisses on it, he said, "Let's go home and make a baby. I want a mini Go-go so badly."

Margo glanced at Kyla and Phoebe, amusement sparkling in her eyes. "Looks like someone's had a little too much to drink."

Phoebe wondered if the newlyweds really were trying to get

pregnant or if that was just the alcohol talking. Although they had been married for only six months or so, Zeke was quite a bit older than his wife, nearing forty. This was his second marriage, and he probably wanted to have children sooner rather than later.

Margo gave them a little wave. "I'll see you later. Happy New Year!" She led her husband away, leaving Phoebe and Kyla alone.

"There's someone I want you to meet," Kyla announced.

"Male or female?" Phoebe asked suspiciously.

A naughty smile curved Kyla's mouth. "Definitely male."

"I already told you that I'm not interested in meeting any guys."

Kyla's smile widened. "Trust me, Phoebe. You want to meet this one. I've told him all about you."

"I should have stayed home," she muttered.

Laughing, Kyla grasped Phoebe's hand. "He's nice. You'll like him. I promise."

With Phoebe's hand gripped snugly within hers, Kyla left the kitchen, weaving her way through the crowd. Phoebe trailed after her, nearly dragging her feet.

She didn't want to meet a nice guy. It would just remind her of the things she wanted desperately but could never have—a long, happy life with a loving husband and a houseful of kids.

Kyla stopped abruptly, and Phoebe careened into her, bobbling her wine. She barely managed not to spill it down her front. As she clutched the plastic goblet, she heard a deep laugh. It reminded her of another laugh … another man. Pleasurable tingles danced up and down her spine.

"I found her," Kyla announced, letting go of Phoebe's hand and shifting to the side.

Phoebe stared at the broad back she had ogled earlier, and the man turned to face her. He was taller than she'd thought, probably close to six-three. Even in her heels, she barely reached his shoulders.

She glanced up, past the onyx buttons on his shirt and the tan column of his strong neck, over a square jaw covered with dark stubble to a set of full lips and a straight, bold nose. Finally, she met his eyes, the same bright turquoise of the Caribbean and edged with long, sooty lashes the exact shade as his thick, shiny hair.

No. It couldn't be.

"Garrett?" she breathed.

All the blood drained from her head, making spots dance in her vision. Closing her eyes, she breathed deeply. His scent overwhelmed her, the spicy notes of his cologne mixing with a darker, more potent aroma that was all him.

She lifted her eyelids and met his gaze, the pulsing music fading into the background. Those amazing eyes widened in shock. "Phoebe?"

"You know each other?" Kyla asked, looking back and forth between them.

With her gaze captured by Garrett's, Phoebe couldn't do anything but nod. Her lips were stiff and dry, so she licked them. His ocean-blue eyes dropped to her mouth before snapping back up.

"You do?" Kyla asked, a bewildered note in her voice. "How?"

CHAPTER TWO

Garrett Gale had never expected to lay eyes on Phoebe Werner again. The last time he'd seen her she'd been curled up in his bed, deliciously naked. And he had been right beside her, equally naked.

"How do you guys know each other?" Kyla asked.

Somehow, he managed to drag his eyes away from Phoebe and focus his attention on Kyla. She moved closer to Jake, and her husband looped his arm around her slender waist and pulled her against his side.

Garrett could barely think … could barely comprehend that the woman he had wanted almost to the point of obsession stood right in front of him. His chest felt tight and achy, just like when he'd had that bad chest cold last year. He took a deep breath, and then another, trying to lessen the pressure.

"How do you guys know each other?" Kyla repeated with sharp impatience.

He shook his head, trying to get his brain and his mouth to work in concert. "We were…"

Classmates. Study partners. Friends. Lovers.

When he couldn't finish his sentence, Phoebe stepped in to

explain, "We went to grad school together at the University of Washington."

"Oh." Disappointment shaded Kyla's voice. "I was so excited to introduce you to each other."

Garrett arched his eyebrows. "*Phoebe* is the friend you wanted me to meet?" he asked, unable to keep the surprise out of his voice.

Kyla had described her friend as cute, sweet, and funny, but painfully shy. Phoebe was all those things and more, but he'd never imagined that Kyla had been talking about the woman who had crawled out of his bed in the middle of the night while he'd slept ... the woman who had ignored his phone calls, emails, and texts after he'd touched every inch of her body.

Jake shifted beside Garrett, drawing his gaze. The other man's hazel eyes gleamed with curiosity, but after a moment, that curiosity morphed into pity. Jake knew what it was like to want a woman so much your guts were constantly twisted into knots.

Although more than three years had passed since Garrett and Phoebe's one and only night together, time hadn't dulled his memories. Not a day went by that he didn't think of her.

But this Phoebe—the one in the low-cut tank top and mini-skirt—didn't look like the woman with whom he'd shared the hottest, most intense sex of his life. He hadn't recognized her, not until she'd said his name, and he'd looked into her moss green eyes.

She'd lost a lot of weight, too much in his opinion. He knew most people would have described the old Phoebe as overweight, but he'd thought she was perfect. Her plump curves had made him harder than any other woman ever had.

Her hair was different, though. When he'd known her, it had been long and straight like a waterfall of dark chocolate. She'd usually worn it in a ponytail or braid, and he'd teased her by tugging on it, just like a little boy in elementary school.

Now her hair was a short cap of springy curls. He wondered how long it had taken her to arrange it into those soft-looking corkscrews.

Bringing his gaze back to Phoebe, he asked, "How do you know Kyla?"

Kyla answered his question instead of Phoebe. "We were in Riley O'Brien & Co.'s management trainee program together."

Familiar with the program, he nodded. When he'd met Kyla, she had been only days from finishing her final rotation. And after she had graduated, she'd taken a gig managing the other trainees.

Kyla continued, "Phoebe has only one more rotation before she graduates and moves on to a permanent position."

Garrett wanted to know more about Phoebe, but he wanted her to respond to his questions, not Kyla. And he wanted to be alone with Phoebe when they talked. Maybe then he would get the answers he really wanted.

Before he could find a way to excuse Phoebe and himself from the group, Jake's best friend, Charlie Shipley, interrupted their conversation. The other man's dark hair was disheveled, and behind his eyeglasses, his coffee-colored eyes were unfocused. He had obviously imbibed more than his fair share of alcohol.

"Ky, you have to put in a good word for me with Vanessa," Charlie wheedled. "I think we're soul mates."

Kyla's older sister, Vanessa, was on the market again after breaking up with her long-time boyfriend Alan Toft. Kyla had detested him, and she was thrilled about her sister's newly single status. But Garrett doubted she would encourage a relationship between Vanessa and Charlie.

"You and Vanessa are not soul mates," Kyla told Charlie matter-of-factly.

Charlie lowered his eyebrows. "How do you know?" he challenged.

"Trust me when I say that she would chew you up and spit you out," Kyla replied.

"It would be my preference if she swallowed."

Garrett slanted a sideways glance at Jake. The other man coughed loudly in a valiant effort to disguise his laughter, but Garrett recognized a fake cough when he heard one.

As Jake pretended to hack into his hand, his hazel gaze gauged his wife's reaction to Charlie's comment. Kyla's eyes were huge, like a cartoon character with its eyes bugging out of its head.

Phoebe, meanwhile, was staring down at the floor. Embarrassed color saturated her cheeks.

Suddenly, all Garrett could think about was Phoebe on her knees in front of him, licking and sucking his cock. It was one of his favorite fantasies, yet it had no basis in reality. But damn, he wished it did.

And now, thanks to Charlie's vulgar, yet honest comment, Garrett's curiosity burned brighter than ever. He was desperate to know if Phoebe swallowed when she went downtown.

Charlie looked up at the ceiling. "Did I say that out loud?"

"Yes, you did," Kyla answered in a tone of voice usually reserved for very small and very naughty children.

Using his index finger, Charlie pushed his glasses up his nose. "I should probably go now," he mumbled before wandering off.

After a moment, Kyla laughed softly. "It would be my preference if she swallowed," she repeated, looking back and forth between Garrett and Jake. "Is that what all guys think?"

Jake subtly nudged Garrett's forearm in a silent warning to keep his mouth shut. But he didn't need it. He hadn't planned to answer Kyla's question anyway. He wasn't an idiot, despite what his past behavior with Phoebe might indicate.

Jake cleared his throat before catching Garrett's eyes. "You and Phoebe should catch up," he suggested before guiding his wife away.

A new song blared through the overhead speakers, "Waste a Moment" by Kings of Leon. The heavy beat reverberated in Garrett's head and echoed the thump of his heart. He saw Phoebe's mouth move, but couldn't hear her. She took a step back, and he abruptly realized she planned to blow him off ... *again*.

Desperate to keep her from leaving, he grasped her elbow, the skin of her inner arm soft and smooth against his fingers. He ushered her toward the sliding doors that opened to the balcony. It stretched along the living room and wrapped around the side of the building, forming an L shape.

As they passed Jake's decrepit recliner, Garrett snagged his sports coat from where he had tossed it earlier. Made of shiny black metallic fabric, it was nothing like the understated clothing he normally wore. But he had wanted to look festive for Jake and Kyla's party, even if he hadn't felt that way on the inside.

Going to the party solo had made him feel a little pathetic, especially since it meant that he wasn't going to get a kiss at midnight. But now that Phoebe was here, maybe he would get that kiss after all.

Once he and Phoebe were outside on the balcony, he led her to a somewhat secluded spot next to one of those tall outdoor heaters that restaurants used to warm their patios. The beat of the music and the buzz of conversation drifted to them, faint but unobtrusive.

He welcomed the chilly air, hoping it would cool his overheated body. Phoebe, however, shivered. Glad that he had thought ahead, he draped his jacket over her shoulders.

With one hand, she gripped the lapels together over her heart. Her other hand was wrapped around the stem of a plastic wineglass full of golden liquid.

She stared up at him, her face clearly visible in the bright lights from nearby skyscrapers. He'd never seen her wear so much makeup. Smoky gray eyeshadow covered her lids, and her dark eyelashes fanned outward, giving her eyes a feline tilt. Slick red gloss shined on her mouth, drawing his attention to the shape of her lips and the tiny brown freckle just above them.

"You look different," he blurted out, struggling to reconcile her sultry appearance with the fresh-faced co-ed he'd known.

Bright pink color bloomed on her smooth cheeks. "I know."

A million questions ping-ponged in his head, but the one that came out surprised even him. "Why did you cut your hair?"

She didn't reply for a long moment. Finally, she said, "Long hair is a hassle."

"Yours was beautiful."

Her lips turned down. "And you don't like short hair."

"I like yours," he replied sincerely.

I like you. I don't care if you have long hair, short hair, or no hair.

He moved closer to her, powerless to resist her pull. She was a magnet, and he was a piece of metal.

A chilly wind blew over them, tossing several curls into her face. He brushed them away, tucking them behind her ear before tracing the delicate shell. She sucked in an audible breath, and he dropped his hand, wondering if now was the right time to say all the things he'd wanted to say three years ago … before she'd disappeared without a word.

As he debated what to do, Phoebe said, "I didn't expect you to be here."

He smiled wryly. "I didn't expect you to be here, either."

Awkward silence welled between them, reminding him of their stilted conversations when their marketing professor had paired them up on the first day of class. Even though he and Phoebe had been in the same MBA program, they hadn't uttered more than two words to each other before that day. She'd been easy to overlook, and he hadn't given her more than a passing glance.

"How do you know Jake and Kyla?" she asked.

He didn't want to talk about Jake and Kyla, but he answered nonetheless. "I ran into Kyla in the hallway of my hotel, and we struck up a conversation."

He omitted the part where he'd asked Kyla out. He wasn't sure why he felt compelled to gloss over it. He had no reason to feel weird or guilty. Jake and Kyla hadn't been together at the time. Garrett was single and unattached, and Kyla was the whole package: smart, sweet, and sexy.

"Kyla introduced me to Jake," he continued, "and now we're all friends."

"Do you live in San Francisco? You always said you'd never leave Seattle."

"I still live there, but I travel to the Bay Area a lot." Bracing his hip against the railing, he looked down into her eyes. "I wondered what happened to you."

When she hadn't shown up for their graduation ceremony, he'd worried that something had happened to her. He had checked with her academic advisor, and the older woman had assured him that Phoebe was fine, but had elected not to walk the stage.

He had suspected that she'd wanted to avoid seeing him. After all, she had ignored all his efforts to contact her. She'd obviously regretted their night together.

"Have you been in San Francisco this whole time?" he asked.

She looked away, glancing out over the city's twinkling skyline. He let his gaze trail over her profile. He'd spent hours studying her when he should have been studying class notes, and he had memorized the feminine tilt of her nose and the lush curve of her lips.

"I moved here ten months ago," she replied before taking a sip of wine.

A droplet shimmered on her lower lip, and she licked it away in an unintentionally sensual move. She was completely unaware of her sex appeal, and her innocent actions drove him crazy.

As she lowered the wine goblet from her mouth, he noticed the red imprint her lips had made on the plastic rim. If he kissed her right now, would her bright lipstick mark him too?

He wanted to kiss her … to lick into her hot mouth … to nibble her plush lips and suck on her wet tongue. But he wanted something else even more: *answers*.

"Why?" he asked, his voice little more than a growl.

Her gaze shot to his. "Why did I move here?"

He shook his head. "Why didn't you return my phone calls or texts?"

She took a hasty step backward, wobbling a little on her high heels, and lost her grip on her goblet. It plummeted to the ground, splashing wine around their feet.

Hooking his arm around her waist, he steadied her. As she placed her palm on his chest, right over where his heart pounded out a fierce rhythm, he said, "I thought we were friends, Phoebe."

He didn't bother to try to disguise the hurt in his voice. He wondered if she could hear it. She had been an important part of his life, and he'd mourned the loss of her friendship.

She looked down, and he stared at the feathery flare of her eyelashes resting on her pink cheeks. "We were friends," she murmured.

"Then why the hell didn't you call me back? Or at least send a goddamn one-line text to let me know you were okay."

After several heartbeats, she lifted her gaze to his. "I—"

Suddenly, a herd of revelers stampeded onto the balcony, some of them wearing paper party hats and most of them carrying colorful horn and kazoo party favors. Laughing and shouting, they crowded around Garrett and Phoebe.

Their presence, not to mention the racket they created, effectively ended the conversation and prevented Garrett from getting the answer to the question that had tormented him for years. Frustration made his blood boil, and he swore under his breath.

"Ten seconds 'til the New Year!" someone yelled.

"Ten!" the crowd chorused, starting the countdown. "Nine! Eight! Seven! Six!"

Phoebe stepped back, but he tightened his arm around her waist and brought her closer. For a moment, she remained rigid and unyielding against him, but then she relaxed until her voluptuous body curved into his.

"Five! Four!"

They stared into each other's eyes as the crowd continued the countdown. Color surged into her face, pinking her cheeks.

"Three!" The volume of the crowd escalated. "Two!"

Her mouth parted, revealing the tempting inner curve of her bottom lip. She sucked in a huge breath that lifted her shoulders.

"One!"

The crowd went wild, yelling "Happy New Year". The rude honk of horns and the off-key wail of kazoos melded with the familiar notes of Auld Lang Syne. Fireworks burst in the inky sky, painting it with drizzles of gold, blue, pink, and green.

"Happy New Year, Phoebe."

He couldn't hear her voice, but he saw her lips move. "Happy New Year, Garrett."

As he debated whether to coax a midnight kiss from her, someone bumped into him from behind. He immediately felt a splash of cold liquid before it began to dribble down his back.

"*Shit!*" he hissed, instinctively turning away to look for the culprit.

Realizing his mistake, he immediately turned back. As he had feared, Phoebe had disappeared, leaving him high and dry, once again.

With his drenched shirt clinging to the clammy skin of his back, he amended his previous thought. Phoebe had left him high and *not-so-dry* this time around.

CHAPTER THREE

Forty-five percent of people made New Year's resolutions, according to the article on Phoebe's Surface Pro tablet. The article also said those who made resolutions were ten times more likely to achieve their goals than those who didn't.

For the past two years, she'd had only one New Year's resolution—*survive*. And she had. She had survived breast cancer.

Scrolling down, she read through the remainder of the article about New Year's resolutions. *Huh.* Only eight percent of people managed to keep a single resolution.

After closing the web browser, she opened a blank document. At the top, she tapped out NEW YEAR'S RESOLUTIONS.

"Number one," she said, stabbing the numeral with her forefinger.

When no resolutions immediately came to mind, she slid deeper into the tufted cushions of her vintage sofa. She'd found it at an estate sale in Boise, and she had loved it so much, she'd shipped it to San Francisco. It had needed new upholstery, and she'd chosen sage green velvet to cover it.

Drumming her fingers against the back of her tablet—which she fondly called Scarface as a play on the word *surface*—she thought about what she wanted to accomplish this year. Before she'd been diagnosed with cancer, her number one New Year's resolution had always been the same: lose weight.

That was something she no longer needed to do. But she needed to take care of her health so she added *exercise at least three times a week* and *eat more fruits and vegetables* to her list.

That got the ideas flowing, and a few minutes later, she had outlined several resolutions including: learn Italian; plant an herb garden; and travel to a place she'd never visited before.

Looking over the list, she nodded in satisfaction. She had some clear goals to work toward this year. She evaluated the last resolution on her list: stop thinking about Garrett Gale. She laughed under her breath, knowing that was one resolution she wasn't going to be able to keep.

As she placed Scarface on the brown leather ottoman that doubled as a cocktail table, the thin silver bangle on her wrist caught the light. She let go of the tablet and traced the bracelet, rubbing her fingers over the smooth platinum surface. Her mother had given it to her the day before Phoebe's lumpectomy. It was inscribed with a quote from Eleanor Roosevelt: "You must do the thing you think you cannot do."

Phoebe hadn't thought she had the strength to fight the cancer. But she had fought, and she'd fought *hard*.

With her parents and older brothers by her side, she'd grieved over the devastating realization that treating the disease would destroy any chance of having children naturally. She'd endured surgery to remove the tumor and cancerous lymph nodes. She'd tolerated countless exams and tests. She'd suffered months of radiation and chemotherapy and the subsequent nausea and hair loss.

And her reward for all that physical and emotional trauma? She was alive and cancer free.

For now.

Her most recent scan had come back clear, but the cancer could return at any time. She had no doubt it would. It was simply a matter of when, not if.

Decades of research proved that younger women who'd survived breast cancer were far more likely to experience a recurrence than older women. Phoebe had been only twenty-seven when her gynecologist had discovered the lump in her right breast during a routine well-woman exam.

She remembered everything about that day more than three years ago, and not just because of the lump. She'd started out the day in Garrett's bed, naked and clinging to him like an aggressive vine. In the unforgiving morning light, she had been horrified by what she'd done the night before.

After imbibing just enough wine to dull her inhibitions, she'd thought it was a good idea to throw herself at the hottest guy in the Northern Hemisphere. And Garrett had taken what she'd offered … several times, in fact.

She'd been too embarrassed to face him the morning after, so she'd snuck out of his apartment while he'd been asleep. For the next few hours, she had agonized over how awkward things would be between them on graduation day. But then Dr. Arley had found the lump in Phoebe's breast, and that had trumped any worries about Garrett.

Having never experienced any health problems before, Phoebe had expected that a diagnosis would take several weeks. To her surprise, the physician had immediately directed her to the closest imaging center for a mammogram.

Aware of the urgency of the situation, the center had squeezed her (and her boobs) in between other appointments. The radiologist had read the x-ray films immediately afterward.

By the time that Phoebe had dressed, the results had been ready—highly suggestive of malignancy and requiring biopsy.

From there, things had seemed to move at the speed of light. Opting to have the biopsy in Boise because she had wanted to have her family close by, she'd hopped a flight to her hometown the next morning.

During that time, Garrett had repeatedly attempted to contact her, but she had ignored him. She hadn't been able to deal with him and the specter of cancer at the same time. And once the biopsy had confirmed what everyone had feared, she'd focused all her energy on surviving.

Eventually, he'd stopped calling and texting, and she had never reached out to him. But she hadn't forgotten him … hadn't forgotten how it had been between them.

She hadn't slept with anyone since Garrett, and before him, she'd been with only one guy. She'd lost her virginity to her college boyfriend, Lowell, and they'd dated for six years before he'd fallen in love with one of his co-workers. He'd dumped Phoebe to marry the other woman.

At the time, Phoebe had been devastated by Lowell's infidelity, but now she thought everything had turned out for the best. If they had stayed together, he would have been stuck with a cancer-stricken wife. And that wasn't something she would wish on anyone, not even the guy who had cheated on her and broken her heart.

A loud chime filled the room, signaling that she had a phone call. She followed the sound into the kitchen where her phone charged. Nabbing it from the counter, she checked the screen, unsurprised to see her mom's image there.

Connecting the call, she exclaimed, "Happy New Year!"

"Happy New Year!" Leslie Werner returned in a sing-song

voice. "Are you hung over? Do you need the recipe for my famous hangover remedy?"

Phoebe laughed. "No, I'm not hung over, Mom. And even if I were I wouldn't touch your hangover remedy." Recalling that the main ingredient was horseradish, she shuddered. "*Yuck.*"

"I had to make it for your dad this morning. We had *way* too much to drink last night."

"I'm sure you did," she replied, shaking her head in amused exasperation.

Her parents were always the life of the party, whether it was a casual backyard barbeque or a black-tie event at the opera. They had hosted a big party to usher in the new year, and they'd been disappointed when Phoebe had decided to come back to San Francisco instead of staying in Boise.

"Did you have fun at Kyla and Jake's New Year's Eve party?" her mom asked.

Not exactly.

Memories of the night before skipped through her mind. Seeing Garrett after all this time had been just as awkward as she'd feared. But at the same time, it had been so *good* to see him again.

As he had pointed out, they'd been friends. In fact, he had become one of Phoebe's best friends over the course of that last semester at U-Dub. The more time she had spent with him, the more she'd liked him.

They had seen each other in class every day and usually shared lunch together in the on-campus cafeteria. More often than not, they'd eaten dinner together too, usually at Phoebe's apartment. And when they hadn't been together, they had called and texted each other incessantly.

"Phoebe? Are you there?"

Her mom's voice jolted Phoebe out of the past and into the present. "Yeah, Mom, I'm here."

"Did you have a good time at the party?"

"Yes," she lied, knowing that her mom would be disappointed if she said otherwise.

Tucking her phone against her chin, she made her way to the refrigerator and pulled open the stainless-steel door. She had been lucky to find an apartment that had been updated with modern, high-end appliances. Most of the places she'd toured in her price range hadn't been renovated since the 1980s.

As Phoebe removed a plastic container of halved strawberries from the fridge, she heard her dad say something in the background. Her mom shouted, "I'm talking to Phoebe." She paused before adding, "Dad wants to talk too. I'm putting you on speaker."

Alex Werner's deep voice came over the line. "Happy New Year, caboose."

Her father was a miniature railroad enthusiast, which explained why he called her caboose. Since she was the youngest of his four children and the only girl, it was an appropriate nickname, or so he said. Her larger-than-normal rear also made the nickname a good choice.

"Hi, Dad," Phoebe replied. "Mom said you needed her hangover remedy this morning."

He chuckled. "She forced it on me. I'm not sure how effective it is."

While her parents squabbled about the efficacy of the hangover remedy, Phoebe popped a piece of strawberry into her mouth. The fruit's intense sweetness made saliva burst on her tongue.

"Did you get a kiss at midnight?" her dad asked abruptly.

Phoebe choked on her mouthful of strawberry. Coughing, she managed to gasp out, "No."

The shouting and fireworks had made it impossible for Phoebe and Garrett to continue their conversation, and she had been relieved. Even if they hadn't been interrupted, she still wouldn't have answered his questions. She would have deflected, and if he had persisted, she would have lied straight to his face.

Only a few people knew she was a breast cancer survivor. While some women were proud to advertise it, Phoebe wanted to keep that part of her life to herself. She didn't like the curiosity and the pity it caused. And she loathed the fact that people treated her differently after they found out.

She didn't want Garrett to know about her cancer. *Ever.*

CHAPTER FOUR

Garrett strode across the lobby of the Hudson San Francisco, his black leather dress shoes tapping on the marble floor. As he passed an antique table topped with a large arrangement of fragrant white blooms and a stack of crisp newspapers, he swiped a finger along the shiny surface to check for dust.

When he found not even a speck, he smiled in satisfaction and nabbed a *Wall Street Journal.* He checked the date on the masthead, January 2nd, before tucking it under his arm.

Waving to the associates manning check-in, he made his way into the hotel's main dining area. With its espresso-stained hardwood floors, bright white tablecloths, and black-and-white striped chairs, the space was minimalist, yet still inviting.

At the front, the hostess was absent, and at least a dozen customers crowded the entrance waiting to be seated. Garrett frowned, his eyes sweeping around the restaurant. He usually ate breakfast in his room, and he hoped this poor service was an anomaly.

Pulling back the starched cuff of his long-sleeve shirt, Garrett checked his Patek Philippe watch. His grandfather had given it to him a couple of months ago, to celebrate his thirty-second birthday. It was one of the few material things he cherished. The white Arabic numerals on the black face indicated it was just after seven-thirty, and he clocked the time it took for the young hostess to return to her station.

Four minutes, thirty-eight seconds.

Where the hell had she been?

The hotel staff knew better than to leave customers unattended for even ten seconds. He made a mental note to talk to the restaurant manager after visiting with Jake.

Garrett didn't recognize the hostess, and he took note of the name on the metal badge on her chest—Samantha. When she saw him standing on the fringe of the small group, her brown eyes widened, first with recognition and then with alarm.

"Mr. Gale," she said, her breathless voice clearly conveying her discomfort, "I'll seat you right away."

Slowly shaking his head, he cast a meaningful glance at the other customers. He owned this hotel, and he wanted his guests to be taken care of first.

Samantha immediately switched her attention to the other people waiting for a table. He noted she didn't apologize for the wait, nor did she call for backup with her microphone and earbud, technology all hotel staff members wore to improve efficiency and customer service.

"Samantha," he said, just loudly enough to catch her attention.

Her head snapped toward him, her light brown ponytail tangling with her silver hoop earring, and he beckoned her over with his forefinger. When she got close enough, he bent down and murmured, "Call for backup. These guests have waited long enough, and they need to be seated. *Now.*" She nodded and started to move away, but he stopped her with a light touch on her shoulder. "Who's in charge this morning?"

"Dimitri."

Dimitri Makarov was a recent employee to Gale Hotel Group, joining the company only a few months ago. The head of food and beverage operations had made the hire. From what Garrett could remember, Dimitri had managed one of the restaurants in the Four Seasons San Francisco. He should be accustomed to providing flawless service.

Deciding that he needed to talk with the restaurant manager immediately, Garrett said, "Get Dimitri up here."

Once the hostess got some help, it took less than three minutes to seat everyone. Dimitri finally emerged from the back, strolling leisurely around the perimeter of the restaurant. When he saw Garrett, his pace increased, but just barely.

Stopping next to Garrett, Dimitri said, "It's delightful to see you this morning, Mr. Gale." He held out his bony hand, and Garrett gave it a perfunctory shake, looking down at the shorter man. "Let me show you to a table."

"Thank you," Garrett responded. "And I'd like you to join me for a cup of coffee."

Dimitri's thin gray eyebrows rose. "It would be my pleasure."

It didn't take them long to get settled in a half-table, half-booth at the back of the restaurant. Garrett took the booth seat so he could see the entrance and spot Jake when he arrived.

Glancing at his watch, Garrett timed how long it took for a server to arrive. Two minutes, fifty-three seconds ... about two minutes too long.

He wasn't an impatient guy. In fact, he thought he was very patient. Proof: he had waited *months* to get Phoebe naked. But this wasn't about him. It was about providing service that attracted upscale clientele. And those guests didn't expect to wait for one second, let alone one hundred and seventy-three seconds.

Once the server had poured two steaming cups of Brazilian Arabica, Garrett added two spoonfuls of sugar to his. He had a fierce sweet tooth in the morning, and he preferred sweet, dark coffee along with pancakes, waffles, or French toast instead of something healthy like an egg-white omelet.

As he gulped down a scalding mouthful of coffee, he eyed Dimitri across the table. The other man was impeccably dressed in a gray Armani suit with a light blue dress shirt, gray and blue paisley tie, and light blue kerchief. He wore a pair of glasses with thin black rims around the lens.

Very urbane. Very European.

Lowering the porcelain cup to the saucer, Garrett said, "When I arrived this morning, the hostess was missing, no fewer than a dozen people were waiting for seats, and half the tables in the dining room were empty. They waited nearly five minutes *without even a greeting.*"

He paused, giving Dimitri an opportunity to respond. But the restaurant manager said nothing. Instead, he picked up his coffee and took a dainty sip.

Garrett leaned forward, angered by the other man's lack of concern. "When the hostess finally showed up, she offered no smile, no apology. *Nothing.* And she didn't do anything to make sure they were seated promptly. She didn't call for reinforcements." He drilled Dimitri with a hard look. "That is unacceptable."

Dimitri returned his cup to the saucer. "She's new—"

"That's an excuse, and I don't want to hear it. Everything in this restaurant, from the crumbs under my chair … did you even notice them, by the way? … to the hostess, is your responsibility."

Spotting Jake across the dining room, Garrett waved at him before bringing his gaze back to the restaurant manager. "My breakfast appointment just arrived so I'm going to have to cut this short."

Dimitri stood, his face pinched and his hazel eyes narrowed behind the rectangular lens of his glasses. He fairly bristled with enmity.

"One more thing," Garrett told the scowling manager. "I want you to stop by each table and personally apologize to the guests who had to wait. Offer a free voucher for breakfast tomorrow, and if they're checking out today, breakfast this morning is on us."

"Of course, Mr. Gale," Dimitri replied flatly. "Enjoy your breakfast."

Garrett watched Dimitri walk away, certain the Hudson San Francisco would need a new restaurant manager. He had no doubt the older man would go back to his office and start making calls to land another gig. And that was more than fine with Garrett. He didn't want anyone on his team who messed up and then refused to take responsibility for it.

As Jake arrived at the table, Garrett closed a mental door on Dimitri and rose to greet his friend. "Hey, boss," he said, slapping the other man's broad back.

Jake's mouth lifted in a half-smile. "I told you to stop calling me that, douche. I'm not your boss."

The nickname was a joke between them. Jake had been Kyla's boss when he and Garrett had met.

"I'll stop calling you *boss* if you stop calling me *douche*. Deal?"

Jake's smile widened. "Sorry, douche, no deal."

Chuckling, Garrett picked up Dimitri's coffee and handed it to a passing server before requesting another cup for Jake. "How's your morning going?"

"It would have been better if I had stayed in bed with my

wife instead of meeting you for breakfast," Jake grumbled, shrugging off his black motorcycle jacket and revealing the long-sleeved maroon thermal tee underneath.

Garrett resumed his seat, uncomfortably aware that he envied Jake ... not because of Kyla, but because Jake had someone special. Garrett didn't have anyone special.

What he did have was a no-strings-attached arrangement with Becca Holloway, a woman he'd met at a hotel investment conference a couple of years ago. She lived in Chicago, and whenever he visited the Windy City to check on his hotels, they hooked up.

"I would have blown you off if I'd had a beautiful woman in my bed," Garrett joked.

"And that's why I call you *douche*."

After draping his jacket on the back of the chair, Jake dropped down into the seat Dimitri had vacated. He ran a hand over his reddish-brown hair, smoothing the short strands before leaning back and propping his ankle on his opposite knee. The silver buckle on his black motorcycle boots peeked out from beneath the frayed hem of his jeans.

Jake looked like a biker, but in this case, looks were deceiving. He served as CFO of one of the largest apparel brands in the world. And with an MBA from Stanford University, he had a more impressive academic pedigree than Garrett.

"So, you're flying home tomorrow?" Jake asked, picking up the breakfast menu.

"I'm not going back to Seattle. I'm going to Boston. There's a hotel in the Back Bay that we're thinking about buying. It's not in great shape, and it's mismanaged. My acquisitions team thinks we could make a shitload of money if we rehabbed it and brought in a new management team."

Jake nodded thoughtfully. "Same as this hotel."

"Yeah. We don't have any properties in Boston, and I want to expand into new markets. But we just closed on The Pacifica here in the Bay Area, and I don't want us to get overextended."

"That place is a dump."

"We're spending close to forty million dollars to rehab it."

Jake whistled. "That's an extreme makeover. How long will it take?"

"Two years. Maybe three." He took a sip of coffee, grimacing at the lukewarm temperature. The server should have already warmed it up. "I'm coming back to San Francisco in a couple of weeks to meet with the design team. I'll probably be here more than I'll be at home. There's a lot of—"

"You can tell me about the plans for your new hotel later." Jake set the menu on the table. "Tell me about Phoebe."

Garrett's eyebrows arched at Jake's unexpected request. "I hadn't seen her in more than three years, boss. You probably know more about her than I do."

Jake smiled wryly. "I doubt it. You know her *biblically*."

"What makes you say that, Reverend Lilliard?" Garrett asked, his voice mocking.

"Because you couldn't take your eyes off her, and she could barely look at you."

Garrett rolled his tight shoulders, more than a little embarrassed that his feelings had been so obvious. "I was surprised to see her."

"I think she was surprised to see you too ... *unpleasantly* surprised."

Jake's observation shot an arrow of pain through Garrett. He wished Phoebe had been so happy to see him that she'd thrown herself into his arms and kissed him senseless.

"Did you do her and dump her?" Jake asked, pouring a splash

331

of cream into his coffee. "Fuck her and forget her?"

"Not exactly."

Jake picked up his spoon and lazily stirred his coffee. "Then what, exactly?"

"Why are you so interested?"

Jake looked up, his greenish-gold eyes glinting with amusement. "Isn't it obvious? I want to know all your secrets so I can use them against you."

"That's what I thought."

Jake laughed. "Fine. Don't tell me."

"She's the one who fucked me and forgot me."

Jake's laughter abruptly stopped. "Really?"

"Yes," Garrett answered curtly.

"Were you dating, or was it just a one-night stand?"

"We were friends, but technically I guess it was a one-night stand."

Garrett hated to characterize the night he'd spent with Phoebe as a one-night stand. It had meant a lot more than that … to him, at least.

He pictured that night in his mind. The expensive restaurant. Phoebe all dressed up, looking so luscious in her tight black dress that he'd had a hard-on all through dinner. A nice bottle of red wine. Strolling back to his condo building with their hands linked.

As they'd stood in the elevator, she had risen on her tiptoes and kissed him. It had been just a peck, nothing more, but after wanting her for months, he'd kind of lost it.

He'd backed her against the wall and slammed his mouth down on hers. And then he'd slid his hands under her dress and found heaven between her legs. He probably would have fucked here then and there if the elevator hadn't stopped to admit a sweaty guy who'd been working out in the eleventh-floor gym.

"Did you want more than one night?" Jake asked.

After a long moment, Garrett nodded slowly. "Yeah, I wanted more. A lot more."

"I figured."

"I still want more," Garrett admitted.

"I figured that too." Jake's mouth quirked. "So, what are you going to do about it?"

CHAPTER FIVE

"I don't think my feet have ever looked so good," Phoebe mused, eyeing the candy apple red polish on her toenails.

"I like that color," Kyla said from her position in the pedicure chair next to Phoebe. "I always pick some shade of pink. Maybe I should try red next time."

Kyla had invited Phoebe for a spa day at the Hudson San Francisco. She had been hesitant to accept Kyla's invitation because of the expense, but Kyla had told Phoebe not to worry about it.

Phoebe had attended a couple of luncheons at the historic hotel, but she had never been pampered in its luxurious spa. Earlier in the day, she and Kyla had enjoyed full-body massages. The massage therapist had used jasmine-scented oil, and Phoebe's skin had soaked it in like a water-deprived plant.

As the nail tech gathered her supplies and left the room, Phoebe let her eyes wander around. She and Kyla had the space to themselves.

The soothing grayish-blue walls reminded Phoebe of the saltwater of Puget Sound. Music drifted from speakers overhead, something light-hearted with flutes and chimes.

Tucking her bulky white robe between her knees, Phoebe glanced at Kyla. Lime green goo covered the other woman's face, and a white towel was wrapped around her hair, turban-style.

"You look like Jim Carrey in that old movie *The Mask*," Phoebe noted, adjusting her own turban.

Kyla glanced sideways at Phoebe. "You look like the little girl who turned into a blueberry in *Willy Wonka and the Chocolate Factory*."

Phoebe gestured to the bluish-purple goo coating her face. "Violet, you're turning violet," she said, quoting the movie.

Kyla smiled, her teeth blindingly white against the backdrop of her lime green face. "I'd rather be violet than orange like those oompa-loompas." She gave a contented sigh. "I'm so glad we did this. I really needed it after the past couple of weeks."

Right after the holidays, a nasty flu bug had swept through the Riley O'Brien & Co. headquarters. Although Phoebe had managed to avoid it—*thank you, hand sanitizer*—Kyla had caught it. She'd missed an entire week of work, and this was the first time they'd been able to enjoy any girl time since New Year's Eve.

"I've been wondering …" Kyla began.

Phoebe tilted her head toward the other woman. "What?"

"Is Garrett as good as he looks?"

Kyla's question surprised Phoebe so much her head jerked back involuntarily. It was the first time her friend had mentioned Garrett, and Phoebe had hoped Kyla wouldn't want any details about him.

"What do you mean?" Phoebe asked, playing dumb.

Kyla rolled her eyes. "*Please*. You know exactly what I mean. You've had sex with him." She leaned toward Phoebe and tapped her forearm. "Don't make me beg."

Knowing Kyla wasn't going to let the subject drop, Phoebe admitted, "Yes, he's as good as he looks."

"Why did you two break up?"

"We didn't *break up*. We were never a couple."

Kyla's eyebrows arched. "Friends with benefits?"

"No."

Before that night, Garrett had never shown even the slightest interest in her as anything other than a friend. In fact, she'd often wondered if he had even noticed she was female.

"So, what was it?" Kyla persisted.

"A lapse in judgment," Phoebe answered flatly. "An alcohol-induced impulse."

She hadn't been more than a little tipsy, but Garrett must have been far more inebriated than she. Otherwise he never would have had sex with her.

Phoebe wasn't Garrett's type. She'd seen him with various women at school events, and his companions had been tall, thin, and gorgeous. Phoebe, in contrast, was plain, shy, and overweight ... or at least she had been before the cancer had taken its toll.

Kyla didn't respond for several moments. Finally, she said, "I thought there might be more to it. At the party, it seemed that you ..."

Phoebe shifted in her seat so she wouldn't have to strain her neck to see Kyla. "Seemed that I *what*?"

Kyla shrugged. "That you liked him."

Phoebe almost laughed. She *liked* her mother's meatloaf. She *liked* Impressionist art. She *liked* to knit.

But she had been in love with Garrett. She'd known he was way out of her league, but that hadn't stopped her from falling for him.

"How did it happen?" Kyla asked.

"How did what happen?"

Kyla expelled an exasperated breath. "How did you end up in bed with Garrett?"

"We went out to dinner to celebrate. We had some wine, and it just happened." She lifted her shoulders in a shrug. "It just happened."

"What were you celebrating?"

"We rocked our final presentation for our data-driven marketing class. It was nearly one hundred percent of our grade. The professor had invited executives from local businesses to evaluate our presentations, so there was a lot of pressure. We worked all semester on the project." Phoebe couldn't help but smile at the memory. "Garrett is amazing in front of an audience. He wowed everyone."

"He's very charismatic," Kyla agreed. "Whose idea was it to go out to dinner to celebrate?"

"Garrett's. After the presentation, he was insistent that we celebrate. I wanted to go to a bar near campus and grab a beer. But he wanted to have dinner at this fancy new restaurant near his condo."

"A fancy new restaurant?" Kyla repeated before smiling slowly. "He wanted to take you on a date but was too chicken to ask."

Phoebe snorted. "Yeah, right. You know Garrett. He doesn't lack confidence. If he had wanted to ask me out, he would have."

She, on the other hand, lacked confidence in a big way. She'd felt so awkward in the trendy restaurant where all the women had been thinner than birch branches and dressed in designer clothes and sexy stilettos.

She'd seen the sideways glances, the ones that wondered *What the hell is* she *doing with him?* She had wondered the same thing.

337

"Even the most confident guy gets a little insecure when he doesn't know how a woman feels about him," Kyla said.

Before Phoebe could reply, a tall brunette in a crisp white shirt and black skirt entered the room, a round silver tray balanced on her hand. A dark green bottle sat on the tray, along with two crystal flutes and a plate of chocolate. Smiling widely, she announced, "I have a special treat for you—champagne and dark chocolate truffles made by our chocolatier."

As the woman placed the tray on the side table, Phoebe glanced at Kyla. "Did you order this?"

"No," Kyla answered, but she didn't seem surprised by the refreshments. Maybe they were part of the spa package.

The server deftly filled the flutes and delivered them to Phoebe and Kyla before divvying up the truffles onto two small plates. Depositing them on the trays attached to the pedicure chairs, she chirped, "Enjoy, ladies."

They thanked her in stereo, and as the server gathered her tray and left the room, Phoebe tasted the chilled champagne. The dry fruitiness made her mouth tingle.

"This is delicious," Phoebe said.

Kyla took a swallow and smacked her lips. "Good stuff."

Picking up a truffle, Phoebe studied the smooth, dark surface decorated with thin, pink stripes. She bit into the candy, moaning a little when she got a hint of raspberry flavor. The chocolate melted slowly, so rich her jaw ached.

As Phoebe took another sip from her flute, a deep voice rumbled from the doorway. "How's the champagne?"

She looked up and spotted Garrett standing just inside the room. She blinked, convinced her eyes were playing tricks on her. They'd just been talking about him. Was he a figment of her imagination?

"Garrett!" Kyla exclaimed joyfully.

Oh, my God, he's really here.

Phoebe sucked in a shocked breath, forgetting that she had champagne in her mouth. The bubbly vintage invaded her airway, and she coughed harshly, slapping a hand over her mouth.

The noise drew his attention away from Kyla. His gaze landed on Phoebe, and a sexy smile slowly appeared on his lips.

"Phoebe," he said.

Maybe it was the husky timbre of his voice or maybe it was the affection threaded through it, but something about the way he said her name sent warmth rushing through her. That warmth coalesced into heat and pooled between her legs.

She dropped her hand from her mouth and glimpsed something dark on it. Bewildered, she stared at her fingers. They were stuck together, and she widened them like a starfish. Suddenly she realized exactly where she was and what she looked like.

I'm naked under this robe. I have a towel on my head. And I have bluish-purple gunk on my face.

Her eyes shot to Garrett, and her dismay must have been obvious because he chuckled. Heat washed over her face, and if it hadn't been smeared with an exfoliating blueberry facial, it would have been bright red with embarrassment.

She wiped her hand on the plush terrycloth covering her thigh and set the champagne flute next to the plate of truffles. She hoped no one noticed that her hand shook.

Garrett propped his shoulder against the doorjamb and crossed his arms over his chest. As the sleeves of his black cashmere sweater pulled tight over his broad shoulders and big biceps, Phoebe recalled that Garrett was an avid rower. That explained those impressive muscles.

339

She darted a quick glance at the rest of him. He wore light gray trousers and a pair of black dress shoes with a squared toe and no laces. He was so sexy and polished he could have modeled for *GQ*.

"I hope that goop doesn't stain," he teased in a laughter-tinged voice. "You'll be ultraviolet."

"It's not going to stain," Kyla assured him. "That *goop* …" she pointed at Phoebe's face,"… is going to make Phoebe gorgeous."

"She's already gorgeous," he replied, his gaze locked on Phoebe. His eyes were deep and blue, just like the ocean, and she felt as if she were drowning in them. "She's always been gorgeous."

Did he really just say I've always been gorgeous?

He nodded as if he had heard her silent question. Dragging her eyes from his, she focused on her freshly painted toenails.

After a few seconds of awkward silence, Kyla said, "I didn't know you were in town, Garrett."

"I flew in this morning, and when I heard you were here, I had the kitchen send a snack."

"First you give me a gift card for unlimited spa treatments, and now you give me champagne and chocolate," Kyla said.

Phoebe glanced up, wondering if Garrett's gift card was paying for her spa day. The thought made her twitchy. When a man paid for a woman to be beautified, shouldn't he benefit in some way?

"You spoil me," Kyla added.

"You deserve to be spoiled, cupcake," he replied, a lazy grin flashing across his face.

Phoebe frowned at the flirty nickname, wondering how well Kyla and Garrett knew each other. They seemed really familiar. The thought of them together—*sans* clothing—made Phoebe's chest ache.

"How long will you be in town?" Kyla asked Garrett.

"I'm not sure. A few weeks, at least."

Phoebe winced internally. She hoped she wouldn't run into him again while he was here. And if she did, she hoped she was wearing more than a robe.

"We should go to dinner," Kyla suggested. "You, me, Jake, and Phoebe."

Alarmed, Phoebe jerked her head up. "No!"

Garrett's eyes narrowed. "Why not?"

"Because ... because ..." she sputtered.

Because I still remember how you felt inside me. Because I can't be near you without throwing myself at you.

Because you make me want things I can never have.

CHAPTER SIX

Phoebe obviously didn't want to go to dinner with him, not even with the buffer of Jake and Kyla. Her lack of enthusiasm, if you could call it that, made Garrett feel like shit. There was nothing he wanted more than to spend time with her.

As Phoebe floundered for an excuse to get out of dinner, the manager of the spa, Blair Gibson, appeared next to him. She gave him a friendly smile before entering the room.

"The facialists are ready for you both," Blair announced. "When you're ready, I'll show you to your rooms."

Dropping his arms to his sides, he straightened from his relaxed stance. "That's my cue to leave."

Relief chased across Phoebe's face, obvious despite the goop covering it. His stomach cramped with an unpleasant mix of disappointment and frustration.

"Enjoy your facials," he said, pleased to hear that his voice betrayed no hint of his feelings.

Kyla waved. "I'll text you later."

He nodded before giving Phoebe one last glance. She stared back at him, her eyes brighter than usual against the dark purple goop. He remembered looking into her eyes as he moved deep inside her ... as she came apart around him.

His cock twitched at the memory, and he spun on his heel, aroused and angry. He made his way down the corridor, intending to head back to his suite. As he pushed through the door that led to the reception area, a voice inside him whispered, *Are you going to let her get away? Again?*

His steps slowed, and the voice grew louder. *Don't be an idiot. The universe has given you another chance. Don't waste it.*

Stopping in front of the reception desk, he asked the young woman there to text him when the facialist was done with Phoebe. He left the spa and ambled toward the part of the hotel that housed the grand ballroom and smaller meeting spaces. It was deserted; no one scheduled big conferences in mid-January.

As he wandered the hallways, he thought about Phoebe. Three years ago, he'd allowed her to disappear from his life without a fight.

He could have tracked her down by trolling her social media pages. He could have found out where her parents lived in Boise and tried to reach her. But he hadn't, mostly because of his pride, but also because that kind of behavior bordered on stalking.

He had no idea how things would have played out between them if she hadn't blown him off. He hadn't been ready for a relationship, and if she'd stuck around, he probably would have fucked things up. He'd known she was special, but at the time, he hadn't realized how truly rare and extraordinary a woman like Phoebe was.

But he realized it now.

His phone vibrated against his leg, and he plucked it from his pocket. The text message alerted him that Phoebe's facial was over. He immediately headed back toward the spa, walking as fast as the slick soles of his shoes would allow.

Two minutes later he stood in front of the spa, his heart pounding with anxious excitement. As he entered through the frosted glass door, he caught the receptionist's eyes.

"Where is she?" he asked.

His voice came out harsher than he'd intended, and the woman's eyes widened. "She's in Hyacinth."

It didn't take him long to reach the treatment room. Before he could talk himself out of it, he knocked on the door.

"Come in," Phoebe called out, her voice muffled.

Grasping the knob, he opened the door and crossed the threshold. The room wasn't large, and a sheet-draped table occupied most of the space. The mellow lighting made the dusky purple walls appear even darker.

Phoebe sat on the table, clad in the same white robe she'd worn earlier. The turban was gone, and her dark hair was a messy tangle of curls. The goop was gone too, and her face looked dewy and fresh.

When she caught sight of him, her mouth fell open. "What are you doing here?"

Closing the door with a quiet snick, he said, "I wanted to talk to you."

"How did you get back here?" she burst out. "Do the employees just let you wander around wherever you want?"

A surprised chuckle escaped him. "As a matter of fact, they do."

"*Why?* Did you bribe them or something?"

She obviously didn't know he owned the Hudson San Francisco. His amusement drained away when he realized what that meant: she was so uninterested in him that she hadn't even bothered to Google him or check out his profile on LinkedIn.

Suddenly angry, he snapped, "Yes, I bribed them ... with a paycheck."

"What?"

"I own this hotel."

Her dark eyebrows winged up her forehead. "You own the Hudson San Francisco?"

"The Hudson San Francisco and seven other hotels."

"Wow." Her plump lips lifted in a tiny smile. "That was your dream." Her smile widened. "I knew you could do it, Garrett. I'm so proud of you."

And just like that, his anger drained away. She'd always had the ability to coax him out of a bad mood, to make his day brighter with one of her smiles. More than once, he had relied on her to fulfill his emotional needs, if not his physical needs.

When his grandfather had suffered a stroke nearly four years ago, and Garrett had been afraid that he would lose the man who had raised him, he had turned to Phoebe. He had needed her and no one else. Phoebe, with her soft voice and kind eyes, had soothed the maelstrom inside him in a way that no one else could.

Garrett moved closer, until he stood right in front of her, almost touching her knees. She squirmed, clearly uncomfortable with his proximity.

The panels of her robe widened, revealing the upper curves of her breasts. Her skin gleamed, smooth and creamy like a pearl, and the heady scent of jasmine drifted from her.

He told himself to look away, but he couldn't. He wanted to bury his face in her cleavage and palm her ample breasts. As he stared at her chest, the delicate skin pinked, and he fought the urge to press open-mouthed kisses on it.

To his disappointment, she clutched the lapels of her robe and pulled them together. Taking a deep breath, he lifted his gaze to her face. It was the same shade as her chest.

"Phoebe, we need to talk about what happened that night."

Her face flushed darker. "It's in the past. It has nothing to do with the present."

"If that were true, you wouldn't have a problem going to dinner with me, Jake, and Kyla."

She looked down, her fingers fiddling with the tie of her robe. "There's nothing to talk about, Garrett. A lot of people do things when they're drunk that they wouldn't do when they're sober."

Drunk? What the hell was she talking about?

They had shared a bottle of wine over dinner. That equaled two glasses each, over the course of two hours. It took a hell of a lot more alcohol than that to make him drunk. He'd been as sober as a judge on sentencing day every second he'd been inside her.

"I wasn't even close to drunk, and neither were you." Tilting his head, he reconsidered. "Well, maybe you were a little tipsy. But your buzz had mostly worn off."

Her expression clouded with visible confusion. "Then why did you … why did we …"

He waited for her to finish her sentence, and when she didn't, he filled in the blanks. "Why did we have sex in the hallway?"

Even now, more than three years later, he still couldn't believe he'd fucked her in the hallway, only a few feet from his condo unit. And he couldn't believe she'd let him. They'd behaved recklessly, without a doubt. Anyone could have seen them.

Their brief encounter in the hallway hadn't done much to satiate his hunger. Once he'd pulled her into his condo, he'd bent her over his sofa and done her from behind. Finally, they had ended up in his bed with her bouncing on top of him.

The memories made his stomach muscles tighten and his

cock thicken. "I was so hard for you, it didn't matter where we were," he told her.

She sucked in an audible breath. "What?"

"All I cared about was getting inside you, Phoebe. I couldn't wait any longer." He stared down into her wide eyes. "I know you wish that night hadn't happened. I know you regret it."

She was silent for a long moment. Finally, she whispered, "I don't regret it."

Relief flooded through him. Maybe he had a chance after all. "I'm really glad you don't regret it … because I want to do it again."

She gasped softly. "You do?"

He brought his hands to her knees, sliding them under the terry cloth until he could feel her bare skin, warm and a little damp. "All I can think about is pulling off this robe and sliding inside you."

She trembled under his palms. "*Garrett.*"

Gently, he pushed her knees apart and stepped between them. Leaning down, he placed his mouth against her ear and murmured, "I hope there's nothing but bare skin under your robe."

He skimmed his hands up her thighs, and the higher he moved, the harder he got, his cock throbbing with every beat of his heart.

His fingers grazed the silky hair on her pussy. He stilled, giving her time to pull away … to slap his face.

But she didn't.

Instead, she widened her legs in a silent, but unmistakable invitation. And he took it. He would take everything she gave him and more.

He slid his fingers higher, easing them between the folds of her pussy. She was incredibly, deliciously wet. And hot. So fucking hot he knew she'd burn him up.

Blood roared in his ears, drowning out the New Age music drifting from the built-in speakers. He was so turned on he was shaking.

Finding the place where her juice trickled from her body, he eased a finger inside her. She moaned low in her throat, and he kissed his way from her ear to her mouth. Her skin was smooth and velvety, reminding him of a rose petal.

He swiped his tongue over her lower lip. It was so soft and plush he couldn't resist a little nip. Her lips fell open, and he darted his tongue into the silken interior of her mouth. She was just as sweet as he remembered.

As he licked into her mouth, he slowly withdrew his finger from her pussy. When he pushed back inside, he added another. He pumped his hand in a slow rhythm, swallowing her gasps with his mouth when he discovered a sweet spot deep inside.

Her wet flesh clasped his fingers, pulling them deeper with each plunge. She rocked against his hand, her tongue tangling with his. As he touched his thumb to her clit, she quivered against him. He brushed over the hard little knot, back and forth until she jerked her mouth from his.

Resting his forehead against hers, he continued to work his fingers between her legs, flicking his thumbnail over her clit and increasing the pace of his thrusts. She was panting, little puffs of champagne-scented breath against his lips.

Knowing she was close, he shifted his other hand from her thigh to her hip. He brought her closer and forced her legs wider.

"Come for me," he demanded, thrusting hard into her.

She tensed, little whimpers spilling from her lips, and dug her nails into his biceps. "Now," he rasped. "Take it."

Her pussy clamped down on his fingers, the internal muscles pulsing with her climax. Slamming his mouth over hers, he silenced her husky cry. He pushed deeper, and she screamed, the sound muffled by his lips.

As her orgasm faded, he kissed her, sucking on her tongue and nibbling on her lips. When the last pulses had left her body, he pulled his hands from under her robe and tugged it over her pale thighs.

Raising his head, he met her eyes. They were dark green, like dew-drenched grass, and glassy with the pleasure he'd given her.

"I want to take you to dinner tonight." He stroked his thumb over her bottom lip. "And then I want to bring you back to my suite and make love to you all night long. Does that sound good to you?"

CHAPTER SEVEN

Such a short little word, no. Only two letters.

N-O.

Easy to spell. Easy to read. Easy to say too.

But not so easy for Garrett to hear, especially when it came out of Phoebe's beautiful mouth.

No.

No dinner. No lovemaking in his suite.

She'd turned him down, crushing him like a stinkbug beneath her foot. That had been six days ago.

She hadn't even softened her answer by offering an excuse. Just *no.*

While he'd stood there groping for a response, Phoebe had wiggled off the spa table and left the treatment room without another word.

He had no trouble imagining how his grandfather would respond if Garrett told him what had happened. He could hear Pops's dry, creaky voice saying *She came, and then she went.*

Garrett laughed under his breath, the sound harsh and bitter. It was either that or hurl his tumbler of scotch into the mirrored wall behind the restaurant's long bar.

Bracing an elbow against the glass-topped bar, he tossed back the remainder of his Macallan. When Kyla had suggested dinner at Fig, the city's best Moroccan restaurant, he'd accepted, knowing she would badger him incessantly if he didn't.

But he wasn't in the mood to hang out with Kyla and Jake. Yes, they were two of his favorite people, but they were so damn happy together it was almost painful to be around them.

He shouldn't have come here tonight, not when Phoebe's rejection stung so painfully. Hell, it would probably sting for a while. It still stung that she'd blown him off years ago.

Sensing someone beside him, he glanced sideways. The hostess stood next to him, a flirtatious smile on her face and a stack of menus in the crook of her arm. She brushed a tendril of dark blond hair over her shoulder before placing a slender hand on his forearm.

"Your table is ready." She stroked his forearm with the tips of her fingers. "We can seat you now, and when the rest of your party arrives, we'll send them your way."

He followed her across the black bamboo floor, weaving between low-profile tables and short armless chairs upholstered in brightly striped silk. The vibrant orangey-red walls created a nice contrast with the dark floor and tables.

The leggy hostess led him past a Moroccan folk band playing airy, instrumental music and stopped at a booth near the back of the restaurant. He slid into the squatty banquette, folding his legs under him.

With his knees almost in his armpits, he placed his phone on the table next to the rolled-up napkin. He sighed internally. This was going to be an uncomfortable meal. He hoped the food was worth the contortions.

The hostess handed a menu to him along with a wine list, and he thanked her. He waited for her to leave, but she leaned down until her tits filled his vision. They were nice, and since he was a normal guy, he appreciated the view.

He let his gaze travel from her chest to her face. She was attractive … gorgeous, in fact. Big brown eyes, thick blond hair, a full mouth, and a long, lithe body.

"My name's Lexie," she murmured. "If you need anything, anything at all, just let me know. I'll take care of it. I'll take care of *you*."

He understood what she was offering. Women came on to him all the time. They liked the way he looked, and they really liked his money.

All he had to do was ask, and the hostess would come back to his suite. He knew she'd say yes.

He could have a woman in his bed tonight or every night. But not the one he really wanted: Phoebe.

"Thanks, Lexie. I'm good."

Disappointment shadowed her face. "Are you sure?"

As Garrett opened his mouth to reply, a short man with a mustache stopped next to Lexie. He shifted slightly, gesturing toward the booth, and Phoebe stepped out from behind him.

Suddenly, everything just disappeared … the Moroccan folk music, the sexy hostess, the buzz of conversation, the clink of silverware. His vision narrowed, and Phoebe's tousled curls and bright eyes were all he could see.

Surprised pleasure lit up her face when she saw him, her glossy lips tilting into a smile. A heartbeat later her smile faded, and her expression darkened.

What the hell?

For a moment, she had been happy to see him. But now she looked as if she wanted to hit something … or someone. Probably him.

He had no idea what was going on in her head, but he sincerely wished he did. Maybe then he would know where he'd gone wrong. Maybe then he would know why she'd shut him down.

It barely registered when the hostess and the mustached man left. When Phoebe made no move to sit, Garrett belatedly remembered his manners and surged to his feet.

"Hello," he said, wincing a little as his voice cracked—something that only happened when he was horribly nervous.

She looked up at him, little lines notched between her dark eyebrows. "Kyla neglected to mention that you'd be here."

Suspicion tinged her voice, and he shook his head. "I know what you're thinking, but I didn't know you would be here either."

Her lush lips flattened into a straight line. Clutching her black bag to her side, she glanced away. As her gaze swept the crowded restaurant, he returned to his seat, knowing she was debating whether to stay.

While she deliberated, he gave her an appraising glance, starting with her feet, which were encased in black patent leather flats. Her black pants were nothing special, but her coral-colored suede jacket complemented her rich, dark hair.

The jacket had wide lapels and a diagonal zipper that started on her left breast and ended near her right hip. His fingers twitched with the desire to unzip it and see what was hidden underneath.

Finally, he reached her face. Peach-colored gloss made her lips slick and succulent. He wondered if the gloss was flavored. He'd really like to find out.

She brought her green gaze back to him, and when their eyes met, a current of energy shot through him. Under his long-sleeved shirt, his skin prickled with heat.

With a resigned sigh, she pulled her bag from her shoulder

and tossed it into the seat across from him. She slid in clumsily, knocking her knees against his.

"Sorry," she muttered.

She reached for the tab of her zipper, and he watched as she pulled it down. Inch by inch, she revealed a silky V-neck camisole the same color as her jacket. Delicate lace edged the neckline, drawing his attention to her creamy cleavage.

A vision of her nipples suddenly filled his head, making his cock twitch. He barely bit back a moan.

This whole situation reminded him of their study sessions in grad school when he'd hidden his hard-ons. Back then he hadn't made a move on her because he hadn't wanted to jeopardize their marketing project or damage their friendship.

Really good reasons, right? But if he were being honest, he would admit that those reasons were just excuses.

He hadn't made a move on Phoebe because he had been too chickenshit. She had never flirted with him or given any hint that she was interested in him as more than a friend or study partner. He had been too insecure and uncertain to risk her rejection.

Across the table, Phoebe moved abruptly, shifting to pull her phone from her jacket pocket. As she looked at the screen, a frown pulled her lips down.

"Kyla and Jake aren't coming," she announced flatly, slipping the phone into her bag.

Just then, Garrett's phone vibrated. Picking it up from the table, he read the text from Jake: *You're welcome, douche. Try not to fuck it up this time.*

Garrett returned his phone to the table, wondering how he could make the most of this unexpected boon. Before he could come up with a strategy, Phoebe reached for her bag, obviously intending to leave.

He could only think of one way to stop her. He vaulted to his feet and slid into the booth beside her. It wasn't a spacious seat, and her warm curves pressed against him from shoulder to knee.

Her head snapped toward him, their faces only inches apart. Surprise swirled in her eyes, along with a dozen other emotions he didn't recognize.

"Let me out, Garrett," she demanded.

"It's just dinner. We've had dinner with each other hundreds of times. Remember Mexican Mondays at Tio Julio's and Takeout Tuesdays from Golden Dragon?" He could hear the pleading note in his voice, and he didn't care if she heard it too. "You have to remember Wine Wednesdays. Every bottle you picked tasted like vinegar."

She stared down at the table in silence. After several moments, he scooted out of the booth and stood.

"Damn it, Phoebe," he snapped, desperation sharpening his tone. "We were friends. Why can't we be friends again?"

She looked up at him, her eyes searching his. "You want us to be friends?"

"Yes."

He wasn't lying. He wanted them to be friends. Wisely, he didn't reiterate that he also wanted them to be lovers.

"You think we can be friends again after ..." Her face flushed. "You think we can go back to the way things used to be?"

The way things used to be? Before he'd realized how amazing she was ... before he'd started to obsess about what she looked like naked ... before he'd heard the sounds she made when she came?

No fucking way.

"We can go back to the way things used to be," he said, telling her what she wanted to hear.

"Just friends?"

No fucking way.

"Just friends," he confirmed.

He waited for a lightning bolt to shoot from the sky as punishment for lying. When nothing happened, he expelled a relieved breath. Apparently, the Big Guy upstairs was too busy with other sinners to bother with Garrett.

His prevarication obviously fooled Phoebe because she visibly relaxed. Tapping the wine menu with her forefinger, she said, "You should choose. My wine selecting skills have not improved."

As he returned to his seat, Garrett didn't bother to hide his satisfied smile. She'd let him back in her life, and if things went his way, it wouldn't be long until she was back in his bed.

CHAPTER EIGHT

"What do you think of my selection?" Garrett asked as he refilled Phoebe's wine glass with a Riesling from Oregon's Willamette Valley.

"It's an inspired choice," she answered lightly, "especially since you prefer merlot."

As he returned the bottle to the earthenware bucket sitting at the end of the table, her gaze settled on his large hand. Just a few days ago, that same hand had given her a soul-shaking orgasm.

She hadn't enjoyed even a mediocre orgasm in three long years. She'd wondered if cancer had robbed her of the ability to feel pleasure. Although she had masturbated, she hadn't been able to bring herself to climax, regardless of how long she'd played with herself.

Neither manual stimulation nor battery-powered toys had worked. Yet Garrett and his talented fingers had gotten her off in under five minutes.

The memory of what had happened at the spa danced through her head, warming her belly and dampening her panties. She didn't know what was more unbelievable, the fact that Garrett had wanted to have sex with her again or the fact that she'd had the strength to turn him down.

She desperately wanted a repeat of that long-ago night. But it would be too dangerous for her, emotionally, if not physically.

Friendship was all she could give Garrett. Anything more would just hurt her. And it would hurt him too if he truly had any feelings for her beyond friendship and lust.

His deep voice jolted her out of her morose thoughts. "I thought a Riesling would complement our Moroccan dinner."

Swirling the pale gold liquid in her glass, she said, "By the time our food comes out, we'll be finished with this bottle."

He shrugged. "So, we'll get another."

She barely stopped herself from blurting out, *The last time we shared a bottle of wine, we ended up naked.*

Her thoughts must have been visible on her face because his mouth hitched up in a knowing smile. His eyes glinted with amusement, the skin around them crinkling.

With a blush staining her cheeks, she groped for something to talk about. Work seemed like a nice, safe topic.

"My boss gave me a big project today," she said, "and I'm a little worried about it."

He lifted a dark eyebrow. "What kind of project?"

"An analysis of the best and worst performing Riley O'Brien & Co. stores. I'm supposed to figure out if the best performing stores have anything in common. Type of retail environment, surrounding trade area, other retailers that are nearby. Stuff like that. And I have to do the same thing for the worst performing stores."

"That sounds like a real estate project."

She nodded. "It is."

He frowned, and little lines appeared on his tan forehead. "Jake said you worked in the e-commerce group."

"E-commerce was my previous rotation. I moved to the real estate group last week."

She wondered if Garrett had asked Jake about her or if Kyla's husband had volunteered the information. What else had they talked about?

Tracing the rim of her wineglass with her forefinger, she said, "This is my first project for my new boss. That's why I'm worried."

To her surprise, Garrett grasped her hand. "There's no reason to be worried. You have one of the most analytical minds I've ever come across." He rubbed his thumb over her knuckles, and little tingles skipped up her arm. "You don't give yourself enough credit. And I'll help you if you need it."

His generous offer produced more tingles than his touch. "You have an entire company to worry about. You don't have time to help me."

"For you, Phoebe, I'll make time. Day or night."

Day or night.

They stared at each other, the air around them almost shimmering with sexual tension, like a mirage in the desert. Sucking in a shaky breath, she tugged her hand away from his. His fingers closed into a fist but then he picked up his wine.

After downing a mouthful of Riesling, he asked, "Why did you take a spot in Riley O'Brien's trainee program? Aren't those positions for people who've recently completed their graduate degree? You've been working for three years in addition to the work experience you had before U-Dub."

His question caught her off guard. As she floundered for an answer, he stared at her unblinkingly, his gaze openly curious. He didn't know that she'd spent the last several years fighting cancer instead of climbing the corporate ladder.

"Anyone can apply to the program, regardless of education or experience."

He nodded thoughtfully. "Gale Hotel Group doesn't have a management trainee program, but it's something I've been thinking about."

"You should talk to Kyla. She's made some changes to the program since she took over." Plucking a piece of pita bread from a wicker basket, Phoebe asked, "How many people work for you?"

"Nearly thirteen hundred."

Compared to Riley O'Brien & Co., which employed tens of thousands of people, Garrett's firm wasn't big. But Phoebe was still impressed. He'd started with nothing more than an idea.

She dipped the pita bread into the *bessara* and took a bite. Made of fava beans and seasoned with olive oil, lemon juice, and garlic, the dip reminded her of Lebanese *hummus*, which happened to be one of her favorite foods.

"We have a fairly lean corporate staff in Seattle, around fifty people or so," Garrett continued. "Each hotel employs a couple hundred people. We try to keep the turnover low, but it's hard to hang on to people, especially in housekeeping and foodservice."

"I think every company struggles with turnover of some sort. I know Riley O'Brien & Co. has a lot of turnover with its store associates. Retail hours are long, and the pay isn't that great." She gestured to the *bessara*. "Do you want some? It's really good."

He shook his head. "I don't like anything that tastes like *hummus*."

"Since when? You always ordered *hummus* when we went to that little Mediterranean café near the U-Dub campus."

"I ordered it because you liked it."

Two thoughts struck her simultaneously. One, Garrett was incredibly considerate, and two, she'd eaten those big servings of pita and *hummus* all by herself. No wonder she'd had to shop in the plus size section.

Moments later, the male server arrived with their entrées. She'd ordered chicken tagine with apricot and almond couscous, while Garrett had picked traditional Moroccan beef stew and a chilled salad of zucchini, tomato, and onion.

When the server asked if they needed anything else, Garrett shot her a questioning glance. "Another bottle of wine?"

Content with water, she declined more wine. As the server moved away, Garrett eyed her plate with covetous eyes.

"That looks good," he said, his longing for her food evident.

She gave him a stern glance. "Don't even think about it, mister."

They ate in silence for a few minutes before Garrett spoke. "Where were you living before you moved to San Francisco?"

"Boise."

He placed his fork on the rim of his plate. "You went back home after grad school?"

"Yes."

His jaw tightened, and he glanced away. She sensed that her answer had upset him, but she couldn't imagine why.

"Do you still live in Belltown?" she asked, referring to the trendy neighborhood situated on Seattle's waterfront. When she and Garrett had attended U-Dub, he'd lived in a high-rise overlooking Elliot Bay.

His gaze swung back to her. "No. I moved in with Pops a couple of months after graduation."

Garrett had introduced Phoebe to his grandfather, Ronald, when the older man had been in the hospital after suffering a mild stroke. He had instructed her to call him Pops, and then he'd directed his grandson to "stop screwing around and marry Phoebe".

She had no idea where Ronald had gotten the idea that she and Garrett were a couple. While she'd been embarrassed by the octogenarian's erroneous assumption, mostly because she had secretly wished for the exact same thing, Garrett had just laughed.

"How is Pops?"

Garrett smiled, his love for his grandfather evident. "Let's just say he won the longevity lotto. He'll be ninety-two next month."

She laughed. "You have the same DNA. You'll probably live even longer than Pops."

Her amusement drained away when she realized that Garrett would probably outlive her by a good sixty years, if not longer. She hadn't been lucky enough to win the longevity lotto.

Garrett took a sip of wine before asking, "Did you move to San Francisco because of the opportunity with Riley O'Brien?"

"No. I made the decision to move here, and then I found a job."

"Why didn't you want to stay in Boise? Your family's still there, right? Your parents and brothers?"

"Yes." She fiddled nervously with her knife, wondering how to reply. Realizing that she could answer his question honestly without disclosing her cancer, she said, "I felt a little smothered."

His lips twitched. "I'm sure you did. You're the youngest and the only girl."

Her parents and her brothers had babied her since birth, and her cancer had made them even more overprotective. Though she appreciated the love and support they'd given her, their hovering had started to grate. It was hard enough to deal with cancer hanging over her head like a guillotine without everyone treating her like an invalid.

Garrett picked up his fork, but instead of eating off his own plate, he stabbed a piece of chicken off hers. As he brought it to his mouth, she kicked him under the table, not hard, just a tap.

"If you wanted chicken tagine," she groused, "you should have ordered it."

Although his mouth was busy chewing, she could tell he wanted to smile. This was their old routine—him eating off her plate, her chastising him, and him offering little tidbits of his meal to repay her.

Switching his fork for a spoon, he scooped some stew from the orange bowl in front of him and held it up to her mouth. She parted her lips with no hesitation, the whole situation as comfortable and familiar as her favorite flannel nightgown.

He spooned the food into her mouth. As she chewed the flavorful combination of tender beef, Kalamata olives, raisins, and garbanzo beans, she got hints of cinnamon and cumin and a little kick of lemon.

"Oh, that's good," she murmured, licking her lips. "Give me another bite."

He didn't give her what she wanted. Instead, his eyes dropped to her mouth and stayed there for several heartbeats. She watched as his pupils expanded and his irises darkened from bright turquoise to deep teal.

She had seen that look in his eyes before, but she hadn't recognized it for what it was. She did now. He wanted her naked and exposed for his pleasure ... and hers.

Suddenly, the situation was no longer comfortable. And neither was the ache between her thighs. Feeling a syrupy trickle of arousal into her panties, she silently cursed herself and shifted on the banquette seat.

She'd known it would be impossible for them to go back to

the way things used to be. They had opened Pandora's Box that night in Seattle. Or, to be more accurate, they had opened Phoebe's box.

They'd released a powerful force into their friendship—desire. And that desire simmered beneath the surface like a dormant volcano on the verge of erupting.

CHAPTER NINE

As the drizzle turned into a downpour, Phoebe berated herself for forgetting her umbrella at work and for staying too long at happy hour. If she'd left the cozy pub just a few minutes earlier, she wouldn't have been forced to take shelter under the portico of a shuttered, rundown building.

Through the veil of heavy rain, she watched cars roll by. She searched for a cab with its light on, but the sudden deluge had sent pedestrians scurrying for cover. The cabs were all occupied, and only a few hearty souls trudged along the sidewalks, their shoulders hunched and their faces tucked into their chests.

Droplets of chilly water dribbled onto her face, and she swiped them away before shaking her head. More droplets flew from her hair, and she laughed, imagining herself as a wet dog. At least she didn't smell like one.

Deciding to wait out the rain, she adjusted her knitted scarf so it covered her neck more effectively and slid her hands into the pockets of her tan trench coat. As she leaned back against the building's granite façade, she studied the metal Art Deco design covering the door.

She wondered what the dilapidated building had been like in

its heyday. She loved old structures, and it made her sad when historic gems fell into disrepair.

To her surprise, one of the doors opened, and a short, bald man emerged. Like her, he wore a tan trench coat. A black cylindrical tube hung over his shoulder, like those carried by architects and contractors. He snapped open a plaid umbrella and hurried away, never glancing Phoebe's direction.

Curious, she edged closer, hoping to get a peek inside the building. The door opened again, this time revealing a large, male hand and an arm clad in a light gray dress shirt. As the man pushed through the door, she lurched to the side, trying to make herself invisible. She didn't want to be caught snooping, even if that was what she'd been doing.

He must have sensed her lurking nearby, though, because his dark head swung toward her. All her breath whooshed from her lungs. She gaped at Garrett in disbelief, wondering if this was some kind of cosmic joke.

One million people lived in the city and another six million lived in the entire Bay Area. Yet she kept running into Garrett—the only man who made her heart race and her panties wet.

She groaned under her breath. Of all the buildings in San Francisco, why had she taken shelter under this one?

Garrett did a double-take when he saw her, his handsome face stamped with surprise. But confusion soon replaced it, and his black brows drew together.

"Are you waiting for me?" he asked, clearly baffled by her presence.

Mutely, she shook her head. A frown overtook his face, his brows slashing downward.

"If you're not waiting for me, then what are you doing here?"

Finding her voice, she answered, "Staying dry." She waved

her hand in the general direction of the pub. "I went to happy hour down the street. I was heading for the BART station when it started to rain."

A spark of amusement lit his eyes. "Where's your umbrella, Miss I'm-Always-Prepared-for-Rain?"

She smiled ruefully. "I forgot it at work."

When she'd lived in Seattle, she had carried an umbrella with her everywhere. She'd even stashed extras in her car, her cubby in the business building, and the gym she'd visited diligently. Garrett had always made fun of her umbrella obsession, even though he'd benefited from it more than once.

His gaze moved from her face to her hair, and she barely suppressed a wince. She had no doubt it was a frizzy mess.

Stepping closer, he touched one of the damp curls hanging over her forehead. "Is your hair naturally curly?"

"Yes."

He rubbed the curl between his thumb and forefinger. "How did I never notice that?" he asked softly, almost as if he were talking to himself.

She shrugged uncomfortably. There hadn't been anything to notice. Her pre-chemo hair had been straight and easy to manage. When it had grown back, it had been curly.

She'd invested quite a bit of time and money trying to tame her curly hair. It had taken more than a year, but she had finally figured out the best products and techniques to create a reasonably attractive style.

Garrett gently tugged on her curl, pulling it straight and then letting go. It recoiled tightly, bouncing over her eye, and he chuckled. "*Boing.*"

He reached for the curl again, and she batted his hand away. "Stop it. You're worse than my five-year-old nephew."

His hand fell to his side. "Are you talking about Finn?"

She nodded, floored by his question. She couldn't believe he remembered her nephew's name. She'd only mentioned Finn once or twice when they'd attended U-Dub.

A mischievous smile tilted Garrett's mouth. "Does Finn like to play with Aunt Phoebe's curlicue hair?"

"Yes," she answered, tucking the unruly ringlet behind her ear. "He's not satisfied with looking. He has to touch."

Garrett's smile faded. "I know *exactly* how he feels."

He had that look in his eyes again. The one that made her stomach tingle and her knees shake. The one that made her forget everything except how good he had felt inside her.

Her body swayed toward his, lured by the attraction arcing between them. A horn blared from the street, followed by the screech of brakes and the squeal of tires. She stumbled backward, jerking her head toward the sound. She expected to see an accident, but traffic continued to move along the street, albeit slower than before.

She brought her attention back to Garrett, belatedly noticing the black trench coat draped over his arm and the expensive leather briefcase in his hand. "What are you doing here?" she asked. "Did you have a meeting? I thought this building was vacant."

"It is." He propped his shoulder against the granite façade, seemingly unbothered by the damp, chilly air. "We acquired it just before Christmas."

"What are you going to do with it?" she asked, hoping he planned to rehab the building rather than raze it.

He sighed. "Roll the dice."

"What does that mean?"

"It means I'm taking a huge risk. I'm spending millions to

renovate a building that's been overrun with bugs and rats for thirty years. And before that, the clientele was just as disgusting … albeit two-legged."

She smiled, relieved that Garrett was going to give this beautiful old building the care and attention it deserved. "It just needs a little love."

"*A lot* of love." He huffed out an exasperated laugh. "Forty million dollars' worth, to be specific."

"That is a lot of love," she conceded.

He cocked his head toward the entrance. "Do you want to see the *before?*"

She was interested in his plans to transform the building. But she was more interested in him.

Garrett had always fascinated her, especially the ease in which he interacted with everyone. His friendly charm was alien to her, yet so appealing. She couldn't resist him when he turned the full force of it on her.

Straightening to his full height, he reached out and grabbed the tail of her ruffled scarf. She let him use the pine green wool to tug her closer, and he loosely encircled her waist with the arm that held his coat and briefcase. His delicious scent enveloped her, and she barely resisted the urge to nuzzle her nose into the hollow of his throat.

"Come on, Phoebe," he cajoled in a low voice. "You know you want to. And if you see the *before*, you'll have a much better appreciation when you see the *after.*"

She reminded herself that it wasn't wise to spend even a few minutes with Garrett. It just made her want more. More of his time. More of his attention. More of *him.*

It wouldn't take much for her to become addicted to him. *Again.*

She had fallen into that trap during their time at U-Dub. She'd enjoyed being with him so much that she had manufactured reasons to extend their study dates by an hour or two.

The voice of reason warned her to keep her distance. But then a louder, more insistent voice pointed out one very important fact: she'd endured a lot of crap over the past three-plus years. She deserved a treat … a tall, dark, and handsome treat.

Nodded her acquiescence, she said, "I would like a tour."

Satisfaction blazed in his eyes, and he immediately ushered her inside. After locking the front doors behind them, he dropped his coat and briefcase on a drafting table near the entrance.

She placed her messenger bag next to his stuff but kept her coat and scarf since it wasn't much warmer inside the building. The heat wasn't on, but the electricity was. Chandeliers and wall sconces illuminated the first floor with a mellow glow.

He strolled to the middle of the lobby and faced her. Stretching his arms to the side in an expansive gesture, he boomed, "Welcome to The Pacifica! This ten-story building is one of the few examples of Art Deco design in San Francisco."

She couldn't help but smile at his little speech. He sounded like an overly enthusiastic tour guide.

"The Pacifica was designed by a young architect who made his way to the West Coast after working at the same firm that designed the Empire State Building. By the way, the Empire State Building is considered to be the finest example of Art Deco design in the world."

Behind Garrett, a huge central staircase bisected the main lobby, wider at the bottom and narrowing toward the top. The metal railings formed an intricate Art Deco design, but layers of gray paint detracted from their unique beauty.

There were so many stunning elements in the old building,

but *he* was the most stunning. The thick, shiny hair that was so dark it was almost black. Those mesmerizing aqua eyes. That faint five o'clock shadow along his strong jaw.

And his body ... it was enough to make a nun hot and bothered. Underneath that expensive button-down shirt, Phoebe knew his broad chest was dusted with dark, silky hair that led to tight, chiseled abs. Her eyes lingered on his charcoal pinstriped pants. With their flat-front, they fit his lean waist and long legs perfectly.

"What do you think?" Garrett asked.

For a moment, she was nonplussed. Then she realized he wasn't inquiring about his physique, he was talking about The Pacifica.

"I think it's amazing."

She was complimenting his building *and* his body. Of course, he didn't know that.

"Most people think it's a dump."

"I don't. I see a priceless diamond that needs to be polished." She gave him a knowing glance. "And I think you see the same thing."

"Maybe I do."

"There's no maybe about it," she countered. "You bought The Pacifica because you want to see it sparkle again."

"You know me too well." A slow smile curved his mouth. "I do want to see it sparkle again."

Curious about the building's origins, she asked, "Who built The Pacifica?"

"A group of wealthy businessmen. They saw a need for luxury residences that would appeal to single, professional men. The building welcomed its first residents in the late nineteen-twenties and quickly became *the* address for young lawyers and bankers."

Looking up, she took in the soaring two-story lobby. Layers of dingy, peeling paint marred the beauty of the coffered ceiling, but the craftsmanship of the individual squares was obvious.

"Even during The Great Depression, the building had a waiting list," Garrett said. "But when World War II began, most of the residents were drafted. At that point, the owners had to make a big decision: rent to women or deal with an empty building."

"That must have been a very difficult decision," she noted dryly.

"It was." He smiled crookedly. "Just think of all those women alone in the big city without any men to keep them—"

"To keep them *what*?" She arched her eyebrows, daring him to finish his chauvinistic sentence. "Don't even think of saying *under control* or *in line*."

His smile widened, his straight teeth flashing against his olive-toned skin. "I was going to say *entertained*."

"Sure you were."

Garrett chuckled for a moment but then his expression turned serious. "The women who lived in The Pacifica during the war didn't need to be entertained. They were too busy keeping this city running."

He lifted his gaze to the massive chandelier that hung above the lobby. "Before I bought my first hotel in San Francisco, I never realized the city played a significant role during World War II." He brought his attention back to her. "Did you know The Presidio was the nerve center for Army operations for the West Coast?"

She nodded. "I've toured The Presidio, so I know a little bit of its history."

Today, The Presidio of San Francisco was part of the Golden Gate National Recreation Area. Previously, it had served as an

Army outpost for three nations for more than two hundred years, first Spain, then Mexico, and finally the United States. One of the most notable parts of the installation was Crissy Field, the military's first Air Coast Defense Station on the Pacific Coast.

"Thousands of women migrated to San Francisco for defense-related jobs, and they needed a place to live," Garrett said. "The Pacifica was one of the buildings that housed them."

Phoebe strolled around the lobby, her low-heeled ankle boots made a scratching noise on the dirty marble floor, the grit grinding under her sole. In her mind, she imagined the women who had lived at The Pacifica. She saw their wavy hair and bright red lips and the black lines drawn down the backs of their legs to mimic stockings.

"I think it's ironic that our guys were fighting to liberate Europe from Hitler, but they ended up liberating women here," Phoebe said. "Their absence gave women the freedom to do what they wanted."

Garrett nodded. "Before World War II, women usually lived with their parents until they got married. They rarely lived on their own. If they did, they were criticized and accused of immoral behavior. But the war changed everything."

"Did you know that some women fooled around with enlisted men during the war to show their patriotism?"

His lips twitched almost imperceptibly. "No, I didn't know that."

"They were called Victory Girls, khaki-whackies, and patriotutes."

"I bet The Pacifica housed more than a few Victory Girls, khaki-whackies and patriotutes."

"Rosie the Riveter by day, Patty the Patriotute by night."

"She must have been exhausted from drilling all day and getting drilled all night."

Unable to contain her mirth, she snickered loudly. He sauntered across the scuffed marble and stopped in front of her. As she struggled to get herself under control, he watched her. His eyes shimmered like the water of the Caribbean, warm and inviting.

When she finally caught her breath, he said, "Have dinner with me. We can talk more about female sexuality throughout the decades."

"I'm sure you have a lot of opinions about that subject."

"Have dinner with me." A little smile played around his kissable mouth. "Come on, Phoebe. You know you want to."

CHAPTER TEN

A warm weight pressed on Garrett's crotch, jolting him from a deep slumber. It took him a moment to realize where he was, and when he did, his cock went from sleepy to stiff in a heartbeat.

He was stretched out on Phoebe's huge vintage sofa, the curved arm supporting his neck. Phoebe lay partly on top of him, sandwiched between his body and the sofa. Her head was nestled on his shoulder, and his arm was wrapped around her waist.

Closing his eyes, he savored the press of her soft curves against his side. Her hand rested on his chest, her thigh draped over his hip, and her bent knee nudged his erection.

This was how he'd wanted to wake up three years ago ... well, not exactly. He'd wanted to wake up with Phoebe in his arms *naked.*

Right now, he couldn't feel her silky skin against his because they were clothed. If he possessed magic powers, he'd snap his fingers and make the layers of cotton and wool between them disappear so he could touch and taste her bare skin.

But holding her was better than nothing at all. It was more than he'd expected when he had given her a ride home after dinner.

To his surprise, she'd invited him into her apartment without any prompts or hints. Then she'd asked if he wanted to watch a movie with her. She no longer seemed to want to avoid him, and he hoped that meant they would be spending more time together, both in and out of bed.

Phoebe loved Alfred Hitchcock films, and tonight they'd watched *Vertigo*. He'd seen the movie at least ten times, all with her. He wasn't a big Hitchcock fan, but Garrett never got tired of watching the legendary director's work, especially since it gave him an opportunity to be close to Phoebe. Hell, he'd watch every sugary chick flick ever made if she snuggled up next to him.

The evening had reminded him of their time in Seattle. He'd spent hours on Phoebe's sofa, studying class notes, and watching old movies. His favorite part of the evening had been holding her close when she fell asleep halfway through the flick. He'd never nodded off, though, so this was a first for him.

Slipping his hand under the hem of her sweater, he stroked the smooth skin of her back. His brain chastised him for copping a feel, but his cock encouraged his hands to drift lower, maybe under the waistband of her jeans and into her panties. Since he was a decent guy— or at least he *tried* to be one—he kept his hand out of her pants.

She sighed softly in her sleep. Glancing down, he attempted to make out her feminine features. The TV screen was black, and only a few beams of light shone through the windows from the lampposts outside. Shadows blanketed the room, and her face was nothing but a pale blur.

She shifted, and her hand slid down his chest to his stomach. His cock throbbed, and it took every ounce of willpower he possessed not to roll her under him and take what he needed so badly.

She was *killing* him with this "just friends" bullshit. He'd suffered through the same thing back when they'd been in grad school.

By that point in his life, he had dated a lot of women and had sex with more than a few of them. But he'd never wanted any of them the way he had wanted Phoebe.

Before she'd come into his life, he had never felt the need to see a woman every day or talk to her every night before he went to sleep. But Phoebe had made him feel things he had never felt before, and for the first time in his life, he'd been afraid of being rejected by a woman.

As graduation had neared, he'd schemed for ways to keep her in his life. He had even thought about asking her to join him when he launched Gale Hotel Group.

He'd spent hours talking with her about his dream of owning a portfolio of hotels around the world, and he hadn't been able to think of anyone he trusted more than Phoebe. She was unlike any other woman he'd ever known—strong, yet soft and giving.

Maintaining the pretense that he only wanted to be friends with her was excruciating. He knew she was attracted to him. She tried to hide it, but he could see the desire in her eyes, hear it in the hitch of her breath when he got close, and feel it spark between them.

He didn't understand her insistence on keeping their relationship platonic ... why she kept pushing him away. She wanted him, although he doubted she wanted him as much as he wanted her. He had passed the point of desperation a long fucking time ago.

As Garrett reclined on the sofa, Phoebe shifted again, this time almost crawling on top of him. His cock thickened even more, and sweat pooled in the small of his back. He took a deep breath, hoping to calm himself. Instead, her scent filled his lungs, the smell of plums so sweet and delicious his mouth literally watered.

Groaning softly, he removed her hand from his chest and maneuvered her off him. He deserved a fucking medal for withstanding the temptation to wake her, pull her on top of him, and grind into her softness.

As he slid to the edge of the sofa, she snuffled sleepily. He was so turned on, even that sounded sexy to him.

Her breathing abruptly changed, and her body stiffened, signaling that she'd woken up. He expected her to sit up once she realized where she was, but to his surprise, she relaxed against him. Three years ago, she would have jumped off the sofa like a cat with its tail on fire.

"Are you awake?" she asked softly.

"Yeah."

He was in a precarious situation, teetering on the edge of the sofa. He needed to either get up or move over. He scooted closer to her, and she snuggled up to his side. They lay there for a long time, their breathing the only sound in the room.

Finally, her voice drifted through the darkness. "I have a bad habit of falling asleep on you."

"I wouldn't call it a *bad* habit, although you drool."

She gasped in affront. "I do not."

"You're right. That was another Phoebe. You're the one who gropes me while you sleep."

She lifted her head. "I do *not*, you liar."

"How do you know? You're asleep."

"*Oh, God*," she breathed, dropping her head back to his shoulder. "Do I really grope you in my sleep?"

He chuckled. "Yes, you do."

"I'm sorry."

His laughter died in his throat. "I'm not. You can grope me any time you want, petal."

"Did you just call me *petal?*" she asked, confusion coloring her voice.

"Yes."

"Why?"

"Because your skin reminds me of a rose petal," he explained. "Smooth. Soft. Delicate."

He waited for her to respond, maybe order him not to call her *petal* ever again. But she didn't.

After a long moment, she burrowed closer. "You're so warm."

He wasn't warm. He was burning up. His erection strained against his zipper, and he tried to think about something that would deflate his dick. He forced himself to imagine the colony of rats infesting The Pacifica, but even that couldn't get rid of his hard-on. Phoebe and her luscious body were rat-defying.

Cottony silence cocooned the room—the kind that invited you to share secrets and confess crimes. But he had no secrets to share. She already knew them all. And his only crime had been letting her get away. He wasn't going to be so stupid again.

"I missed you," he admitted. "I missed hanging out with you."

She rubbed her sock-covered foot against the wool material of his pants, creating a hiss of static electricity. "I missed you too."

Then why did you leave me?

"How much did you miss me?" he asked.

"I missed you a lot." After several heartbeats, she asked, "How much did you miss me?"

"A lot. It was hard to go from seeing you every day to not

seeing you at all." He nuzzled his face in her hair, and her springy curls tickled his nose and mouth. "It was like going cold turkey."

She giggled. "You make me sound like an addiction."

He didn't share her amusement. He had been addicted to her. He still was. And he had a feeling he always would be.

"I don't want you to disappear from my life again." She didn't reply, and after a moment, he asked, "Did you hear what I said?"

"Yes."

He dropped a kiss on the top of her head. "Don't disappear on me," he murmured into her curls.

"What time is it?" She exhaled softly. "It must be really late."

She sat up and crawled to the other end of the oversized sofa. He heard her fumbling with something on the end table, and seconds later, a lamp flared to life. Blinking against the sudden brightness, he was finally able to focus on Phoebe. Little ringlets stuck out from her head in chocolaty zigzags.

She picked up her phone. "It's almost four o'clock."

He sat up and swung his legs over the side of the sofa. His neck twinged, and he stretched it side-to-side to work out the crick.

"At least it's Saturday," he said. "We can stay in bed all day if we want."

Her head snapped toward him, her expression filled with both surprise and anticipation. And in that moment, he promised himself that he would put an end to this "just friends" bullshit before the weekend was over.

Giving her his most innocent smile, he asked, "What would you like to do today?"

CHAPTER ELEVEN

"I've never been to a parade at night," Garrett said, his deep voice rumbling right next to Phoebe's ear. "This is fun."

She agreed with him wholeheartedly. Even so, she wished she'd never suggested that they go to the Chinese New Year parade when he'd asked what she would like to do today. She needed to limit her exposure to him, just like a freckly redhead shunned the sun.

Unfortunately, she couldn't avoid him, not at this precise moment. Thousands of spectators clogged the streets, eager to get a glimpse of the parade, and she and Garrett were squashed together like a peanut butter and jelly sandwich.

He stood behind her, his strong body pressed against her back. Like her, he wore dark-washed jeans, tennis shoes, and several layers on top to ward off the chilly air.

As he shifted, the sleeve of his gray quilted North Face jacket brushed against her side before his big hand settled on her hip. She could feel the warmth of his palm through her puffy blue coat, radiating heat to places that were already damp and achy.

She clenched her thighs together, disgusted with herself for ignoring her better judgment. Instead of exploring Chinatown and watching the parade with Garrett, she should have gone alone. Or she should have stayed home, watched the Hitchcock movie marathon on TV, and done her laundry.

But had she done either of those things? No.

Idiot.

She'd taken one look at him sitting on her sofa—his sleepy eyes, mussed hair, and sooty stubble—and her self-control had disappeared like a bowl of guacamole at a Super Bowl party. No, that wasn't true. It had disappeared well before then, probably the second she'd gazed into his gorgeous eyes at Jake and Kyla's party.

The past twenty-four hours had been filled with *I shouldn't haves.* As in, *I shouldn't have accepted Garrett's invitation to tour The Pacifica. I shouldn't have gone to dinner with him. I shouldn't have let him drive me home.*

And the cherry on top of the sundae: *I shouldn't have asked Garrett if he wanted to watch a movie with me.*

When she'd slid into the leather seat of his silver Mercedes last night, she'd told herself to politely thank him for dinner and then wave good-bye. She'd warned herself not to invite him into her apartment, even if he asked to come up. But her mouth hadn't heeded the warning, and now her heart was in danger.

Taking a deep breath of frosty air, she forced herself to focus on the parade. It had begun in the 1860s during the Gold Rush, and now it was the largest Asian event in North America.

Like most parades, this one featured high school marching bands, dance troupes, huge floats, and a beauty queen. But it was unique because it also had smoke, firecrackers, and a three-hundred-foot dragon carried by more than a hundred martial artists.

Garrett bent down until his cheek touched hers. "Look at

that." He pointed to the massive fortune cookie-shaped float in front of them. "I'm thinking the fortune inside says *size matters*. Or maybe *bigger is better*."

She couldn't help but laugh. He turned his head, and they were so close she could see the variegated flecks of sapphire, azure, and turquoise in his ocean-blue eyes.

"What do you think it says?" he asked, his gaze locked on hers.

With him so distractingly close, it took her a moment to remember what they'd been talking about … oh, right, the fortune in the giant fortune cookie float.

"Don't bite off more than you can chew," she said.

Good advice, Phoebe.

"That definitely fits." He shook his head with a frown. "But I don't like that saying."

"Why not?"

"Because it sows the seeds of self-doubt. When people say that, what they really mean is that they don't have faith in you."

"I don't think that's true," she countered. "I think they're saying that you should know your limitations."

His lips quirked. "No one knows their limitations until they slam into them face first."

"So, you'd rather take a huge bite and choke on it."

He laughed. "Well, when you put it that way … *no*."

"That's what I thought."

The Balboa High School marching band passed in front of them, making further conversation impossible. The familiar notes of Lady Gaga's "Bad Romance" blasted their ears, and the crowd shouted the lyrics as the musicians stomped by. The school's dance team followed, dressed in white latex bodysuits and platform boots like those Lady Gaga wore in the "Bad Romance" music video.

Phoebe grimaced. "I feel sorry for those girls. Their feet are probably a blistered, bloody mess inside those boots."

"I would *never* let my teenage daughter out of the house like that," Garrett vowed.

His words made her chest feel funny. In all the time she'd known him, she had never imagined him as a father. Suddenly the image of him surrounded by little girls filled her head. She had no doubt he'd be a wonderful daddy, and if his daughters got his looks, they'd break hearts the moment they came out of the womb.

"Those outfits are *indecent*," he added, sounding more like a spinster aunt than the man who'd had sex with her in the hallway of his condo building.

She looked sideways, and his lips grazed her nose. "Don't most guys like indecent outfits?"

"Not on teenage girls who can't even drive yet." The corner of his mouth hitched up. "I'd like to see you in one of those outfits, though. Or maybe just the boots." He blinked slowly, his smile widening. "Yeah, I'd *really* like that."

She thought about standing in front of Garrett wearing nothing but white leather platform boots and a smile. Heat suffused her entire body, a fiery mix of embarrassment and arousal, and a little moan escaped from her mouth.

As she snapped her head forward, he laughed softly. His warm breath wafted through her knitted cap. Goose bumps lifted on her skin, and her nipples pebbled under the lacy cups of her bra.

Trying to ignore him, she feigned interest in the parade. She watched as another float slid past, this one featuring a replica of the Golden Gate Bridge. A red-and-gold dragon perched on one of the cables, its mouth opened wide to show its sharp teeth.

"According to Chinese lore, dragons scare away evil spirits," she lectured in her most pedagogical voice. "They're supposed get rid of everything bad and unlucky to make room for a healthy, prosperous, and lucky new year. At the end of the parade, we'll see the golden dragon, Gum Lung."

Garrett slid his hand from her hip and placed his palm flat against her stomach, drawing her closer. "Dragons must be pretty powerful if they can scare away evil spirits."

She barely heard him. All she could think was that friends didn't touch each other the way he was touching her. They didn't invade each other's personal space the way he was invading hers.

All of a sudden, loud popping noises filled the air. She jerked in alarm, and he slipped his other arm around her, linking his hands together against her stomach.

Holding her tightly, he crooned, "It's okay, petal. It's just firecrackers."

The nickname, combined with his proximity, made her knees wobble. She told herself to shove his hands away and wiggle out of the cage of his arms. But her body melted against him, just as it had this morning on the sofa.

She still couldn't believe she'd cuddled with him in the hushed darkness of the early morning. Cuddled!

WTF? What were you thinking?

But that was the problem, wasn't it? She hadn't been thinking. She'd been *feeling*.

Garrett always made her feel too much. And when she was drowning in feelings, she ended up doing things she normally wouldn't do. Things like having sex in public and cuddling in the dark with a man who could never be hers.

When she'd woken up this morning, it had taken a single heartbeat for her to realize Garrett lay next to her. She had recognized him by the feel of his body and the scent of his skin.

Her first thought had been: *Too bad we're not naked.* Her second thought had been: *I wish I could stay like this forever.*

More firecrackers popped, the sound like a machine gun, and the smell of sulfur fogged the air. The heavy beat of the drums increased, and the crowd began to chant *Gum Lung.*

Garrett rested his head against hers, and all the noise and odors of the parade faded into the background. Pleasure saturated her cells, overwhelming her senses.

It felt so good to have his arms wrapped around her … to have his warmth surrounding her. And it wasn't just sexual. It went beyond that. It felt as if they fit, like two LEGO pieces snapping together.

Tears welled in her eyes, and she blinked rapidly to keep them from falling. No matter how hard she had tried to keep her feelings for Garrett buried, they had found their way to the surface.

Her love for him had never gone away. It had simply gone dormant, like daffodils or geraniums in winter. But once she'd seen him again that love had started to bloom.

Every moment she spent with him she fell deeper in love. She was more in love with him today than she'd been when she had rolled out of his bed so many years ago.

No matter how much she wanted to be with him, she had to stay away from him. They had no future together because *she* had no future.

CHAPTER TWELVE

After the cacophony of the parade, the streets of Chinatown seemed almost quiet now, despite the crowds of people. The acrid smell of sulfur still lingered in the air, a stinky reminder of the festive firecrackers.

Garrett looked down at Phoebe, smiling at the sight of her dark ringlets peeking out of the bottom of her knitted cap. With its ombré effect in shades of blue, the hat matched the scarf draped around her neck.

"I like your hat. And your scarf."

She glanced up. "Thanks." She touched the scarf with her gloved hand. "I made them. And my gloves."

Surprised, he said, "They don't look handmade."

"I assume you meant that as a compliment," she replied wryly.

He chuckled. "Yes, I meant it as a compliment."

His hats, scarves, and sweaters came from a store. He knew nothing about knitting, except that old women liked to do it. And apparently young women too.

"Have you been knitting for a long time? Where did you learn?"

She bit her lip before saying, "I've been knitting for a few years. I learned after I moved back to Boise."

He eyed Phoebe's handmade scarf with interest. "That looks pretty intricate. How did you get so good, so fast?"

She shrugged. "It's like any hobby. The more you do it, the better you get."

Reaching out, he stroked his fingers over the folds of the scarf. "What kind of material is this?"

"Cotton chenille."

"It's soft." He looked into her eyes as he brought his fingers to her cheek. "But not as soft as you are, petal."

Pink tinted her face, and he smiled at her obvious embarrassment. She was just so *adorable*.

She tugged his fingers away from her face, but didn't let go of his hand. They stood there staring at each other, their breath fogging the air.

"Maybe you can knit a sweater for me," he suggested. "I like sweaters. You can never have too many."

She blinked owlishly. "You want me to knit a sweater for you?"

"Yes," he answered with an emphatic nod. "I like the idea of wearing something you made just for me. I would think of you every time I wore it."

As he imagined her smooth fingers working those metal knitting tools, whatever the hell they were called, his cock twitched. He shook his head in disgust. He had to be only man on the planet who got turned on by *knitting*.

She dropped his hand as if it were a hot coal. "I'm not going to knit a sweater for you," she snapped.

Turning on her heel, she stalked off. He stared after her, wondering why she seemed so angry. Maybe he should have asked for a scarf instead.

He followed her, and since her stride was much shorter than his, he caught up to her in four steps. She didn't even glance in his direction.

They ambled along the sidewalk in silence for several minutes before he noticed a couple of teenage boys racing toward them. The kids shoved people out of the way as they ran, and Garrett rushed to shield Phoebe, not wanting her to be jostled.

One of the gangly boys collided with Garrett with a loud *oomph* and ended up sprawled on his ass. The teenager shook himself like a wet dog before scrambling to his feet and dashing off.

"That was like seeing a bird fly into the side of a mountain," Phoebe noted.

He resumed his place beside her. "Yeah, well, if not for this mountain, your ass ..." he patted her jean-covered rear "... would have been intimately familiar with the concrete."

She gasped softly, and he looked down into her wide green eyes. He was being *intimately familiar* with her, no longer denying his constant urge to touch her.

They resumed their walk. Beside him, she shivered. Draping his around her shoulders, he tucked her against him. He had plenty of body heat to share. Whenever she was around, his temperature spiked.

She immediately ducked out from under his arm, shoving her hands in her pockets. Irritation surged through him when she scooted sideways, putting more space between them. Clearly, she'd rather freeze than touch him.

Spotting a coffee cart a few feet ahead, he asked, "Want some hot chocolate?"

She nodded, and it didn't take long to place their order and be on their way with their beverages. As he took a sip of his salted caramel hot chocolate, he glanced around, studying the colorful storefronts and Chinese signs.

"I always wanted to visit Chinatown, but I never made time," he said. "I was too busy with work."

He abruptly realized he'd never made time to explore any of the cities where he'd bought hotels. The past several years had been all work and no play, except for the occasional hook up. And now that he thought about it, the casual sex had been more about blowing off steam than real gut-clenching desire.

"Other than The Presidio, I haven't been able to sightsee much either," Phoebe said. "I'd like to go to Fisherman's Wharf and watch the sea lions."

As they passed a shop with brightly colored silk tunics displayed in the window, he said, "I'd like to tour Alcatraz. Have you been there?"

"No."

"Maybe we can go together."

He would love to explore San Francisco's tourist attractions with her. He couldn't think of anyone else he'd rather go with. She made everything more interesting, even stopping at the gas station for a fill-up.

She didn't reply to his suggestion that they explore the city together. Instead, she took a sip of her peppermint hot chocolate.

After several moments of uncomfortable silence, he asked, "Do you like living here?"

"Yes."

"Better than Seattle?"

"No. I loved Seattle."

He wondered why she had moved back to Boise if she had loved Seattle so much. He prayed she hadn't moved because of him … because she'd been running from him and the memory of their night together.

"Do you think you'll ever move back?"

"To Seattle?" She glanced up at him. "Why would I move back? There's nothing there for me."

He clenched his jaw. *What about me?* he wanted to shout. *I'm there.*

As they reached the intersection of Powell and Bush Streets, he tossed his salted caramel hot chocolate into a metal trashcan on the corner. The rich drink wasn't sitting well in his stomach. Or maybe it was Phoebe's comment that wasn't sitting well.

"When are you going back to Seattle?" Phoebe asked as they turned left and headed toward the Powell Street BART station.

"This week. But first I'm going to Chicago to check on our property there. It was the second hotel we acquired after the one in Seattle."

She swallowed a mouthful of hot chocolate. He waited for her to respond, wondering if she even cared if or when he was coming back to San Francisco. Apparently not.

"I've never been to Chicago." She looked up at him. "That's one of my New Year's resolutions."

Confused, he asked, "Your New Year's resolution is to go to Chicago?"

She shook her head. "No. My resolution is to go somewhere I've never been before." Her lips turned down. "There are so many places I've never been. So many places I want to go."

They passed a Chinese restaurant, and she detoured to toss her hot chocolate in the garbage can near the eatery's entrance. When she returned to his side, he said, "I'll take you anywhere you want to go. Just tell me where and when."

She huffed out a laugh, the sound laced with incredulity. "That's not going to happen."

391

"Why not? I'll take care of everything. Transportation, lodging, food, entertainment."

Definitely the entertainment.

Stopping in the middle of the sidewalk, she glared up at him. "I'm not going on a trip with you, Garrett."

Aware that they had halted the sidewalk traffic, he tugged her toward a narrow opening between storefronts. He turned her until her back was against the brick wall, and he stood in front of her. He couldn't see her face—the light from the street wasn't strong enough to permeate the darkness—but he could hear her rapid, choppy breaths.

"Why are you so pissed off?" He placed his palms flat on the wall beside her head. "Most women would be happy if a guy offered to take them anywhere they wanted to go."

"I'm not most women," she snapped.

He laughed, the sound edged with frustration. "Clearly." He moved closer until his chest brushed against the front of her puffy jacket. "Friends travel together all the time, you know."

"Friends?" She angrily shoved his chest with both palms. "You didn't offer to take me anywhere I wanted to go because we're friends."

"Now you're catching on," he shot back before dropping his head and finding her mouth in the dark.

As he sucked on her lower lip, he got a taste of peppermint. He traced the seam of her lips with his tongue, but her mouth stayed stubbornly closed.

"Kiss me," he whispered against her lips. "Come on, Phoebe. You know you want to."

With a low moan, her lips fell open. He darted his tongue into the soft recesses of her mouth, licking deeply, before seeking out her tongue. Finding it, he sucked it into his mouth.

She moaned again and clutched his waist under his coat, digging her nails into his sides.

Dropping his hands to her ass, he lifted her against him until his erection settled into the apex between her thighs. She widened her legs, and he rocked into her softness as their tongues tangled. When that wasn't enough, he clenched his fingers in her ass cheeks and ground against her.

She gasped, inhaling the breath from his lungs, and jerked her mouth from his. He growled in protest, following her lips with his. Nudging her mouth open, he pushed his tongue past her lips and devoured her sweet depths.

As she writhed against his hard on, she sucked on his tongue … wet, delicious pulls that made his cock pulse. Tingles shot down his spine to the tip of his penis, and he pulled his mouth from hers, willing himself to calm down.

Gulping in oxygen, he loosened his hands and let her slide down until her feet touched the ground. She pushed her palms against his chest, and he released her.

"We can't do this," she said huskily.

"Why the fuck not?" He winced, realizing he sounded like an absolute douche. "*God.* I'm sorry. I'm just so…" He rubbed his hands over his face. "*Shit*, Phoebe. I don't understand you. I know you want me."

"No, I don't."

"You're lying." Crowding her against the wall, he cupped his hand over her mound. "If I stripped off your jeans right now, you'd be wet." He pressed his palm against the thick denim seam, and a strangled moan escaped her "You're wet, aren't you?"

"Yes," she panted.

"You want me." Bending down, he licked the corner of her mouth. "Say it."

393

She shuddered. "I want you."

"I know you do. I also know that I can make you come so hard that you'll scream until your voice is gone. And I know that once I get inside you, I'm going to stay there for a long, long time." Almost choking with frustration, he shook his head. "I *know* those things. But I don't know why you keep saying no. Explain it to me."

He stepped back, crossed his arms over his chest, and waited for her to say something ... anything. To his surprise, she lunged sideways and sprinted toward the street. It took him a second to process what had happened. By the time he reached the sidewalk, she was gone, swallowed up by the crowd.

Phoebe had left him. Again.

CHAPTER THIRTEEN

Garrett swiped his wrist over his sweaty forehead before grabbing some water from the mini fridge. As he twisted off the cap, he nudged the door closed with his knee.

Leaning against the granite bar, he chugged the ice-cold liquid, parched from his long workout. He'd spent nearly two hours in the hotel gym, making use of the rowing machine and free weights. He preferred to row outside, but the temperature in Chicago in early February barely topped twenty degrees, and he wasn't a fan of rowing with numb fingers.

Although he had hoped the exercise would take his mind off Phoebe, he'd thought about her with every lift and pull. After she'd abandoned him in Chinatown five days ago, he had decided not to chase after her, literally or figuratively. She might want him, but she didn't want to be *with* him.

After draining the plastic bottle, he crushed it with both hands and dropped it into the recycle bin next to the bar. He toed off his tennis shoes and headed across the large suite toward the bedroom. Halfway there, he heard a loud knock.

He moved to the door and checked the peephole by habit. Becca Holloway stood on the other side, her long strawberry blond hair loose around her shoulders and an overnight bag slung over her arm.

Shit. He'd been so fixated on a certain curly-haired brunette he had forgotten about Becca. They'd been hooking up for more than a year, enjoying vigorous, meaningless sex whenever he was in town. She was sexy, intelligent, and best of all, flexible.

This visit to the Windy City had been on his schedule since Christmas. Becca always confirmed his travel plans with his assistant and then showed up at his suite on his first night in town.

Opening the door, he said, "Becca, it's good to see you again."

She gave him a once over, her cornflower blue eyes heating. "Looks like you've been working out."

He nodded, and her glossy lips tipped into a coquettish smile. "I hope you still have some energy left."

Standing on her tiptoes, she brushed her mouth over his in a brief kiss. Her lips were full and smooth, but they didn't feel right against his.

They weren't Phoebe's lips.

He stepped back and ushered her into the suite. "Give me ten minutes to shower," he said, taking her bag, "and then we can grab some dinner."

After placing her bag next to the cushy arm chair, he strode toward the bedroom. Stopping at the threshold, he looked over his shoulder. "There's wine in the mini-bar if you want some. Or liquor if you prefer something harder."

She laughed. "Yes, Garrett, I prefer something harder. *Much harder.*"

Shaking his head in amusement, he closed the door behind him. As he walked to the en-suite bathroom, he stripped off his workout clothes.

All the bathrooms in his hotels were luxurious, but this one was particularly decadent. Black slate tiles covered the floor, and along with the requisite toilet and sink, it also featured a huge jetted tub and a glassed-in spa shower that could accommodate at least five people.

Using the digital touchpad on the wall next to the shower, he programmed the temperature and intensity of the water flow. A moment later, hot water streamed from the shower head and body jets, filling the bathroom with steamy fog.

He stepped into the shower and braced his hands against the white tumbled marble tile. Dropping his head, he let the hot water pour over him. What was he going to do about the gorgeous woman in his hotel suite?

As he shampooed his hair, his mind drifted to another gorgeous woman: Phoebe. She was probably just now leaving work. He wondered if she'd had a good day and how she planned to spend her evening.

He wished he was with her, eating takeout and watching an old Hitchcock flick. Maybe *Rearview Window*. He liked that one better than *Vertigo*.

Just as he reached for his body wash, cool air drifted over him. Glancing behind him, he saw Becca step into the shower, naked of course, with her long hair twisted on top of her head.

This wasn't the first time she'd joined him in the shower. It was one of his favorite places to fuck. He liked the feel of slippery smooth skin under his hands, slick with sudsy bubbles.

As he turned toward Becca, she moved closer, under the spray of the water. Droplets drenched her shoulders and dribbled over her firm breasts and rosy nipples. He waited for that spark of sexual interest, the familiar pressure in his penis, the sharp twinge in his testicles, but it wasn't there.

Placing her palms flat on his pecs, she kneaded gently before trailing one hand down his stomach. When she reached for his cock, he grasped her hand and held it immobile between them.

She looked up and met his gaze. They stared at each other for several heartbeats, silent and unmoving. After a moment, she wiggled her hand loose from his grip. Without a word, she turned and left the shower.

With a loud sigh, he lathered up his body and rinsed. When he exited the shower, the bathroom was empty, and the door was closed. After turning off the water with the touchpad, he nabbed a plush white towel from the sleek chrome towel bar and wrapped it around his waist.

As he opened the door and stepped over the threshold, he spotted Becca standing in front of the floor-to-ceiling windows. Clad in one of the hotel's white robes, she was looking out on the Chicago skyline. The high-rises sparkled against the dark backdrop of the night sky.

He padded across the room, stopping behind her. He could see her reflection in the windows, but couldn't see her expression.

Knowing he owed her an apology, he said, "I'm sorry, Becca."

She sighed. "What's her name?" He hesitated, but she persisted. "What's her name, Garrett?"

"Phoebe."

"That's a pretty name." She placed her palm on the window. "Is she the one?"

The one?

"What do you mean?" he asked.

She turned to face him. Staring at his bare chest, she said, "Put on some clothes, babe. A girl can only take so much temptation."

He hurried toward the dresser and pulled out a pair of black track pants. As he stepped into them, she asked, "Do you remember the night we met?"

Surprised, he glanced up. "Of course."

Becca was one of the top hotel brokers in the country, representing sellers in large transactions. She and Garrett had met at a cocktail party at the Americas Lodging Investment Summit in Los Angeles.

She was looking out the window again, her face in profile. "Do you remember what you said when I suggested that we get together the next time you came to Chicago?"

"No." He tied the drawstring on his waistband. "What did I say?"

"You said, 'Why not? I don't belong to anyone.'"

He pulled on a heather gray U-Dub T-shirt and made his way to her side. "I don't remember saying that, but it's true."

She laughed softly. "No, it's not. You belong to *her*. I knew you were in love with someone. I just didn't know her name."

He stared at their reflections, his pulse pounding in his ears and his heart thudding against his sternum. Taking his hand, she pulled him around until they faced each other.

"Is Phoebe the one? Do you belong to her? Are you in love with her?" Becca looked up him, her eyes softer than he'd ever seen them. "She is, isn't she?"

"Yes," he answered hoarsely, finally accepting the depth of his feelings for Phoebe. "But she doesn't feel the same. She doesn't belong to me. She doesn't love me."

Becca's hand tightened on his. "There's not a woman on this planet who wouldn't love you, Garrett." She led him to the seating area in the corner. "Sit."

As he dropped down into one of the overstuffed chairs, she left the room. She was only gone for a moment, and when she returned, she held two glasses.

"Scotch or vodka?" she asked, handing one of the tumblers to him.

"Scotch."

"Perfect. I'm in the mood for vodka."

She pulled two mini bottles of liquor from the pocket of her robe, and he plucked the scotch from her hand. He poured his drink, and she did the same before climbing into the other chair.

As she tucked one leg under her, she said, "Tell me about Phoebe."

He swallowed a mouthful of scotch. "What do you want to know?" he asked, the liquor warming his stomach.

"Everything."

So, he told Becca everything, even though it was weird to talk with his lover about the woman he loved. She listened silently, sipping her vodka. When he'd finished, they had burned through all the scotch and vodka, plus the whiskey, and they had scarfed down all the M&Ms, plain and peanut.

"Phoebe is sending you some crazy mixed signals, isn't she?"

He laughed harshly. "I think ditching me in the middle of Chinatown was a pretty clear message."

"What's your plan now?"

"I don't know." He scrubbed his hands over his face. "Move on with my life. Forget her."

"Garrett." His name was an exasperated sigh. "You've had more than three years to move on with your life. You've had plenty of time to forget her. But you haven't. You *can't*." She clicked her crimson fingernails against her empty glass. "I think I know what the problem is."

He arched an eyebrow. "Enlighten me."

"You've never told Phoebe how you feel about her. You've never told her that you want a relationship with her. You've just said that you want to have sex with her again. If I were her, I would think you wanted to be friends with benefits. Or that you just wanted a fling. Most women aren't interested in that."

Eying her thoughtfully, he said, "You were."

"That's all you were willing to give me, and I thought that was better than nothing at all." She smiled, a hint of sadness twisting her lips. "I knew you belonged to someone else, but that didn't stop me from falling in love with you too."

Her admission stunned him. "Becca … I …" he stuttered to a stop, unsure how to respond to her declaration of love.

Not once had he considered that their time together had meant something more to her. Now he felt like a real asshole for spending the last two hours babbling about Phoebe.

"I tried to keep things purely sexual, but you're so easy to love." Becca shook her head. "If I thought I could make you happy, Garrett, I'd fight for you. But Phoebe is the only woman who can do that. Tell her you love her. Tell her you want more than a fling."

He imagined baring his soul to Phoebe. Then he imagined her ordering him to leave her alone. His trepidation must have been evident on his face because Becca laughed.

"I just told you I loved you even though I know you're in love with someone else," she pointed out dryly. "If I can do that, you can be honest with Phoebe."

CHAPTER FOURTEEN

For a single, unattached woman like Phoebe, Valentine's Day was just another day. There had been no red roses or dark chocolate, although she had indulged in a small bowl of peanut butter fudge ice cream after finishing off her pasta primavera. And there had been no fragrant candles or sexy lingerie, although she had taken a long bubble bath and donned her favorite flannel pajamas afterward.

Now she was relaxing on her sofa, watching reruns of *The Big Bang Theory* and knitting a sweater that just happened to be the same size Garrett wore and the same color as his beautiful eyes.

Yep, just another day.

A buzzing noise filled her apartment, the sound indicating she had a visitor at the front door. Since she wasn't expecting anyone, she ignored it, sure the person downstairs would realize he had pushed the button for the wrong unit.

But the buzzer sounded again, this time longer and more insistent. She put her knitting aside and stomped to the intercom. Pushing the button, she shouted, "You have the wrong apartment!"

"No, I don't." Garrett's deep voice drifted from the speaker. "May I come up?"

Joy sparked inside her before she could tamp it down. She hadn't seen or heard from him in more than two weeks, not since the Chinese New Year parade.

She had missed him, and she really wanted to see him now. But she had promised herself that she would stay away from him.

As she debated whether to let him in, his voice came through the speaker again. "Please let me in. I need to talk to you."

She glanced down, evaluating her cozy pajamas. With their whimsical design of bright red cardinals, delicate tree branches, and egg-filled nests against a pale blue background, they weren't exactly sexy. They covered her from neck to ankle and were loose enough to disguise her lack of bra and underwear.

"Okay," she replied, pressing the button to unlock the exterior door.

She opened her front door and heard fast footsteps on the hardwood stairs as Garrett made his way up. Her pulse raced as she waited for him to round the corner.

And then … there he was, even more gorgeous than she remembered. His glossy hair was shorter than usual, as if he'd recently had it cut, and his face was cleanly shaven.

Her heart seemed to expand in her chest. She was so happy to see him a huge smile curved her mouth.

As he walked toward her, she appreciated the way his black trousers fit his long legs and the way his eggplant-colored sweater clung to his muscular chest and broad shoulders. A large black gift bag with little white polka dots dangled from his hand, and she wondered what was in it.

He stopped in front of her. His gaze roamed over her face, his blue eyes gleaming brightly despite the lack of illumination in the corridor. They stared at each other, their breathing fast and audible.

She wanted his strong arms to enfold her and pull her into his big body. She wanted to rest her head against his chest and breathe in his spicy, citrusy scent. Instead, she said, "Come in."

Accepting her invitation, he entered her apartment. She closed the door behind him and gestured to the living area. "Have a seat."

She curled up on one end of the vintage sofa, her knees drawn up against her chest. He placed the gift bag on the floor and sat down on the other end of the sofa, his body angled toward her and his eyes locked on her face.

After what seemed like hours of silence, she asked, "How long have you been in town?"

"A couple of days."

"How was your trip to Chicago?"

"Enlightening," he answered curtly.

Leaning sideways, he lifted the gift bag from the floor. He set it on the cushion between them.

"This is for you," he announced, his voice a little rough. "Happy Valentine's Day."

Surprised by the gift, she only managed to mutter, "Oh."

He nudged the bag toward her. "I was going to give you a necklace. One with a jeweled butterfly pendant. It reminded me of you. I don't know why." He shrugged. "I was just about to hand over my credit card when I realized most women like jewelry. Since we've already established you're not *most women*, I decided to give you something else."

She shook her head. "You shouldn't have bought me a Valentine's Day gift." She looked down at her lap. "I'm not your Valentine."

A sound emerged from his throat, a low growl that raised the fine hairs on her body. "Open it," he demanded.

The tone of his voice warned her that she had better open the bag *or else*. She tugged it closer and tipped it toward her so she could delve inside. She dug through hot pink tissue paper until she reached the contents: at least a dozen skeins of yarn.

Looking up, she met Garrett's eyes over the gift bag. "You bought me yarn?"

He nodded, his face flushed dark red. "Luxury yarn. Silk. Cashmere. Angora. Llama. Qiviut." He huffed out a soft laugh. "Who knew the most expensive yarn in the world is called qiviut and comes from a muskox? I don't even know what the hell a muskox is."

She couldn't help but smile. "A muskox is a mix between a goat and an antelope. They have thick, shaggy coats and large curved horns. They're arctic mammals, native to the tundra of North America and Greenland."

She decided not to tell Garrett that the name *muskox* came from the strong odor that male animals emitted during rutting season. She didn't want to say the words *odor* or *rutting* in his presence. She would never admit it out loud, but she was turned on by the thought of the odor Garrett might emit when he was rutting.

And now I'm comparing Garrett to a muskox. I'm such a pervert!

She pulled out a couple of skeins, one a sumptuous cashmere yarn in a gorgeous periwinkle color, and the other a lovely silk yarn in various shades of green, from mint to pine.

"They're all hand-dyed," he added.

Rubbing her fingers over the soft strands, she said, "They're beautiful." She returned the skeins to the bag and met his gaze. "Thank you, Garrett. This was really thoughtful."

"I would never give yarn to another woman. Only you." His blue eyes speared into her. "Phoebe, I—"

And then, suddenly, the gift bag was on the floor, and she was in his lap, her mouth fused to his and her hands tangled in his thick hair. His lack of response to her kiss, coupled with the stillness of his body, revealed his surprise.

Starving for him, she ravaged his mouth, licking and biting his lips. When his mouth opened under hers, she thrust her tongue inside, aggressively stroking over his teeth and the interior of his cheeks.

Arousal bloomed at her center, flooding her pajama bottoms. She widened her legs, moaning when his erection pressed into the notch between her thighs.

When she rocked against him, he gasped against her lips and jerked his head back. Dropping her hands to his shoulders, she stared into his eyes. They were heavy-lidded with lust, the pupils enlarged.

"How is this going to end, Phoebe?" he rasped. "With you kicking me out of your apartment? With you running away from me? With me never seeing you again?"

They had no future together. She knew that. But she wanted to live in the present, just for a little while. She loved this man, and right now, she needed him more than she needed air.

"No." She traced his lower lip with her fingers. "It's going to end with us naked."

He smiled slowly. "That's the beginning." Palming her butt, he rose from the sofa with her legs wrapped around his waist and her arms twined around his neck. "Where's your bedroom?"

"Down the hall. Second door on the right."

As he carried them out of the living room, she leaned forward and nuzzled her nose into his neck. He smelled so delicious she just had to taste him. She swiped her tongue over his skin, tracing little circles under his ear before sucking his earlobe into her mouth.

His hands clenched on her rear, and he picked up the pace, almost jogging. He stopped just inside her bedroom, and she flipped the switch to light her bedside lamps. Their bodies cast shadows on the pastel blue walls.

He brought her to the queen-sized bed, and she let herself fall backwards onto her blue-and-brown toile duvet.

"Do you have any condoms?" he asked, his voice so gravelly it sounded painful.

Propping herself up on her elbows, she shook her head regretfully. "I'm sorry. I haven't had a reason to buy any."

To her surprise, he smiled. "Don't apologize, petal. I'm glad you haven't had a reason." His smile widened. "But you have one now."

After kicking off his expensive black dress shoes, he grabbed the neck of his sweater and pulled it over his head, revealing his bare chest. "I have two condoms in my wallet. We'll have to make them last."

She barely heard what he said. She didn't know if her memory was faulty or if he was even more built than he'd been three years ago, but *snap*, his body was amazing. His skin gleamed dark gold in the glow of the lamps, his shoulders and arms dense with muscle.

Under a light dusting of dark hair, his chest looked as if it had been chiseled out of granite. Well-defined pectoral muscles topped a tight six pack split by a trail of silky-looking hair.

She sat up and hooked her fingers in his waistband. Tugging him closer, she placed a constellation of kisses on his stomach. His abdominal muscles jumped reflexively.

He laughed huskily. "I have a feeling those two condoms aren't going to last as long as I'd hoped. Mostly because *I'm* not going to last."

As she licked a circle around his belly button, she unbuckled his black leather belt. His erection tented the front of his pants, and she slid to the floor in front of him, eager to put her mouth on him. She hadn't had the opportunity three years ago.

He wove his fingers through her hair, playing with the curls. "Maybe I shouldn't admit this, but I fantasize about you going down on me all the time."

"What else do you fantasize about?" she asked, her hands busy unfastening his pants.

"What *don't* I fantasize about?" A laugh rustled in his throat. "They're always about you, in case you wondered."

"Really?" she asked, surprised and flattered.

He nodded, his expression nakedly sincere. "Always."

She pushed his pants and underwear past his hips, and his erection sprang free. Long and thick, it pointed toward his stomach.

She eyed it like a chocoholic drooling over brownies, her gaze zeroing in on the plump head. Fluid trickled from the tiny slit, creating a corresponding trickle between her legs. Leaning forward, she swiped her tongue over the tip, gathering his pre-cum. His taste burst in her mouth, rich and salty, and she cupped his testicles, learning the weight and texture of them.

As she wrapped her mouth around the flushed head of his penis, his fingers tightened in her hair. She sucked strongly before grasping the base of his erection. With more eagerness than finesse, she slid her mouth up and down his length. Finding a rhythm that consisted of sucks, swirls, and licks, she did her best to bring him to the edge.

With a deep groan, he tilted his hips forward, a silent request to take him deeper. She widened her mouth, and he touched the back of her throat. Humming at the fullness, she gently squeezed his sac.

He gasped. "Stop."

She looked up at him, wondering if he didn't like her technique. He brushed a couple of curls away from her forehead.

"I love what you're doing, but I don't want to finish this way." As he stepped back, his penis slid from her lips. "I want to be inside you."

He pulled her to her feet and had her pajamas off before she could blink. With a quick movement, he tugged back the comforter and dumped her on the lavender-scented sheets.

After kicking off his clothes and tossing the condoms on her nightstand, he came down on top of her. His hairy chest tickled her breasts, while his lower body settled snugly between her legs.

Bracing his hands beside her head on the mattress, he stared down into her eyes. Such intense emotion swirled in those aqua-colored depths, she shivered.

"Phoebe." The way he said her name was almost reverent. "You have no idea how much I want this ... how much I want you."

His words created a sweet ache in her chest. "I want you too."

Reaching between them, he trailed his hand down her stomach to the damp place between her thighs. She widened her legs in encouragement, and he eased his fingers between her folds, stroking the sensitive flesh with a light touch.

"You're soaked," he murmured, his tone tinged with satisfaction. "I love knowing that I make you this wet."

When his fingers grazed her clit, she couldn't hold back a moan. He wedged his hand deeper between her legs and dipped two fingers inside her. With his fingers slicked in her arousal, he returned to the knot of nerves at the top of her sex.

"Sensitive little nub." He massaged it gently. "So sweet and hard." He plucked at it, sending sparks up and down her spine.

"I can feel it throbbing with your heartbeat."

He lightly scraped his fingernail back and forth across her clit, intensifying the ache inside her. As he squeezed her nub between his fingers, a powerful orgasm shook her, darkening her vision. She closed her eyes, her entire body quaking with pleasure.

He rolled to the side, and she heard him tear open the condom. A second later, he was back, his erection positioned at her opening. Lifting her lids, she met his gaze. His eyes were so hot she thought her skin might sizzle.

"Are you ready?" he asked, his voice guttural. "Are you ready for me to fill you with my cock?"

Unable to form any words, she nodded. He palmed her butt and pressed forward. Her flesh resisted before softening around the head of his penis.

His breath hissed between his teeth. "Fuck, you feel good." He pumped forward and withdrew, going a little deeper with each tiny thrust. "Tight. Hot. *Perfect.*"

Tilting her hips, she took everything he gave her. She wrapped her arms and legs around him, her heart and body filled with Garrett.

"I can't…" He sucked in a huge breath. "I can't hold on."

"Then let go," she whispered, caressing the lean muscles of his back. "Just let go."

A groan vibrated his chest, and he began to move in deep, fast plunges that pushed her up the mattress. She gripped the metal headboard in both hands and met his hard thrusts. With each wet slide, his penis hit a sensitive spot, setting fire to her insides.

He increased his pace, slamming into her and forcing the headboard against the wall. He stilled suddenly, his entire body tensing.

Holding her butt in a crushing grip, he came. He shouted something unintelligible, his penis pulsing inside her. The vibrations hurled her into another orgasm, one so powerful her body arched off the bed.

She cried out his name as her vaginal muscles clenched around his length. He grunted and rooted deeper, still hard. Pleasure-pain ripped through her, making her ears ring and black spots dance in her vision.

He collapsed on top of her, panting, his face tucked into the side of her neck. When she finally noticed she couldn't breathe, she lightly slapped his shoulder.

"Move," she gasped.

Groaning, he pulled out and rolled onto his back. He reached for her, drawing her against his side.

"You're the one," he murmured. "You always have been."

CHAPTER FIFTEEN

When Phoebe entered the spacious waiting room for Oncology Associates of Northern California, she wasn't surprised to see that nearly every chair was occupied. The multi-physician practice was one of the largest cancer-care providers in the entire state. More important, it was one of the best.

She had an appointment with Dr. Dalal to check her tumor markers, which would indicate whether her cancer had returned. Her oncologist would also review the PET scan she'd had earlier in the week.

Dr. Dalal conducted these tests every three months. If they continued to come back clear for the next year, he would probably extend the testing schedule to six-month intervals.

After checking in with the front desk, Phoebe took a seat between a gaunt, older man and a forty-something woman with a navy blue silk scarf wrapped around her head. The woman looked up from the parenting magazine in her hands and smiled as Phoebe sat down.

Placing her canvas bag on the floor between her feet, she settled in for a long wait. Unlike a lot of physicians, Dr. Dalal didn't rush through his appointments. That meant he ran behind schedule by at least an hour, usually more.

Phoebe's oncologist in Boise had highly recommended Dr. Dalal, and this was her second appointment with him. She hadn't been prepared for the long wait the first time, but today she'd remembered to bring something to keep her busy.

Rummaging through her bag, she pulled out an unfinished knitting project. She hadn't made much progress on the cabled crewneck sweater. She'd been too busy to knit.

Over the past month, she had spent every non-working minute with Garrett. After Valentine's Day, he'd decided to stay in San Francisco indefinitely, and she knew it was because of her.

Except for one overnight trip to Houston that he hadn't been able to cancel, they had spent every night together, indulging in bone-melting, mind-numbing sex until they were nearly comatose. They alternated between her apartment and his suite in the Hudson San Francisco. She'd become a familiar face at the hotel, and most of the staff greeted her by name now.

She and Garrett had also spent time together out of bed. A couple of weeks ago he had surprised her with a romantic dinner at The Ellington Club, a romantic restaurant located on the top floor of the Hudson San Francisco. Additionally, they had visited Alcatraz, driven up to Napa to tour the wineries, and strolled through the recently opened Violet O'Brien Gold Rush History Museum.

"What are you making?"

The question came from the woman on her right.

Meeting the woman's friendly brown gaze, Phoebe answered, "A sweater."

"Really? It's so big I thought it was the beginnings of a blanket."

Smiling, Phoebe explained, "He's a big guy."

"My guy has a gut too." The woman nodded sagely. "A little too much beer during football season."

An image of Garrett's ripped abs and ridged V-cut flashed through Phoebe's mind, and she couldn't help but laugh. "I should have said *tall*," she clarified. "Or *broad-shouldered*."

The woman's light laughter joined Phoebe's before she held out her right hand. "Melanie Tavin."

Dropping the sweater to her lap, she took Melanie's hand. "Phoebe Werner."

With the introduction complete, Melanie asked, "Are you knitting the sweater for your boyfriend?"

A wave of yearning crashed over Phoebe. She wished Garrett could be her boyfriend, but that title implied permanence. And the only thing permanent in her life was cancer.

"No, it's not for my boyfriend."

"A relative, then?"

"No."

Melanie eyed her thoughtfully. "I really like the color you chose. My husband took me to Bora Bora for our fifteenth anniversary, and the water was the same shade as that yarn."

Phoebe fingered the soft aqua-colored wool in her lap. "It matches his eyes."

"Tall. Broad shoulders. Gorgeous eyes." Melanie crossed her jean-clad legs, the denim making a rasping sound as it rubbed together. "He sounds hot. Lucky for you, he's not a relative."

Yes, Garrett was hot ... beyond hot, in fact. *Scorching.* He could have any woman he wanted, and Phoebe still found it hard to believe he wanted her. She still found it hard to believe that she was the one who turned him on so much he trembled and gasped and moaned.

He definitely turned her on. But she loved more than his hot body. She loved *him*—everything about him, even though he could be stubborn, arrogant, and impatient. His innate kindness, gentle charm, and playful sense of humor more than made up for those things.

Melanie spoke again, regaining Phoebe's attention. "I tried to learn to knit, years ago, but I guess I don't have the patience. Or the dexterity."

Phoebe studied the unfinished sweater in her lap. She'd chosen a complicated pattern, but had decided to use a basic ribbed stitch because she didn't want the garment to be bulky. A ribbed stitch offered a lot of elasticity and conformed to the wearer.

"I learned to knit while undergoing chemo," Phoebe divulged, surprising herself because she rarely spoke about her cancer, not even to people who had gone through the same thing. "I was going crazy, just sitting there for hours with the meds dripping into me. I was too on edge to focus enough to read or do crossword puzzles or sudoku. One of the nurses suggested knitting. For some reason, I picked it up pretty easily."

"What kind of cancer do you have?"

"Breast."

"Me too."

They sat silently for a while until Melanie asked, "When were you diagnosed?"

"Almost four years ago."

"How old were you? You look really young."

"Twenty-seven."

"That *is* young. I was older than you when I was diagnosed. I had just turned thirty-five." Melanie laughed sadly. "I had a four-year-old son and two-year-old twin daughters at home. I was exhausted and bitchy all the time. I'm grateful to this day that my doctor took the time to check me over instead of just prescribing the anti-depressants I asked for. He felt a lump in my left breast. That was almost ten years ago."

Phoebe glanced at the scarf covering Melanie's head. "Have you been fighting that whole time?"

"No. I was cancer-free for eight years."

A hollow feeling spread through Phoebe's chest. If her cancer followed the same path as Melanie's, she had only seven more years of cancer-free living. She'd be thirty-eight when the cancer came back. She might die before her fortieth birthday.

Or Dr. Dalal could tell you today that your tumor markers are up and your scan was spotty. Then the real countdown would begin.

"I truly believed it wouldn't come back," Melanie murmured. "But it did, even worse than before. It's more aggressive. It means business this time." She sighed softly. "My husband's a mess. In seventeen years of marriage, he's only cried three times—when our kids were born, and when Dr. Cornish told us the cancer was back and had spread to my lungs. My kids are having such a hard time. They're dealing with typical teenage drama plus a sick mom."

Phoebe didn't reply. What could she say?

I'm sorry, Melanie. It sucks that you're going to die. It sucks that your husband is going to be a widower and your kids will have to go through life without their mother. Yeah, it really sucks.

Melanie kicked her crossed leg forward and backward in a steady rhythm. "They're never going to get over this."

Phoebe didn't need to ask what *this* was. She knew what Melanie meant. Her death would scar her husband and children. They would never be whole again, no matter how many years passed.

"I wish I could go back in time and change things," Melanie said.

"What would you change?"

Melanie shrugged. "Sometimes I think it would be better if my husband and I had never met ... if he had never spilled beer down my back at that 49ers game in Candlestick Park." A smile ghosted over her mouth. "Adam's clumsy, but he's a great guy. Funny. Thoughtful. Sweet. I know he would have met someone else. He would have married another woman and had children with her ... someone who didn't have a ticking time bomb inside her."

Ticking time bomb.

The words reverberated within Phoebe like an earthquake, creating huge fissures in her heart. Like Melanie, Phoebe had a ticking time bomb inside her. If she continued to spend time with Garrett, she would blow his life apart.

"But then I remind myself that if I'd never met Adam, my kids wouldn't exist," Melanie added. "And I could never wish for that, no matter what." She glanced at Phoebe, her face etched with sorrow. "I just wish I wasn't the cause of all their pain."

Phoebe's heart splintered into a million jagged pieces. She didn't want to cause Garrett pain, either. She had been selfish when she'd given in to her desire to be with him.

She had to tell him about her cancer. She had to—

"Phoebe Werner."

At the sound of her name, Phoebe jerked her head up. Dr. Dalal's nurse stood across the room, using her body to hold open the door that led to the exam rooms.

"We're ready for you, Phoebe," the petite nurse announced.

Phoebe waved in acknowledgment before unhooking the steel knitting needles from the wad of yarn and dropping them into her bag. After tucking the yarn under her arm, she grabbed her bag and stood. She glanced at Melanie, knowing she would never see the cancer-stricken woman again.

"Good luck, Melanie. I hope you…"

Beat the odds. Survive. Live to see your grandchildren.

Knowing that was unlikely, Phoebe simply said, "I hope you have a nice day."

As she hurried toward the nurse and the open door, she spotted a small metal trash can. Stopping beside it, she stepped on the pedal. The lid popped up, and she shoved the unfinished sweater deep into the bin. She stared at it, her throat tight with misery, before lifting her foot.

The lid snapped shut, burying both the sweater she'd knitted for Garrett and the naïve hope that she could be with him, if only for a little while.

CHAPTER SIXTEEN

Garrett glanced at his watch. He had fifteen minutes before his weekly operations conference call kicked off, so he decided to call his grandfather. He checked in with Pops every day, just to see how the old guy was doing.

He closed the door to his windowless office before placing the call. The administrative offices in the Hudson San Francisco were located on the second floor, and he had picked a tiny one in the back. It didn't make sense for him to occupy a larger space. He did a lot of work in his suite, and moreover, he wasn't here every day.

Pops answered on the first ring with a raspy *hello*.

"Hey, Pops," Garrett replied, adjusting his headset so it sat more comfortably against his ear.

"Hey yourself, Trout."

Garrett smiled at the nickname. Pops had begun calling him *Trout* just after his fifth birthday. He had taken Garrett on a fishing trip to Bonaparte Lake in the Okanogan-Wenatchee National Forest, and over the course of the three-day trip, Garrett had caught more than twenty trout. Pops, meanwhile, had managed to catch only three.

419

"How's it going today?" Garrett asked.

"Fair to middling. Simone made Reuben sandwiches with homemade sauerkraut. And tonight we're having lobster mac-n-cheese."

Simone Merlait's official title was elder care companion, but she did everything around the house, from cooking to changing light bulbs. And she watched out for Pops as if he were her own father. Without her, Garrett could never be away from home so much.

"How's your day?" Pops asked.

"Fair to middling."

In truth, Garrett's day had been almost perfect. There was no way it could have started any better. He'd woken up with Phoebe's mouth wrapped around his morning wood, and she'd gifted him with an orgasm that had damn near blown off his head.

Afterward he had pulled her into the shower and lathered up every inch of her curvy body, paying special attention to the sweet flesh between her legs. Then he'd picked her up and fucked her so hard the guests in the suite next door had called the front desk to report a disturbance.

The hotel manager had passed along the complaint with a knowing grin. Garrett had made a mental note to talk to the facilities manager about adding some soundproofing to Garrett's suite. He planned to make Phoebe scream a lot more.

"What's new in the world of Gale Hotel Group?" Pops asked.

His question was more than just idle curiosity. Having invested millions in his grandson's company, Pops had some serious skin the game.

Garrett forcefully redirected his thoughts away from Phoebe. "Well, let's see ... we've almost finalized the design plans for

The Pacifica, and the demolition is nearly finished. This morning Christine told me the meeting and special event space across the portfolio is ninety-eight percent booked for the next fourteen months."

"You should talk with Christine about pricing. The space might be sold out so far in advance because the rates are too low."

"Good point," Garrett said, picking up his tablet and adding that to his never-ending to-do list.

Pops cleared his throat. "How are things with Phoebe?"

There wasn't much that Garrett didn't tell his grandfather. They'd always been close, and they'd grown even closer when Garrett's parents had died in a seaplane crash when he was nine. He had moved into Pops's big house on the shores of Lake Washington, and his grandfather had been his anchor ever since.

"Things are good," Garrett answered.

Garrett couldn't remember ever feeling this way ... so lighthearted he thought he might float away like an un-tethered balloon. He woke up happy, and he went to sleep happy.

He walked around with stars in his eyes, a silly smile on his face, and a spring in his step. He'd even caught himself whistling as if he were the eighth dwarf, one named Smitten. He greatly feared he would involuntarily burst into song, likely something operatic.

And it was all because of Phoebe, with her sweet smile and kind heart. Her infectious laugh and analytical brain. Her smooth skin and lush lips.

Yeah, things were good. But Garrett wanted more. He wanted Phoebe to tell him that she loved him.

Of course he hadn't told her how he felt either. Maybe they were both too afraid to say those three little words because they had a lot of power. They could change everything.

"How good?" Pops persisted. "Good enough for me to get your grandmother's engagement ring out of the safe deposit box?"

"Are you that eager for great-grandchildren?"

"Hell, yes," Pops barked.

Drumming his fingers on the top of his desk, Garrett said, "We've only been together for a few weeks, Pops."

"Don't bullshit me, Trout. You've had a hard-on for that girl for years."

Garrett laughed. "That's true."

"You've had plenty of time to figure out what you want."

"That's also true." Garrett rubbed his hand over the top of his head. "If I thought she would say yes, I *would* ask her to marry me. But I don't think she's there yet."

The older man made a rude sound. "Then get her there," he shot back.

Pops muttered something else under his breath, but Garrett wasn't stupid enough to ask him to repeat it. He was pretty sure his grandfather had just called his manliness into question.

Before Pops could castigate Garrett further, the office door opened a crack, and the hotel's administrative assistant, Patricia Keith, stuck her head around it. He beckoned her inside with a wave of his hand.

Crossing the room, she passed him a Post-It note. It read: Phoebe wants to see you.

Surprised, he glanced up. "Now?" he mouthed to Patricia, and she nodded.

It was only three o'clock. Phoebe should still be at work. She hadn't mentioned anything about getting off early, and he hadn't expected to see her until this evening.

He held up a finger to Patricia, indicating he needed her to wait a second. "Sorry, Pops," he said into the headset, "I gotta run. I love you."

His grandfather grunted. "Love you too," he replied gruffly, as he always did.

After disconnecting the call, Garrett tossed the headset on his desk. "Bring her back," he told Patricia, his mind wondering why Phoebe was here, and his body humming at the prospect of seeing her.

As Patricia left his office, he texted his assistant in Seattle, asking her to reschedule the operations conference call for tomorrow morning. Once she had acknowledged his request, he put his phones and tablet on do-not-disturb mode. He didn't want to be interrupted. Phoebe deserved his undivided attention.

Seconds later, Patricia ushered Phoebe through the door and closed it with a quiet click. As he rose, he gave her a thorough review, starting with the top of her curly head. His gaze flicked over her cowl-necked cherry red sweater and black skirt before ending at her black leather knee boots.

Part of him had feared that her unexpected visit heralded bad news, maybe something to do with work or her family. But she looked absolutely fine, clear-eyed and pink-cheeked. He breathed a sigh of relief.

Wrapping his arms around her, he pulled her into his body. Her canvas bag hit his ankle, but he ignored it. He nuzzled his face in her hair, the sweet scent making his mouth water.

"This is a pleasant surprise, petal."

He knew his comment sounded trite. But that didn't mean it wasn't true.

She said something, but his chest muffled her words. He stepped back so he could look down into her face.

"What?" he asked.

She licked her upper lip, and he followed the movement with his eyes, his cock twitching at the erotic sight of her pink tongue. He stroked the glistening bow at the top of her mouth, and her breath rushed over his fingers. He barely noticed when her bag fell from her hand and landed on his foot.

It had only been eight hours since he'd touched her petal-soft skin and slid inside her tight pussy, but he craved her incessantly. Right now, his body shouted its primal need for hers, demanding and insistent. He would never get enough of her, not even if he had an entire lifetime to indulge his desire.

Ignoring the voice of reason inside him—the one telling him this was neither the time nor the place—he walked backward toward his chair, bringing her with him. After dropping into it, he pulled her onto his lap.

With her knees spread on either side of his thighs, he gripped her ass in one hand and brought her closer until his cock notched between her thighs. She gasped, obviously surprised by his erection.

She pressed her palms against his chest. "Garrett, I need to—

Cupping his other hand around the back of her head, he forced her mouth to his, cutting off her words. She resisted his kiss for a moment, but then her lips softened and her arms snaked around his neck.

He brought his hand from her nape to one of her breasts, shaping the firm mound with his fingers while he played with her mouth. She moaned deep in her throat, and he slipped his hand under her sweater, dying to touch her bare skin.

As he licked and sucked at her lips, he tugged the lace cups of her bra down until her breasts spilled out. He gently brushed his thumb over one tight nipple before rolling it between his thumb and forefinger, fascinated by its velvety texture. He gave her other nipple the same attention until she arched her back in invitation.

With his blood rushing through his veins like lava, he grabbed the hem of her sweater and pushed it up to her neck. He stared down at her breasts, the skin so pale it was almost translucent.

Palming one of the mounds, he brought her pebbled nipple to his mouth and sucked it into his mouth. She wove her fingers through his hair and held his face against her breast.

He circled the stiff bud with his tongue, and she squirmed on his lap, pressing her mound against his erection. As he laved her nipple, he lightly scraped his fingernail over the other tight peak.

"*Please*," she breathed. "*Please*."

He didn't know what she wanted, but he knew exactly what *he* wanted. Reaching under her skirt, he encountered the silky fabric of her panties. He delved inside them, sliding his fingers past her damp slit into her hot center. Her juice spilled over his hand, proof that she wanted him as much as he wanted her.

His cock thickened, his pulse pounding furiously in his ears. With desire clouding his mind, only one thought shone through: *I need to be inside her. Now.*

"Up," he growled, too turned on to say anything more.

She lifted her lower body just enough for him to free his erection from his trousers. He pulled her panties to the side, and then he was inside her ... where he belonged.

A groan tore loose from his chest as her flesh clasped his cock, tighter and hotter than ever before. She widened her legs and took him even deeper, the tip of his erection nudging her cervix.

A fire ignited in his pelvis, making his skin prickle with heat. Panting, he stared into her lust-hazed eyes.

"How do you want it?" he asked, his voice raw.

She rested her forehead against his. "Slow."

Gripping her hips in both hands, he lifted her off his cock, so slowly he could feel her pussy ripple around him. Loosening his grip, he let her slide back down, rolling his pelvis as he eased his erection into her, one slick inch at a time.

Lazily, he worked her over his cock, his hands tight on her curves. She would have bruises there tomorrow if he didn't loosen his grip.

He continued the easy rhythm, and with every slide, she grew wetter … softer. The ridges of his penis dragged over her slippery flesh, and sweat bloomed on his skin, soaking his cotton undershirt.

Pressure built in his groin, his balls tightening with his looming orgasm. He placed his forefinger on her clit and rubbed circles around the stiff little nub as he pumped slowly into her.

Little whimpers drifted from her mouth. He stroked her clit with a firmer touch, but somehow managed to keep the pace of his thrusts unhurried even though he wanted to slam furiously into her.

Just as his tenuous control snapped, she tensed. He covered her mouth with his and swallowed her cry of release as she came, her pussy squeezing his length in voluptuous clenches.

He let go then, dropping his head back against the chair and emptying himself inside her with blinding intensity. In that moment, she was the only thing that existed … the only thing that mattered.

"*Phoebe*," he groaned.

His orgasm went on and on, his cock jerking violently until there was nothing left inside him. She had taken everything, maybe even his soul.

Phoebe slumped against him, burying her face in his shoulder. Bringing his hands to her back, he hugged her to him. They stayed like that until their hearts regained their normal rhythm and their breathing slowed.

Finally, she lifted her head. He leaned forward and gave her a gentle kiss, their lips clinging. When they broke apart, he opened his mouth to tell her how much he loved her. But she scooted backward before he could get any words out.

His spent penis slipped from her body, and warm fluid trickled over him. Realization dawned, and he clenched his jaw. No wonder her pussy had felt so good. He'd had her without the barrier of latex.

In his eagerness to get inside Phoebe, he had forgotten to use a condom.

CHAPTER SEVENTEEN

Phoebe clumsily wiggled off Garrett's lap. Her legs wobbled as she stood, and he steadied her with a hand around her forearm. When she found her balance, he let go, and she put some space between them.

She turned away from his scrutiny, tears prickling the backs of her eyes. She had come here to tell him about her cancer, not to have sex with him. But he had pounced on her like a starving lion, and she hadn't resisted. She'd been starving for him too.

Swallowing hard, she tucked her breasts back into her bra. She heard a rustle behind her as she tugged down her sweater. By the time she had smoothed her skirt over her hips and turned to face him, he'd fastened his pants.

He rose from his office chair and moved in front of her. Looking down into her face, he said, "I didn't use a condom, petal."

It took her a moment to digest his words. When she did, she became aware of the warm stickiness between her thighs.

Protection hadn't crossed her mind. But as long as he was clean—and she was sure he was—there wasn't any concern. Because of the chemo and radiation, it was almost impossible for her to get pregnant.

"Did you hear me?" he asked.

"Yes, I heard you."

"I'm sorry. I wasn't thinking. But you need to know I've never forgotten a condom before." His words came out so fast they seemed to pile up. "This is the first time I've ever had sex without one. I haven't been with anyone but you since I had my annual physical. I was tested for everything, even TB. I'm clean. Are you?"

She nodded. "There's nothing to worry about."

"Good. We're both healthy."

Well, not exactly.

He blew out a gusty breath. "I know you're not using any other form of birth control."

"No, I'm not. But—"

Grasping her hand, he said, "I would be happy if you were pregnant. More than happy. I'd be thrilled. I want to have children with you."

She gasped, not only because she was surprised by his words, but also because they hurt worse than a dull razor slicing into her skin. She would have loved to be the mother of his children. But that was never going to happen.

With his eyes locked on her face, he said, "I'm in love with you."

Invisible bands squeezed her chest, crushing her with agonizing pain. She tried to shake off his hand, but he tightened it around hers.

"I love you, Phoebe."

Deep inside her, something big and ugly escaped from the cage she'd put it in. Something that cried in the night at the unfairness of it all.

"I don't want you to love me!" she yelled. "It doesn't change anything!"

His face paled to a sickly gray, his stubble standing out like little dots of black ink on newsprint. His grip slackened just enough for her to jerk her hand free. They stared at each other, the air in the room almost vibrating with emotion.

She forced the beast back inside its cage and locked it up tight. Calmer now, she said, "I came here today to end things."

"Why…" His voice cracked on the end of the word, and he cleared his throat roughly. "Why do you want to end things? Everything seemed fine this morning. And it seemed pretty damn great a few minutes ago."

She flushed at his pointed reference to the office chair sex. "We don't have a future together. It's better if we just say good-bye now."

A muscle ticked in his jaw. "What did I do wrong?" he asked, his lips barely moving.

"You didn't do anything wrong. It's me. I have—"

"It's not you. It's me." He barked out a laugh, the sound sharp and bitter. "That's classic. Next you'll say you hope we can stay friends." He shook his head. "The answer is no."

"It's me," she repeated. "I have breast cancer."

He stared at her unblinkingly for several moments. Finally, he whispered, "What did you just say?"

"I have breast cancer."

"*No.*" He dropped heavily onto the side of the desk. "Tell me I didn't hear you right."

Almost four years ago, her oldest brother had said the exact same thing when she'd told him about her diagnosis. When she had confirmed that he had indeed heard her right, he'd broken down and cried like a little boy.

"I had an appointment with my gynecologist the day after our big presentation. I thought about canceling it because you're not supposed to have sex right before. The lubrication on condoms can mess with the results of the Pap smear, and we'd had a lot of sex the night before."

Garrett stared at her, a baffled expression on his handsome face. She knew she was babbling, but telling him about her cancer was a lot harder than she'd imagined. She felt as if she were confessing a horrible crime.

"I decided to go to the appointment anyway, and my doctor found a lump in my right breast. I flew home and was diagnosed with stage IIB ductal carcinoma a few days later. I had a three-centimeter tumor, and the cancer had spread to four lymph nodes."

"*Oh, God,*" he muttered, his dark head drooping forward.

"That's why I never returned your texts or called you back."

His head snapped up, and he speared her with his ocean-blue gaze. "You should have told me."

"I just couldn't deal with you and the cancer. It was too much. I had a lumpectomy, six months of chemo, and radiation."

"Oh, Phoebe," he murmured.

Gesturing to her midsection, she said, "I didn't lose all that weight because I watched what I ate or because I worked out. I lost it because the chemo made me so sick I couldn't eat. I puked nonstop."

She pointed to her hair. "And this? I didn't cut it. It fell out. And when it grew back in, it was curly." She pulled on a tight ringlet. "I hate it! It's uncontrollable! The fog makes it frizzy!"

Slowly, he rose from his perch on the side of his desk. "I like your curls."

She ignored him. It didn't matter if he liked her curls or not. And it didn't matter if she liked them either.

"Last year my scan finally came back clear, and my tumor markers dropped."

"You said you *have* cancer." His gaze locked on her face, intense and unwavering. "Is it back?"

"Not yet."

"So you're cured?"

She laughed mirthlessly. "That's not how cancer works, Garrett."

"Then how does it work? Explain it to me so I understand what we're up against."

What we're up against.

He said it like they were a team. Like they could handle anything as long as they stuck together. But that wasn't true. They couldn't handle cancer.

"I'm cancer-free *right now*. But it's going to come back."

"How do you know?" he asked, a frown darkening his face.

"I just know."

His eyes narrowed. "Is that why you said we don't have a future together? Because you *had* cancer and it *might* come back?"

She nodded. "It's going to come back. That's why I didn't want to get involved with you. You're better off with another woman. A healthy woman."

He studied her for a long moment. His scrutiny made her feel like a virus under a microscope, and she barely resisted the urge to squirm.

"Would we have a future together if you weren't a cancer survivor?"

She hesitated, but then said, "That's a stupid question. I *am* a cancer survivor."

He smiled, but there was little humor in it. "Here's another stupid question: do you love me?"

"I need to go," she choked out.

Bending down, she nabbed the handles of her canvas bag and

rushed toward the door. Just as she reached it, Garrett placed his palm flat against the wood surface, keeping it shut.

"You didn't answer my question."

"No, I don't love you," she said without turning around. It was much easier to lie when she couldn't see his face.

He sighed softly, his breath stirring her hair. "I fell in love with you at U-Dub. I didn't realize it at the time because … well, because I'm a guy, and most of us have a hard time understanding our feelings."

He brought his other arm around her, caging her in. "I've had a lot of time to think about it, and I'm pretty sure I know the exact moment it happened. One day we were walking across campus, and it started to sprinkle. You looked up, and a couple of droplets fell on your lips. I wanted to suck the rain off them."

She rested her forehead against the door, tears pooling in her eyes. "Please stop."

He continued as if she hadn't spoken. "While I stood there thinking about kissing you, you opened your umbrella and almost poked my eye out."

She remembered that day very clearly, as if it had been branded on her memory. She'd been so worried she had hurt him, but he'd laughed it off.

"Since I had kissing on the brain, I joked that you should kiss it all better. You kissed your fingers and pressed them on my cheek, near my eye. And that's when it happened … that's when I fell in love with you." He brushed the hair off her neck and pressed his mouth to her nape. "I have loved you for years, Phoebe. And I think you love me too."

He carefully turned her until her back was against the door. Cupping her cheek in his hand, he lifted her face to his. "Am I right?"

"Yes," she admitted, tears leaking from her eyes. "I didn't think I could love someone as much as I love you."

Smiling slowly, he brushed her tears away with his thumb. "Yeah, that's pretty much how I feel."

"I love you, and that's why I'm ending things."

His smile faded, his mouth tightening into a straight line. "That's one of the stupidest things I've ever heard," he said flatly. "It makes no sense."

"It makes perfect sense. I want you to have a happy life, Garrett. One filled with joy and laughter. Not one filled with sadness and tears. And that's what you'll get with me. You'll get doctors' appointments and hospital stays and visits to the cemetery…" She touched his cheek with her fingertips. "I'm doing this for you."

He pulled her hand away, almost crushing it in his grip. "I don't want you to do this for me," he snarled. "I can make my own goddamn decisions. I don't want anyone else. I want *you*."

Grasping her shoulders, he said, "Listen to me. *Please*. The way I feel about you … it will never fade." His eyes drilled into her. "You said you want me to have a happy life. *You* make me happy. I'm only half alive when I'm not with you."

His last sentence made her think about Melanie's poor husband. She didn't want Garrett to go through the same thing.

"I had an appointment with my oncologist this afternoon. I met a woman in the waiting room. Melanie. She was forty-five. She had a husband and three teenagers. She'd been cancer-free for eight years. She thought it was gone forever. But it came back. She said it meant business this time. It had spread to her lungs." A few tears leaked from her eyes. "They won't be able to stop it. It's going to kill her."

"Phoebe—"

"How are you going to feel when my cancer comes back?"

He growled in frustration, tilting his head toward the ceiling as if he were seeking divine intervention before returning his gaze to her. "You don't know for sure that it *is* going to come back. No one knows what the future holds. And if it comes back, we'll deal with it."

"No." She shook her head. "*No.* I don't want you to have to deal with it."

"*I love you.* Do you understand what that means? It means I love everything about you, even your fucking cancer. The good, the bad, and the ugly."

Her chest felt tight, like she couldn't get a deep breath, so she inhaled and exhaled slowly. "Do you know what Melanie said? She wished she could go back in time and change things. She thought it would be better if she and her husband had never met. She wanted to spare him the pain she had brought into his life."

A loud knock vibrated the wood against her back. Seeing an opportunity to escape, Phoebe spun around and opened the door.

"I'm sorry to interrupt, Mr. Gale," Patricia apologized, looking over Phoebe's shoulder, "but you asked me to let you know when Mr. Lambert called."

"Tell him I'll call him back," Garrett replied curtly.

"Put him through in two minutes," Phoebe told Patricia. "I'm leaving."

Patricia looked back and forth between Phoebe and Garrett. "I'll ask Mr. Lambert if he can hold for a few minutes," she said before heading back down the hall.

Phoebe moved into the open doorway and faced Garrett. "Eventually you're going to thank me for this. I have a ticking time bomb inside me, and if you're around when it goes off,

435

you'll be hurt too." She clenched her fingers around the straps of her bag. "I love you too much to let that happen."

He opened his mouth, but she held up her hand. "There's nothing you could say that will change my mind. This is good-bye."

CHAPTER EIGHTEEN

Condensation had beaded on Garrett's glass of iced tea, and he traced a pattern in it with his forefinger. Block letters emerged on the slick surface without conscious thought.

PHOEBE

As if he needed more proof she had taken over his subconscious. Even if he wanted to forget her, he couldn't. She was a part of him.

Out of the corner of his eye, Garrett saw the server place the bill folder on the table. He opened it, added a generous tip, and signed the credit card slip.

"Thanks for lunch," Jake said.

Tucking his credit card back into his wallet, Garrett replied, "You're welcome, boss. Thanks for meeting me. I know you're busy."

Garrett had texted Jake this morning and invited him to lunch. Knowing Jake's schedule was jam packed, Garrett had been prepared to beg or bribe him for his time, whatever worked. He desperately needed the other's man help with Phoebe.

Garrett hadn't seen or talked to her since she'd rushed out of his office. That had been three days ago. Seventy-two miserable hours during which he'd called and texted her with no reply.

He'd dropped by her place several times, but she hadn't answered his buzz. And this morning he'd shown up on her doorstep at six-thirty, hoping to catch her as she left for work.

He had felt like a stalker, lurking around her building in his hooded sweatshirt. After three hours, she still hadn't emerged, so he'd returned to his suite, numb with cold and determined to find another way to see her.

Jake was the key. He had access to Phoebe. They worked in the same building, and his wife was one of Phoebe's best friends.

"Are you heading back to the Hudson now?" Jake asked.

"No. I'm going to stop by The Pacifica. I need to pick up some sample boards from the interior designer."

"I'll walk with you. It's on the way back to Riley Plaza."

Nodding, Garrett rose and shrugged on his black leather car coat. He followed Jake from the restaurant, and they headed east toward The Pacifica. The sun had finally made its appearance, softening the sharp bite of the wind.

As they waited for the signal to cross the street, Garrett said, "I need your help."

"I won't help you kill anyone," Jake replied, absolutely deadpan. "Sorry."

Garrett chuckled. "How disappointing."

"What do you need?"

"I need to talk to Phoebe. I need you to get me access."

Jake shot him a knowing look. "Fucked it up again, huh?" He shoved his hands in the pockets of his motorcycle jacket. "What happened?"

Garrett had no idea if Jake knew about Phoebe's cancer. He doubted it. She was a private person.

Unwilling to disclose such personal information, he said, "That's between us."

Jake barked out a laugh. "Sorry, douche. If you want me to put my ass on the line for you, I need details."

"How would you be putting your ass on the line?" Garrett demanded.

"You've obviously never been in a long-term relationship, or you would understand the risk. If Phoebe had a good reason for kicking your ass to the curb, and Kyla finds out I helped you, I'll be sleeping alone."

Garrett snorted. "Maybe for one night."

"That's one night too many," Jake shot back, scowling fiercely. "Plus, I like Phoebe. She's a sweetheart. I don't want to help you if you've done something to hurt her."

The light finally turned green, and they continued on. Garrett weighed his desire to keep Phoebe's cancer confidential against his need for Jake's help. It only took him a few steps to make up his mind.

"Jake, I'll give you the details. But you have to forget them when this conversation is over. You have to scrub them from your brain."

Jake's eyes widened. "It's that bad? What the hell did you do?" His face darkened. "Maybe you shouldn't tell me. Because then I might feel compelled to beat the shit out of you."

"Yeah, you could try," Garrett bit out, more than a little insulted by Jake's assumption that he had mistreated Phoebe. "I didn't do anything. This is about Phoebe."

Jake nodded slowly. "Okay."

"Phoebe is a breast cancer survivor."

"*What?*" Jake stumbled to a stop, his gaze shooting to Garrett's face. "Phoebe had *breast cancer?*"

Garrett stopped beside Jake. "Yes. Stage IIB ductal carcinoma."

"I don't know much breast cancer, but that sounds fucking terrifying."

"I did some research after she told me. It's a very serious diagnosis."

After Phoebe had left Garrett's office, he had gone back to his suite and spent the rest of the night online researching breast cancer. The complexity and quantity of information had overwhelmed him, and he'd had even more questions the next morning.

He had called one of his college buddies, a good guy named Ryan Fournier who practiced neuro-oncology at MD Anderson Cancer Center in Houston. Ryan had put Garrett in touch with one of his colleagues who specialized in breast cancer, a Brazilian-born doctor named Renata Cabral. Last night, Garrett and Dr. Cabral had video chatted for more than an hour, and he now had a much better understanding of Phoebe's situation.

Jake cleared his throat. "When was Phoebe diagnosed?"

"Almost four years ago. That's why she never returned my phone calls or texts after that one night. She's been cancer-free for more than a year."

"I thought it was really rare for a young woman to get breast cancer."

"It is rare. But it does happen. Most doctors don't recommend mammograms until age forty. Dr. Cabral said it's important for all women to do self-exams."

Jake nodded thoughtfully. "I need to make sure Kyla is doing that."

A skinny guy with a goatee and brown fedora skirted around Jake and Garrett. "You're blocking the entire sidewalk," he snapped. "Can't you have your domestic dispute somewhere else?"

Staring after the rude dude, Jake muttered, "*Dickhead.*"

They continued along the sidewalk. The sun had disappeared

again, slipping behind a screen of gray clouds. The weather suited Garrett's mood, gloomy and depressed with occasional rays of hope.

"When did Phoebe tell you about her cancer? Did you know about it before you got together?"

"No. She told me three days ago." Garrett figured he might as well tell Jake everything. "She stopped by my office unexpectedly, and we had sex."

Laughter rustled in Jake's throat. "Been there, done that."

"I forgot to use a condom."

"Been there," Jake repeated ruefully, "done that." They exchanged a look of shared camaraderie before he asked, "Did you flip out?"

"No. I told her I wanted to have children with her. But that was the worst thing I could have said."

In his mind, he could see Phoebe standing in his office, looking as if he had slapped her. At the time, he hadn't understood her response, but now he did.

Dr. Cabral had explained that Phoebe probably couldn't have children. That knowledge had smothered him like a volcano's pyroclastic flow, hot and choking. He could only imagine how Phoebe felt.

"The worst thing?" Jake repeated. "Why?"

"Because chemo and radiation damages the ovaries. It causes infertility. It's unlikely Phoebe can have children."

Jake exhaled roughly. "Oh, man." He glanced sideways at Garrett. "How do you feel about that?"

Garrett met Jake's sympathetic gaze. "How would you feel if Kyla couldn't have children?"

Jake was silent for several steps before he said, "Devastated. Heartbroken. For Kyla. For myself. But it wouldn't change how

I feel about her. I would still want to be with her."

"Yeah, that's exactly how I feel." They hooked a right at the intersection and continued their trek to The Pacifica. "I told Phoebe that I loved her. I'd never said that to a woman before."

"How did she respond?"

"She yelled at me that she didn't want me to love her ... that it didn't change anything. And then she said she had come to my office to end things ... that we didn't have a future together."

He remembered the whole conversation almost verbatim because it had hurt so badly to hear those horrible words.

"Oh, fuck, Garrett." Jake's face twisted in a grimace. "I'm sorry."

"That's when she told me about the cancer. At first I thought she had just been diagnosed because she said, 'I have breast cancer.' Present tense."

Jake's mouth fell open. "If Kyla said that to me, I probably would pass out. Did you pass out?"

"Almost."

"*Have* versus *had*," Jake mused. "That one word makes a huge fucking difference, doesn't it?"

"It makes a difference to you, and it makes a difference to me. But it doesn't make a difference to Phoebe. She doesn't think of her cancer as being past tense."

Jake frowned. "What do you mean?"

"She's convinced her cancer is going to come back. That's why she thinks we don't have a future together."

Dr. Cabral had confirmed that Phoebe's fears were not unfounded, especially given the age when she had been diagnosed. But the physician had also said there was no way of knowing whether the cancer would return.

"Could Phoebe's cancer come back?" Jake asked.

"Yes. It *could*. But there are a lot of things that *could* happen. The Earth *could* be invaded by aliens."

Jake's lips quirked. "It could." He rolled his shoulders. "I understand why Phoebe is afraid. I would be too. And if it were Kyla, I would be terrified the cancer might come back."

"Phoebe thinks she has a ticking time bomb inside her. Those were her exact words. She said she doesn't want me to get hurt when it goes off. That she loves me too much to let that happen."

Jake's face softened. "Selfless love," he murmured. "A deep and genuine wish for the happiness of others without wanting anything in return."

The familiar portico of The Pacifica appeared in front of them. Garrett pulled open one of the Art Deco doors and gestured for Jake to precede him. They stopped just inside the lobby. The buzz of power tools echoed throughout the space as construction workers painstakingly removed decades of abuse from the walls, floor, and woodwork.

"It's quieter on the upper floors," Garrett said.

Once they were inside the elevator and away from the noise, Garrett resumed their conversation. "Phoebe thinks she's doing the right thing by walking away, but she's not. I need to talk to her ... to make her understand. But she won't answer my phone calls or texts. And I can't get into her apartment building."

"What do you need me to do?"

"Help me get her alone so we can talk. It needs to be a place where she can't run away ... where she'll have to listen to me."

"Like an elevator?" Jake suggested, glancing around pointedly.

Garrett laughed. "Yeah. That would be perfect."

"It *would* be perfect." Jake's eyes narrowed in consideration. "I could probably persuade the security guy in our condo building to shut down one of the elevators with you guys in it. Kyla could invite Phoebe over. You could be waiting on our floor, and when the elevator arrives with Phoebe in it, you could jump in. The door closes. The elevator shuts down. And then you have her to yourself for as long as you want."

"I like that plan." Garrett nodded his approval. "Will Kyla go along with it?"

"Yeah, I think—"

A loud noise filled the elevator, a mechanical groan that made the hair on the back of Garrett's neck stand up. The floor trembled, and Jake's eyes shot to Garrett.

"What was that?" Jake asked, apprehension stamped all over his face.

Before Garrett could respond, something heavy hit the top of the elevator. The cab jerked, and he lost his balance, slamming against the wall. Jake grabbed the railing as an ear-splitting squeal echoed above them, metal grinding against metal.

And then everything went dark.

CHAPTER NINETEEN

Phoebe stared at her monitor, willing herself to concentrate on the data neatly presented on the spreadsheet. The project comparing Riley O'Brien & Co.'s best performing stores to its worst performing stores was due in two weeks, and she still had a lot of data left to analyze, not to mention writing the report and creating the presentation.

The numbers on the screen blurred, and she tiredly rubbed her eyes. She hadn't slept well last night. Or the night before. Or the night before that.

She missed Garrett. She missed curling up next to him in bed and talking in the dark. She missed waking up next to him and making love before breakfast.

This morning she'd dragged herself out of bed at five, dressed for the day, and gone to a twenty-four-hour diner to work on her project. Despite her early start, she hadn't made a lot of progress. She couldn't focus on work. All she could think about was Garrett and what he'd said the last time they had spoken.

You make me happy. I'm only half alive when you're not with me.

She wanted him to be happy, and she hated that she'd hurt him so badly when she had ended things. Her head told her that she'd done the right thing. But her heart insisted that she'd made a mistake.

"Phoebe!"

Spinning around in her office chair, she spotted Kyla standing just outside her cube. The blonde's face was ashen, her silvery-gray eyes wild with fear.

Phoebe jumped to her feet. "What's wrong?"

"Jake and Garrett were in an accident."

It took a moment for Kyla's words to penetrate Phoebe's stunned brain. When they did, the bottom dropped out of her stomach.

"What kind of accident? Are they okay?"

"I don't know." Kyla's gaze flicked around Phoebe's cube. "Where's your purse? We have to go." She clamped her hand around Phoebe's forearm and jerked her forward. "*Now, Phoebe.*"

Phoebe grabbed her purse, and they sprinted for the elevators. Kyla stabbed the down button, her hand shaking.

"Tell me what you know," Phoebe said, her heart pounding in a frantic rhythm.

"Someone from Saint Francis Memorial's ER called. She said the paramedics had just brought Jake and Garrett in. The doctors were assessing their condition. That's all I know."

The elevator dinged, and they rushed into it. Just a couple of minutes later they were outside.

Kyla glanced desperately up and down the street. "*God!* Why are there never any taxis when you need them?"

Spotting one on the other side of the street, Phoebe darted into traffic with her arm raised to flag it down. Horns honked and tires squealed, but she ignored them. She only cared about one thing: getting to Garrett.

She clambered into the taxi, and Kyla slid in behind her.

"Saint Francis Memorial," Kyla told the driver. "Take us to the Emergency Room."

Bracing her hand on the headrest in front of her, Phoebe leaned forward. "I'll give you a hundred bucks if you can get us there in less than five minutes."

With a nod, the taxi driver accelerated into traffic. Phoebe collapsed against the black vinyl seat, her mind whirling.

"What were they doing together?" she asked Kyla.

"They met for lunch at Fog City Grill. Jake texted me when he left the restaurant. That was more than two hours ago. I haven't heard from him since then."

Phoebe looked out the window. The buildings were nothing but a blur as they passed, but she wasn't sure if it was because of the taxi's speed or the mist of tears in her eyes.

"We're here," the driver said as he guided the taxi in front of the ER entrance. "Four minutes."

By the time Phoebe had dug the money out of her wallet and paid the driver, Kyla had already disappeared through the sliding doors. Phoebe followed, her purse thumping against her side as she ran into the hospital.

People packed the waiting room, and she ducked and dodged her way to where Kyla stood at the check-in desk. With her hands fluttering in agitation, Kyla explained to the dark-haired woman behind the glass partition that someone from the ER had called.

"Last name?" the hospital staffer asked.

"Lilliard. Jake Lilliard," Kyla answered, her voice tight with fear. "And Garrett Gale."

Along with Kyla, Phoebe waited impatiently for the hospital staffer to check her computer. Finally, the woman pointed to her left. "See those doors? Wait there. Someone will be back to get you in a minute."

It seemed as if years passed before doors opened, revealing a tall, skinny guy wearing dark green scrubs. His shaggy blond head dipped down to look at the tablet computer in his hand.

"Lilliard?" he asked.

"Yes," Kyla said tremulously.

"Come with me. I'll take you to him." He turned, his tennis shoes squeaking on the beige tile flooring. "I'm Trevor, by the way. I'm one of the ER nurses."

As they walked down a corridor with pale blue walls, Kyla asked, "Is Jake okay?"

Trevor glanced over his shoulder at Kyla. "He's pretty banged up. But he'll be okay. He—"

"What about Garrett?" Phoebe asked, her chest so tight she could barely breathe.

The nurse's gaze shifted to Phoebe. "We sent him upstairs for a CT scan."

All the air left her lungs. "Why?" she wheezed. "What's wrong with him?"

"We're not sure yet," he replied. "He was unconscious when he came in."

She absorbed this information silently, trying not to panic. But the fear sucked her down, and her body flashed hot and cold.

Trevor stopped suddenly and pulled back a striped curtain. "You have visitors," he announced, shifting to the side to admit Kyla and Phoebe.

Jake reclined on a hospital gurney, his face colored in bruises and his lower lip pinched with stitches. His left arm was in a sling, and his lower left leg was stabilized in a splint.

His eyes lit up when he saw Kyla. He held out his good arm to her, and she flew across the room, diving into his embrace. Touching her forehead to his, she said something too quietly for

Phoebe to hear, her hand cupped around his bruised cheek.

Phoebe turned toward Trevor. "I want to see Garrett. Please."

Shaking his head regretfully, he said, "I'm sorry. You can't. The priority right now is determining the severity of his brain injury and the best way to treat it."

"Brain injury?" she repeated faintly.

Her knees turned to JELL-O, and she threw out an arm, groping for anything to stop her from falling. Trevor caught her upper arm in a hard grip.

"Steady," he cautioned, guiding her to a chair next to Jake's gurney. "We don't want you to fall and hit your head too."

Garrett has a brain injury. A brain injury.

Her chest caved in, and her shoulders slumped forward. The nurse knelt in front of her.

"What's your name, honey?"

"Phoebe."

"Phoebe, I promise we're taking good care of your guy. As soon as I hear anything, I will let you know." He stood and looked toward Jake. "You need anything?"

"Nah," Jake answered. "I've got everything I need right here."

Trevor left, pulling the privacy curtain closed behind him. Kyla dropped down into the vacant chair next to Phoebe, her hand entwined with Jake's. She looked a little ragged, her long golden hair straggling from her up-do, and her eyes ringed with mascara.

"What happened?" Kyla asked Jake.

One corner of his mouth hitched up—the one without the stitches. "We were unlucky enough to be in an elevator when it decided to fall seven stories."

Phoebe and Kyla gasped in unison.

"Seven stories?" Phoebe repeated at the same time Kyla asked, "Where were you?"

"The Pacifica."

"Why?" Kyla asked.

"Garrett needed to pick up something, and I tagged along." Jake shrugged. "Wrong place, wrong time."

"You could have died," Kyla said, her voice nearly a wail.

He slowly nodded. "I could have. But I didn't." He glanced at Phoebe. "A lot of things *could* happen. You never know." His greenish-gold eyes pierced her. "Life's a gamble. Sometimes you just have to push all the chips in and hope for the best."

She stared at Jake, knowing his words were a special message just for her. Garrett must have told him what had happened between them.

Just then the curtain fluttered, and Charlie slipped into the room. He wore a white doctor's coat over jeans and a plaid button-down shirt. His pediatric practice was located just a few blocks away.

Charlie's dark brown eyes swept over Phoebe and Kyla before stopping on Jake. "*Dude.*" A grimace flashed over his face. "You look like you've been trampled by a herd of cattle."

Jake chuckled, but then winced. "Don't make me laugh. It hurts."

"Yeah. Two busted ribs, a dislocated shoulder, and a broken leg. You'll be hurting for a few weeks."

"Did you check on Garrett?" Jake asked Charlie.

Charlie nodded, his expression grim. "He has a severe concussion. His CT scan shows some swelling in the brain, but no bleeding."

"That's good, right?" Kyla speculated.

"Yes and no," Charlie answered. "Bleeding is definitely the

biggest concern. But edema—swelling—isn't good either because it puts pressure on the brain. They have to get it under control."

Phoebe swallowed thickly. "What are they doing for him?"

Charlie's gaze swung to her. "They're trying oxygenation and medication first. And if that doesn't work the next step is surgery."

"Is he still unconscious?" she asked.

"Yes, because he's sedated. That allows the brain to rest."

Phoebe covered her face with her hands. She felt Charlie's big hand settle on her shoulder, offering comfort and lending strength. He was a good guy.

"Garrett is in the ICU," Charlie explained quietly. "They're pretty strict with visiting hours, but I'll talk with the nurses so you can spend as much time with him as you want."

She'd spent the last three days miserable and alone when she could have spent them with Garrett. She could have spent that time showing him how much she loved him.

She could have…

CHAPTER TWENTY

When Garrett woke up, he stayed perfectly still until he had assessed the pain in his head. The first time he'd woken up after the elevator accident, he'd made the mistake of turning his head. That small movement had set off World War III inside his skull, forcing a pained groan from his throat and compelling his nurse to shoot him full of sedatives.

Fortunately, the pain had dropped from DEFCON level one (imminent nuclear war) to level four (heightened security measures). He blew out a relieved breath, glad his brain wasn't planning to do battle with rest of his body.

He gingerly rolled his head to the side, hoping to see Phoebe sitting in the chair next to his hospital bed. She had been there every time he'd woken up. This time was no different, except she wasn't alone. Pops sat in the chair across from her, and a chessboard lay on the table between them.

Warmth spread throughout Garrett's chest as he gazed at the two people he loved most in the world. Late afternoon sunlight filtered through the windows, drenching Phoebe and Pops in shimmering gold.

His grandfather's tortoiseshell glasses hung precariously on the tip of his nose as he waited for Phoebe to make her move. His silvery hair poked out from his head in sparse tufts, reminding Garrett of steel wool.

Phoebe shifted in her seat, a frown of concentration marring the smooth skin between her eyebrows. The sunlight glinted off her dark curls, highlighting strands of mahogany and auburn.

She tapped her forefinger against her bottom lip in a steady rhythm, drawing Garrett's attention to the lush curve. As he stared at her pink mouth, his blood heated and pooled in his groin.

Finally. Something other than my brain is swollen.

Phoebe pushed her queen across the board, putting Pops's king at risk. "Check," she murmured.

"Nice move," Garrett praised, his voice raspy from disuse.

Almost simultaneously Phoebe and Pops's heads snapped toward Garrett. More than sixty years of living separated them, but in that moment their expressions were identical: absolute joy.

Phoebe vaulted to her feet and edged around her chair to stand next to his bed. "You're awake."

She nabbed an insulated drink mug from a nearby tray and placed the flexible straw between his lips. He sucked down the cool water, letting it lubricate his cottony mouth and throat.

After returning the mug to the tray, she brought her attention back to him. "How are you feeling?"

"A lot better." He licked his cracked lips. "Almost normal."

Pops stood up, a hint of a smile lurking around his mouth. "Well, Trout, it looks like your brain is going to stay in your skull."

"Dr. Bettaney stopped by earlier," Phoebe chimed in. "He says the brain edema is almost completely gone."

Garrett sent up a quick prayer of thanks that he had

recovered from his head injury. According to the doctors, brain trauma was tricky to diagnose and difficult to treat. He had been lucky the swelling hadn't required surgery.

Pops's gaze bounced back and forth between Garrett and Phoebe. "I'm a little hungry," he announced cheerfully. "I think I'll head down to the cafeteria and see what they have. Can I get you anything, Phee?"

Phoebe smiled and shook her head. "I'm good. Thanks for asking."

Pops dropped a kiss on Phoebe's head before heading toward the door. Garrett watched him, saying another silent prayer of thanks, this one for his amazing grandfather.

Just before Pops reached the threshold, he stopped and looked over his shoulder. He cut his eyes toward Phoebe, waggled his eyebrows, and then winked at Garrett. Fortunately, she was oblivious to the old man's antics.

As Pops left the room with a jaunty wave, Phoebe pulled the chair closer to Garrett's bed and sat down. "Depending on how your next CT scan looks, you might be able to go home tomorrow."

"I can't wait to get out of here." Garrett sighed. "How many days has it been now? Four?"

"Six." She grasped his hand, her fingers tangling with his. "Six very long days."

He studied her face as she stared down at their entwined hands. She looked exhausted, tiny bruises shadowing the delicate skin under her eyes.

"You've been here the entire time," he noted. "Almost twenty-four-seven."

She met his gaze. "Yes. It's given me a lot of time to think."

Hope bloomed inside Garrett. There was nothing like a near-death experience to open someone's eyes.

"What have you been thinking about while I impersonated Sleeping Beauty?"

A breathy laugh floated from her, and she shook her head, clearly exasperated. "I can't believe you're joking about it. You could have died."

"I know."

"Garrett…"

He waited for her to continue, but she didn't. He counted ten beeps of the heart monitor before he prodded her. "What, Phoebe? Tell me."

"I was so scared," she said, her voice barely above a whisper. "I thought I had lost you … that you wouldn't wake up. And that if you *did* wake up, you'd be…"

"It's okay. *I'm* okay." He squeezed her fingers. "Give me a day or two, and I'll be happy to prove how *okay* I really am."

She didn't even crack a smile at his sexual innuendo. To his surprise, tears filled her eyes.

"When I heard how badly you were hurt … when I realized you could die … all I could think about was the time I had wasted by pushing you away." She pulled in a shaky breath. "That was time I could have spent showing you how much I love you."

She blinked, and tears spilled over her lower lashes. "You said no one knows what the future holds, and you're right. When I registered for that data-driven marketing class, I never imagined the professor would pair us up." She sniffed. "I never imagined I would run into you at Jake and Kyla's New Year's Eve party."

"Sometimes life throws you a curveball." He rubbed his thumb over her knuckles. "Your cancer was one hell of a curveball."

"It was," she agreed, swiping at the tears trickling down her face. "You said there's no way to know for sure that my cancer will come back, and you're right. But there's a really good chance it *will* come back."

"I know. After you told me about your cancer, I did a lot of research. I talked to a breast cancer specialist at MD Anderson. Dr. Cabral explained things to me. She said a lot of cancer survivors are weighted down by *what ifs*."

Her lips drooped in a frown. "I have a lot of those."

"Dr. Cabral said cancer casts a shadow over people's lives. But she counsels her patients to stand in the light instead of the darkness. She said it's a choice."

Phoebe swallowed, her smooth throat rippling with the movement. "You said you wanted to have children with me, and I—"

He cut her off because he knew what she was going to say, and he didn't want her to have to say it. He wanted to spare her pain whenever he could.

"I know radiation and chemo damages the ovaries," he said. "I know you can't get pregnant. But that doesn't mean we can't have children if we want them. There are other ways for us to be parents. Adoption. Egg donation. Surrogacy."

She exhaled softly. "You'd be willing to go through that?"

"I'm willing to do anything you want me to ... anything except give up on us."

After a long silence, she said, "I took steps to preserve my fertility. I froze my eggs. I wasn't going to, but my mom was insistent. She said I might change my mind ... that I might find a guy who would convince me to try."

Happiness trickled through him like honey, sweet and sticky. "So, you put your eggs on ice."

She nodded slowly. "But there's no guarantee—"

"I don't need a guarantee, Phoebe. I need you."

"I'm so sorry," she said, tears glittering in her deep green eyes.

Her words made his breath seize in his lungs. "What are you sorry for?"

"I'm sorry for pushing you away … for ending things. I should have listened to you." She wrapped both of her hands around his, carefully avoiding his IV. "I don't want to spend even one day without you, Garrett. I love you."

Emotion clogged his throat, and he cleared it roughly. "I love you too." He tugged her closer, until she perched on the edge of her chair. "Cancer has cast a shadow over your life for a long time, but I want you to make the choice to stand in the light."

Her hands tightened around his. "I'll stand in the light if you stand beside me."

"I will," he promised.

EPILOGUE

Nine months later

Phoebe settled deeper into the plush gray sofa and propped her sock-covered feet on the sleek coffee table. As she picked up her tablet, her bracelets clinked together. She gave the platinum bangles a brief glance.

In addition to wearing the one her mother had given her, she also wore the one Garrett had given to her for Christmas a week ago. It was inscribed with a quote from Anais Nin: *Don't let one cloud obliterate the whole sky.*

She turned her attention back to her tablet. After opening a blank document on the screen, she typed NEW YEAR'S RESOLUTIONS at the top. With the cursor blinking at her, she debated what she wanted to achieve this year.

Thanks to Garrett, she had marked off two resolutions from last year's list. He had helped her plant an herb garden, most of which was still alive, and he had surprised her with trips to Chicago and Miami, two places she'd never visited before.

She had come up with five resolutions by the time Garrett let himself back into the hotel suite. He held a drink caddy in one hand and a white pastry bag in the other.

When he spotted her on the sofa, a sexy smile curved his mouth. "Happy New Year." He held up the pastry bag. "I grabbed some coffee and pastries from the kitchen. I got your favorite: strawberry cream cheese."

Coffee and pastries sounded delicious. But not as delicious as the man standing in front of her.

His thick hair was still a little damp from his earlier shower, and dark stubble shadowed his lower face. His oatmeal-colored sweater clung to his broad chest and dark-washed jeans emphasized his long legs. She had made the shawl-collared sweater with some of the yarn he'd given her. He wore it so often one of the cuffs had unraveled.

"I stopped by the restaurant," he said. "They're slammed with people coming in for the New Year's Day brunch buffet, but they can squeeze us in around one thirty. I figured the pastries could tide us over until then."

She checked the time on her tablet, unsurprised to see it was almost noon. She and Garrett hadn't gone to bed until nearly three in the morning after attending a New Year's Eve party at Jake and Kyla's house. When they'd finally woken up, they had celebrated the new year with slow, soul-shaking sex.

Garrett passed one of the to-go cups to her, and she thanked him before swallowing a sip of coffee. As always, he had put the perfect amount of sugar and cream in it.

After nabbing the remaining to-go cup from the holder, he dropped down beside her, his body angled toward her. He gulped down a mouthful of coffee before setting it on the end table.

Tilting his head toward her tablet, he asked, "What are you reading, petal?"

"Nothing. I'm making a list of New Year's resolutions."

The corner of his mouth hitched up. "What's on your list?"

"Just some things I've been thinking about for a few months." She pulled her legs to her chest and repositioned herself so she could look at him without getting a crick in her neck. "What are you going to put on your list?"

He pushed back one of his sleeves, revealing a muscular forearm dusted with dark hair, and draped his arm along the back of the sofa. "I don't make New Year's resolutions."

Freezing with her coffee cup halfway to her lips, she asked, "You don't?"

"No."

"People who make resolutions are ten times more likely to achieve their goals," she informed him, sounding just a tad superior.

He gave her an indulgent glance, his crystalline blue eyes gleaming with amusement. "In that case, I should make at least one resolution." He stood abruptly. "I need pen and paper."

He strode to the desk where he'd left his black leather briefcase. She watched him as he rummaged around in the briefcase, her stomach warming when her gaze zeroed in on his tight butt.

Seconds later he was back, a spiral-bound notepad and retractable pen in hand. He sat down, propped his ankle over his opposite knee, and flipped open the notepad. With it balanced on his thigh, he clicked the pen and scribbled something on the paper. After reviewing what he had written, he tore out the sheet and folded it in half.

"That's it?" she asked.

He met her eyes. "Yes." He placed the paper on the sofa between them. "There's only one thing I want to accomplish this year."

"You only have one resolution?" she asked incredulously. "How is that possible? You own ten hotels and employ thousands of people."

He clicked the pen off and tossed it and the notepad on the coffee table. "I have a five-year strategic plan for Gale Hotel Group. I don't need resolutions."

Garrett's company continued to grow. Last month, he had closed on the acquisition of his first hotel in Denver. It was located in the city's trendy LoDo district, and they planned to fly to Colorado next weekend so Garrett could show the historic property to her.

Here in San Francisco, renovations at The Pacifica were on schedule. But they were a little over budget because Garrett had replaced all three elevators in the Art Deco building.

Curious about Garrett's one-and-only resolution, she reached for the folded-over paper. To her surprise, he slapped his right hand down on top of it. She jerked her eyes to his, and he tilted his head toward her tablet.

"I want to see yours before I show you mine," he said.

Now she was really intrigued. Blowing out an exasperated breath, she held out her tablet to Garrett. He grabbed it with his left hand, leaving his right on top of the folded-over paper. She opened her mouth to protest, but he just gave her a narrow-eyed look before shifting his attention to the tablet.

"Stand in the light," he said, reading her number one resolution.

Every day she made a choice to stand in the light. It wasn't always easy, especially when she had an appointment with Oncology Associates of Northern California, a place where cancer cast a huge shadow.

But she didn't go to the appointment alone; Garrett came with her. Fortunately, her scans continued to come back clean and her tumor markers remained unchanged.

"Adopt a dog," Garrett said, continuing to read her list. "Take ballroom dance lessons. Go on a cruise. Move back to Seattle."

He looked up, his eyes locking on her face. "Move back to Seattle?"

Garrett tried to split his time between Seattle and San Francisco, but she knew it was hard on him. When he was in Seattle, he missed her. And when he was in San Francisco, he worried about Pops.

It was hard on her too. She hated to be away from Garrett, even for one day. He obviously felt the same way because when he had to travel, he wanted her to come with him. Of course, her job at Riley O'Brien & Co. prevented her from taking out-of-town trips.

"You need to be in Seattle," Phoebe told him. "For Pops. For Gale Hotel Group. And I need to be with you."

His mouth tightened. "What about your job? You love it."

After Phoebe had finished her management trainee rotation with Riley O'Brien & Co., she had taken a permanent position in the e-commerce group. She worked closely with the marketing group to drive traffic to the company's website.

"I like my job," she said. "But I love you. And Pops."

Garrett shook his head. "I don't want you to give up a job you *like*. We can figure something else out. Maybe—"

She placed her fingers over his lips. "I'm going to ask my boss if I can telecommute. Hopefully he'll say yes. That way I can work anywhere, Seattle or any other city you're traveling to. But if he says no, you'll have to find something for me to do at Gale Hotel Group."

Garrett's mouth moved her under fingers as he smiled. "I can do that."

She dropped her hand to her lap. "I want to move by the end of the month. I've already told my landlord."

His smile widened. "If that's what you want, petal."

She glanced pointedly at his large hand covering the folded paper. "I showed you mine. Now you show me yours."

He picked up the paper and gave it to her. Unfolding it, she read his resolution: *Marry Phoebe.*

She inhaled sharply, her ears filled with a roar like a jet engine. The paper slipped from her numb fingers, and she watched it float to her lap before bringing her gaze to Garrett. He was absolutely still, his eyes assessing her reaction.

She'd wondered when he would propose. In all honesty, she had expected him to do it way before now. They had made vows to each other in that hospital room after his accident, and he wasn't a particularly patient guy.

"Is that ..." she pointed down at the paper "... a proposal?"

"It is if you plan to say yes."

She couldn't help but laugh at his answer. "And if I don't?"

"Then it's just a simple resolution—a goal to work toward." He plucked the paper from her lap. "So, tell me ... is this a proposal or a resolution?"

"Oh, it's definitely a proposal."

He grinned hugely, the skin around his gorgeous eyes crinkling. "Yes?"

"Yes," she confirmed.

To her surprise, he slid from the sofa to kneel at her feet. He delved into the right front pocket of his Rileys and pulled out a blue velvet ring case.

"This was my grandmother's engagement ring," he said as he opened the case and removed the ring.

He held it out to her, and she gasped in delight. The round

center diamond was at least four carats, and small round diamonds created a halo around it. The platinum band was also encrusted with round diamonds.

"Wow," she breathed. "Pops has great taste in jewelry."

She extended her left hand, and Garrett slid the ring onto her finger. He stared down at it, rubbing his thumb over the large diamond.

"I've wanted to see you wearing this ring for a long time now." He glanced up at her, his eyes shimmering with satisfaction. "It looks perfect."

She wiggled her fingers, and the diamonds shot prisms of color across the room. "It really sparkles."

"That's because you're standing in the light."

Don't Miss These Full-Length Riley O'Brien & Co. Novels!

All the Right Places
Book 1 in the Riley O'Brien & Co. series
Available now

Amelia Winger is a small-town girl with big dreams of becoming a successful designer. When she gets a gig designing accessories for denim empire Riley O'Brien & Co., it's a dream come true. Amelia can handle the demanding job, but she isn't quite prepared for sexy CEO Quinn O'Brien. She's doing her best to keep things professional, but the attraction sparking between them makes it personal. And so does the secret project she's working on behind his back...

Quinn's not interested in the new accessories, but he is interested in the woman designing them. Amelia is smart, sexy, and talented, and he hasn't been able to stop thinking about her since they met. Mixing business and pleasure isn't wise, but that doesn't stop him from coming up with excuses to spend time with her. He thinks he understands the risk he's taking when he gets involved with Amelia. But he doesn't know he's risking a lot more than his heart.

Coming Apart at the Seams
Book 2 in the Riley O'Brien & Co. series
Available now

Teagan O'Brien, heiress to the Riley O'Brien & Co. denim empire, is anything but a spoiled rich girl. She's worked hard to secure her place in the family business and can hold her own, in and out of the office. Only one man has ever been able to get under her skin—sexy football star Nick Priest. Years ago, they crossed the line from friends to lovers, but he left her heartbroken. Since then, she's been determined to keep him at arm's length—no matter how tempting he looks in his jeans!

Nick has fortune, fame, and looks that make most women hot and bothered. But he doesn't have the woman he really wants. He knows he screwed up when he walked away from Teagan, and now that he has a second chance, he'll do whatever it takes to win her over—no matter how tongue-tied he gets…

Hanging by a Thread
Book 3 in the Riley O'Brien & Co. series
Available now

Thirty-year-old Bebe Banerjee is desperate to get rid of two things: her fiancé and her virginity. Escaping her arranged marriage might be impossible, but she refuses to give her firsts to an entitled jerk who lives on another continent. Instead, she devises a plan that guarantees another man will get her momentous firsts. But she never imagined that man would be Cal O'Brien, the gorgeous heir to the Riley O'Brien & Co. denim empire...

Although Cal has always been fascinated by Bebe's brilliant mind and beautiful eyes, he's never pursued her. She can't stand the sight of him, and every time they're in the same room, they end up trading insults. Yet when he finds out about Bebe's bold plan, he makes his move, unaware of her upcoming nuptials. He promises to make her firsts unforgettable, but he doesn't know how hard it will be to forget her when their arrangement ends.

About the Author

Jenna Sutton is a former award-winning journalist who traded fact for fiction when she began writing novels. Surprisingly, the research she conducted for her articles provided a lot of inspiration for her books.

Jenna is the author of the Riley O'Brien & Co. romances. She has a Bachelor's degree in Journalism from Texas Christian University and a Master's degree in Integrated Marketing Communications from Northwestern University.

Jenna and her husband live in Texas in a 105-year-old house affectionately known as "The Money Pit".

You can find out more about Jenna and her books by visiting www.jennasutton.com or you can connect with her on Facebook at www.facebook.com/jennasuttonauthor or Twitter @jsuttonauthor.

www.ingramcontent.com/pod-product-compliance
Lightning Source LLC
Chambersburg PA
CBHW031942260626
47157CB00017B/2022